The Interpreter
A Tale of the War

by

G. J. Whyte-Melville

Double 9
BOOKS

The Interpreter
A Tale of the War
by G. J. Whyte-Melville

Copyright © 2024

All Rights reserved.

ISBN: 978-93-64282-95-6

Published by

DOUBLE 9 BOOKS

2/13-B, Ansari Road
Daryaganj, New Delhi – 110002
info@double9books.com
www.double9books.com
Tel. 011-40042856

ABOUT THE AUTHOR

G. J. Whyte-Melville (1821-1888) was a notable British author known for his novels and works of fiction, particularly those set in the context of military and adventure. His writing reflects his experiences and interests, often focusing on themes of heroism, military life, and adventure. Some of his notable works are **"The Interpreter: A Tale of the War"** (1867): One of his most recognized works, this novel offers a detailed portrayal of military life and espionage during wartime. **"Katerfelto: A Story of Exmoor"** (1860): A novel set in the English countryside, showcasing Whyte-Melville's skill in depicting rural life and adventure. **"Satanella"** (1868): A novel featuring elements of romance and intrigue, set against a backdrop of political and social drama. **"The Gloved Hand"** (1865): Another example of his engaging storytelling, blending romance with adventure and mystery. G. J. Whyte-Melville's contributions to literature are notable for their detailed and engaging portrayal of military and adventure themes. His novels remain of interest for their historical and narrative depth, and his ability to blend romance with adventure has earned him a place in 19th-century British literature.

Whyte-Melville passed away on November 7, 1888, but his works continue to be appreciated for their vivid storytelling and exploration of themes related to heroism, duty, and military life.

CONTENTS

CHAPTER I
THE OLD DESK

Not one of my keys will fit it: the old desk has been laid aside for years, and is covered with dust and rust. We do not make such strong boxes nowadays, for brass hinges and secret drawers have given place to flimsy morocco and russian leather; so we clap a Bramah lock, that Bramah himself cannot pick, on a black bag that the veriest bungler can rip open in five seconds with a penknife, and entrust our notes, bank and otherwise, our valuables, and our secrets, to this faithless repository with a confidence that deserves to be respected. But in the days when George the Third was king, our substantial ancestors rejoiced in more substantial workmanship: so the old desk that I cannot succeed in unlocking, is of shining rosewood, clamped with brass, and I shall spoil it sadly with the mallet and the chisel.

What a medley it holds! Thank Heaven I am no speculative philosopher, or I might moralise for hours over its contents. First, out flies a withered leaf of geranium. It must have been dearly prized once, or it would never have been here; maybe it represented the hopes, the wealth, the all-in-all of two aching hearts: and they are dust and ashes now. To think that the flower should have outlasted them! the symbol less perishable than the faith! Then I come to a piece of much-begrimed and yellow paper, carefully folded, and indorsed with a date,--a receipt for an embrocation warranted specific in all cases of bruises, sprains, or lumbago; next a gold pencil-case, with a head of Socrates for a seal; lastly, much of that substance which is generated in all waste places, and which the vulgar call "flue." How it comes there puzzles equally the naturalist and the philosopher; but you shall find it in empty corners, empty drawers, empty pockets, nay, we believe in its existence in the empty heads of our fellow-creatures.

In my thirst for acquisition, regardless of dusty fingers, I press the inner sides of the desk in hopes of discovering secret springs and hoarded repositories: so have poor men ere now found thousand-pound notes hid away in chinks and crannies, and straightway, giddy with the possession of boundless wealth, have gone to the Devil at a pace such as none but the beggar on horseback can command; so have old wills been fished out, and frauds discovered, and rightful heirs re-established, and society in general disgusted, and all concerned made discontented and uncomfortable--

so shall I, perhaps--but the springs work, a false lid flies open, and I do discover a packet of letters, written on thin foreign paper, in the free straggling characters I remember so well. They are addressed to Sir H. Beverley, and the hand that penned them has been cold for years. So will yours and mine be some day, perhaps ere the flowers are out again; *O beate Sexti!* will you drink a glass less claret on that account? Buxom Mrs. Lalage, shall the dressmaker therefore put unbecoming trimmings in your bonnet? The "shining hours" are few, and soon past; make the best of them, each in your own way, only try and choose the right way:--

> For the day will soon be over, and the minutes are of gold,
>
> And the wicket shuts at sundown, and the shepherd leaves the fold.

LETTER I

"Those were merry days, my dear Hal, when we used to hear the 'chimes at midnight' with poor Brummell and Sir Benjamin;[#] very jolly times they were, and I often think, if health and pockets could have stood it, I should like to be going the pace amongst you all still. And yet how few of us are left. They have dropped off one by one, as they did the night we dyed the white rose red at the old place; and you, and I, and stanch old 'Ben,' were the only three left that could walk straight. Do you remember the corner of King-street, and 'Ben' stripped 'to the buff,' as he called it himself, 'going-in' right royally at the tall fellow with the red head? I never saw such right-and-lefters, I never thought he had so much 'fight' in him; and you don't remember, Hal, but I do, how 'the lass with the long locks' bent over you when you were floored, like Andromache over a debauched Hector, and stanched the claret that was flowing freely from your nostrils, and gave you gin in a smelling-bottle, which you sucked down as though it were mother's milk, like a young reprobate as you were; nor do you remember, nor do I very clearly, how we all got back to 'The Cottage,' and finished with burnt curagoa, and a dance on the table by daylight. And now you and I are about the only two left, and I am as near ruined as a gentleman can be; and you must have lost your pen-feathers, Hal, I should think, though you were a goose that always could pick a living off a common, be it never so bare. Well, we have had our fun; and after all, I for one have been far happier since than I ever was in those roystering days; but of this I cannot bear to speak."

[#] The dandy's nickname for the Prince Regent.

"Nor am I so much to be pitied now. I have got my colours and my sketch-book, after all; and there never was such a country as this for a man who has half an eye in his head. On these magnificent plains the lights and shades are glorious. Glorious, Hal, with a little red jagged in here and there towards sunset, and the ghostly maize waving and whispering, and the feathery acacias trembling in the lightest air, the russet tinge of the one and the fawn-coloured stems of the other melting so softly into the neutral tints of the sandy soil. I could paint a picture here that should be perfectly true to Nature--nay, more natural than the old dame herself--and never use but two colours to do it all! I am not going to tell you what they are: and this reminds me of my boy, and of a want in his organisation that is a sad distress to me. The child has not a notion of colour. I was painting out of doors yesterday, and he was standing by--bless him! he never leaves me for an instant--and I tried to explain to him some of the simplest rudiments of the godlike art. 'Vere,' said I, 'do you see those red tints on the tops of the far acacias, and the golden tinge along the back of that brown ox in the foreground?' 'Yes, papa!' was the child's answer, with a bewildered look. 'How should you paint them, my boy?' 'Well, papa, I should paint the acacias green, because they *are* green, and'--here he thought he had made a decided hit--'I should put the red into the ox, for he is almost more red than brown.' Dear child! he has not a glimmering of colour; but composition, that's his forte; and drawing, drawing, you know, which is the highest form of the art. His drawing is extraordinary--careless, but great breadth and freedom; and I am certain he could compose a wonderful picture, from his singular sensibility to beauty. Young as he is, I have seen the tears stand in his eyes when contemplating a fine view, or a really exquisite 'bit,' such as one sees in this climate every day. His raptures at his first glimpse of the Danube I shall never forget; and if I can only instil into him the principles of colour, you will see Vere will become the first painter of the age. The boy learns languages readily enough. He has picked up a good deal of Hungarian from his nurse. Such a woman, Hal! magnificent! Such colouring: deep brown tones, and masses of the richest grey hair, with superb, solemn, sunken eyes, and a throat and forehead tanned and wrinkled into the very ideal of a Canidia, or a Witch of Endor, or any fine old sorceress, 'all of the olden time.' I have done her in chalks, and in sepia, and in oils. I adore her in the former. She is, I fancy, a good, careful woman, and much attached to Vere, who promises to be an excellent linguist; but of this I cannot see the advantage. There is but one pursuit, in my opinion, for an intellectual being who is not obliged to labour in the fields for his daily bread, and that is Art. I have wooed the heavenly maid all my life. To me she has been sparing of her favours; and yet a single smile from her has gilded my path for many a long and weary day. She has beckoned me on and on till I feel I could follow her to the end of the world; she shielded me *in the dark hour*; she has brightened my lot ever since; she led me to nature, her grand reflection--for you know my theory, that art is reality, and nature but the embodiment of art; she has made me independent of the frowns of that other jade, Fortune, and taught me the most difficult lesson of all--to be content. What is wealth? You and I have seen it lavished with both hands, and its possessor weary, satiate, languid, and disgusted. What is rank? a mark for envy, an idol but for fools. Fame? a few orders on a tight uniform; a craving for more and more; even when we know the tastelessness of the food, to be still hungry for applause. Love? a sting of joy and a heartache for ever. Are they not all vanity of vanities? But your artist is your true creator. He can embody the noblest aspirations of his mind, and give them a reality and a name. You, Hal, who are the most practical, unimaginative, business-like fellow that ever hedged a bet or drove a bargain, have had such dreams betwixt sleeping and waking as have given you a taste of heaven, and taught you the existence of a fairy-land of which, to such as you, is only granted a far-away and occasional glimpse. What would you give to be able to embody such blissful visions and call them up at will? Let me have a camel's-hair brush, a few dabs of clay, and, behold! I am the magician before whose wand these dreams shall reappear tangibly, substantially, enduringly: alas! for mortal shortcomings, sometimes a little out of drawing, sometimes a little hard and cold; but still, Hal, I can make my own world, such as it is, and people it for myself; nor do I envy any man on earth, except, perhaps, a sculptor. To have perfected and wrought out in the imperishable marble the ideal of one's whole life, to walk round it, and smoke one's cigar and say, 'This will last as long as St. Paul's Cathedral or the National Debt, and this is mine, I made it'--must be a sensation of delight that even we poor painters, with our works comparatively of a day, can hardly imagine; but then, what we lose in durability we gain in reproduction: and so once more I repeat, let who will be statesman, warrior, stock-jobber, or voluptuary, but give me the pallet and the easel, the *délire d'un peintre*, the line of beauty and the brush!

"Can you wonder that I should wish my boy to tread the same path? Had I but begun at his age, and worked as I *should* have worked, what might I have been now? Could I but make amends to him by leading him up the path to real fame, and see Vere the regenerator of modern art, I should die happy.

"And now, Hal, I must ask you of your own pursuits and your own successes. I do not often see an English paper; but these are a fine sporting people, with a dash of our English tastes and love of horseflesh; and in a small pothouse where we put up last week, in the very heart of the Banat, I found a print of Flying Childers, and a *Bell's Life* of the month before last. In this I read that your Marigold colt was first favourite for the Derby, and I can only say that I hope he will win, as fervently as I should have done some years back, when he would have carried a large portion of my money, or at least of my credit, on his back. I have also gathered that your shorthorns won the prize at the great cattle-show. 'Who drives fat oxen must himself be fat.' I trust, therefore, that you are flourishing and thriving; also, that Constance, the most stately little lady I ever beheld at two years old, still queens it at the Manor-house. I will write again shortly, but must leave off now, as my boy is calling me to go out. He grows more like his poor mother every day, especially about the eyes.--Adieu, Hal; ever yours,

"PHILIP EGERTON."

LETTER II

"The longer I linger here the more I become wedded to the land in which, after all, I have known the few hours of real happiness I ever spent. Yes, Hal, with all its guilt, with all its anxieties, with everything and everybody battling against me--that was my golden year, such as I shall never see again. She was so generous, so gentle, and so true; she sacrificed all so willingly for me, and never looked back. Such courage, such patience, and oh! such beauty; and to lose her after one short year. Well, it is my punishment, and I bear it; but if it had to be done again I would do it. Surely I was not so much to blame. Had she but lived I would have made her such amends. And after all she is mine--mine in her lonely grave under the acacias, and I shall meet her again. If the universe holds her I shall meet her again. Wearily the years have dragged on since I lost her, but every birthday is a milestone nearer home; and in the meantime I have Vere and my art. And we wander about this wild country, and scamper across its boundless plains, and I paint and smoke, and try to be happy.

"We arrived here last night, and I need scarcely tell you that Edeldorf is as English as any place out of England can be, and my old friend but little altered during the last twenty years. You remember De Rohan at Melton and Newmarket, at Rome and at Paris. Wherever he lived he was quite the Englishman, and always rode a thoroughbred horse. It would indeed be ungrateful on your part to forget him. Need I remind you of the dinner at the old Club, and the procession afterwards, with some fourteen wax candles, to inspect The Switcher in your stables, at the risk of burning down the greater part of the town, and converting some of the best horses in England into an exceedingly tough grill. I can see the Count's face of drunken gravity now, as he felt carefully down the horse's forelegs, undeterred by the respectful stare of your groom, or the undisguised astonishment of the animal itself. 'Vat is his name?' was the only question he asked of the polite Mr. Topthorn. 'The Switcher, my lord,' was the reply. 'Ver' nice name,' said the Count, and bought him forthwith at a price that you yourself can best appreciate; but from that day to this he never could pronounce the animal's appellation;

and although he rode 'The Svishare' both in England and here, and has got prints and pictures of him all over the house, 'The Svishare' he will continue to be till the end of time.

"All this Anglo-mania, however, is not much appreciated in high places; and I can see enough without looking much below the surface to satisfy me that the Count is eyed jealously by the authorities, and that if ever they catch him tripping they will not spare his fortunes or his person. I fear there will be a row before long, and I would not trust the wild blood of my friends here if once they get the upper hand. Only yesterday an incident occurred that gave me a pretty correct idea of the state of feeling in this country, and the disaffection of the peasant to his imperial rulers. Vere and I were travelling along in our usual manner, occupying the front seat of a most dilapidated carriage, which I purchased at Bucharest for twenty ducats, with the nurse and the baggage behind. We had stopped for me to sketch an animated group, in the shape of a drove of wild horses being drafted and chosen by their respective owners, and Vere was clapping his hands and shouting with delight at the hurry-skurry of the scene (by the way, there was a white horse that I caught in a beautiful attitude, who comes out admirably and lights up the whole sketch), when an officer and a couple of Austrian dragoons rode into the midst of the busy horse-tamers, and very rudely proceeded to subject them to certain inquiries, which seemed to meet with sulky and evasive answers enough. After a time the Austrian officer, a handsome boy of twenty, stroking an incipient moustache, ordered the oldest man of the party to be pinioned; and placing him between his two soldiers, began to interrogate him in a most offensive and supercilious manner. The old man, who was what we should call in England a better sort of yeoman farmer, of course immediately affected utter ignorance of German; and as the young Austrian was no great proficient in Hungarian, I was compelled most unwillingly to interpret between them, Vere looking on meanwhile with his mouth wide open, in a state of intense bewilderment. The following is a specimen of the conversation:--

"*Austrian Sub-Lieutenant*, in German--'Thou hast been hiding deserters; and so shalt thou be imprisoned, and fined, and suffer punishment.' I have to modify these threats into Hungarian.--'Brother, this noble officer seeks a deserter. Knowest thou of such an one?'

"*Old Man*--'My father, I know nothing.'

"*Austrian Officer*, with many expletives, modified as before by your humble servant--'You shall be punished with the utmost rigour if you do not give him up.'

"*Old Man*, again--'My father, I know nothing.'

"*Officer*, losing all patience, and gesticulating wildly with his sword--'Slave, brute, dog, tell me this instant which way he took, or I will have you hanged to that nearest tree, your family shall be imprisoned, and your village burnt to the ground.'

"*Old Man*, as before--'My father, I know nothing.'

"The case was getting hopeless; but the young officer had now thoroughly lost his temper, and ordered his men to tie the peasant up, and flog him soundly with a stirrup-leather. Here I thought it high time to interpose; I saw the wild Hungarian blood beginning to boil in the veins of some dozen dark scowling fellows, who had been occupied tending the horses. Eyes were flashing at the Austrians, and hands clutching under the sheepskin where the long knife lies. Fortunately the officer was a gentleman and an admirer of the English. With much difficulty I persuaded him to abandon his cruel intention, and to ride on in prosecution of his search; but it was when his back was turned that the tide of indignation against himself and his country swelled to the highest. The peasants' faces actually became convulsed with rage, their voices shook with fury, and threats and maledictions were poured on their masters enough to make one's very blood run cold. If ever they do get the upper hand, woe to the oppressor! There is nothing on earth so fearful as a Jacquerie. God forbid this fair land should ever see one.

"We journeyed on in a different direction from the dragoons, but we caught occasional glimpses of their white coats as they gleamed through the acacias that skirted the road; and I was just thinking how well I could put them in with a dab or two of chalk against a thunder-storm, or a dark wood in the midst of summer, when the bright sun makes the foliage almost black, and debating in my own mind whether the officer would not have made a better sketch if his horse had been a light grey, when my postilion pulled up with a jerk that nearly chucked Vere out of the carriage, and, pointing to something in the road, assured 'my Excellency' that the horse was dying, and the rider, in all probability, lying killed under his beast. Sure enough, an over-ridden horse was prostrate in the middle of the road, and a young man vainly endeavouring to raise him by the bridle, and calling him by all the terms of endearment and abuse in the Hungarian vocabulary, without the slightest effect. Seeing our carriage, he addressed me in German, and with a gentlemanlike voice and manner begged to know in what direction I was travelling. 'I hope to get to Edeldorf to-night,' was my answer. He started at the name. 'Edeldorf!' said he; 'I, too, am bound for Edeldorf; can you favour me with a seat in your carriage?' Of course I immediately complied; and Vere and I soon had the stranger between us, journeying amicably on towards my old friend's chateau. You know my failing, Hal, so I need not tell you how it was that I immediately began to study my new acquaintance's physiognomy, somewhat, I thought, to his discomfiture, for at first he turned his head away, but after a while seemed to think better of it, and entered into conversation with much frankness and vivacity. The sun was getting low, and I think I could have sketched him very satisfactorily in that warm, soft light. His head was essentially that of a soldier; the brow deficient in ideality, but with the bold outlines which betoken penetration and forethought. Constructiveness fully developed, combativeness moderate, but firmness very strongly marked; the eye deep set, and, though small, remarkably brilliant; the jaw that of a strong, bold man, while the lines about the mouth showed great energy of character and decision. From the general conformation of his head I should have placed forethought as the distinguishing quality of his character, and I should have painted the rich brown tones of his complexion on a system of my own, which such a portrait would be admirably calculated to bring out. However, I could not well ask him to sit to me upon so short an acquaintance; so, while he and Vere chatted on--for they soon became great friends, and my new acquaintance seemed charmed to find a child speaking German so fluently--I began to speculate on the trade and character of this mysterious addition to our party. 'Hair cut short, moustache close clipped,' thought I, 'perfect German accent, and the broad Viennese dialect of the aristocracy, all this looks like a soldier; but the rough frieze coat, and huge shapeless riding boots could never belong to an officer of that neatest of armies--"the Imperial and Kingly." Then his muscular figure, and light active gait, which I remarked as he sprang into the carriage, would argue him one who was in the habit of practising feats of strength and agility. There is no mistaking the effects of the gymnasium. Stay, I have it, he is a fencing-master; that accounts for the military appearance, the quick glance, the somewhat worn look of the countenance, and he is going to Edeldorf, to teach De Rohan's boy the polite art of self-defence. So much the better. I, too, love dearly a turn with the foils, so I can have a glorious "set-to" with him to-morrow or the next day; and then, when we are more intimate, I can paint him. I think I shall do him in oils. I wish he would turn his head the least thing further this way.' I had got as far as this when my new friend did indeed turn his head round, and looking me full in the face, thus addressed me:--'Sir, you are an Englishman, and an honourable man. I have no right to deceive you. You incur great danger by being seen with me. I have no right to implicate you; set me down, and let me walk.' Vere looked more astonished than ever. I begged him to explain himself. 'I tell you,' said he, 'that I am a thief and a deserter. My name is posted at every barrack-gate in the empire. I am liable to be hanged, if taken. Are you not afraid of me now?' 'No,' exclaimed Vere, his colour heightening and his eyes glistening (oh! so like her). 'Papa and I will take care of you; don't be afraid.' My boy had anticipated what I was going to say; but I assured him that as I had taken him into my carriage I considered him as my guest, and come what would I never could think of abandoning him till we reached our destination. 'Of course,' I added, 'you are then free to come and go as you please. If you have done anything disgraceful, we need never know each other again. I do not wish to hear of it. You are to me only a belated traveller; permit me to add, a gentleman, to whom I am delighted to be of service. Will you smoke? Let me offer you a cigar.' The blood rushed to his face as he declined the proffered courtesy; for an instant he looked half offended, and then, seizing my hand, he exclaimed, 'If you knew all, you would pity me--nay, more, you would approve of what I have done.' He turned suddenly to Vere, and rather startled him by abruptly exclaiming, 'Boy, do you love your father? is he all the world to you?' 'Yes,' said Vere, colouring up again, 'of course I love papa, and Nurse "Nettich" too.' That worthy woman was fast asleep in the rumble. 'Well,' said the stranger, more composedly, 'I love my father, too; he is all I have in the world, and for his sake I would do the same thing again. I will tell you all about it, and you shall judge between me and my crime.' But my new friend's story I must defer, my dear Hal, to another letter. So for the present, *Vive valeque*."

CHAPTER II
THE DESERTER

Dim and strange are the recollections that steal over me while I read these time-worn letters of one who, with all his faults, was the kindest, fondest, and best of enthusiasts. It seems like a dream; I cannot fancy that I am the child alluded to. It seems as though all this must have happened to some one else, and that I stood by and watched. Yet have I a vague and shadowy remembrance of the warm autumnal evening; the road soft and thick with dust; the creaking, monotonous motion of the carriage, and my waking up from an occasional nap, and finding myself propped by the strong arm of a stranger, and nestling my head upon his broad shoulder, whilst my father's kind face and eager eyes were turned towards my new acquaintance with the earnest comprehensive look I remember so well. My father always seemed to take in at a glance, not only the object that attracted his attention, but all its accessories, possible as well as actual. I believe he never left off painting in his mind. I remember nothing very distinctly; and no wonder, for my little brain must have been a strange chaos of shifting scenes and unexpected events, foreign manners and home ideas, to say nothing of a general confusion of tongues; for I could prattle French, German, and Hungarian, with a smattering of Turkish, not to mention my own native language; and I used them all indiscriminately. But my father's letters bring back much that I had otherwise forgotten, and whilst I read the story of the renegade, I can almost fancy I am leaning against his upright soldierlike form, and listening to the clear decided tones in which he told his tale.

LETTER III

"'I am a soldier, sir,' said my new acquaintance, whilst I leant back in the carriage smoking my cigar, and, *more meo*, Hal, made the most of my 'study.' 'I am an Austrian soldier--at least I was a week ago--I would not give much for my chance if ever I come into the clutches of the "Double Eagle" again. Shall I tell you why I entered the Imperial army? All my life I have thought it best to be on the winning side. If I had been born an Englishman, oh, what happiness! I would have asked no better lot than to wander about with my dog and my gun, and be free. But a Croat, no, there is no liberty in Croatia. We must have masters, forsooth! territorial dues and seignorial rights; and we must bow and cringe and be trampled on by our own nobility. But these, too, have *their* masters, and I have seen the lord of many thousand acres tremble before a captain of dragoons. So I determined that if a military despotism was to be the order of the day, why I, too, would make a part of the great engine, perhaps some time I might come to wield it all. My father was appointed steward to a great lord in Hungary--perhaps, had he remained, I might never have left home, for I am his only child, and we two are alone in the world; besides, is not a son's first duty to obey his father?--but I could not bear to exchange the free open air, and my horse, and my gun, and my dogs (I had the best greyhounds in Croatia), for a leathern stool and an inkstand, and I said, "Father, I too will become an Austrian, and so some day shall I be a great man, perhaps a colonel, and then will I return once a year to see you, and comfort you in your old age." So I was sworn to obey the Emperor, and soon I learnt my exercise, and saw that to rise even in the Austrian army was not difficult for one who could see clearly before him, and could count that two and two make four, and never five.

"'Very few men are soldiers at heart, and those who love the profession and would fain shine, can only see one way to success, and that must be the old-established track that has always been followed. If I wanted to move across that stream and had no boats, what should I do? I would try if it be too deep to wade. But the regulation says, soldiers shall not wade if the water be over a certain depth. So for six inches of water I must be defeated. That should not be my way; if it came no higher than their chins my men should cross; and if we could keep our muskets dry, where would be the harm? Well, I soon rose to be a corporal and a sergeant; and whilst I practised fencing and riding and gymnastics, I learnt besides something of gunnery and fortification, and the art of supplying an army with food. At last I was made lieutenant and paymaster of the regiment, for I could always calculate readily, and never shrank from trouble or feared responsibility. So I had good pay and good comrades, and was getting on. Meanwhile my poor father was distressing himself about my profession, and imagining all sorts of misfortunes that would happen to me if I remained a soldier. In his letters to me he always hinted at the possibility of some great success--at his hopes of, before long, placing me in an independent position; that I should leave the army to come and live with him, and we would farm an estate of our own, and never be parted any more. Poor old man! what do you think he built on? why, these foolish lotteries. Ticket after ticket did he purchase, and ticket after ticket came up a blank. At last, in his infatuation, he raised a sum of money--enough to obtain him all the numbers he had set his heart upon--for he mixed calculation with his gambling, which is certain ruin-- and for this purpose he embezzled two thousand florins of his employer's property, and wasted it as he had done the rest. In his despair he wrote to me. What could I do? two thousand florins were in the pay-chest. I have it here in this leathern bag. I have saved my father; he is steward at Edeldorf. I shall see him to-night; after that I must fly the country. I will go to England, the land of the free. I am ruined, degraded, and my life is not worth twelve hours' purchase; but I do not regret it. Look at your boy, sir, and tell me if I am not right.' He is a fine fellow this, Hal, depend upon it; and though my own feelings as a gentleman were a little shocked at a man talking thus coolly of robbery in anything but the legitimate way on the turf, I could scarcely remonstrate with him now the thing was done; so I shook him by the hand, and promised him at any rate a safe convoy to Edeldorf, which we were now rapidly approaching. You like a fine place, Hal; you always did. I remember when you used to vow that if ever Fortune smiled upon you-- and faith, it is not for want of wooing that you have missed the goddess's favours--how you would build and castellate and improve Beverley Manor, till, in my opinion as an artist and a man of associations, you would spoil it completely; but I think even your fastidious taste would be delighted with Edeldorf. The sun was just down as we drove into the park, and returned the salute of the smart Hussar mounting guard at the lodge; and the winding road, and smooth sward dotted with thorns, and those eternal acacias, reminded one of a gentleman's place in Old England, till we rounded the corner of a beautifully-dressed flower-garden, and came in view of the castle itself, with all its angles and turrets and embrasures, and mullioned windows, and picturesque ins-and-outs; the whole standing boldly out in a chiaro-oscuro against the evening sky, fast beginning to soften into twilight. Old De Rohan was on the steps to welcome me, his figure upright and noble as ever; his countenance as pleasing; but the beard and moustache that you and I remember so dark and glossy, now as white as snow; yet he is a very handsome fellow still. In mail or plate, leaning his arm on his helmet, with his beard flowing over a steel cuirass inlaid with gold, he would make a capital seneschal, or marshal of a tournament, or other elderly dignitary of the middle ages; but I should like best to paint him in dark velvet, with a skull-cap, as Lord Soulis, or some other noble votary of the magic art; and to bring him out in a dusky room, with one ray of vivid light from a lamp just over his temples, and gleaming off that fine, bold, shining forehead, from which the hair is now completely worn away."

There are no more of the old dusty letters. Why these should have been tied up and preserved for so many years is more than I can tell. They have, however, reminded me of much in my youth that I had well-nigh forgotten. I must try back on my vague memories for the commencement of my narrative.

CHAPTER III
"PAR NOBILE"

"You shall play with my toys, and break them if you like, for my papa loves the English, and you are my English friend," said a handsome blue-eyed child to his little companion, as they sauntered hand-in-hand through the spacious entrance-hall at Edeldorf. The boy was evidently bent on patronising his friend. The friend was somewhat abashed and bewildered, and grateful to be taken notice of.

"What is your name?--may I call you by your Christian name?" said the lesser child, timidly, and rather nestling to his protector, for such had the bigger boy constituted himself.

"My name is Victor," was the proud reply, "and *you* may call me Victor, because I love you; but the servants must call me Count, because my papa is a count; and I am not an Austrian count, but a Hungarian. Come and see my sword." So the two children were soon busy in an examination of that very beautiful, but not very destructive plaything.

They were indeed a strange contrast. Victor de Rohan, son and heir to one of the noblest and wealthiest of Hungary's aristocracy, looked all over the high-bred child he was. Free and bold, his large, frank blue eyes, and wide brow, shaded with clustering curls of golden brown, betokened a gallant, thoughtless spirit, and a kind, warm heart; whilst the delicate nostril and handsomely-curved mouth of the well-born child betrayed, perhaps, a little too much pride for one so young, and argued a disposition not too patient of contradiction or restraint. His little companion was as unlike him as possible, and indeed most people would have taken Victor for the English boy, and Vere for the foreign one. The latter was heavy, awkward, and ungainly in his movements, timid and hesitating in his manner, with a sallow complexion, and dark, deep-set eyes, that seemed always looking into a world beyond. He was a strange child, totally without the light-heartedness of his age, timid, shy, and awkward, but capable of strong attachments, and willing to endure anything for the sake of those he loved. Then he had quaint fancies, and curious modes of expressing them, which made other children laugh at him, when the boy would retire into himself, deeply wounded and unhappy, but too proud to show it. As he looks now at Victor's sword, with which the latter is vapouring about the hall, destroying imaginary enemies, Vere asks--

"What becomes of the people that are killed, Victor?"

"We ride over their bodies," says Victor, who has just delivered a finishing thrust at his phantom foe.

"Yes, but what *becomes* of them?" pursues the child, now answering himself. "I think they come to me in my dreams; for sometimes, do you know, I dream of men in armour charging on white horses, and they come by with a wind that wakes me; and when I ask 'Nettich' who they are, she says they are the fairies; but I don't think they are fairies, because you know fairies are quite small, and have wings. No, I think they must be the people that are killed."

"Very likely," replies Victor, who has not considered the subject in this light, and whose dreams are mostly of ponies and plum-cake--"very likely; but come to papa, and he will give us some grapes." So off they go, arm-in-arm, to the great banqueting-hall; and Vere postpones his dream-theories to some future occasion, for there is a charm about grapes that speaks at once to a child's heart.

So the two boys make their entrance into the banqueting-hall, where De Rohan sits in state, surrounded by his guests. On his right is placed Philip Egerton, whose dark eye gleams with pleasure as he looks upon his son. Who but a father would take delight in such a plain, unattractive child? Vere glides quietly to his side, shrinking from the strange faces and gorgeous uniforms around; but Victor walks boldly up to the old Count, and demands his daily glass of Tokay, not as a favour, but a right.

"I drink to Hungary!" says the child, looking full into the face of his next neighbour, a prince allied to the Imperial family, and a General of Austrian cavalry. "Monsieur le Prince, your good health! Come, clink your glass with me."

"Your boy is a true De Rohan," says the good-natured Austrian, as he accepts the urchin's challenge, and their goblets ring against each other. "Will you be a soldier, my lad, and wear the white uniform?"

"I will be a soldier," answers the child, "but not an Austrian soldier like you: Austrian soldiers are not so brave as Hungarians."

"Well said, my little patriot," replies the amused General. "So you do not think our people are good for much? Why, with that sword of yours, I should be very sorry to face you with my whole division. What a Light

Dragoon the rogue will make, De Rohan! see, he has plundered the grapes already." And the jolly prince sat back in his chair, and poured himself out another glass of "Imperial Tokay."

"Hush, Victor!" said his father, laughing, in spite of himself, at his child's forwardness. "Look at your little English friend; he stands quiet there, and says nothing. I shall make an Englishman of my boy, Egerton; he shall go to an English school, and learn to ride and box, and to be a man. I love England and the English. Egerton, your good health! I wish my boy to be like yours. *Sapperment!* he is quiet, but I will answer for it he fears neither man nor devil."

My father's face lighted up with pleasure as he pressed me to his side. Kind father! I believe he thought his ugly, timid, shrinking child was the admiration of all.

"I think the boy has courage," he said, "but for that I give him little credit. All men are naturally brave; it is but education that makes us reflect; hence we learn to fear consequences, and so become cowards."

"Pardon, *mon cher*," observed the Austrian General, with a laugh. "Now, my opinion is that all men are naturally cowards, and that we alone deserve credit who overcome that propensity, and so distinguish ourselves for what we choose to call bravery, but which we ought rather to term self-command. What say you, De Rohan? You have been in action, and 'on the ground,' too, more than once. Were you not cursedly afraid?"

De Rohan smiled good-humouredly, and filled his glass.

"Shall I tell you my opinion of courage?" said he, holding up the sparkling fluid to the light. "I think of courage what our Hungarian Hussars think of a breast-plate. 'Of what use,' say they, 'is cuirass and back-piece and all that weight of defensive armour? Give us a pint of wine in our stomachs, and we are *breastplate all over*.' Come, Wallenstein, put your breastplate on--it is very light, and fits very easily."

The General filled again, but returned to the charge.

"You remind me," said he, "of a conversation I overheard when I was a lieutenant in the first regiment of Uhlans. We were drawn up on the crest of a hill opposite a battery in position not half-a-mile from us. If they had retired us two hundred yards, we should have been under cover; but we never got the order, and there we stood. Whish! the round-shot came over our heads and under our feet, and into our ranks, and we lost two men and five horses before we knew where we were. The soldiers grumbled sadly, and a few seemed inclined to turn rein and go to the rear. Mind you, it is not fair to ask cavalry to sit still and be pounded for amusement; but the officers being *cowards by education*, Mr. Egerton, did their duty well, and kept the men together. I was watching my troop anxiously enough, and I heard one man say to his comrade, 'Look at Johann, Fritz! what a bold one he is; he thinks nothing of the fire; see, he tickles the horse of his front-rank man even now, to make him kick.'"

"Exactly my argument," interrupted my father; "he was an uneducated man, consequently saw nothing to be afraid of. Bravery, after all, is only insensibility to danger."

"Fritz did not think so," replied Wallenstein. "Hear his answer--'Johann is a blockhead,' he replied, 'he has never been under fire before, and does not know his danger; but you and I, old comrade, we deserve to be made corporals; for we sit quiet here on our horses, *though we are most cursedly afraid.*'"

The guests all laughed; and the discussion would have terminated, but that De Rohan, who had drunk more wine than was his custom, and who was very proud of his boy, could not refrain from once more turning the conversation to Victor's merits, and to that personal courage by which, however much he might affect to make light of it in society, he set such store.

"Well, Wallenstein," said he; "you hold that Nature makes us cowards; if so, my boy here ought to show something of the white feather. Come hither, Victor. Are you afraid of being in the dark?"

"No, papa!" answered Victor, boldly; but added, after a moment's consideration, "except in the Ghost's Gallery. I don't go through the Ghost's Gallery after six o'clock."

This *naïve* confession excited much amusement amongst the guests; but De Rohan's confidence in his boy's courage was not to be so shaken.

"What shall I give you," said he, "to go and fetch me the old Breviary that lies on the table at the far end of the Ghost's Gallery?"

Victor looked at me, and I at him. My breath came quicker and quicker. The child coloured painfully, but did not answer. I felt his terrors myself. I looked upon the proposed expedition as a soldier might on a forlorn hope; but something within kept stirring me to speak; it was a mingled feeling of emulation, pity, and friendship, tinged with that inexplicable charm that coming danger has always possessed for me--a charm that the constitutionally brave are incapable of feeling. I mastered my shyness with an effort, and, shaking all over, said to the master of the house, in a thick, low voice--

"If you please, Monsieur le Comte, if Victor goes, I will go too."

"Well said, little man!" "Bravo, boy!" "Vere, you're a trump!" in plain English from my father; and "In Heaven's name, give the lads a breastplate apiece, in the shape of a glass of Tokay!" from the jolly General, were the acclamations that greeted my resolution; and for one delicious moment I felt like a little hero. Victor, too, caught the enthusiasm; and, ashamed of showing less courage than his playfellow, expressed his readiness to accompany me,--first stipulating, however, with praise-worthy caution, that he should take his sword for our joint preservation; and also that two large bunches of grapes should be placed at our disposal on our safe return, "if," as Victor touchingly remarked, "we ever came back at all!" My father opened the door for us with a low bow, and it closed upon a burst of laughter, which to us, bound, as we fancied, on an expedition of unparalleled danger, sounded to the last degree unfeeling.

Hand-in-hand we two children walked through the ante-room, and across the hall; nor was it until we reached the first landing on the wide, gloomy oak staircase, that we paused to consider our future plans, and to scan the desperate nature of our enterprise. There were but two more flights of steps, a green-baize door to go through, a few yards of passage to traverse, and then, Victor assured me, in trembling accents, we should be in the Ghost's Gallery. My heart beat painfully, and my informant began to cry.

We laid our plans, however, with considerable caution, and made a solemn compact of alliance, offensive and defensive, that no power, natural or supernatural, was to shake. We were on no account whatsoever to leave go of each other's hands. Thus linked, and Victor having his sword drawn,--for the furtherance of which warlike attitude I was to keep carefully on his left,--we resolved to advance, if possible, talking the whole way up to the fatal table whereon lay the Breviary, and then snatching it up hastily, to return backwards, so as to present our front to the foe till we reached the green-baize door, at which point *sauve qui peut* was to be the order; and we were to rush back into the dining-room as fast as our legs could carry us. But in the event of our progress being interrupted by the ghost (who appeared, as Victor informed me, in the shape of a huge black dog with green eyes,--a description at which my blood ran cold,--and which he added had been seen once by his governess and twice by an old drunken Hussar who waited on him, and answered to the name of "Hans"), we were to lie down on our faces, so as to hide our eyes from the ghostly vision, and scream till we alarmed the house; but on no account, we repeated in the most binding and solemn manner--on no account were we to let go of each other's hands. This compact made and provided, we advanced towards the gallery, Victor feeling the edge and point of his weapon with an appearance of confidence that my own beating heart told me must be put on for the occasion, and would vanish at the first appearance of danger.

And now the green door is passed and we are in the gallery; a faint light through the stained windows only serves to show its extent and general gloom, whilst its corners and abutments are black as a wolfs mouth. Not a servant in the castle would willingly traverse this gallery after dark, and we two children feel that we are at last alone, and cut off from all hopes of assistance or rescue. But the Breviary lies on the table at the far end, and, dreading the very sound of our own footsteps, we steal quietly on. All at once Victor stops short.

"What is that?" says he, in trembling accents.

The question alone takes away my breath, and I feel the drops break out on my lips and forehead. We stop simultaneously and listen. Encouraged by the silence, we creep on, and for an instant I experience that vague tumultuous feeling of excitement which is almost akin to pleasure. But hark!--a heavy breath!!--a groan!!! My hair stands on end, and Victor's hand clasps mine like a vice. I dare scarce turn my head towards the sound,--it comes from that far corner. There it is! A dark object in the deepest gloom of that recess seems crouching for a spring. "The ghost!--the ghost!!" I exclaim, losing all power of self-command in an agony of fear. "The dog!--the dog!!" shrieks Victor; and away we scour hard as our legs can carry us, forgetful of our solemn agreements and high resolves, forgetful of all but that safety lies before, and terror of the ghastliest description behind; away we scour, Victor leaving his sword where he dropped it at the first alarm, through the green door, down the oak staircase, across the hall, nor stop till we reach the banqueting-room, with its reassuring faces and its lights, cheering beyond measure by contrast with the gloom from which we have escaped.

What shouts of laughter met us as we approached the table. "Well, Victor, where's the Breviary?" said the Count. "What! my boy, was Nature too strong for you in the dark, with nobody looking on?" asked the General. "See! he has lost his sword," laughed another. "And the little Englander,-- he, too, was panic-struck," remarked the fourth. I shrank from them all and took refuge at my father's side. "Vere, I am ashamed of you," was all he said; but the words sank deep into my heart, and I bowed my head with a feeling of burning shame, that I had disgraced myself in my father's eyes for ever. We were sent to bed, and I shared Victor's nursery, under the joint charge of Nettich and his own attendant; but, do what I would, I could not sleep. There was a stain upon my character in the eyes of the one I loved best on earth, and I could not bear it. Though so quiet and undemonstrative, I was a child of strong attachments. I perfectly idolised my father, and now he was ashamed of me;--the words seemed to burn in my little heart. I tossed and tumbled and fretted myself into a fever, aggravated by the sounding snores of Nettich and the other nurse, who slept as only nurses can.

At last I could bear it no longer. I sat up in bed and peered stealthily round. All were hushed in sleep. I determined to do or die. Yes, I would go to the gallery; I would fetch the Breviary and lay it on my father's table before he awoke. If I succeeded, I should recover his good opinion; if I encountered the phantom dog, why, he could but kill me, after all. I would wake Victor, and we would go together;--or, no,--I would take the whole peril, and have all the glory of the exploit, myself. I thought it over every way. At last my mind was made up; my naked feet were on the floor; I stole from the nursery; I threaded the dark passages; I reached the gallery; a dim light was shining at the far end, and I could hear earnest voices conversing in a low, guarded tone. Half-frightened and altogether confused, I stopped and listened.

CHAPTER IV
FATHER AND SON

The Count's old steward has seen all go to rest in the castle; the lords have left the banqueting-room, and the servants, who have been making merry in the hall, are long ere this sound asleep. It is the steward's custom to see all safe before he lights his lamp and retires to rest; but to-night he shades it carefully with a wrinkled hand that trembles strangely, and his white face peers into the darkness, as though he were about some deed of shame. He steals into the Ghost's Gallery, and creeps silently to the farther end. There is a dark object muffled in a cloak in the gloomiest corner, and the light from the steward's lamp reveals a fine young man, sleeping with that thorough abandonment which is only observable in those who are completely outwearied and overdone. It is some minutes ere the old man can wake him.

"My boy!" says he; "my boy, it is time for us to part. Hard, hard is it to be robbed of my son--robbed----" and the old man checks himself as though the word recalled some painful associations.

"Ay, father," was the reply, "you know our old Croatian proverb, 'He who steals is but a borrower.' Nevertheless, I do not wish the Austrians to 'borrow' me, in case I should never be returned; and it is unmannerly for the lieutenant to occupy the same quarters as the general. I must be off before dawn; but surely it cannot be midnight yet."

"In less than an hour the day will break, my son. I have concealed you here because not a servant of the household dare set foot in the Ghost's Gallery till daylight, and you are safe; but twenty-four more hours must see you on the Danube, and you must come here no more. Oh, my boy! my boy!--lost to save me!--dishonoured that I might not be disgraced!--my boy! my boy!"--and the old man burst into a passion of weeping that seemed to convulse his very frame with agony.

The son had more energy and self-command; his voice did not even shake as he soothed and quieted the old man with a protecting fondness like that of a parent for a child. "My father," said he, "there is no dishonour where there is no guilt. My first duty is to you, and were it to do again, I would do it. What? it was but a momentary qualm and a snatch at the box; and *now* you are safe. Father, I shall come back some day, and offer you a home. Fear not for me. I have it *here* in my breast, the stuff of which men make fortunes. I can rely upon myself. I can obey orders; and, father, when others are bewildered and confused, I can *command*. I feel it; I know it. Let me but get clear of the 'Eagle's' talons, and fear not for me, dear father, I shall see you again, and we will be prosperous and happy yet. But, how to get away?--have you thought of a plan? Can I get a good horse here? Does the Count know I am in trouble, and will he help me? Tell me all, father, and I shall see my own way, I will answer for it."

"My gallant boy!" said the steward, despite of himself moved to admiration by the self-reliant bearing of his son; "there is but one chance; for the Count could not but hand you over to Wallenstein if he knew you were in the castle, and then it would be a pleasant jest, and the nearest tree. The General is a jovial comrade and a good-humoured acquaintance; but, as a matter of duty, he would hang his own son and go to dinner afterwards with an appetite none the worse. No, no. 'Trust to an Austrian's mercy and confess yourself!' I have a better plan than that. The Zingynies are in the village; they held their merrymaking here yesterday. I saw their Queen last night after you arrived. I have arranged it all with her. A gipsy's dress, a dyed skin, and the middle of the troop; not an Austrian soldier in Hungary that will detect you then. Banishment is better than death. Oh, my boy! my boy!" and once more the old man gave way and wept.

"Forward, then, father!" said the young man, whom I now recognised as my travelling acquaintance; "there is no time to lose now. How can we get out of the castle without alarming the household? I leave all to you now; it will be my turn some day." And as he spoke he rose from the steps on which he had been lying when his recumbent form had so alarmed Victor and myself, and accompanied his father down a winding staircase that seemed let into the massive wall of the old building. My curiosity was fearfully excited. I would have given all my playthings to follow them. I crept stealthily on, naked feet and all; but I was not close enough behind, and the door shut quietly with a spring just as my hand was upon it, leaving me alone in the Ghost's Gallery. I was not the least frightened now. I forgot all about ghosts and Breviaries, and stole back to my nursery and my bed, my little head completely filled with a medley of stewards and soldiers and gipsies, and Austrian generals and military executions, and phantom dogs and secret staircases, and all the most unlikely incidents that crowd together in that busy organ--a child's brain.

CHAPTER V
THE ZINGYNIES

The morning sun smiles upon a motley troop journeying towards the Danube. Two or three lithe, supple urchins, bounding and dancing along with half-naked bodies, and bright black eyes shining through knotted elf-locks, form the advanced guard. Half-a-dozen donkeys seem to carry the whole property of the tribe. The main body consists of sinewy, active-looking men, and strikingly handsome girls, all walking with the free, graceful air and elastic gait peculiar to those whose lives are passed entirely in active exercise, under no roof but that of heaven. Dark-browed women in the very meridian of beauty bring up the rear, dragging or carrying a race of swarthy progeny, all alike distinguished for the sparkling eyes and raven hair, which, with a cunning nothing can overreach, and a nature nothing can tame, seem to be the peculiar inheritance of the gipsy. Their costume is striking, not to say grotesque. Some of the girls, and all the matrons, bind their brows with various coloured handkerchiefs, which form a very picturesque and not unbecoming head-gear; whilst in a few instances coins even of gold are strung amongst the jetty locks of the Zingynie beauties. The men are not so particular in their attire. One sinewy fellow wears only a goatskin shirt and a string of beads round his neck, but the generality are clad in the coarse cloth of the country, much tattered, and bearing evident symptoms of weather and wear. The little mischievous urchins who are clinging round their mothers' necks, or dragging back from their mothers' hands, and holding on to their mothers' skirts, are almost naked. Small heads and hands and feet, all the marks of what we are accustomed to term high birth, are hereditary among the gipsies; and we doubt if the Queen of the South herself was a more queenly-looking personage than the dame now marching in the midst of the throng, and conversing earnestly with her companion, a resolute-looking man scarce entering upon the prime of life, with a gipsy complexion, but a bearing in which it is not difficult to recognise the soldier. He is talking to his protectress--for such she is--with a military frankness and vivacity, which even to that royal personage, accustomed though she be to exact all the respect due to her rank, appear by no means displeasing. The lady is verging on the autumn of her charms (their summer must have been scorching indeed!) and though a masculine beauty, is a beauty nevertheless. Black-browed is she, and deep-coloured, with eyes of fire, and locks of jet, even now untinged with grey. Straight and regular are her features, and the wide mouth, with its strong, even dazzling teeth, betokens an energy and force of will which would do credit to the other sex. She has the face of a woman that would dare much, labour much, everything but *love* much. She ought to be a queen, and she is one, none the less despotic for ruling over a tribe of gipsies instead of a civilised community.

"None dispute my word here," says she, "and my word is pledged to bring you to the Danube. Let me see a soldier of them all lay a hand upon you, and you shall see the gipsy brood show their teeth. A long knife is no bad weapon at close quarters. When you have got to the top of the wheel you will remember me!"

The soldier laughed, and lightly replied, "Yours are the sort of eyes one does not easily forget, mother. I wish I were a prince of the blood in your nation. As I am situated now I can only be dazzled by so much beauty, and go my ways."

The woman checked him sternly, almost savagely, though a few minutes before she had been listening, half amused, to his gay and not very respectful conversation.

"Hush!" she said, "trifler. Once more I say, when the wheel has turned, remember me. Give me your hand; I can read it plainer so."

"What, mother?" laughed out her companion. "Every gipsy can tell fortunes; mine has been told many a time, but it never came true."

She was studying the lines on his palm with earnest attention. She raised her dark eyes angrily to his face.

"Blind! blind!" she answered, in a low, eager tone. "The best of you cannot see a yard upon your way. Look at that white road, winding and winding many a mile before us upon the plain. Because it is flat and soft and smooth as far as we can see, will there be no hills on our journey, no rocks to cut our feet--no thorns to tear our limbs? Can you see the Danube rolling on far, far before us? Can you see the river you will have to cross some day, or can you tell me where it leads? I have the map of our journey here in my brain; I have the map of your career here on your hand. Once more I say, when the chiefs are in council, and the hosts are melting like snow before the sun, and the earth quakes, and the heavens are filled with thunder, and the shower that falls scorches and crushes and blasts--remember me! I follow the line of wealth: Man of gold! spoil on; here a horse, there a diamond; hundreds to uphold the right, thousands to spare the wrong; both hands full, and broad lands near a city of palaces, and a king's favour, and a nation of slaves beneath thy foot. I follow the line of pleasure: Costly amber; rich embroidery; dark eyes melting for the Croat; glances unveiled for the shaven head, many and loving and beautiful; a garland of roses, all for one--rose by rose plucked and withered and thrown away; one tender bud remaining; cherish it till it blows, and wear it till it dies. I follow the line of blood: it leads towards the rising sun--charging squadrons with lances in rest, and a wild shout in a strange tongue; and the dead wrapped in grey, with charm and amulet that were powerless to save; and hosts of many nations gathered by the sea--pestilence, famine, despair, and victory. Rising on the whirlwind, chief among chiefs, the honoured of leaders, the counsellor of princes--remember me! But ha! the line is crossed. Beware! trust not the sons of the adopted land; when the lily is on thy breast, beware of the dusky shadow on the wall; beware and remember me!"

The gipsy stopped, and clung to him exhausted. For a few paces she was unable to support herself; the prophetic mood past, there was a reaction, and all her powers seemed to fail her at once; but her companion walked on in silence. The eagerness of the Pythoness had impressed even his strong, practical nature, and he seemed himself to look into futurity as he muttered, "If man can win it, I will."

The gipsies travelled but slowly; and although the sun was already high, they had not yet placed many miles between the fugitive and the castle. This, however, was of no great importance. His disguise was so complete, that few would have recognised in the tattered, swarthy vagrant, the smart, soldier-like traveller who had arrived the previous evening at Edeldorf. From the conversation I had overheard in the Ghost's Gallery, I was alone in the secret, which, strange to say, I forbore to confide even to my friend Victor. But I could not forget the steward and his son; it was my first glimpse into the romance of real life, and I could not help feeling a painful interest in his fortunes, and an eager desire to see him at least safe off with his motley company. I was rejoiced, therefore, at Victor's early proposal, made the very instant we had swallowed our breakfasts, that we should take a ride; and notwithstanding my misgivings about a strange pony, for I was always timid on horseback, I willingly accepted his offer of a mount, and jumped into the saddle almost as readily as my little companion, a true Hungarian, with whom,

> Like Mad Tom, the chiefest care
> Was horse to ride and weapon wear.

Of course, Victor had a complete establishment of ponies belonging to himself; and equally of course, he had detailed to me at great length their several merits and peculiarities, with an authentic biography of his favourite--a stiff little chestnut, rejoicing in the name of "Gold-kind," which, signifying as it does "the golden-child," or darling, he seemed to think an exceedingly happy allusion to the chestnut skin and endearing qualities of his treasure.

Fortunately, my pony was very quiet; and although, when mounted, my playfellow went off at score, we were soon some miles from Edeldorf, without any event occurring to upset my own equilibrium or the sobriety of my steed. Equally fortunately, we took the road by which the gipsies had travelled. Ere long, we overtook the cavalcade as it wound slowly along the plain. Heads were bared to Victor, and blessings called down upon the family of De Rohan; for the old Count was at all times a friend to the friendless, and a refuge to the poor.

"Good luck to you, young Count! shall I tell your fortune?" said one.

"Little, honourable cavalier, give me your hand, and cross it with a 'zwantziger,'" said another.

"Be silent, children, and let me speak to the young De Rohan," said the gipsy queen; and she laid her hand upon his bridle, and fairly brought Gold-kind to a halt.

Victor looked half afraid, although he began to laugh.

"Let me go," said he, tugging vigorously at his reins; "papa desired me not to have my fortune told."

"Not by a common Zingynie," urged the queen, archly; "but I am the mother of all these. My pretty boy, I was at your christening, and have held you in my arms many a time. Let me tell your happy fortune."

Victor began to relent. "If Vere will have his told first, I will," said he, turning half bashfully, half eagerly to me.

I proffered my hand readily to the gipsy, and crossed it with one of the two pieces of silver which constituted the whole of my worldly wealth. The gipsy laughed, and began to prophesy in German. There are some events a child never forgets; and I remember every word she said as well as if it had been spoken yesterday.

"Over the sea, and again over the sea; thou shalt know grief and hardship and losses, and the dove shall be driven from its nest. And the dove's heart shall become like the eagle's, that flies alone, and fleshes her beak in the slain. Beat on, though the poor wings be bruised by the tempest, and the breast be sore, and the heart sink; beat on against the wind, and seek no shelter till thou find thy resting-place at last. The time will come--only beat on."

The woman laughed as she spoke; but there was a kindly tone in her voice and a pitying look in her bright eyes that went straight to my heart. Many a time since, in life, when the storm has indeed been boisterous and the wings so weary, have I thought of those words of encouragement, "The time will come--beat on."

It was now Victor's turn, and he crossed his palm with a golden ducat ere he presented it to the sibyl. This was of itself sufficient to insure him a magnificent future; and as the queen perused the lines on his soft little hand, with its pink fingers, she indulged in anticipations of magnificence proportioned to the handsome donation of the child.

"Thou shalt be a 'De Rohan,' my darling, and I can promise thee no brighter lot,--broad acres, and blessings from the poor, and horses, and wealth, and honours. And the sword shall spare thee, and the battle turn aside to let thee pass. And thou shalt wed a fair bride with dark eyes and a queenly brow; but beware of St. Hubert's Day. Birth and burial, birth and burial--beware of St. Hubert's Day."

"But I want to be a soldier," exclaimed Victor, who seemed much disappointed at the future which was prognosticated for him; "the De Rohans were always soldiers. Mother, can't you make out I shall be a soldier?" still holding the little hand open.

"Farewell, my children," was the only answer vouchsafed by the prophetess. "I can only read, I cannot write: farewell." And setting the troop in order, she motioned to them to continue their march without further delay.

I took advantage of the movement to press near my acquaintance of the day before, whom I had not failed to recognise in his gipsy garb. Poor fellow, my childish heart bled for him, and, in a happy moment, I bethought me of my remaining bit of silver. I stooped from my pony and kissed his forehead, while I squeezed the coin into his hand without a word. The tears came into the deserter's eyes. "God bless you, little man! I shall never forget you," was all he said; but I observed that he bit the coin with his large, strong teeth till it was nearly double, and then placed it carefully in his bosom. We turned our ponies, and were soon out of sight; but I never breathed a syllable to Victor about the fugitive, or the steward, or the Ghost's Gallery, for two whole days. Human nature could keep the secret no longer.

CHAPTER VI
SCHOOL

In one of the pleasantest valleys of sweet Somersetshire stands a large red-brick house that bears unmistakably impressed on its exterior the title "School." You would not take it for a "hall," or an hospital, or an almshouse, or anything in the world but an institution for the rising generation, in which the ways of the wide world are so successfully imitated that, in the qualities of foresight, cunning, duplicity, and general selfishness, the boy may indeed be said to be "father to the man." The house stands on a slope towards the south, with a trim lawn and carefully-kept gravel drive, leading to a front door, of which the steps are always clean and the handles always bright. How a ring at that door-bell used to bring all our hearts into our mouths. Forty boys were we, sitting grudgingly over our lessons on the bright summer forenoons, and not one of us but thought that ring might possibly announce a "something" for him from "home." Home! what was there in the word, that it should call up such visions of happiness, that it should create such a longing, sickening desire to have the wings of a dove and flee away, that it should make the present such a blank and comfortless reality? Why do we persist in sending our children so early to school? A little boy, with all his affections developing themselves, loving and playful and happy, not ashamed to be fond of his sisters, and thinking mamma all that is beautiful and graceful and good, is to be torn from that home which is to him an earthly Paradise, and transferred to a place of which we had better not ask the urchin his own private opinion. We appeal to every mother--and it is a mother who is best capable of judging for a child--whether her darling returns to her improved in her eyes after his first half-year at school. She looks in vain for the pliant, affectionate disposition that a word from her used to be capable, of moulding at will, and finds instead a stubborn self-sufficient spirit that has been called forth by harsh treatment and intercourse with the mimic world of boys; more selfish and more conventional, because less characteristic than that of men. He is impatient of her tenderness now, nay, half ashamed to return it. Already he aspires to be a man, in his own eyes, and thinks it manly to make light of those affections and endearments by which he once set such store. The mother is no longer all in all in his heart, her empire is divided and weakened, soon it will be swept away, and she sighs for the white-frock days when her child was fondly and entirely her own. Now, I cannot help thinking the longer these days last the better. Anxious parent, what do you wish your boy to become? A successful man in after life?--then rear him tenderly and carefully at first. You would not bit a colt at two years old; be not less patient with your own flesh and blood. Nature is the best guide, you may depend. Leave him to the women till his strength is established and his courage high, and when the metal has assumed shape and consistency, to the forge with it as soon as you will. Hardship, buffetings, adversity, all these are good for the *youth*, but, for Heaven's sake, spare the *child*.

Forty boys are droning away at their tasks on a bright sunshiny morning in June, and I am sitting at an old oak desk, begrimed and splashed with the inkshed of many generations, and hacked by the knives of idler after idler for the last fifty years. I have yet to learn by heart some two score lines from the Æneid. How I hate Virgil whilst I bend over those dog's-eared leaves and that uncomfortable desk. How I envy the white butterfly of which I have just got a glimpse as he soars away into the blue sky--for no terrestrial objects are visible from our schoolroom window to distract our attention and interfere with our labours. I have already accompanied him in fancy over the lawn, and the garden, and the high white-thorn fence into the meadow beyond,--how well I know the deep glades of that copse for which he is making; how I wish I was on my back in its shadow now. Never mind, to-day is a half-holiday, and this afternoon I will spend somehow in a dear delicious ramble through the fairy-land of "out of bounds." The rap of our master's cane against his desk--a gentlemanlike method of awakening attention and asserting authority--startles me from my day-dream. "March," for we drop the Mr. prefixed, in speaking of our pedagogue, "March is a bit of a Tartar, and I tremble for the result."

"Egerton to come up."

Egerton goes up accordingly, with many misgivings, and embarks, like a desperate man, on the loathed *infandum Regina jubes*.

The result may be gathered from March's observations as he returns me the book.

"Not a line correct, sir; stand down, sir; the finest passage of the poet shamefully mangled and defaced; it is a perfect disgrace to Everdon. Remain in till five, sir; and repeat the whole lesson to Mr. Manners."

"Please, sir, I tried to learn it, sir; indeed I did, sir."

"Don't tell me, sir; *tried* to learn it, indeed. If it had been French or German, or--or any of these useless branches of learning, you would have had it by heart fast enough; but Latin, sir, Latin is the foundation of a gentleman's education; Latin you were sent here to acquire, and Latin, sir" (with an astounding rap on the desk), "you *shall* learn, or I'll know the reason why."

I may remark that March, though an excellent scholar, professed utter contempt for all but the dead languages.

I determined to make one more effort to save my half-holiday.

"Please, sir, if I might look over it once more, I could say it when the second class goes down; please, sir, won't you give me another chance?"

March was not, in schoolboy parlance, "half a bad fellow," and he did give me another chance, and I came up to him once more at the conclusion of school, having repeated the whole forty lines to myself without missing a word; but, alas! when I stood again on the step which led up to the dreaded desk, and gave away the book into those uncompromising hands, and heard that stern voice with its "Now, sir, begin," my intellects forsook me altogether, and while the floor seemed to rock under me, I made such blunders and confusion of the chief's oration to the love-sick queen, as drove March to the extremity of that very short tether which he was pleased to call his "patience," and drew upon myself the dreaded condemnation I had fought so hard to escape.

"Remain in, sir, till perfect, and repeat to Mr. Manners, without a mistake--Mr. Manners, you will be kind enough to see, *without a mistake!* Boys!" (with another rap of the cane) "school's up." March locks his desk with a bang, and retires. Mr. Manners puts on his hat. Forty boys burst instantaneously into tumultuous uproar, forty pairs of feet scuffle along the dusty boards, forty voices break into song and jest and glee, forty spirits are emancipated from the prison-house into freedom and air and sunshine-- forty, all save one.

So again I turn to the *infandum Eegina Jubes*, and sit me down and cry.

I had gone late to school, but I was a backward child in everything save my proficiency in modern languages. I had never known a mother, and the little education I had acquired was picked up in a desultory manner here and there during my travels with my father, and afterwards in a gloomy old library at Alton Grange, his own place in the same county as Mr. March's school. My father had remained abroad till his affairs made it imperative that he should return to England, and for some years we lived in seclusion at Alton, with an establishment that even my boyish penetration could discover was reduced to the narrowest possible limits. I think this was the idlest period of my life. I did no lessons, unless my father's endeavour to teach me painting, an art that I showed year after year less inclination to master, could be called so. I had but few ideas, yet they were very dear ones. I adored my father; on him I lavished all the love that would have been a mother's right; and having no other relations--none in the world that I cared for, or that cared for me, even nurse Nettich having remained in Hungary--my father was all-in-all. I used to wait at his door of a morning to hear him wake, and go away quite satisfied without letting him know. I used to watch him for miles when he rode out, and walk any distance to meet him on his way home. To please him I would even mount a quiet pony that he had bought on purpose for me, and dissemble my terrors because I saw they annoyed my kind father. I was a very shy, timid, and awkward boy, shrinking from strangers with a fear that was positively painful, and liking nothing so well as a huge arm-chair in the gloomy oak wainscoted library, where I would sit by the hour reading old poetry, old plays, old novels, and wandering about till I lost myself in a world of my own creating, full of beauty and romance, and all that ideal life which we must perforce call nonsense, but which, were it reality, would make this earth a heaven. Such was a bad course of training for a boy whose disposition was naturally too dreamy and imaginative, too deficient in energy and practical good sense. Had it gone on I must have become a madman; what is it but madness to live in a world of our own? I shall never forget the break-up of my dreams, the beginning, to me, of hard practical life.

I was coiled up in my favourite attitude, buried in the depths of a huge arm-chair in the library, and devouring with all my senses and all my soul the pages of the *Morte d'Arthur,* that most voluminous and least instructive of romances, but one for which, to my shame be it said, I confess to this day a sneaking kindness. I was gazing on Queen Guenever, as I pictured her to myself, in scarlet and ermine and pearls, with raven hair plaited over her queenly brow, and soft violet eyes, looking kindly down on mailed Sir Launcelot at her feet. I was holding Arthur's helmet in the forest, as the frank, handsome, stalwart monarch bent over a sparkling rill and cooled his sunburnt cheek, and laved his chestnut beard, whilst the sunbeams flickered through the green leaves and played upon his gleaming corslet and his armour of proof. I was feasting at Camelot with the Knights of the Round Table, jesting with Sir Dinadam, discussing grave subjects of high import with Sir Gawain, or breaking a lance in knightly courtesy with Sir Tristram and Sir Bore; in short, I was a child at a spectacle, but the spectacle came and went, and grew more and more gorgeous at will. In the midst of my dreams in walked my father, and sat down opposite the old arm-chair.

"Vere," said he, "you must go to school."

The announcement took away my breath: I had never, in my wildest moments, contemplated such a calamity.

"To school, papa; and when?" I mustered up courage to ask, clinging like a convict to the hope of a reprieve.

"The first of the month, my boy," answered my father, rather bullying himself into firmness, for I fancy he hated the separation as much as I did; "Mr. March writes me that his scholars will reunite on the first of next month, and he has a vacancy for you. We must make a man of you, Vere; and young De Rohan, your Hungarian friend, is going there too. You will have lots of playfellows, and get on very well, I have no doubt; and Everdon is not so far from here, and--and--you will be very comfortable, I trust; but I am loth to part with you, my dear, and that's the truth."

I felt as if I could have endured martyrdom when my father made this acknowledgment. I could do anything if I was only coaxed and pitied a little; and when I saw he was so unhappy at the idea of our separation, I resolved that no word or look of mine should add to his discomfort, although I felt my heart breaking at the thoughts of bidding him good-bye and leaving the Grange, with its quiet regularity and peaceful associations, for the noise and bustle and discipline of a large school. Queen Guenever and Sir Launcelot faded hopelessly from my mental vision, and in their places rose up stern forms of harsh taskmasters and satirical playfellows, early hours, regular discipline, Latin and Greek, and, worst of all, a continual bustle and a life in a crowd.

There were two peculiarities in my boyish character which, more than any others, unfitted me for battling with the world. I had a morbid dread of ridicule, which made me painfully shy of strangers. I have on many an occasion stood with my hand on the lock of a door, dreading to enter the room in which I heard strange voices, and then, plunging in with a desperate effort, have retired again as abruptly, covered with confusion, and so nervous as to create in the minds of the astonished guests a very natural doubt as to my mental sanity. The other peculiarity was an intense love of solitude. I was quite happy with my father, but if I could not enjoy his society, I preferred my own to that of any other mortal. I would take long walks by myself--I would sit for hours and read by myself--I had a bedroom of my own, into which I hated even a servant to set foot--and perhaps the one thing I dreaded more than all besides in my future life was, that I should never, never, be *alone*.

How I prized the last few days I spent at home; how I gazed on all the well-known objects as if I should never see them again; how the very chairs and tables seemed to bid me good-bye like old familiar friends. I had none of the lively anticipations which most boys cherish of the manliness and independence arising from a school-life; no long vista of cricket and football, and fame in their own little world, with increasing strength and stature, to end in a tailed coat, and even whiskers! No, I hated the idea of the whole thing. I expected to be miserable at Everdon, and, I freely confess, was not disappointed.

CHAPTER VII
PLAY

Dinner was over, and play-time begun for all but me, and again I turned to the *infandum Regina jubes*, and sat me down to cry.

A kind hand, grimed with ink, was laid on my shoulder, a pair of soft blue eyes looked into my face, and Victor de Rohan, my former playfellow, my present fast friend and declared "chum," sat down on the form beside me, and endeavoured to console me in distress.

"I'll help you, Egerton," said the warm-hearted lad; "say it to me; March is a beast, but Manners is a good fellow; Manners will hear you now, and we shall have our half-holiday after all."

"I can't, I can't," was my desponding reply. "Manners won't hear me, I know, till I am perfect, and I never can learn this stupid sing-song story. How I hate Queen Dido--how I hate Virgil. You should read about Guenever, Victor, and King Arthur! I'll tell you about them this afternoon;" and the tears came again into my eyes as I remembered there was no afternoon for me.

"Try once more," said Victor; "I'll get Manners to hear you; leave it to me; I know how to do it. I'll ask Ropsley." And Victor was off into the playground ere I was aware, in search of this valuable auxiliary.

Now, Ropsley was the mainspring round which turned the whole of our little world at Everdon. If an excuse for a holiday could be found, Ropsley was entreated to ask the desired favour of March. If a quarrel had to be adjusted, either in the usual course of ordeal by battle, or the less decisive method of arbitration, Ropsley was always invited to see fair play. He was the king of our little community. It was whispered that he could spar better than Manners, and construe better than March: he was certainly a more perfect linguist--as indeed I could vouch for from my own knowledge--than Schwartz, who came twice a week to teach us a rich German-French. We saw his boots were made by Hoby, and we felt his coats could only be the work of Stulz, for in those days Poole was not, and we were perfectly willing to believe that he wore a scarlet hunting-coat in the Christmas holidays, and had visiting cards of his own. In person he was tall and slim, with a pale complexion, and waving, soft brown hair: without being handsome, he was distinguished-looking; and even as a boy, I have seen strangers turn round and ask who he was; but the peculiar feature of his countenance was his light grey eye, veiled with long black eyelashes. It never seemed to kindle or to waver or to wink; it was always the same, hard, penetrating, and unmoved; it never smiled, though the rest of his features would laugh heartily enough, and it certainly never wept. Even in boyhood it was the eye of a cool, calculating, wary man. He knew the secrets of every boy in the school, but no one ever dreamt of cross-questioning Ropsley. We believed he only stayed at Everdon as a favour to March, who was immensely proud of his pupil's gentlemanlike manners and appearance, as well as of his scholarly proficiency, although no one ever saw him study, and we always expected Ropsley was "going to leave this half." We should not have been the least surprised to hear he had been sent for by the Sovereign, and created a peer of the realm on the spot; with all our various opinions, we were unanimous in one creed--that nothing was impossible for Ropsley, and he need only try, to succeed. For myself, I was dreadfully afraid of this luminary, and looked up to him with feelings of veneration which amounted to positive awe.

Not so Victor; the young Hungarian feared, I believe, nothing on earth, and *respected* but little. He was the only boy in the school who, despite the difference of age, would talk with Ropsley upon equal terms; and if anything could have added to the admiration with which we regarded the latter, it would have been the accurate knowledge he displayed of De Rohan's family, their history, their place in Hungary, all their belongings, as if he himself had been familiar with Edeldorf from boyhood. But so it was with everything; Ropsley knew all about people in general better than they did themselves.

Victor rushed back triumphantly into the schoolroom, where I still sat desponding at my desk, and Ropsley followed him.

"What's the matter, Vere?" he asked, in a patronising tone, and calling me by my Christian name, which I esteemed a great compliment. "What's the matter?" he repeated; "forty lines of Virgil to say; come, that's not much."

"But I *can't* learn it," I urged. "You must think me very stupid; and if it was French, or German, or English, I should not mind twice the quantity, but I cannot learn Latin, and it's no use trying."

The older boy sneered; it seemed so easy to him with his powerful mind to get forty lines of hexameters by heart. I believe he could have repeated the whole *Æneid* without book from beginning to end.

"Do you want to go out to-day, Vere?" said he.

I clasped my hands in supplication, as I replied, "Oh! I would give anything, *anything*, to get away from this horrid schoolroom, and 'shirk out' with Victor and Bold."

' The latter, be it observed, was a dog in whose society I took great delight, and whom I kept in the village, at an outlay of one shilling per week, much to the detriment of my personal fortune.

"Very well," said the great man; "come with me to Manners, and bring your book with you."

So I followed my deliverer into the playground, with the *infandum Regina* still weighing heavily on my soul.

Manners, the usher, was playing cricket with some dozen of the bigger boys, and was in the act of "going for a sixer." His coat and waistcoat were off, and his shirt-sleeves tucked up, disclosing his manly arms bared to the elbow; and Manners was in his glory, for, notwithstanding the beard upon his chin, our usher was as very a boy at heart as the youngest urchin in the lower class. A dandy, too, was Manners, and a wight of an imaginative turn of mind, which chiefly developed itself in the harmless form of bright visions for the future, teeming with romantic adventures, of which he was himself to be the hero. His past he seldom dwelt upon. His aspirations were military--his ideas extravagant. He was great on the Peninsula and Lord Anglesey at Waterloo; and had patent boxes in his high-heeled boots that only required the addition of heavy clanking spurs to complete the illusion that Mr. Manners ought to be a cavalry officer. Of his riding he spoke largely; but his proficiency in this exercise we had no means of ascertaining. There were two things, however, on which Manners prided himself, and which were a source of intense amusement to the urchins by whom he was surrounded:--these were, his personal strength, and his whiskers; the former quality was encouraged to develop itself by earnest application to all manly sports and exercises; the latter ornaments were cultivated and enriched with every description of "nutrifier," "regenerator," and "unguent" known to the hairdresser or the advertiser. Alas! without effect proportioned to the perseverance displayed; two small patches of fluff under the jaw-bones, that showed to greatest advantage by candlelight, being the only evidence of so much painstaking and cultivation thrown away. Of his muscular prowess, however, it behoved us to speak with reverence. Was it not on record in the annals of the school that when the "King of Naples," our dissipated pieman, endeavoured to justify by force an act of dishonesty by which he had done Timmins minor out of half-a-crown, Manners stripped at once to his shirt-sleeves, and "went in" at the Monarch with all the vigour and activity of some three-and-twenty summers against three-score? The

Monarch, a truculent old ruffian, with a red neckcloth, half-boots, and one eye, fought gallantly for a few rounds, and was rather getting the best of it, when, somewhat unaccountably, he gave in, leaving the usher master of the field. Ropsley, who gave his friend a knee, *secundum artem*, and urged him, with frequent injunctions, to "fight high," attributed this easy victory to the forbearance of their antagonist, who had an eye to future trade and mercantile profits; but Manners, whose account of the battle I have heard more than once, always scouted this view of the transaction.

"He went down, sir, as if he was shot," he would say, doubling his arm, and showing the muscles standing out in bold relief. "Few men have the biceps so well developed as mine, and he went down *as if he was shot*. If I had hit him as hard as I could, sir, I *must* have killed him!"

Our usher was a good-natured fellow, notwithstanding.

"I'll hear you in ten minutes, Egerton," said he, "when I have had my innings;" and forthwith he stretched himself into attitude, and prepared to strike.

"Better give me your bat," remarked Ropsley, who was too lazy to play cricket in a regular manner. Of course, Manners consented; nobody ever refused Ropsley anything; and in ten minutes' time I had repeated the *infandum Regina*, and Ropsley had added some dozen masterly hits to the usher's score. Ropsley always liked another man's "innings" better than his own.

Now the regulations at Everdon, as they were excessively strict, and based upon the principle that Apollo should always keep the bow at the utmost degree of tension, so were they eluded upon every available opportunity, and set at nought and laughed at by the youngest urchins in the school. We had an ample playground for our minor sports, and a meadow beyond, in which we were permitted to follow the exhilarating pastime of cricket, the share of the younger boys in that exciting amusement being limited to a pursuit of the ball round the field, and a prompt return of the same to their seniors, doubtless a necessary ingredient in this noble game, but one which is not calculated to excite enthusiastic pleasure in the youthful mind. From the playground and its adjacent meadow it was a capital offence to absent oneself. All the rest of Somersetshire was "out of bounds"; and to be caught "out of bounds" was a crime for which corporal punishment was the invariable reward. At the same time, the offence was, so to speak, "winked at." No inquiries were made as to how we spent half-holidays between one o'clock and seven; and many a glorious ramble we used to have during those precious six hours in all the ecstasy of "freedom,"--a word understood by none better than the schoolboy. A certain deference was, however, exacted to the regulations of the establishment; by a sort of tacit compact, it seemed to be understood that our code was so far Spartan as to make, not the crime, but the being "found out," a punishable offence, and boys were always supposed to take their chance. If seen in the act of escaping, or afterwards met by any of the masters in the surrounding country, we were liable to be flogged; and to do March justice, we always *were* flogged, and pretty soundly, too. Under these circumstances, some little care and circumspection had to be observed in starting for our rambles. Certain steps had been made in the playground wall, where it was hidden from the house by the stem of a fine old elm, and by dropping quietly down into an orchard beyond--an orchard, be it observed, of which the fruit was always plucked before it reached maturity--and then stealing along the back of a thick, high hedge, we could get fairly away out of sight of the school windows, and so make our escape.

Now, on the afternoon in question we had planned an expedition in which Victor, and I, and my dog Bold had determined to be principal performers. Of the latter personage in the trio I must remark, that no party of pleasure on which we embarked was ever supposed to be perfect without his society. His original possessor was the "King of Naples," whom I have already mentioned, and who, I conclude, stole him, as he appeared one day tied to that personage by an old cotton handkerchief, and looking as wobegone and unhappy as a retriever puppy of some three months old, torn from his mamma and his brothers and sisters, and the comfortable kennel in which he was brought up, and transferred to the tender mercies of a drunken, poaching, dog-stealing ruffian, was likely to feel in so false a position. The "King" brought him into our playground on one of his tart-selling visits, as a specimen of the rarest breed of retrievers known in the West of England. The puppy seemed so thoroughly miserable, and looked up at me so piteously, that I forthwith asked his price, and after a deal of haggling, and a consultation between De Rohan and myself, I determined to become his purchaser, at the munificent sum of one sovereign, of which ten shillings (my all) were to be paid on the spot, and the other ten to remain, so to speak, on mortgage upon the animal, with the further understanding that he should be kept at the residence of the "King of Naples," who, in consideration of the regular payment of one shilling per week, bound himself to feed the same and complete his education in all the canine branches of plunging, diving, fetching and carrying, on a system of his own, which he briefly described as "fust-rate."

With a deal of prompting from Manners, I got through my forty lines; and he shut the book with a good-natured smile as Ropsley threw down the bat he had been wielding so skilfully, and put on his coat.

"Come and lunch with me at 'The Club,'" said he to Manners, whom he led completely by the nose; "I'll give you Dutch cheese, and sherry and soda-water, and a cigar. Hie! Vere, you ungrateful little ruffian, where are you off to? I want you."

I was making my escape as rapidly as possible at the mention of "The Club," a word which we younger boys held in utter fear and detestation, as being associated in our minds with much perilous enterprise and gratuitous suffering. The Club consisted of an old bent tree in a retired corner of the playground, on the trunk of which Ropsley had caused a comfortable seat to be fashioned for his own delectation; and here, in company with Manners and two or three senior boys, it was his custom to sit smoking and drinking curious compounds, of which the ingredients, being contraband, had to be fetched by us, at the risk of corporal punishment, from the village of Everdon, an honest half-mile journey at the least.

Ropsley tendered a large cigar to Manners, lit one himself, settled his long limbs comfortably on the seat, and gave me his orders.

"One Dutch cheese, three pottles of strawberries--now attend, confound you!--two bottles of old sherry from 'The Greyhound,'--mind, the OLD sherry; half-a-dozen of soda-water, and a couple of pork-pies. Put the whole into a basket; they'll give you one at the bar, if you say it's for me, and tell them to put it down to my account. Put a clean napkin over the basket, and if you dirty the napkin or break the bottles, I'll break *your* head! Now be off! Manners, I'll take your two to one he does it without a mistake, and is back here under the five-and-twenty minutes."

I did not dare disobey, but I was horribly disgusted at having to employ any portion of my half-holiday in so uncongenial a manner. I rushed back into the schoolroom for my cap, and held a hurried consultation with Victor as to our future proceedings.

"He only got you off because he wanted you to 'shirk out' for him," exclaimed my indignant chum; "it's a shame, *that* it is. Don't go for him, Vere; let's get out quietly, and be off to Beverley. It's the last chance, so old 'Nap' says" (this was an abbreviation for the "King of Naples," who was in truth a great authority both with Victor and myself); "and it's *such* a beautiful afternoon."

"But what a licking I shall get from Ropsley," I interposed, with considerable misgivings; "he's sure to say I'm an ungrateful little beast. I don't like to be called ungrateful, Victor, and I don't like to be called a little beast."

"Oh, never mind the names, and a licking is soon over," replied Victor, who learned little from his *Horace* save the *carpe diem* philosophy, and who looked upon the licking with considerably more resignation than did the probable recipient. "We shall just have time to do it, if we start now. Come on, old fellow; be plucky for once, and come on."

I was not proof against the temptation. The project was a long-planned one, and I could not bear the thoughts of giving it up now. Many a time in our rambles had we surmounted the hill that looked down upon Beverley Manor, and viewed it from afar as a sort of unknown fairyland. What a golden time one's boyhood was! A day at Beverley was our dream of all that was most exciting in adventure, most voluptuous in delight; and now "Nap" had promised to accompany us to this earthly Paradise, and show us what he was pleased to term its "hins-an'-houts." Not all the cheeses of Holland should prevent my having one day's liberty and enjoyment. I weighed well the price: the certain licking, and the sarcastic abuse which I feared even more; and I think I held my half-holiday all the dearer for having to purchase it at such a cost.

We were across the playground like lapwings. Ropsley, who was deep in his cigar and a copy of *Bell's Life*, which forbidden paper he caused Manners to take in for him surreptitiously, never dreamed that his behests could be treated with contempt, and hardly turned his head to look at us. We surmounted the wall with an agility born of repeated practice; we stole along the adjacent orchard, under covert of the well-known friendly hedge, and only breathed freely when we found ourselves completely out of sight of the house, and swinging along the Everdon lane at a schoolboy's jog, which, like the Highlander's, is equivalent to any other person's gallop. No pair of carriage horses can step together like two schoolboy "chums" who are in the constant habit of being late in company. Little boys as we were, Victor and I could do our five miles in the hour without much difficulty, keeping step like clockwork, and talking the whole time.

In five minutes we were at the wicket of a small tumble-down building, with dilapidated windows and a ruinous thatched roof, which was in fact the dwelling of no less a personage than the "King of Naples," but was seldom alluded to by that worthy in more definite terms than "the old place," or "my shop"; and this only when in a particularly confidential mood--its existence being usually indicated by a jerk of the head towards his blind side, which was supposed to infer proper caution, and a decorous respect for the sanctity of private life. It was indeed one of those edifices of which the word "tenement" seems alone to convey an adequate description.

The garden produce consisted of a ragged shirt and a darned pair of worsted stockings, whilst a venerable buck rabbit looked solemnly out from a hutch on one side of the doorway, and a pair of red-eyed ferrets shed their fragrance from a rough deal box on the other. "Nap" himself was not to be seen on a visitor's first entrance into his habitation, but generally appeared after a mysterious delay, from certain back settlements, of which one never discovered the exact "whereabout." A grimy old woman, with her skirts pinned up, was invariably washing the staircase when we called, and it was only in obedience to her summons that "Nap" himself could be brought forward. This dame possessed a superstitious interest in the eyes of us boys, on account of the mysterious relationship in which she stood to "Nap." He always addressed her as "mother"--but no boy at Everdon had yet ascertained whether this was a generic term significant of age and sex, an appellation of endearment to a spouse, or a tribute of filial reverence from a son.

"Come, 'Nap,' look alive," halloed Victor, as we rushed up the narrow path that led from the wicket to the door, in breathless haste not to lose the precious moments of our half-holiday. "Now, mother, where is he?" added the lively young truant. "Time's up; 'Nap'--'Nap'!"--and the walls echoed to Victor's rich, laughing voice, and half-foreign accent. As usual, after an interval of a few minutes, "Nap" himself appeared at the back door of the cottage, with a pair of greased half-boots in one hand, and a ferret, that nestled confidingly against his cheek, in the other.

"Sarvice, young gen'elmen," said "Nap," wiping his mouth with the back of his hand--"Sarvice, my lord; sarvice, Muster Egerton," repeated he, on recognising his two stanchest patrons. "Here, Bold! Bold!--you do know your master, sure*lie*," as Bold came rollicking forth from the back-yard in which he lived, and testified his delight by many ungainly gambols and puppy-like freedoms, which were responded to as warmly by his delighted owner. My scale of affections at this period of life was easily defined. I loved three objects in the world--viz., my father, Victor, and Bold. I verily believe I cared for nothing on earth but those three; and certainly my dog came in for his share of regard. Bold, although in all the awkwardness of puppyhood, was already beginning to show symptoms of that sagacity which afterwards developed itself into something very few degrees inferior to reason, if indeed it partook not of that faculty which we men are anxious to assume as solely our own. He would already obey the slightest sign--would come to heel at a whisper from his owner or instructor--would drag up huge stones out of ten feet of water, with ludicrous energy and perseverance; and stand waiting for further orders with his head on one side, and an expression of comic intelligence on his handsome countenance that was delightfully ridiculous. He promised to be of great size and strength; and even at this period, when he put his forepaws on my shoulders and licked my face, he was considerably the larger animal of the two. Such familiarities, however, were much discouraged by "Nap."

"If so be as you would keep a 'dawg,' real sporting and dawg-like, master," that philosopher would observe, "let un know his distance; I strikes 'em whenever I can reach 'em. Fondlin' of 'em only spiles 'em--same as women."

CHAPTER VIII
THE TRUANTS

So the day to which we had looked forward with such delight had arrived at last. Our spirits rose as we got further and further from Everdon, and we never stopped to take breath or to look back till we found ourselves surmounting the last hill above Beverley Manor. By this time we had far outstripped our friend "Nap"--that worthy deeming it inconsistent with all his maxims ever to hurry himself. "Slow and sure, young gentlemen," he observed soon after we started--"slow and sure wins the day. Do'ee go on ahead, and wait for I top of Buttercup Close. I gits on better arter a drop o' drink this hot weather. Never fear, squire, I'll not fail ye! Bold! Bold! you go on with your master." So "Nap" turned into the "Cat and Fiddle," and we pursued our journey alone, not very sorry to be rid of our companion for the present; as, notwithstanding our great admiration for his many resources, his knowledge of animal life, his skilful method with rats, and general manliness of character, we could not but be conscious of our own inferiority in these branches of science, and of a certain want of community in ideas between two young gentlemen receiving a polite education at Everdon, and a rat-catching, dog-stealing poacher of the worst class.

"It's as hot as Hungary," said Victor, seating himself on a stile, and taking off his cap to fan his handsome, heated face. "Oh, Vere, I wish I was back in the Fatherland! Do you remember the great wood at Edeldorf, and the boar we saw close to the ponies? And oh, Vere, how I should like to be upon Gold-kind once again!"

"Yes, Victor, I remember it all," I answered, as I flung myself down among the buttercups, and turned my cheek to the cool air that came up the valley--a breeze that blew from the distant hills to the southward, and swept across many a mile of beauty ere it sighed amongst the woods of Beverley, and rippled the wide surface of the mere; "I shall never forget Edeldorf, nor my first friend, Victor. But what made you think of Hungary just now?"

"Why, your beautiful country," answered Victor, pointing to the luxuriant scene below us--a scene that could exist in England only--of rich meadows, and leafy copses, and green slopes laughing in the sunlight, dotted with huge old standard trees, and the deep shades of Beverley, with the white garden-wall standing out from amongst yew hedges, and rare pines, and exotic evergreens; while the grey turrets of the Manor House peeped and peered here and there through the giant elms that stirred and flickered in the summer breeze. The mere was glittering at our feet, and the distant uplands melting away into the golden haze of summer. Child as I was, I could have cried, without knowing why, as I sat there on the grass, drinking in beauty at every pore. What is it that gives to all beauty, animate or inanimate, a tinge of melancholy?--the greater the beauty, the deeper the tinge. Is it an instinct of mortality? the "bright must fade" of the poet? a shadowy regret for Dives, who, no more than Lazarus, can secure enjoyment for a day? or is it a vague yearning for something more perfect still?--a longing of the soul for the unattainable, which, more than all the philosophy in the universe, argues the necessity of a future state. I could not analyse my feelings. I did not then believe that others experienced the same sensations as myself. I only knew that, like Parson Hugh, I had "great dispositions to cry."

"I wish I were a man, Vere," remarked Victor, as he pulled out his knife, and began to carve a huge V on the top bar of the stile. "I should like to be grown up now, and you too, Vere; what a life we would lead! Let me see, I should have six horses for myself, and three--no, four for you; and a pack of hounds, like Mr. Barker's, that we saw last half, coming home from hunting; and two rifles, both double-barrelled. Do you know, I hit the bull's-eye with papa's rifle, when Prince Vocqsal was at Edeldorf, and he said I was the best shot in Hungary for my age. Look at that crow, Vere, perching on the branch of the old hawthorn--I could put a bullet into him from here. Oh! I wish I had papa's rifle!"

"But should you not like to be King of Hungary, Victor?" said I, for I admired my "chum" so ardently, that I believed him fit for any position, however exalted. "Should you not like to be king, and ride about upon a white horse, with a scarlet tunic and pelisse, and ostrich feathers in your hat, bowing right and left to the ladies at the windows, with a Hungarian body-guard clattering behind you, and the people shouting and flinging up their caps in the street?" I saw it all in my mind's eye, and fancied my friend the hero of the procession. Victor hesitated, and shook his head.

"I think I had rather be a General of Division, like Wallenstein, and command ten thousand cavalry; or better still, Vere, ride and shoot as well as Prince Vocqsal, and go up into the mountains after deer, and kill bears and wolves and wild boars, and do what I like. Wouldn't I just pack up my books, and snap my fingers at March, and leave Everdon to-morrow, if I could take you with me. But you, Vere, if you could have your own way, what would you be?"

I was not long answering, for there was scarcely a day that I did not consider the subject; but my aspirations for myself were so humble, that I hesitated a little lest Victor should laugh at me, before I replied.

"Oh, I will do whatever my father wishes, Victor; and I hope he will sometimes let me go to you; but if I could do exactly what I liked, if a fairy was at this moment to come out of that bluebell and offer me my choice, I should ask to be a doctor, Victor, and to live somewhere on this hill."

"*Sappramento!*" exclaimed Victor, swearing, in his astonishment, his father's favourite oath--"a doctor, Vere! and why?"

"Well," I answered, modestly, "I am not like you, Victor; I wish I were. Oh, you cannot tell how I wish I were you! To be high-born and rich, and heir to a great family, and to have everybody making up to one and admiring one--that is what I should call happiness. But I can never have the chance of that. I am shy and stupid and awkward, and--and, Victor"--I got it out at last, blushing painfully--"I know that I am ugly--*so ugly*! It is foolish to care about it, for, after all, it is not my fault; but I cannot help wishing for beauty. It is so painful to be remarked and laughed at, and I know people laugh at *me*. Why, I heard Ropsley say to Manners, only yesterday, after I had been fagging for him at cricket, 'Why, what an ugly little beggar it is!' and Manners said, 'Yes,' and 'he thought it must be a great misfortune.' And Ropsley laughed so, I felt he must be laughing at me, as if I could help it! Oh, Victor, you cannot think how I long to be loved; that is why I should like to be a doctor. I would live up here in a small cottage, from which I could always see this beautiful view; and I would study hard to be very clever-- not at Greek and Latin, like March, but at something I could take an interest in; and I would have a quiet pony, not a rantipole like your favourite Gold-kind; and I would visit the poor people for miles round, and never grudge time nor pains for any one in affliction or distress. I would *make* them fond of me, and it would be such happiness to go out on a day like this, and see a kind smile for one on everybody's face, good or bad. Nobody loves me now, Victor, except papa and you and Bold; and papa, I fear, only because he is my papa. I heard him say one day, long ago, to my nurse (you remember nurse Nettich?), 'Never mind what the boy is like--he is my own.' I fear he does not care for me for myself. You like me, Victor, because you are used to me, and because I like *you* so much; but that is not exactly the sort of liking I mean; and as for Bold--here, Bold! Bold! Why, what has become of the dog? He must have gone back to look for 'Nap.'"

The Interpreter | 53

Sure enough Bold was nowhere visible, having made his escape during our conversation; but in his place the worthy "King of Naples" was to be seen toiling up the hill, more than three parts drunk, and with a humorous twinkle in his solitary eye which betokened mischief.

"Now, young gents," observed the poacher, settling himself upon the stile, and producing from the capacious pockets of his greasy velveteen jacket an assortment of snares, night-lines, and other suspicious-looking articles; "now, young gents, I promised to show you a bit of sport comin' here to Beverley, and a bit of sport we'll have. Fust and foremost, I've agot to lift a line or two as I set yesterday in the mere; then we'll just take a turn round the pheasantry, for you young gentlemen to see the fowls, you know; Sir 'Arry, he bain't a comin' back till next week, and Muster Barrells, the keeper, he's off into Norfolk, arter pinters, and such like. You keep the dog well at heel, squire. Why, whatever has become o' Bold?"

Alas, Bold himself was heard to answer the question. Self-hunting in an adjoining covert, his deep-toned voice was loudly awakening the echoes, and scaring the game all over the Manor, to his own unspeakable delight and our intense dismay. Forgetful of all the precepts of his puppyhood, he scampered hither and thither; now in headlong chase of a hare; now dashing aside after a rabbit, putting up pheasants at every stride, and congratulating himself on his emancipation and his prowess in notes that could not fail to indicate his pursuits to keepers, watchers, all the establishment of Beverley Manor, to say nothing of the inhabitants of that and the adjoining parishes.

Off we started in pursuit, bounding down the hill at our best pace. Old "Nap" making run in his own peculiar gait, which was none of the most graceful. Victor laughing and shouting with delight; and I frightened out of my wits at the temporary loss of my favourite, and the probable consequences of his disobedience.

Long before we could reach the scene of Bold's misdoings, we had been observed by two men who were fishing in the mere, and who now gave chase--the one keeping along the valley, so as to cut us off in our descent; the other, a long-legged fellow, striding right up the hill at once, in case we should turn tail and beat a retreat. "Nap" suddenly disappeared--I have reason to believe he ensconced himself in a deep ditch, and there remained until the danger had passed away. Victor and I were still descending the hill, calling frantically to Bold. The keeper who had taken the lower line of pursuit was gaining rapidly upon us. I now saw that he carried a gun under his arm. My dog flashed out of a small belt of young trees in hot pursuit of a hare--tongue out, head down, and tail lowered, in full enjoyment of the chase. At the instant he appeared the man in front of me stopped dead short. Quick as lightning he lifted his long shining barrel. I saw the flash; and ere I heard the report my dog tumbled heels over head, and lay upon the sunny sward, as I believed in the agony of that moment, stone dead. I strained every nerve to reach him, for I could hear the rattle of a ramrod, as the keeper reloaded,--and I determined to cover Bold with my body, and, if necessary, to die with him. I was several paces ahead of Victor; whom I now heard calling me by name, but I could think of nothing, attend to nothing, but the prostrate animal in front. What a joy it Was when I reached him to find he was not actually killed. His fore-leg was frightfully mangled by the charge; but as I fell breathless by the side of my darling Bold, he licked my face, and I knew there was a chance for him still.

A rough grasp was laid on toy shoulder, and a hoarse voice roused me:

"Come, young man; I thought I'd drop on to you at last. Now you'll just come with me to Sir 'Arry, and we'll see what *he* has to say to this here."

And on looking up I found myself in the hands of a strong, square-built fellow, with a velveteen jacket, and a double-barrelled gun under his arm, being no less a person than Sir Harry Beverley's head keeper, and the identical individual that had been watching us from the mere, and had made so successful a shot at Bold.

"Come, leave the dog," he added; giving me another shake, and scrutinising my apparel, which was evidently not precisely of the description he had expected; "leave the dog--it's no great odds about him; and as for *you*, young gentleman, if you *be* a young gentleman, you *had* ought to be ashamed of yourself. It's not want as drove you to this trade. Come, none of that; you go quietly along of me; it's best for you, I tell you."

I was struggling to free myself from his hold, for I could not bear to leave my dog. A thousand horrible anticipations filled my head. Trial, transportation, I knew not what, for I had a vague terror of the law, and had heard enough of its rigours in regard to the offence of poaching, to fill me with indescribable alarm; yet, through it all, I was more concerned for Bold than myself. My favourite was dying, I believed, and I could not leave him.

I looked up in the face of my captor. He was a rough, hairy fellow; but there was an expression of kindliness in his homely features which encouraged me to entreat for mercy.

"Oh, sir," I pleaded, "let me only take my dog; he's not so very heavy; I'll carry him myself. Bold, my darling Bold! He is my own dog, and I'd rather you'd kill me too than force me to leave him here."

The man was evidently mollified, and a good deal puzzled into the bargain. I saw my advantage, and pressed it vigorously.

"I'll go to prison willingly,--I'll go anywhere you tell me,--only do try and cure Bold. Papa will pay you anything if you'll only cure Bold. Victor! Victor!" I added, seeing my chum now coming up, likewise in custody, "help me to get this gentleman to save Bold."

Victor looked flushed, and fiercer than I ever remembered to have seen that pretty boyish face. His collar was torn and his dress disordered. He had evidently struggled manfully with his captor, and the latter wiped his heated brow with an expression of mingled amusement and astonishment, that showed he was clearly at his wit's end what to make of his prize.

"Blowed if I know what to say o' this here, Mr. Barrells," said he to his brother functionary. "This little chap's even gamer nor t'other one. *Run!* I never see such a one-er to run. If it hadn't been for the big hedge at the corner of the cow-pasture, I'd never a cotched 'un in a month o' Sundays; and when I went to lay hold, the young warmint out with his knife and offered to whip it into me. He's a rare boy this; I could scarce grip him for laughing; but the lad's got a sperret, bless'd if he ain't. I cut my own knuckles gettin' of it out of his hands." And he showed Victor's knife to his comrade as he spoke.

Mr. Barrells was a man of reflection, as keepers generally are. He examined the knife carefully, and spoke in an undertone to his friend.

"Do you see this here?" he remarked, pointing to the coronet which was inlaid in the steel; "and do you see that there?" he added, with a glance at Victor's gold watch-chain, of Parisian fabric. "Put this here and that there together, Bill, which it convinces me as these here little chaps is not them as we was a lookin' for. Your cove looks a gentleman all over; I knows the breed, Bill, and there's no mistake about the real thing; and my precious boy here, he wouldn't leave the dawg, not if it was ever so, though he's a very little 'un; he's a gentleman too; but that don't make no odds, Bill: gentlemen hadn't ought to be up to such-like tricks, nor haven't half the excuse of poor folks; and, gentlemen or no gentlemen, they goes before Sir 'Arry, dog and all, as sure as my name's Barrells!"

Victor and I looked at each other in hopeless despair; there was, then, nothing for it but to undergo the extreme penalty of the law. With hanging heads and blushing cheeks we walked between our captors; Bill, who seemed a good-natured fellow enough, carrying the unfortunate Bold on his shoulders. We thought our shame had reached its climax, but we were doomed to suffer even more degradation in this our first visit to Beverley Manor.

As we threaded the gravel path of a beautiful shrubbery leading to the back offices of the Manor House, we met a young girl taking her afternoon's walk with her governess, whose curiosity seemed vividly excited by our extraordinary procession. To this day I can remember Constance Beverley as she stood before me then, the first time I ever saw her. She was scarcely more than a child, but her large serious dark eyes, her noble and somewhat sad expression of countenance, gave her an interest which mere childish beauty could never have possessed. There are some faces that we can discern even at such a distance as renders the features totally indistinct, as if the expression of countenance reached us by some magnetic process independent of vision, and such a face was that of Constance Beverley. I have often heard her beauty disputed. I have even known her called plain, though that was generally by critics of her own sex, but I never heard any one deny that she was *uncommon-looking*, and always certain to attract attention, even where she failed in winning admiration. Victor blushed scarlet, and I felt as if I must sink into the earth when this young lady walked up to the keeper, and asked him "what he was going to do with those people, and why he was taking them to papa?"

Miss Constance was evidently a favourite with Mr. Barrells, for he stopped and doffed his hat with much respect whilst he explained to her the circumstance of our pursuit and capture. So long as he alluded only to our poaching offences, I thought the little lady looked on us with eyes of kindly commiseration; but when he hinted his suspicions of our social position, I observed that she immediately assumed an air of marked coldness, and transferred her pity to Bold.

"So you see, Miss, I does my duty by Sir 'Arry without respect to rich or poor," was Mr. Barrells' conclusion to a long-winded oration addressed partly to the young lady, partly to her governess, and partly to ourselves, the shame-faced culprits; "and therefore it is as I brings these young gentlemen up to the justice-room, if so be, as I said before, they *be* young gentlemen; and so, Miss Constance, the law must take its course."

"But you'll take care of the poor dog, Barrells; promise me you'll take care of the poor dog," was the young lady's last entreaty as she walked on with her governess; and a turn in the shrubbery hid her from our sight.

"*What* a half-holiday this has been!" whispered I to my comrade in distress, as we neared the house that had so long been an object of such curiosity.

"Yes," replied Victor, "but it's not over yet."

Sir Harry was at the farm; we must wait for his return. Meantime we were shown into the servants' hall; a large stone chamber devoid of furniture, that reminded me of our schoolroom at Everdon--much as we hated the latter, what would we have given to be there now! Cold meat and ale were offered us; but, as may well be imagined, we had no appetite to partake of them, although in that respect our captors set us a noble example; remaining, however, on either side of us as turnkeys watch those who are ordered for execution. The servants of the household came one after another to stare at the unfortunate culprits, and made audible remarks on our dress and general appearance. Victor's beauty won him much favour from the female part of the establishment; and a housemaid with a wonderfully smart cap brought him a cup of tea, which he somewhat rudely declined. There was considerable discussion as to our real position in society carried on without the slightest regard to our presence. The under-butler, whose last place was in London, and whose professional anxiety about his spoons may have somewhat prejudiced him, gave it as his opinion that we belonged to what he called "the swell mob"; but Mr. Barrells, who did not seem to understand the term, "pooh-poohed" this suggestion with so much dignity as at once to extinguish that official, who incontinently retired to his pantry and his native obscurity. The women, who generally lean to the most improbable version of a story, were inclined to believe that we were sailors, and of foreign extraction; but the most degrading theory of all, and one that I am bound to confess met with a large majority of supporters, was to the effect that we were run-away 'prentices from Fleetsbury, and would be put in the stocks on our return to that market town. We had agreed not to give our names except as a last resource, my friend clinging, as I thought somewhat hopelessly, to the idea that Sir Harry would let us off with a reprimand, and we might get back to Everdon without March finding it out. So the great clock ticked loudly in the hall, and there we sat in mute endurance. As Victor had before remarked, "it was not over yet."

CHAPTER IX
ROPSLEY

Ropsley smoked his cigar on the trunk of the old tree, and Manners drank in worldly wisdom from the lips of his junior, whom, however, he esteemed as the very guide-book of all sporting and fashionable life. It was the ambition of our usher to become a thorough man of the world; and, had he been born to a fortune and a title, there was no reason why he should not have formed a very fair average young nobleman. His tastes were frivolous enough, his egotism sufficiently developed, his manner formed on what he conceived the best model. All this was only absurd, I presume, because he was an usher; had he been a marquis, he would have shown forth as a "very charming person." His admiration of Ropsley was genuine, the latter's contempt for his adorer equally sincere, but better concealed. They sit puffing away at their cigars, watching the smoke wreathing up into the summer sky, and Manners coaxes his whiskers and looks admiringly at his friend. Ropsley's cigar is finished, and he dashes it down somewhat impatiently.

"What can have become of that little wretch?" says he, with a yawn and a stretch of his long, well-shaped limbs; "he's probably made some stupid mistake, and I shall have to lick him after all. Manners, what have you done with the old dog-whip we used to keep for the lower boys?"

"Safe in my desk," replies Manners, who, being a good-natured fellow, likes to keep that instrument of torture locked up; "but Egerton's a good little fellow; you mustn't be too hard upon him this time."

"I never could see the difference between a good fellow and a bad one," replies Ropsley. "If I want a thing done I choose the most likely person to do it; and if he fails it's his fault and not mine, and he must suffer for it. I've no prejudices, my good friend, and no feelings--they're only different words for the same thing; and, depend upon it, people get on much better without them. But come: let's walk down to the village, and look after him. I'll go and ask March if he wants anything 'down the road.'"

Luckily for me, my chastiser had not proceeded half a mile upon his way, ere he met the "King of Naples" in person, hot and breathless, flustered with drink and running, and more incoherent than usual in his conversation and demeanour. He approached Ropsley, who was the most magnificent of his patrons, with hat in hand, and somewhat the air of a dog that knows he has done wrong.

"What's up now, you old reprobate?" said the latter, in his most supercilious manner--a manner, I may observe, he adopted to all whom he could influence without conciliating, and which made the conciliation doubly winning to the favoured few--"What's up now? Drunk again, I suppose, as usual?"

"Not drunk, squire--not drunk, as I'm a livin' man," replied the poacher, sawing the air in deprecation with a villainously dirty hand; "hagitated, perhaps, and over-anxious about the young gentlemen--Oh! them lads, them lads!" and he leered at his patron as much as to hint that he had a precious story to tell, if it was only made worth his while.

"Come, no nonsense!" said Ropsley, sternly; "out with it. What's the matter? You've got De Rohan and Egerton into some scrape; I see it in your ugly old face. Tell me all about it this instant, or it will be worse for you."

"Doan't hurry a man so, squire; pray ye, now, doan't. I be only out o' breath, and the lads they be safe enough by this time; but I wanted for you to speak up for me to the master, squire. I bain't a morsel to blame. I went a-purpose to see as the young gents didn't get into no mischief; I did, indeed. I be an old man now, and it's a long walk for me at my years," whined the old rascal, who was over at the Manor three nights a week when he thought the keepers were out of the way. "And the dog, he was most to blame, arter all; but the keepers they've got the young gents safe, enough,-- and that's all about it." So saying, he stood bolt upright, like a man who has fired his last shot, and is ready to abide the worst. Truth to tell, the "King of Naples" was horribly afraid of Ropsley.

The latter thought for a moment, put his hand in his pocket, and gave the poacher half-a-crown. "You hold your tongue," said he, "or you'll get into worse trouble than any of them. Now go home, and don't let me hear of your stirring out for twenty-four hours. Be off! Do you hear?"

Old "Nap" obeyed, and hobbled off to his cottage, there to spend the term of his enforced residence in his favourite occupation of drinking, whilst Ropsley walked rapidly on to the village, and directed his steps to that well-known inn, "The Greyhound," of which every boy at Everdon School was more or less a patron.

In ten minutes' time there was much ringing of bells and general confusion pervading that establishment; the curly-headed waiter (why do all waiters have curly hair?) rushed to and fro with a glass-cloth in his hand; the barmaid drooped her long ringlets over her own window-sill, within which she was to be seen at all hours of the day and night, like a pretty picture in its frame; the lame ostler stumped about with an activity foreign to his usual methodical nature, and a chaise and pair was ordered to be got ready immediately for Beverley Manor.

Richard the Third is said to have been born with all his double teeth sharp set, and in good masticatory order. It is my firm belief that Ropsley was also ushered into the world with his wisdom teeth in a state of maturity. He had, indeed, an old head upon young shoulders; and yet this lad was brought up and educated by his mother until he was sent to school. Perhaps he was launched into the world too early; perhaps his recollections of home were not vivid enough to soften his character or awaken his feelings. When I first knew him he had been an orphan for years; but I am bound to say that the only being of whom he spoke with reverence was his mother. I never heard him mention her name but twice, and each time a soft light stole over his countenance and altered the whole expression of his features, till I could hardly believe it was the same person. From home, when a very little boy, he was sent to Eton; and after a long process of hardening in that mimic world, was transferred to Everdon, more as a private pupil than a scholar. Here it was that I first knew him; and great as was my boyish admiration for the haughty, aristocratic youth just verging upon manhood, it is no wonder that I watched and studied his character with an intensity born of my own ardent disposition, the enthusiasm of which was all the stronger for having been so repressed and concealed in my strange and solitary childhood. Most children are hero-worshippers, and my hero for the time was Ropsley.

He was, I think, the only instance I can recollect of a mere boy proposing to himself a certain aim and end in life, and going steadily forward to its attainment without pause or deviation. I often think now, what is there that a man with ordinary faculties might not attain, would he but propose to himself at fourteen that position which he would wish to reach at forty? Show me the hill that six-and-twenty years of perseverance would fail to climb. But no; the boy never thinks of it at all--or if he does, he believes the man of forty to be verging on his grave, and too old to enjoy any of the pleasures of existence, should he have the means of indulging them. He will not think so when he has reached that venerable period; though, after all, age is a relative term, and too often totally irrespective of years. Many a heart is ruined and worn out long ere the form be bent or the head grown grey. But the boy thinks there is time enough; the youth grudges all that interferes with his pleasures; and the man only finds the value of energy and perseverance when it is too late to avail himself of them. Oh!

opportunity!--opportunity!--phantom goddess of success, that not one in a million has decision to seize and make his own:--if hell be paved with good intentions, it might be roofed with lost opportunities.

Ropsley, however, was no morbid whiner over that which is irretrievable. He never lost a chance by his own carelessness; and if he failed, as all must often fail, he never looked back. *Aide-toi, et Dieu t'aidera*, is a motto that comprises in five words the noblest code of philosophy; the first part of the sentence Ropsley had certainly adopted for his guidance, and to do him justice, he never was remiss in any sense of the word in helping himself.

Poor, though of good family, his object was to attain a high position in the social world, power, wealth, and influence, especially the latter, but each and all as a means towards self-aggrandisement. The motive might not be amiable or noble, but it was better than none at all, and he followed it out most energetically. For this object he spared no pains, he feared no self-denial, he grudged no sacrifice. He was a scholar, and he meant to make the most of his scholarship, just as he made the most of his cricket-playing, his riding, his skill in all sports and exercises. He knew that his physical good looks and capabilities would be of service to him hereafter, and he cultivated them just as he stored and cultivated that intellect which he valued not for itself, but as a means to an end.

"If I had fifty thousand a year," I once heard him say to Manners, "I should take no trouble about anything. Depend upon it, the real thing to live for is enjoyment. But if I had only forty-five thousand I should work like a slave--it would not *quite* give me the position I require."

Such was Ropsley at this earliest period of our acquaintance.

"Drive to Beverley Manor," said he, as he made himself thoroughly comfortable amongst the cushions, let down all the windows, and settled himself to the perusal of the last daily paper.

Any other boy in the school would have gone in a gig.

CHAPTER X
BEVERLEY MANOR

Why does a country gentleman invariably select the worst room in the house for his own private apartment, in which he transacts what he is pleased to call his "business," and spends the greater part of his time? At Beverley Manor there were plenty of rooms, cheerful, airy, and well-proportioned, in which it would have been a pleasure to live, but none of these were chosen by Sir Harry for his own; disregarding the charms of the saloon, the drawing-room, the morning-room, the billiard-room, and the hall itself, which, with a huge fire-place and a thick carpet, was by no means the least comfortable part of the house,--he had retired to a small, ill-contrived, queer-shaped apartment, dark, dusty, and uncomfortable, of which the only recommendation was that it communicated directly with a back-staircase and offices, and did not require in its own untidiness any apology on the part of muddy visitors, who had not thought of wiping their boots and shoes as they came up. A large glass gun-case, filled with double-barrels, occupied one side of the room, flanked by book-shelves, loaded with such useful but not entertaining works as the *Racing Calendar, White's Farriery,* and *Hawker's Instructions to Young Sportsmen.* In one corner was a whip-stand, hung round with many an instrument of torture. The knotted dog-whip that reduced Ponto to reason in the golden stubbles; the long-thonged hunting-whip, that brought to mind at once the deep, fragrant woodland in November, with its scarlet coats flitting down the distant ride; and the straight, punishing "cut-and-thrust," that told of Derby and St. Leger, Ditch-In, Middle-Mile, and all the struggles of Epsom and Newmarket. In another was an instrument for measuring land, and a roll of plans by which acres were to be calculated and a system of thorough draining established, with a view to golden profits.

"Draining!" remarked Sir Harry, in his younger days, to an assemblage of country gentlemen, who stood aghast at the temerity of his proposition, "I am no advocate for draining:"--voices were raised, and hands uplifted in pious horror and deprecation--"all I can say is, gentlemen, that I have drained my property till *I cannot get a farthing from it*" was Sir Harry's conclusive reasoning, which must have satisfied Mr. Mechi himself.

A coloured engraving of the well-known Beverley shorthorn "Dandy" hung on one side of the fire-place, and on the other, a print of "Flying Childers," as he appeared when going at the rate of a mile in a minute, apparently ridden by a highwayman in huge jack-boots and a flowing periwig. In the centre of the room was fixed a large leather-covered writing-table, and at this table sat Sir Harry himself, prepared to administer justice and punish all offenders. He was a tall, thin man, somewhat bent, and bald, with a hooked nose, and a bright, searching eye, evidently a thorough man of the world in thought, opinion, and feeling; the artificial will become second nature if long enough persisted in, and Sir Harry had served no short apprenticeship to the trade of fashion. His dress was peculiarly neat and gentleman-like, not the least what is now termed "slang," and yet with a something in it that marked the horseman. He was busy writing when we were ushered into the awful presence, and Victor and I had time to steal a look at each other, and to exchange a reassuring pressure of the hand. The young Hungarian raised his head frank and fearless as usual; I felt that I should like to sink into the ground, but yet was determined to stand by my friend.

Mr. Barrells commenced a long oration, in which he was rapidly losing himself, when his master, whose attention was evidently occupied elsewhere, suddenly looked up, and cut him short with the pertinent inquiry--

"What's all this about, Barrells? and why are these lads here?"

"We are gentlemen, and not poachers;" and "Indeed, sir, it was Bold that got away!" exclaimed Victor and I simultaneously.

At this instant a card was brought in by the butler, and placed in Sir Harry's hand; he looked at it for a moment, and then said--

"Immediate! very well, show the gentleman in."

I thought I knew the step that came along the passage, but never was failing courage more grateful for assistance than was mine to recognise in Sir Harry's visitor the familiar person of my schoolfellow, Ropsley; I cared not a farthing for the promised licking now.

"I have to apologise for disturbing you, Sir Harry," said he, standing as composed and collected as if he were in our schoolroom at Everdon;--even in the anxiety of the moment I remember thinking, "What would I give to possess 'manner' such as his;"--"I have to apologise for my rudeness" (Sir Harry bowed, and said, "Not at all;" I wondered what he meant by *that*), "but I am sure you will excuse me when I tell you that I am a pupil of Mr. March's at Everdon" (Sir Harry looked at the tall, well-dressed figure before him, and seemed surprised), "and these two young friends of mine belong to the same establishment. I heard quite accidentally, only an hour ago, of the scrape they had got into, and I immediately hurried over here to assure you that they can have had no evil intentions in trespassing on your property, and to apologise for their thoughtlessness, partly out of respect to you, Sir Harry, and partly, I am bound to say, for the credit of the school. I am quite sure that neither Egerton nor De Rohan----"

Sir Harry started. "Egerton! De Rohan!" he exclaimed; "not the son of my old friend Philip Egerton, not young Count de Rohan?--really, Mr.----" (he looked at the card he held in his hand), "really, Mr. Ropsley, I am very much obliged to you for rectifying this extraordinary mistake;" but even whilst he was speaking, I had run round the table to where he sat, and seizing his hand--I remember how cold it felt between my own little hot, trembling ones--exclaimed--

"Oh! do you know my papa? then I am sure you will not punish us; only let us off this time, and give me back Bold, and we will promise never to come here again."

The Baronet was not a demonstrative person, nor had he much patience with those who were; he pushed me from him, I thought rather coldly, and addressed himself once more to Ropsley.

"Why, these boys are sons of two of the oldest friends I have in the world. I would not have had such a thing happen for a thousand pounds. I must apologise to you, young gentlemen, for the rudeness of my servants--Good heavens! ou were kept waiting in the hall: why on earth did you not give your names? Your father and I were at college together, Egerton; and as for you, Monsieur le Comte, had I known you were at Everdon, I would have made a point of going over to call upon you myself; but I have only just returned to the country, and that must be my excuse."

Victor bowed gracefully: notwithstanding his torn jacket and disordered collar, he looked "the young Count" all over, and so I am sure thought Sir Harry. Ropsley was perfectly *gentlemanlike*, but Victor was naturally *high bred*.

"Barrells, where are you going, Barrells?" resumed his master, for that discreet person, seeing the turn things were taking, was quietly leaving the room; "you always were the greatest fool that ever stood upon two legs: now let this be a warning to you--every vagabond in the county helps himself to my game whenever he pleases, and you never lay a finger on one of them; at last you insult and abuse two young gentlemen that any one but a born idiot could see were gentlemen, and bring them in here for poachers--*poachers!* as if you didn't know a poacher when you see one. Don't stand gaping there, you fool, but be off, and the other blockhead too. Hie! here; let the dog be attended to, and one of the watchers must lead him back to Everdon when he's well again. Now see to that, and never make such a stupid mistake again."

"May I go and see Bold, sir?" said I, summoning up courage as my late captors quitted the room.

"Quite right, my little man," replied the Baronet, "so you shall, this evening; but in the meantime, I hope you'll all stay and dine with me. I'll write to your master--what's his name?--and send you back in the carriage at night; what say you, Mr. Ropsley? I can give you a capital bottle of claret."

So here were we, who one short hour before had been making up our minds to endure with fortitude the worst that could happen,--who had expected to be driven with ignominy from Beverley, and handed over to condign punishment on our return to school, if indeed we were fortunate enough to escape committal and imprisonment in the County Gaol,--now installed as honoured guests in the very mansion which we had so long looked upon as a *terra incognita* of fairyland, free to visit the "hins-and-houts" of Beverley, with no thanks to the "King of Naples" for his assistance, and, in short, raised at one step from the abyss of schoolboy despair to the height of schoolboy gratification. Victor's delight was even greater than mine as we were shown into a pretty little dressing-room overlooking the garden, to wash our hands before dinner. He said it reminded him of home, and made him feel "like a gentleman" once more.

What a dinner that was to which we sat down in the stately old dining-room, served upon massive plate by a butler and two footmen, whose magnificence made me feel quite shy in my comparative insignificance. Ropsley of course seemed as much at home as if he was in the habit of dining there every day, and Victor munched away with an appetite that seemed to afford our good-natured host immense gratification. Soup and fish, *entrées* of every description, hashed venison, iced champagne--how grateful after our hot pursuit in the summer sun--and all the minor luxuries of silver forks, clean napkins, finger-glasses, etc., were indeed a contrast to the plain roast mutton and potatoes, the two-pronged fork, and washy table-beer of our Everdon bill-of-fare. What I liked, though, better than all the eatables and drinkables, was a picture opposite which I sat, and which riveted my attention so much as to attract the observation of Sir Harry himself.

"Ha! Egerton," said he, "you are your father all over, I see. Just like him, wild about painting. Now I'll bet my life you're finding fault with the colouring of that picture. The last time he was here he vowed, if I would let him, he would paint it all over again; and yet it's one of the best pictures in England at this moment. What do you think of it, my boy? Could you paint as good a one?"

"No, sir," I replied modestly, and rather annoyed at my reverie being interrupted; "my father tries to teach me, but--but I cannot learn to paint."

Sir Harry turned away, and Ropsley whispered something about "very odd"--"poor little fellow." The dessert had just been put on the table, and Victor was busy with his strawberries and cream. There must be some truth in magnetism, there must be something in the doctrine of attraction and repulsion: why do we like some people as we dislike others, without any shadow of a reason? Homoeopathists tell us that the nausea which contracts our features at the smell of a drug, is a provision of Nature to guard us against poison. Can it be that these antipathies are implanted in our being to warn us of those who shall hereafter prove our enemies? it is not a charitable theory nor a Christian-like, and yet in my experience of life I have found many instances in which it has borne a strange semblance of truth.

"Men feel by instinct swift as light

The presence of the foe,

Whom God has marked in after years

To strike the mortal blow.

The other, though his brand be sheathed,

At banquet or in hall,

Hath a forebodement of the time

When one or both must fall."

So sings "the minstrel" in his poem of *Bothwell*, but *Bothwell* was not written at the time of which I speak, and the only poetry I had ever heard to justify my antipathies was the homely quatrain of *Dr. Fell*. Still I felt somehow from that moment I hated Ropsley; it was absurd, it was ungrateful, it was ungentlemanlike, but it was undeniable.

So I buried myself in the contemplation of the picture, which possessed for me a strange fascination. The subject was Queen Dido transfixed on her funeral pyre, the very *infandum regina* to whose history I owed so many school-room sorrows. I began to think I should never hate Virgil again. The whole treatment of the picture was to the last degree unnatural, and the colouring, even to my inexperienced eye, faulty and overdone. Yet that face of mute sorrow and resignation spoke at once to the heart; the Queen lay gazing on the distant galleys which were bearing away her love, and curling their beaks and curvetting, so to speak, up-hill on a green sea, in a manner that must have made the task of Palinurus no easy one when he undertook to steer the same. Her limbs were disposed stiffly, but not ungracefully, on the fatal couch, and her white bosom was pierced by the deadly blade. Yet on her sweet, sad countenance the artist had depicted with wonderful skill the triumph of mental over bodily anguish; and though the features retained all woman's softness and woman's beauty, you read the breaking heart beneath. I could have looked at that picture for hours, I was lost in it even then, but the door opened, and whilst Ropsley got up with a flourish and his most respectful bow, in walked the young lady whom we had met under far different circumstances some three hours before in the shrubbery, and quietly took her place by the side of her papa.

As I looked from Queen Dido to Miss Constance I quite started; there was the very face as if it had walked out of the canvas. Younger, certainly, and with a more childish expression about the mouth, but the same queenly brow, the same sad, serious eyes, the same delicate features and oval shape; the fascination was gone from the picture now, and yet as I looked at the child--for child she was then--I experienced once more the old well-known pang of self-humiliation which so often poisoned my happiness; I felt so dull and awkward amongst these bright faces and polished manners, so ungainly and out of place where others were gay and at their ease. How I envied Victor's self-possession as he addressed the young lady with his pleasant, foreign accent, and a certain assurance that an English boy never acquires till he is verging on manhood. How willingly would I have exchanged places with any one of the party. How I longed to cast the outward slough of timidity and constraint, to appear as I felt myself in reality, an equal in mind and station and feelings to the rest. For the first time in my life, as I sat a mere child at that dinner-table, came the thrilling, maddening feeling to my heart--

"Oh! that something would happen, something dreadful, something unheard of, that should strip from each of us all extraneous and artificial advantages, that should give us all a fair start on equal terms--something that should try our courage or our fortitude, and enable me to prove myself what I really am."

It was the first spark of ambition that ever entered my boyish breast, but when once kindled, such sparks are never completely extinguished. Fortunate is it that opportunities are wanting to fan them into a flame, or we should ere long have the world in a blaze.

Miss Constance took very little notice of us beyond a cold allusion to the well-being of my dog, and it was not till Sir Harry bade her take charge of Victor and myself, and lead us out through the garden to visit our wounded favourite, that we had any conversation with this reserved young lady. Sir Harry rang for another bottle of claret, and composed himself for a good chat upon racing matters with Ropsley, who was as much at home with everything connected with the turf as if he spent his whole time at Newmarket. Ropsley had even then a peculiar knack of being "all things to all men," and pleaded guilty besides to a very strong *penchant* for horse-racing. This latter taste raised him considerably in Sir Harry's estimation, who, like the rest of mankind, took great pleasure in beckoning the young along that path of pleasure which had nearly led to his own ruin. Well, we are all children to the last; was there one whit more wisdom in the conversation of the Baronet and his guest as to the relative merits of certain three-year-olds and the weight they could carry, than in the simple questions and answers of us three children, walking soberly along the soft garden sward in the blushing sunset? At first we were very decorous: no brocaded courtier of Queen Anne, leading his partner out to dance a minuet, could have been more polite and respectful than Victor; no dame of high degree, in hoop and stomacher, more stately and reserved than Miss Constance. I said little, but watched the pair with a strange, uncomfortable fascination. Ere long, however, the ice began to thaw, questions as to Christian names, and ages, and respective birthdays, brought on increased confidence and more familiar conversation. Constance showed us her doves, and was delighted to find that we too understood thoroughly the management of these soft-eyed favourites; the visit to Bold was another strong link in our dawning friendship; the little girl was so gentle and so pitiful, so caressing to the poor dog, and so sympathising with its master, that I could not but respond to her kindness, and overcame my timidity sufficiently to thank her warmly for the interest she took in poor Bold. By the time we had all enjoyed in turn the delights of a certain swing, and played a game at battledore and shuttlecock in the echoing hall, we were becoming fast friends, and had succeeded in interesting our new acquaintance extremely in all the details of schoolboy life, and our own sufferings at Everdon. I remarked, however, that Constance took far less notice of me than of Victor; with him she seemed frank and merry and at her ease; with me, on the contrary, she retained much of her early reserve, and I could not help fancying, rather avoided my conversation than otherwise. Well, I was used to being thrown in the background, and it was pleasure enough for me to watch that grave, earnest countenance, and speculate on the superhuman beauty of Queen Dido, to which it bore so strange a resemblance.

It was getting too dark to continue our game. We had already lost the shuttlecock three times, and it was now hopelessly perched on the frame of an old picture in the hall; when the dining-room door opened, and Sir Harry came out, still conversing earnestly with his guest on the one engrossing topic.

"I am much obliged to you for the hint," said the Baronet. "It never struck me before; and if your information is really to be depended on, I shall certainly back him. Strange that I should not have heard of the trial."

"My man dare not deceive me, I assure you," answered Ropsley, his quiet, distinct tones contrasting with Sir Harry's, who was a little flushed and voluble after his claret. "He used to do odd jobs for me when I was in the sixth form at Eton, and I met him unexpectedly enough the other day in the High-street at Bath. He is a mason by trade, and is employed repairing Beckford's tower; by the way, he had heard of *Vathek*--I am not sure that he hasn't read it, so the fellow has some brains about him. Well, I knew he hadn't been hanging about Ascot all his life for nothing, so I described the colt to him, and bade him keep his eyes open when perched in mid-air these bright mornings, with such a command of Lansdowne. Why, he knew the horse as well as I did, and yesterday sent me a full account of the trial. I destroyed it immediately, of course, but I have it all here" (pointing to his forehead, where, indeed, Ropsley carried a curious miscellany of information). "He beat the mare at least fifty yards, and she was nearly that distance ahead of 'Slap-Jack,' so you may depend upon it he is a real flyer. I have backed him to win a large stake, at least, for a boy like me," added Ropsley, modestly; "and I do not mean to hedge a farthing of it."

Sir Harry was delighted; he had found a "young one," as he called it, after his own heart; he declared he would not wish him "good-bye"; he must come over again and see the yearlings; he must accompany him to the Bath races. If he was to leave Everdon at the end of the half-year, he must come and shoot in September; nay, they would go to Doncaster together; in short, Sir Harry was fascinated, and put us all into the carriage, which he had ordered expressly to take us back to Everdon, with many expressions of hospitality and good-will.

Bold was lifted on to the box, from whence he looked down with his tongue hanging out in a state of ludicrous helplessness and dismay. Miss Constance bade us a quiet "good-night" in tones so sweet that they rang in my ears half way home, and so we drove off in state from the front door, as though we had not that very afternoon been brought in as culprits at the back.

Ropsley was unusually silent during the whole journey. He had established his footing at Beverley Manor, perhaps he was thinking how "to make the most of it."

CHAPTER XI
DULCE DOMUM

I must skip a few years; long years they were then to me; as I look back upon them now, they seem to have fleeted away like a dream. Victor and I are still at Everdon, but we are now the two senior boys in the school. De Rohan has grown into one of the handsomest youths you will often see. His blue eye is as clear and merry as ever, but the chestnut curls have turned dark and glossy, and the light, agile form is rapidly developing itself into a strong, symmetrical young man. He is still frank, gay, and unsophisticated; quick enough at his studies, but utterly without perseverance, and longing ardently for the time when he shall be free to embark upon a course of pleasure and dissipation. I am much altered too. With increasing growth and the assumption of the *toga virilis*, or that manly garment which schoolboys abruptly denominate "tails," I have acquired a certain degree of outward equanimity and self-command, but still suffer much from inward misgivings as to my own appearance and personal advantages. Hopelessly I consult the glass in our joint bed-room--the same glass that daily reflects Victor's handsome face and graceful figure--and am forced unwillingly to confess that it presents to me the image of a swarthy, coarse-featured lad, with sunken eyes and scowling eyebrows, sallow in complexion, with a wide, low forehead overhung by a profusion of bushy black hair; this unprepossessing countenance surmounting a short square figure, broad-shouldered, deep-chested, and possessed of great physical strength. Yes, I was proud of my strength. I shall never forget the day when first I discovered that nature had gifted me with one personal advantage, that I, of all others, was disposed most to appreciate. A lever had been left in the playground, by which the workmen, who were repairing the wall, intended to lift the stem of the well-known tree which had formerly constituted what we called "The Club." We boys had come out of school whilst the men were gone to dinner. Manners, the muscular, was delighted with such an opportunity of displaying his prowess; how foolish he looked when he found himself incapable of moving the huge inert mass--he said it was impossible; two boys attempted it, then three, still the great trunk remained motionless. I asked leave to try, amidst the jeers of all, for I was usually so quiet and undemonstrative that no one believed Egerton had, in schoolboy parlance, either "pith or pluck" in him. I laid my weight to it and heaved "with a will"; the great block of timber vibrated, moved, and rolled along the sward. What a triumph it was, and how I prided myself on it. I, too, had my ideal of what I should like to be, although I would not have confessed it to a soul. I wished to be like some *preux chevalier* of the olden time; my childish longing to be loved had merged into an ardent desire to be admired; I would have been brave and courteous and chivalrous and strong. Yes, in all the characters of the olden time that I so loved to study, strength was described as one of the first attributes of a hero. Sir Tristram, Sir Launcelot, Sir Bevis, were all "strong," and my heart leapt to think that if the opportunity ever arrived, my personal strength might give me a chance of distinguishing myself, when the beautiful and the gallant were helpless and overcome. But there was another qualification of which in my secret soul I had hideous misgivings,--I doubted my own courage: I knew I was nervous and timid in the common every-day pursuits of a schoolboy's life; I could not venture on a strange horse without feeling my heart in my mouth; I did not dare stop a ball that was bowled swiftly in to my wicket, nor fire a gun without shutting both eyes before I ventured to pull the trigger. What if I should be a coward after all? A *coward!* the thoughts of it almost drove me mad; and yet how could I tell but that I was branded with that hideous curse? I longed, yet dreaded, to know the worst.

In my studies I was unusually backward for a boy of my age. Virgil, thanks to the picture of Dido, never to be forgotten, I had completely mastered; but mathematics, arithmetic--all that are termed the exact sciences--I appeared totally incapable of learning. Languages I picked up with extraordinary facility, and this alone redeemed me from the character of an irreclaimable dunce.

"You *can* learn, sir, if you will," was March's constant remark, after I had arrived at the exalted position of a senior boy, to whom flogging and such coercive measures were inappropriate, and for whom "out of bounds" was not. "You *can* learn, or else why do I see you poring over Arabic and Sanscrit during play-hours, when you had much better be at cricket? You must have brains somewhere, but to save my life I can't find them. You can speak half-a-dozen languages, as I am informed, nearly as well as I can speak Latin, and yet if I set you to do a 'Rule of Three' sum, you make more blunders than the lowest little dunce in the school! Egerton, I can't make you out."

It was breaking-up day at Everdon. Victor and I walked with our arms over each other's shoulders, up and down, up and down, in the old playground, and as we paced those well-worn flags, of which we knew every stone, my heart sank within me to think it was for the last, *last* time. What is there that we are not sorry to do for the last time? I had hated school as much as any schoolboy could; I had looked forward to my emancipation as the captive looks forward to the opening of his prison-door; and now the time was come, and I felt grieved and out of spirits to think that I should see the old place no more.

"You must write to me constantly, Vere," said Victor, with an affectionate hug, as we took our hundredth turn. "We must never forget each other, however far apart, and next winter you must come again to Edeldorf; I shall be there when the shooting begins. Oh, Vere, you will be very dull at home."

"No," I replied; "I like Alton Grange, and I like a quiet life. I am not of your way of thinking, Victor; you are never happy except in a bustle; I wish I were more like you;" and I sighed as I thought of the contrast between us.

I do not know what brought it to my mind, but I thought of Constance Beverley, and the first time we saw her when we were all children together at Beverley Manor. Since then our acquaintance had indeed progressed but little; we scarcely ever met except on certain Sundays, when we took advantage of our liberty as senior boys to go to church at Fleetsbury, where from the gallery we could see right into the Beverley pew, and mark the change time had wrought on our former playfellow. After service, at the door we might perhaps exchange a stiff greeting and a few words before she and her governess got into the carriage; and this transcendent pleasure we were content to purchase with a broiling walk of some five miles on a dusty high-road, and a patient endurance of the longest sermon from the worthy rector of Fleetsbury, an excellent man, skilled in casuistry, and gifted with extraordinary powers of discourse. Victor, I think, took these expeditions in his own good-natured way, and seemed to care but little whether he went or not. One hot Sunday, I recollect he suggested that we should dispense with afternoon church altogether, and go to bathe instead, a proposal I scouted with the utmost indignation, for I looked forward to our meetings with a passionate longing for which I could not account even to myself, and which I never for an instant dreamed of attributing to the charms of Miss Beverley. I know not now what tempted me to ask the question, but I felt myself becoming bright scarlet as I inquired of my school-fellow whether he had not *other* friends in Somersetshire besides myself whom he would regret leaving. His reply ought to have set my mind at ease, if I was disturbed at the suspicion of his entertaining any *penchant* for Miss Beverley, for he answered at once in his own off-hand way--"None whatever that I care a sixpence about, not even that prim little girl and her governess, whom you drag me five miles every Sunday to see. No, Vere, if I could take you with me, I should sing for joy the whole way from here to London. As it is, I shall not break my heart: I am so glad to get away from this dull, dreadful place."

Then he did not care for Miss Beverley, after all. Well, and what difference could that possibly make to me? Certainly, I was likely to see her pretty constantly in the next year or two, as our respective abodes would be but a short distance apart; but what of that? There could be nothing in common between the high-born, haughty young lady, and her awkward, repulsive neighbour. Yet I was glad, too, that Victor did not care for her. All my old affection for him came back with a gush, and I wrung his hand, and cried like a fool to think we were so soon to be parted, perhaps for years. The other boys were singing *Dulce domum* in the schoolroom, hands joined, dancing round and round, and stamping wildly with the chorus, like so many Bacchanals; they had no regrets, no misgivings; they were not going to leave for *good*. Even Manners looked forward to his temporary release with bright anticipations of amusement. He was to spend the vacation with a clerical cousin in Devonshire, the cousin of whom we all knew so much by report, and who, indeed, to judge by his relative's account, must have been an individual of extraordinary talents and attainments. The usher approached us with an expression of mingled pleasure and pain on his good-looking, vacant countenance. He had nearly finished packing his things, and was now knocking the dust out of those old green slippers I remembered when first I came to Everdon. He was a good-hearted fellow, and was sorry to lose his two old friends.

"We shall miss you both very much next half," said he; "nothing but little boys here now. Everdon is not what it used to be. Dear me, we never have such a pupil as Ropsley now. When you two are gone there will be no one left for me to associate with: this is not a place for a man of energy, for a man that feels he is a man," added Manners, doubling his arm, and feeling if the biceps was still in its right place. "Here am I now, with a muscular frame, a good constitution, a spirit of adventure, and a military figure" (appealing to me, for Victor, as usual, was beginning to laugh), "and what chances have I of using my advantages in this circumscribed sphere of action? I might as well be a weak, puny stripling, without an atom of nerve, or manliness, or energy, for all the good I am likely to do here. I must cut it, Egerton; I must find a career; I am too good for an usher--an usher," he repeated, with a strong expression of disgust; "I, who feel fit to fight my way anywhere--I have mistaken my profession--I ought to have been an officer--a cavalry officer; that would have suited me better than this dull, insipid life. I must consult my cousin about it; perhaps we shall meet again in some very different scenes. What say you, De Rohan, should you not be surprised to see me at the head of a regiment?"

Victor could conceal his mirth no longer, and Manners turned somewhat angrily to me. "You seem to be very happy as you are," I answered, sadly, for I was contrasting his well-grown, upright figure and simple fresh-coloured face, with my own repulsive exterior, and thinking how willingly I would change places with him, although he *was* an usher; "but wherever we meet, I am sure *I* shall be glad to see you again." In my own heart I thought Manners was pretty certain to be at Everdon if I should revisit it that day ten years, as I was used to these visionary schemes of his for the future, and had heard him talk in the same strain every vacation regularly since I first came to school.

But there was little time now for such speculations. The chaises were driving round to the door to take the boys away. March bid us an affectionate farewell in his study. Victor and I were presented respectively with a richly-bound copy of *Horatius Flaccus* and *Virgilius Maro*--copies which, I fear, in after life, were never soiled by too much use. The last farewell was spoken--the last pressure of the hand exchanged--and we drove off on our different destinations; my friend bound for London, Paris, and his beloved Hungary; myself, longing to see my father once more, and taste the seclusion and repose of Alton Grange. To no boy on earth could a school-life have been more distasteful than to me; no boy could have longed more ardently for the peaceful calm of a domestic hearth, and yet I felt lonely and out of spirits even now, when I was going home.

CHAPTER XII
ALTON GRANGE

A dreary old place was Alton Grange, and one which would have had a sobering, not to say saddening, effect, even on the most mercurial temperament. To one naturally of a melancholy turn of mind, its aspect was positively dispiriting. Outside the house the grounds were overgrown with plantations and shrubberies, unthinned, and luxuriating into a wilderness that was not devoid of beauty, but it was a beauty of a sombre and uncomfortable character. Every tree and shrub of the darkest hues, seemed to shut out the sunlight from Alton Grange. Huge cedars overshadowed the slope behind the house; hollies, junipers, and yew hedges kept the garden in perpetual night. Old-fashioned terraces, that should have been kept in perfect repair, were sliding into decay with mouldering walls and unpropped banks, whilst a broken stone sun-dial, where sun never shone, served but to attract attention to the general dilapidation around.

It was not the old family place of the Egertons. That was in a northern county, and had been sold by my father in his days of wild extravagance, long ago; but he had succeeded to it in right of his mother, at a time when he had resolved, if possible, to save some remnant from the wreck of his property, and, when in England, he had resided here ever since. To me it was home, and dearly I loved it, with all its dulness and all its decay. The inside corresponded with the exterior. Dark passages, black wainscotings, everywhere the absence of light; small as were the windows, they were overhung with creepers, and the walls were covered with ivy; damp in winter, darkness in summer, were the distinguishing qualities of the old house. Of furniture there was but a scanty supply, and that of the most old-fashioned description: high-backed chairs of carved oak, black leathern *fauteuils*, chimney-pieces that the tallest housemaid could never reach to dust, would have impressed on a stranger ideas of anything but comfort, whilst the decorations were confined to two or three hideous old pictures, representing impossible sufferings of certain fabulous martyrs; and one or two sketches of my father's, which had arrived at sufficient maturity to leave the painting-room, and adorn the every-day life of the establishment.

The last-named apartment was cheerful enough: it was necessarily supplied with a sufficiency of daylight, and as my father made it his own peculiar den, and spent the greater part of his life in it, there were present many smaller comforts and luxuries which might have been sought elsewhere in the house in vain. But no room was ever comfortable yet without a woman. Men have no idea of order without formality, or abundance without untidiness. My father had accumulated in his own particular retreat a heterogeneous mass of articles which should have had their proper places appointed, and had no business mixed up with his colours, and easel, and brushes. Sticks, whips, cloaks, umbrellas, cigar-boxes, swords, and fire-arms were mingled with lay-figures, models, studies, and draperies, in a manner that would have driven an orderly person out of his senses; but my father never troubled his head about these matters, and when he came in from a walk or ride, would fling his hat down in one corner of the room, the end of his cigar in another, his cloak or whip in a third, and begin painting again with an avidity that seemed to grow fiercer from the enforced abstinence of a few hours in taking necessary exercise. My poor father! I often think if he had devoted less attention to his art, and more to the common every-day business of life, which no one may neglect with impunity, how much better he would have succeeded, both as a painter and a man.

He was hard at work when I came home from school. I knew well where to find him, and hurried at once to the painting-room. He was seated at his easel, but as I entered he drew a screen across the canvas, and so hid his work from my inquiring gaze. I never knew him do so before; on the contrary, it had always seemed his greatest desire to instil into his son some of his own love for the art; but I had hardly time to think of this ere I was in his arms, looking up once more in the kind face, on which I never in my whole life remembered to have seen a harsh expression. He was altered, though, and thinner than when I had seen him last, and his hair was now quite grey, so that the contrast with his flashing dark eye--brighter it seemed to me than ever--was almost unearthly. His hands, too, were wasted, and whiter than they used to be, and the whole figure, which I remembered once a tower of strength, was now sunk and fallen in, particularly about the chest and shoulders. When he stood up, it struck me, also, that he was shorter than he used to be, and my heart tightened for a moment at the thought that, he might be even now embarking on that long journey from which there is no return. I remembered him such a tall, handsome, stalwart man, and now he seemed so shrunk and emaciated, and quite to totter and lean on me for support.

"You are grown, my boy," said he, looking fondly at me; "you are getting quite a man now, Vere; it will be sadly dull for you at the Grange:

but you must stay with your old father for a time--it will not be for long--
not for long," he repeated, and his eye turned to the screened canvas, and
a glance shot from it that I could hardly bear to see--so despairing, yet so
longing--so wild, and yet so fond. I had never seen him look thus before,
and it frightened me.

Our quiet meal in the old oak parlour--our saunter after dinner through
the dark walks and shrubberies--all was so like the olden time, that I felt
quite a boy again. My father lighted up for a time into his former good
spirits and amusing sallies, but I remarked that after every flash he sank
into a deeper dejection, and I fancied the tears were in his eyes as he wished
me good-night at the door of the painting-room. I little thought when I went
to bed that it was now his habit to sit brooding there till the early dawn of
morning, when he would retire for three or four hours to his rest.

So the time passed away tranquilly and dully enough at Alton Grange.
My father was ever absorbed in his painting, but studied now with the door
locked, and even I was only admitted at stated times, when the mysterious
canvas was invariably screened. My curiosity, nay more, my interest, was
intensely excited; I longed, yet feared, to know what was the subject of this
hidden picture; twenty times was I on the point of asking my father, but
something in his manner gave me to understand that it was a prohibited
subject, and I forbore. There was that in his bearing which at once checked
curiosity on a subject he was unwilling to reveal, and few men would have
dared to question my father where he did not himself choose to bestow his
confidence.

I read much in the old library; I took long walks once more by myself; I
got back to my dreams of Launcelot and Guenever, and knights and dames,
and "deeds of high emprize." More than ever I experienced the vague
longing for something hitherto unknown, that had unconsciously been
growing with my growth, and strengthening with my strength,--the restless
craving of which I scarcely guessed the nature, but which weighed upon
my nervous, sensitive temperament till it affected my very brain. Had I but
known then the lesson that was to be branded on my heart in letters of fire,-
-could I but have foreseen the day when I should gnaw my fetters, and yet
not wish to be free,--when all that was good, and noble, and kindly in my
nature should turn to bitter self-contempt, and hopeless, helpless apathy,--
when love, fiercer than hatred, should scorch and sting the coward that had
not strength nor courage to bear his burden upright like a man,--had I but
known all this, I had better have tied a millstone round my neck, and slept
twenty feet deep below the mere at Beverley, than pawned away hope, and
life, and energy, and manhood, for a glance of her dark eyes, a touch of her
soft hand, from the heiress of Beverley Manor.

Yes, Alton Grange was distant but a short walk from Beverley. Many a time I found myself roaming through the old trees at the end of the park, looking wistfully at the angles and turrets of the beautiful Manor House, and debating within myself whether I ought or ought not to call and renew an acquaintance with the family that had treated me so kindly after the scrape brought on by Bold's insubordination. That favourite was now a mature and experienced retriever, grave, imperturbable, and of extraordinary sagacity. Poor Bold! he was the handsomest and most powerful dog I ever saw, with a solemn expression of countenance that denoted as much intellect as was ever apparent on the face of a human being. We were vastly proud of Bold's beauty at the Grange, and my father had painted him a dozen times, in the performance of every feat, possible or impossible, that it comes within the province of a retriever to attempt. Bold was now my constant companion; he knew the way to Beverley as well as to his own lair in my bed-room, where he slept. Day after day he and I took the same road; day after day my courage failed me at the last moment, and we turned back without making the intended visit. At last, one morning, while I strolled as usual among the old trees at one extremity of the park, I caught sight of a white dress rounding the corner of the house, and entering the front door. I felt sure it could only belong to one, and with an effort that quite surprised even myself, I resolved to master my absurd timidity, and walk boldly up to call.

I have not the slightest recollection of my ringing the door-bell, nor of the usual process by which a gentleman is admitted into a drawing-room; the rush of blood to my head almost blinded me, but I conclude that instinct took the place of reason, and that I demeaned myself in no such incoherent manner as to excite the attention of the servants, for I found myself in the beautiful drawing-room, which I remembered I had thought such a scene of fairyland years before, and seated, hat in hand, opposite Miss Beverley.

She must have thought me the stupidest morning visitor that ever obtained entrance into a country-house; indeed, had it not been for the good-natured efforts of an elderly lady with a hooked nose, who had been her governess, and was now a sort of companion, Miss Beverley would have had all the conversation to herself; and I am constrained to admit that once or twice I caught an expression of surprise on her calm sweet face, that could only have been called up by the very inconsequent answers of which I was guilty in my nervous abstraction. I was so taken up in watching and admiring her, that I could think of nothing else. She was so quiet and self-possessed, so gentle and ladylike, so cool and well-dressed. I can remember the way in which her hair was parted and arranged to this day. She seemed to me a being of a superior order, something that never could by any possibility belong to the same sphere as myself. She was more like the picture of Queen Dido than ever, but the queen, happy and fancy free, with kindly eyes and unruffled brow; not the deceived, broken-hearted woman on her self-selected death-bed. I am not going to describe her-- perhaps she was not beautiful to others--perhaps I should have wished the rest of the world to think her positively hideous--perhaps she was *then* not so transcendently beautiful even to me; nay, as I looked, I could pick faults in her features and colouring. I had served a long enough apprenticeship to my father to be able to criticise like an artist, and I could see here a tint that might be deepened, there a plait that might be better arranged--I do not mean to say she was perfect--I do not mean to say that she was a goddess or an angel; but I do mean to say that if ever there was a face on earth which to me presented the ideal of all that is sweetest and most lovable in woman, that face was Constance Beverley's.

And yet I was not in love with her; no, I felt something exalting, something exhilarating in her presence--she seemed to fill the void in my life, which had long been so wearisome, but I was not in love with her-- certainly not then. I felt less shy than usual, I even felt as if I too had some claim to social distinction, and could play my part as well as the rest on the shifting stage. She had the happy knack of making others feel in good spirits and at their ease in her society. I was not insensible to the spell, and when Sir Harry came in, and asked kindly after his old friend, and promised to come over soon and pay my father a visit, I answered frankly and at once; I could see even the thoughtless Baronet was struck with the change in my manner, indeed he said as much.

"You must come over and stay with us, Mr. Egerton," was his hospitable invitation; "or if your father is so poorly you cannot leave him, look in here any day about luncheon-time. I am much from home myself, but you will always find Constance and Miss Minim. Tell your father I will ride over and see him to-morrow. I only came back yesterday. How you're grown, my lad, and improved--isn't he, Constance?"

I would have given worlds to have heard Constance's answer, but she turned the subject with an inquiry after Bold (who was at that instant waiting patiently for his master on the door-step), and it was time to take leave, so I bowed myself out, with a faithful promise, that I was not likely to forget, of calling again soon.

"So she has not forgotten Bold," I said to myself, at least twenty times, in my homeward walk; and I think, fond as I had always been of my dog, I liked him that day better than ever.

"Father," I said, as I sat that evening after dinner, during which meal I felt conscious that I had been more lively, and, to use an expressive term, "better company," than usual; "I must write to London for a new coat, that black one is quite worn out."

"Very well, Vere," answered my father, abstractedly; "tell them to make it large enough--you grow fast, my boy."

"Do you think I am grown, father? Indeed, I am not so very little of my age now; and do you know, I was the strongest boy at Everdon, and could lift a heavier weight than Manners the usher; but, father"--and here I hesitated and stammered, till reassured by the kind smile on his dear old face,--"I don't mind asking you, and I *do* so wish to know--am I so *very, very*--ugly?" I brought out the hated word with an effort--my father burst out laughing.

"What an odd question--why do you wish to know, Vere?" he asked. I made no reply, but felt I was blushing painfully. My father looked wistfully at me, while an expression as of pain contracted his wan features; and here the conversation dropped.

CHAPTER XIII
"LETHALIS ARUNDO"

That week I went over again to Beverley; the next, I had a book to fetch for Constance from Fleetsbury, that she had long wished to read, and I took it to her a volume at a time. My father was still busy with his painting--Sir Harry had gone off to Newmarket--Miss Minim seemed delighted to find any one who could relieve the monotony of the Manor House, and Constance herself treated me, now that the first awkwardness of our re-introduction was over, like an old playmate and friend. I was happier than I had ever been in my life. I felt an elasticity of spirits, a self-respect and self-reliance that I had thought myself hitherto incapable of entertaining. Oh, the joy of that blindfold time! whilst our eyes are wilfully shut to the future that we yet know *must* come, whilst we bask in the sunshine and inhale the fragrance of the rose, nor heed the thunder-cloud sleeping on the horizon, and the worm creeping at the core of the flower. I looked on Constance as I would have looked on an angel from heaven. I did not even confess to myself that I loved her, I was satisfied with the intense happiness of the present, and trembled at the bare idea of anything that might break the spell, and interrupt the calm quiet of our lives. With one excuse or another, I was at Beverley nearly every day; there were flowers to be dried, for Constance was a great botanist, and I had taken up that study, as I would have taken up shoe-making, could I have seen her a minute a day longer for the pursuit,--there was music to be copied, and if I could do nothing else, I could point off those crabbed hieroglyphics like a very engraver. Then Miss Minim broke her fan, and I walked ten miles in the rain to get it mended, with an alacrity and devotion that must have convinced her it was not for *her* sake: and yet I loved Miss Minim dearly, she was so associated in my mind with Constance, that except the young lady's own, that wizened old face brought the blood to my brow more rapidly than any other in the world. Oh! my heart aches when I think of that beautiful drawing-room, opening into the conservatory, and Constance playing airs on the pianoforte that made my nerves tingle with an ecstasy that was almost painful. Miss Minim engaged with her crotchet-work in the background, and I, the awkward, ungainly youth, saying nothing, hardly breathing, lest I should break the spell; but gazing intently on the fair young face, with its soft kind eyes, and its thrilling smile, and the smooth, shining braids of jet-black hair parted simply on that pure brow. Mine was no love at first sight, no momentary infatuation that has its course and burns itself out, the fiercer the sooner, with its own unsustained violence. No; it grew and stole upon me by degrees, I drank it in with every breath I breathed--I fought against it till every moment of my life was a struggle; and yet I cherished and pressed it to my heart when all was done. I knew I was no equal for such as Miss Beverley, I knew I had no right even to lift my eyes to so much beauty and so much goodness--I, the awkward, ugly schoolboy, or at best the shrinking, unattractive youth, in whose homage there was nothing for a woman to take pride, even if she did not think it ridiculous; but yet--God! how I loved her. Not a blossom in the garden, not a leaf on the tree, not a ray of sunshine, nor a white cloud drifting over the heaven, but was associated in my mind with her who was all the world to me. If I saw other women, I only compared them with *her*; if I read of beauty and grace in my dear old romances, or hung over the exquisite casts and spirited studies of my father's painting-room, it was but to refer the poet's dream and the artist's conception back to my own ideal. How I longed for beauty, power, talent, riches, fame, everything that could exalt me above my fellows, that I might fling all down at *her* feet, and bid her trample on it if she would. It was bitter to think I had nothing to offer; and yet I felt sometimes there ought to be something touching in my self-sacrifice. I looked for no return--I asked for no hope, no favour, not even pity; and I gave my all.

At first it was delightful: the halcyon days flitted on, and I was happy. Sir Harry, when at home, treated me with the greatest kindness, and seemed to find pleasure in initiating me into those sports and amusements which he himself considered indispensable to the education of a gentleman. He took me out shooting with him, and great as was my natural aversion to the slaying of unoffending partridges and innocent hares, I soon conquered my foolish nervousness about firing a gun, and became no mean proficient with the double-barrel. My ancient captor, the head keeper, now averred that "Muster Egerton was the *cooollest* shot he ever see for so young a gentleman, and *coool* shots is generally deadly!" The very fact of my not caring a straw whether I killed my game or not, removed at once that over-anxiety which is the great obstacle to success with all young sportsmen. It was sufficient for me to know that a day's shooting at her father's secured two interviews (morning and afternoon) with Constance, and I loaded, and banged, and walked, and toiled like the veriest disciple of Colonel Hawker that ever marked a covey. All this exercise had a beneficial effect on my health and spirits; I grew apace, I was no longer the square, clumsy-built dwarf; my frame was gradually developing itself into that of a powerful, athletic man. I was much taller than Constance now, and not a little proud of that advantage. Having no others with whom to compare myself, I began to hope that I was, after all, not much worse-looking than the rest of my kind; and by degrees a vague idea sprang up in my mind, though I never presumed to give it shape and consistency, that Constance might some day learn to look kindly upon me, and that perhaps, after many, many years, the time would come when I should dare to throw myself at her feet and tell her how I had worshipped her; not to ask for a return, but only to tell her how true, and hopeless and devoted had been my love. After that I thought I could die happy.

Weeks grew to months, and months to years, and still no change took place in my habits and mode of life. My father talked of sending me to Oxford, for I was now grown up, but when the time came he was loth to part with me, and I had such a dread of anything that should take me away from Alton, that I hailed the abandonment of the scheme with intense joy. Constance went to London with Sir Harry during the season, and for two or three months of the glorious summer I was sadly low and restless and unhappy; but I studied hard during this period of probation, to pass the time, and when she came again, and gave me her hand with her old kind smile, I felt rewarded for all my anxieties, and the sun began to shine for me once more.

I was a man now in heart and feelings, and loved with all a man's ardour and singleness of purpose, yet I never dreamed she could be mine. No; I shut my eyes to the future, and blindfold I struggled on; but I was no longer happy; I grew restless and excited, out of temper, petulant in trifles, and incapable of any fixed application or sustained labour. I was leading an aimless and unprofitable life; I was an idolater, and I was beginning to pay the penalty; little did I know then what would be my sufferings ere the uttermost farthing should be exacted. Something told me the time of my happiness was drawing to a close; there is a consciousness before we wake from a moral as well as a physical sleep, and my awakening was near at hand.

It was a soft grey morning early in August, one of those beautiful summer days that we have only in England, when the sky is clouded, but the air pure and serene, and the face of nature smiling as though in a calm sleep. Not a breath stirred the leaves of the grand old trees in the park at Beverley, nor rippled the milk-white surface of the mere. The corn was ready for cutting, but scarce a sheaf had yet fallen before the sickle; it was the very meridian and prime of the summer's beauty, and my ladye-love had returned from her third London season, and was still Constance Beverley. It was later than my usual hour of visiting at the Manor, for my father had been unwell during the night, and I would not leave him till the doctor had been, so Constance had put on her hat and started for her morning's walk alone. She took the path that led towards Alton, and Bold and I caught sight at the same moment of the well-known white dress flitting under the old oaks in the park. My heart used to stop beating when I saw her, and now I turned sick and faint from sheer happiness. Not so Bold: directly he caught sight of the familiar form away he scoured like an arrow, and in less than a minute he was bounding about her, barking and frisking, and testifying his delight with an ardour that was responded to in a modified degree by the young lady. What prompted me I know not, but instead of walking straight on and greeting her, I turned aside behind a tree, and, myself unseen, watched the form of her I loved so fondly, as she stepped gracefully on towards my hiding-place; she seemed surprised, stopped, and looked about her, Bold meanwhile thrusting his nose into her small gloved hand.

"Why, Bold," said she, "you have lost your master." And as she spoke she stooped down and kissed the dog on his broad, honest forehead. My heart bounded as if it would have burst; never shall I forget the sensations of that moment; not for worlds would I have accosted her then--it would have been sacrilege, it would have seemed like taking advantage of her frankness and honesty. No; I made a wide detour, still concealed behind the trees, and struck in upon the path in front of her as if I came direct from home. Why was it that her greeting was less cordial than usual? Why was it no longer "Vere" and "Constance" between us, but "Mr. Egerton" and "Miss Beverley"? She seemed ill at ease, too, and her tone was harder than usual till I mentioned my father's illness, when she softened directly. I thought there were *tears in her voice* as she asked me--

"How could I leave him if he was so poorly?"

"Because I knew you came back yesterday, Miss Beverley, and I would not miss being one of the first to welcome you home," was my reply.

"Why do you call me Miss Beverley?" she broke in, with a quick glance from under her straw hat. "Why not 'Constance,' as you used?"

"Then why not call me 'Vere'?" I retorted; but my voice shook, and I made a miserable attempt to appear unconcerned.

"Very well, 'Constance' and 'Vere' let it be," she replied, laughing; "and now, Vere, how did you know I came back yesterday?"

"Because I saw the carriage from the top of Buttercup Hill--because I watched there for six hours that I might make sure--because----"

I hesitated and stopped; she turned her head away to caress Bold. Fool! fool that I was! Why did I not tell her all then and there? Why did I not set my fate at once upon the cast? Another moment, and it was too late. When she turned her face again towards me it was deadly pale, and she began talking rapidly, but in a constrained voice, of the delights of her London season, and the gaieties of that to me unknown world, the world of fashionable life.

"We have had so many balls and operas and dissipations, that papa says he is quite knocked up; and who do you think is in London, Vere, and who do you think has been dancing with me night after night?" (I winced), "who but your old schoolfellow, your dear old friend, Count de Rohan!"

"Victor!" I exclaimed, and for an instant I forgot even my jealousy at the idea of any one dancing night after night with Constance, in my joy at hearing of my dear old schoolfellow. "Oh, tell me all about him--is he grown? is he good-looking? is he like what he was? is he going to stay in England? did he ask after me? is he coming down to see me at Alton?"

"Gently," replied Constance, with her own sweet smile. "One question at a time, if you please, Vere, and I can answer them. He is grown, of course, but not more than other people; he is *very* good-looking, so everybody says, and *I* really think he must be, too; he is not nearly so much altered from what he was as a boy, as some one else I know" (with a sly glance at me), "and he talks positively of paying us a visit early in the shooting season, to meet another old friend of yours, Mr. Ropsley, who is to be here to-day to luncheon; I hope you will stay and renew your acquaintance, and talk as much 'Everdon' as you did when we were children; and now, Vere, we must go in and see papa, who has probably by this time finished his letters." So we turned and bent our steps (mine were most unwilling ones) towards the house.

We had not proceeded far up the avenue, ere we were overtaken by a postchaise laden with luggage, and carrying a most irreproachable-looking valet on the box; as it neared us a well-known voice called to the boy to stop, and a tall, aristocratic-looking man got out, whom at first I had some difficulty in identifying as my former school-fellow, Ropsley, now a captain in the Guards, and as well known about London as the Duke of York's Column itself. He sprang out of the carriage, and greeted Constance with the air of an old friend, but paused and surveyed me for an instant from head to foot with a puzzled expression that I believe was only put on for the occasion,--then seized my hand, and declared I was so much altered and improved he had not known me at first. This is always gratifying to a youth, and Ropsley was evidently the same as he had always been--a man who never threw a chance away--but what good could *I* do him? Why should it be worth his while to conciliate such as me? I believe he never forgot the fable of the Lion and the Mouse.

When the first salutations and inquiries after Sir Harry were over, he began to converse with Constance on all those topics of the London world with which women like so much to be made acquainted,--topics so limited and personal that they throw the uninitiated listener completely into the background. I held my tongue and watched my old schoolfellow. He was but little altered since I had seen him last, save that his tall figure had grown even taller, and he had acquired that worn look about the eyes and mouth which a few seasons of dissipation and excitement invariably produce even in the young. After detailing a batch of marriages, and a batch of "failures," in all of which the names of the sufferers were equally unknown to me, he observed, with a peculiarly marked expression, to Constance, "Of course you know there never was anything in that report about De Rohan and Miss Blight; but so many people assured me it was true, that if I had not known Victor as well as I do, I should have been almost inclined to believe it."

I watched Constance narrowly as he spoke, and I fancied she winced. Could it have been only my own absurd fancy? Ropsley proceeded, "I saw him yesterday, and he desired his kindest regards to you, and I was to say he would be here on the 3rd."

"Oh! I am so glad!" exclaimed Constance, her whole countenance brightening with a joyous smile, that went like a knife to my foolish, inexperienced heart, that OUGHT to have reassured and made me happier than ever. Does a woman confess she is "delighted" to see the man she is really fond of? Is not that softened expression which pervades the human face at mention of the "one loved name" more akin to a tear than a smile? "He is so pleasant and so good-natured, and will enliven us all so much here;" she added, turning to me, "Vere, you must come over on the 3rd, and meet Count de Rohan; you know he is the oldest friend you have,--an older friend even than I am."

I was hurt, angry, maddened already, and this kind speech, with the frank, affectionate glance that accompanied it, filled my bitter cup to overflowing. Has a woman no compunction? or is she ignorant of the power a few light commonplace words may have to inflict such acute pain? Constance *cannot* have guessed the feelings that were tearing at my heart; but she must have seen my altered manner, and doubtless felt herself aggrieved, and thought she had a right to be angry at my unjustifiable display of temper.

"I thank you," I replied, coldly and distantly; "I cannot leave my father until he is better; perhaps De Rohan will come over and see us if he can get away from pleasanter engagements. I fear I have stayed too long already. I am anxious about my father, and must go home. Good-bye, Ropsley; good-morning, Miss Beverley. Here--Bold! Bold!"

She looked scared for an instant, then hurt, and almost angry. She shook hands with me coldly, and turned away with more dignity than usual. Brute, idiot that I was! even Bold showed more good feeling and more sagacity than his master. He had been sniffing round Ropsley with many a low growl, and every expression of dislike which a well-nurtured dog permits himself towards his master's associates; but he looked wistfully back at Constance as she walked away, and I really thought for once he would have broken through all his habits of fidelity and subordination, and followed her into the house.

What a pleasant walk home I had I leave those to judge who, like me, have dashed down in a fit of ill-temper the structure that they have taken years of pain, and labour, and self-denial to rear on high. Was this, then, my boasted chivalry--my truth and faith that was to last for ever--to fight through all obstacles--to be so pure, and holy, and unwavering, and to look for no return? I had failed at the first trial. How little I felt, how mean and unworthy, how far below my own standard of what a man should be--my ideal of worth, that I had resolved I would attain. And Ropsley, too--the cold, calculating, cynical man of the world--Ropsley must have seen it all. I had placed myself in his power--nay, more, I had compromised *her* by my own display of bitterness and ill-temper. What right had I to show any one how I loved her? nay, what right had I to love her at all? The thought goaded me like a sting. I ran along the foot-path, Bold careering by my side--I sprang over the stiles like a madman, as I was; but physical exertion produced at last a reaction on the mind. I grew gradually calmer and more capable of reasoning; a resolution sprang up in my heart that had never before taken root in that undisciplined soil. I determined to win her, or die in the attempt.

"Yes," I thought, "from this very day I will devote all my thoughts, all my energies, to the one great work. Beautiful, superior, unattainable as she is, surely the whole devotion of a life must count for something--surely God will not permit a human being to sacrifice his very soul in vain." (Folly! folly! Ought I not to have known that this very worship was idolatry, blasphemy of the boldest, to offer the creature a tribute that belongs only to the Creator--to dare to call on His name in witness of my mad rebellion and disloyalty?) "Surely I shall some day succeed, or fall a victim to that which I feel convinced must be the whole aim and end of my existence. Yes, I will consult my kind old father--I will declare myself at once honestly to Sir Harry. After all, I, too, am a gentleman; I have talents; I will make my way; with such a goal in view I can do anything; there is no labour I would shrink from, no danger I should fear to face, with Constance as the prize of my success;" and I reached the old worn-out gates of Alton Grange repeating to myself several of those well-known adages that have so many premature and ill-advised attempts to answer for--"Fortune favours the bold;" "Faint heart never won fair lady;" "Nothing venture, nothing have," etc.

CHAPTER XIV
THE PICTURE

My father was very weak, and looked dreadfully ill: the doctor had recommended repose and absence of all excitement; "especially," said the man of science, "let us abstain from painting. Gentle exercise, generous living, and quiet, absolute quiet, sir, can alone bring us round again." Notwithstanding which professional advice, I found the patient in his dressing-gown, hard at work as usual with his easel and colours, but this time the curtain was not hastily drawn over the canvas, and my father himself invited me to inspect his work.

I came in heated and excited; my father was paler than ever, and seemed much exhausted. He looked very grave, and his large dark eyes shone with an ominous and unearthly light.

"Vere," said he, "sit down by me. I have put off all I had to say to you, my boy, till I fear it is too late. I want to speak to you now as I have never spoken before. Where have you been this morning, Vere?"

I felt my colour rising at the question, but I looked him straight in the face, and answered boldly, "At Beverley Manor, father."

"Vere," he continued, "I am afraid you care for Miss Beverley,--nay, it is no use denying it," he proceeded; "I ought to have taken better care of you. I have neglected my duty as a father, and my sins, I fear, are to be visited upon my child. Look on that canvas, boy; the picture is finished now, and my work is done. Vere, that is your mother."

It was the first time I had ever heard that sacred name from my father's lips. I had often wished to question him about her, but I was always shy, and easily checked; whilst he from whom alone I could obtain information, I have already said, was a man that brooked no inquiries on a subject he chose should remain secret, so that hitherto I had been kept in complete ignorance of the whole history of one parent. As I looked on her likeness now, I began for the first time to realise the loss I had sustained.

The picture was of a young and gentle-looking woman, with deep, dark eyes, and jet-black hair; a certain thickness of eyebrows and width of forehead denoted a foreign origin; but whatever intensity of expression these peculiarities may have imparted to the upper part of her countenance, was amply redeemed by the winning sweetness of her mouth, and the delicate chiselling of the other features. She was pale of complexion, and looked somewhat sad and thoughtful; but there was a depth of trust and affection in those fond eyes that spoke volumes for the womanly earnestness and simplicity of her character. It was one of those pictures that, without knowing the original, you feel at once must be a likeness. I could not keep down the tears as I whispered, "Oh, mother, mother, why did I never know you?"

My father's face grew dark and stern: "Vere," said he, "the time has come when I must tell you all. It may be that your father's example may serve as a beacon to warn you from the rock on which so many of us have made shipwreck. When I was your age, my boy, I had no one to control me, no one even to advise. I had unlimited command of money, a high position in society, good looks--I may say so without vanity now--health, strength, and spirits, all that makes life enjoyable, and I enjoyed it. I was in high favour with the Prince. I was sought after in society; my horses won at Newmarket, my jests were quoted in the Clubs, my admiration was coveted by the 'fine ladies,' and I had the ball at my foot. Do you think I was happy? No. I lived for myself; I thought only of pleasure, and of pleasure I took my fill; but pleasure is a far different thing from happiness, or should I have wandered away at the very height of my popularity and success, to live abroad by myself with my colours and sketch-book, vainly seeking the peace of mind which was not to be found at home? I was bored, Vere, as a man who leads an aimless life always is bored. Fresh amusements might stave off the mental disease for a time, but it came back with renewed virulence; and I cared not at what expense I purchased an hour's immunity with the remedy of fierce excitement. But I never was faithless to my art. Through it all I loved to steal away and get an hour or two at the easel. Would I had devoted my lifetime to it. How differently should I feel now.

"One winter I was painting in the Belvidere at Vienna. A young girl timidly looked over my shoulder at my work, and her exclamation of artless wonder and admiration was so gratifying, that I could not resist the desire of making her acquaintance. This I achieved without great difficulty. She was the daughter of a bourgeois merchant, one not moving in the same society as myself, and, consequently, unknown to any of my associates. Perhaps this added to the charm of our acquaintance; perhaps it imparted the zest of novelty to our intercourse. Ere I returned to London, I was fonder of Elise than I had ever yet been of any woman in the world. Why did I not make her mine? Oh! pride and selfishness; I thought it would be a *mésalliance*--I thought my London friends would laugh at me--I thought I should lose my liberty.--Liberty, forsooth! when one's will depends on a fool's sneer. And yet I think if I had known her faith and truth, I would have given up all for her, even then. So I came back to England, and the image of my pale, lovely Elise haunted me more than I liked. I rushed deeper into extravagance and dissipation; for two years I gambled and speculated, and rioted, till at the end of that period I found ruin staring me in the face. I saved a competency out of the wreck of my property; and by Sir Harry's advice--our neighbour, Vere; you needn't wince, my boy--I managed to keep the old house here as a refuge for my old age. Then, and not till then, I thought once more of Elise--oh, hard, selfish heart!--not in the wealth and luxury which I ought to have been proud to offer up at her feet, but in the poverty and misfortune which I felt would make her love me all the better. I returned to Vienna, determined to seek her out and make her my own. I soon discovered her relatives; too soon I heard what had become of her. In defiance of all their wishes, she had resolutely refused to make an excellent marriage provided for her according to the custom of her country. She would give no reasons; she obstinately denied having formed any previous attachment; but on being offered the alternative, she preferred 'taking the veil,' and was even then a nun, immured in a convent within three leagues of Vienna. What could I do? Alas! I know full well what I ought to have done; but I was headstrong, violent, and passionate: never in my life had I left a desire ungratified, and now could I lose the one ardent wish of my whole existence for the sake of a time-worn superstition and an unmeaning vow? Thus I argued, and on such fallacious principles I acted.

"Vere, my boy, right is right, and wrong is wrong. You always know in your heart of hearts the one from the other. Never stifle that instinctive knowledge, never use sophistry to persuade yourself you may do that which you feel you ought not. I travelled down at once to the convent. I heard her at vespers; I knew that sweet, silvery voice amongst all the rest. As I stood in the old low-roofed chapel, with the summer sunbeams streaming across the groined arches and the quaint carved pews, and throwing a flood of light athwart the aisle, while the organ above pealed forth its solemn tones, and called us all to repentance and prayer, how could I meditate the evil deed? How could I resolve to sacrifice her peace of mind for ever to my own wild happiness? Vere, I carried her off from the convent--I eluded all pursuit, all suspicion--I took her with me to the remotest part of Hungary, her own native country. For the first few weeks I believe she was deliriously happy, and then--it broke her heart. Yes, Vere, she believed she had lost her soul for my sake. She never reproached me--she never even repined in words; but I saw, day after day, the colour fading on her cheek, the light growing brighter in her sunken eye. She drooped like a lily with a worm at its core. For one short year I held her in my arms; I did all that man could to cheer and comfort her--in vain. She smiled upon me with the wan, woful smile that haunts me still; and she died, Vere, when you were born." My father hid his face for a few seconds, and when he looked up again he was paler than ever.

"My boy," he murmured, in a hoarse, broken voice, "you have been sacrificed. Forgive me, forgive me, my child; *you are illegitimate.*" I staggered as if I had been shot--I felt stunned and stupefied--I saw the whole desolation of the sentence which had just been passed upon me. Yes, I was a bastard; I had no right even to the name I bore. Never again must I hold my head up amongst my fellows; never again indulge in those dreams of future distinction, which I only now knew I had so cherished; *never, never* think of Constance more! It was all over now; there was nothing left on earth for me.

There is a reaction in the nature of despair. I drew myself up, and looked my father steadily in the face.

"Father," I said, "whatever happens, I am your son; do not think I shall ever reproach you. Even now you might cast me off if you chose, and none could blame you; but I will never forget you,--whatever happens, I will always love you the same." He shook in every limb, and for the first time in my recollection, he burst into a flood of tears; they seemed to afford him relief, and he proceeded with more composure--

"I can never repay the injury I have done you, Vere; and now listen to me and forgive me if you can. All I have in the world will be yours; in every respect I wish you to be my representative, and to bear my name. No one knows that I was not legally married to *her*, except Sir Harry Beverley. Vere, your look of misery assures me that I have told you *too late*. I am indeed punished in your despair. I ought to have watched over you with more care. I had intended to make you a great man, Vere. In your childhood I always hoped that my own talent for art would be reproduced in my boy, and that you would become the first painter of the age, and then none would venture to question your antecedents or your birth. When I found I was to be disappointed in this respect, I still hoped that with the competency I shall leave you, and your own retired habits, you might live happily enough in ignorance of the brand which my misconduct has inflicted on you. But I never dreamed, my child, that you should set your heart on *his* daughter, who can alone cast this reproach in your teeth. It is hopeless--it is irretrievable. My boy, my boy! your prospects have been ruined, and now I fear your heart is breaking, and all through me. My punishment is greater than I can bear."

My father stopped again. He was getting fearfully haggard, and seemed quite exhausted. He pointed to the picture which he had just completed.

"Day after day, Vere," he murmured, "I have been working at that likeness, and day after day her image seems to have come back more vividly into my mind. I have had a presentiment, that when it was quite finished it would be time for me to go. It is the best picture I ever painted. Stand a little to the left, Vere, and you will get it in a better light. I must leave you soon, my boy, but it is to go to her. Forgive me, Vere, and think kindly of your old father when I am gone. Leave me now for a little, my boy; I must be alone. God bless you, Vere!"

"'My father was apparently asleep . . . !'"

The Interpreter)

"'My father was apparently asleep...!*

I left the painting-room, and went into the garden to compose my mind, and recover, if possible, from the stunning effects of my father's intelligence. I walked up and down, like a man in a dream. I could not yet realise the full extent of my misery. The hours passed by, and still I paced the gravel walk under the yew-trees, and took no heed of time or anything else. At length a servant came to warn me that dinner was waiting, and I went back to the painting-room to call my father. The door was not locked, as it had hitherto been, and my father was apparently asleep, with his head resting on one arm, and the brush, fallen from his other hand, on the floor. As I touched his shoulder to wake him, I remarked that hand was clenched and stiff. Wake him! he would never wake again. How I lived through that fearful evening I know not. There was a strange confusion in the house,--running up and down stairs, hushed voices, ghostly whisperings. The doctors came. I know not what passed. They called it aneurism of the heart; I recollect that much; but everything was dim and indistinct till, a week afterwards, when the funeral was over, I seemed to awake from a dream, and to find myself alone in the world.

CHAPTER XV
BEVERLEY MERE

What contrasts there are in life! Light and shade, Lazarus and Dives, the joyous spirit and the broken heart, always in juxtaposition. Here are two pictures not three miles apart.

A pale, wan young man, dressed in black, with the traces of deep grief on his countenance, and his whole bearing that of one who is thoroughly overcome and prostrated by sorrow, sits brooding over an untasted breakfast; the room he occupies is not calculated to shed a cheering influence on his reflections: it is a long, low, black-wainscoted apartment, well stored with books, and furnished in a curious and somewhat picturesque style with massive chairs and quaintly carved cabinets. Ancient armour hangs from the walls, looming ghostly and gigantic in the subdued light, for although it is a bright October morning out-of-doors, its narrow windows and thick walls make Alton Grange dull and sombre and gloomy within. A few sketches, evidently by the hand of a master, are hung in favourable lights. More than one are spirited representations of a magnificent black-and-white retriever--the same that is now lying on the floor, his head buried between his huge, strong paws, watching his master's figure with unwinking eyes. That master takes no notice of his favourite. Occasionally he fixes his heavy glance on a picture hanging over the chimney-piece, and then withdraws it with a low stifled moan of anguish, at which the dog raises his head wistfully, seeming to recognise a too familiar sound. The picture is of a beautiful foreign-looking woman; its eyes and eyebrows are reproduced in that sorrow-stricken young man. They are mother and son; and they have never met. Could she but have seen me then! If ever a spirit might revisit earth to console the weary pilgrim here, surely it would be a mother's, bringing comfort to a suffering child. How I longed for her love and her sympathy. How I felt I had been robbed--yes, *robbed*--of my rights in her sad and premature death. Reader, have you never seen a little child, after a fall, or a blow, or some infantine wrong or grievance, run and hide its weeping face in its mother's lap? Such is the first true impulse of our childish nature, and it is never completely eradicated from the human breast. The strong, proud man, though he may almost forget her in his triumphs and successes, goes to his mother for consolation when he is overtaken by sorrow, deceived in his affections, wounded in his feelings, or sad and sick at heart. There he knows he is secure of sympathy and consolation; there he knows he will not be judged harshly, and as the world judges; there he knows that, do what he will, is a fountain of love and patience, never to run dry; and for one blessed moment he is indeed a child again. God help those who, like me, have never known a mother's love. Such are the true orphans, and such He will not forget.

Bold loses patience at last, and pokes his cold, wet nose into my hand. Yes, Bold, it is no use to sit brooding here. "Hie, boy! fetch me my hat." The dog is delighted with his task: away he scampers across the hall--he knows well which hat to choose--and springing at the crape-covered one, brings it to me in his mouth, his fine honest countenance beaming with pride, and his tail waving with delight. We emerge through a glass door into the garden, and insensibly, for the first time since my father's death, we take the direction of Beverley Manor.

This is a dark and sadly-shaded picture; let us turn to one of brighter lights and more variegated colouring. The sun is streaming into a beautiful little breakfast-room opening on a conservatory, with flowers, and a fountain of gold-fish, and all that a conservatory should have. The room itself is richly papered and ornamented, perhaps a little too profusely, with ivory and gilding. Two or three exquisite landscapes in water-colours adorn the walls; and rose-coloured hangings shed a soft, warm light over the furniture and the inmates. The former is of a light and tasteful description--low, soft-cushioned *fauteuils*, thin cane chairs, bright-coloured ottomans and footstools, Bohemian glass vases filled with flowers--everything gay, vivid, and luxurious; a good fire burning cheerfully on the hearth, and a breakfast-table, with its snowy cloth and bright silver belongings, give an air of homely comfort to the scene. The latter consists of four persons, who have met together at the morning meal every day now for several weeks. Constance Beverley sits at the head of the table making tea; Ropsley and Sir Harry, dressed in wondrous shooting apparel, are busily engaged with their breakfast; and Miss Minim is relating to the world in general her sufferings from rheumatism and neuralgia, to which touching narrative nobody seems to think it necessary to pay much attention. Ropsley breaks in abruptly by asking Miss Beverley for another cup of tea. He treats her with studied politeness, but never takes his cold grey eye off her countenance. The girl feels that he is watching her, and it makes her shy and uncomfortable.

"Any news, Ropsley?" says Sir Harry, observing the pile of letters at his friend's elbow; "no *officials*, I hope, to send you back to London."

"None as yet, thank Heaven, Sir Harry," replies his friend; "and not much in the papers. We shall have war, I think."

"Oh, don't say so, Mr. Ropsley," observes Constance, with an anxious look. "I trust we shall never see anything so horrid again."

Miss Minim remarks that "occasional wars are beneficial, nay, necessary for the welfare of the human race," illustrating her position by the familiar metaphor of thunderstorms, etc.; but Ropsley, who has quite the upper hand of Miss Minim, breaks in upon her ruthlessly, as he observes, "The funds gone down a fraction, Sir Harry, I see. I think one ought to sell. By-the-bye, I've a capital letter from De Rohan, at Paris. You would like to hear what he is about, Miss Beverley, I am sure."

Constance winced and coloured. It was Ropsley's game to assert a sort of matter-of-course *tendresse* on her part for my Hungarian friend, which he insisted on so gradually, but yet so successfully, as to give him the power of making her uneasy at the mention of "De Rohan's" name. He wished to establish an influence over her, and this was the only manner in which he could do so; but Ropsley was a man who only asked to insert the point of the wedge, he could trust himself to do the rest. Yet, with all his knowledge of human nature, he made this one great mistake, he judged of women by the other half of mankind; so he looked pointedly at Constance as he added, "I'll read you what he says, or, perhaps, Miss Beverley, you would like to see his letter?"

He had now driven her a little too far, and she turned round upon him.

"Really, Mr. Ropsley, I don't wish to interfere with your correspondence. I hate to read other people's letters; and Count de Rohan has become such a stranger now that I have almost forgotten him."

She was angry with herself immediately she had spoken. It seemed so like the remark of a person who was piqued. Ropsley would be more than ever convinced now that she cared for him. Sir Harry, too, looked up from his plate, apparently at his daughter's unusual vehemence. The girl bit her lips, and wished she had held her tongue. Ropsley saw he had marked up another point in the game.

"Very true," said he, with his quiet, well-bred smile: "old playfellows and old school-days cannot be expected to last all one's life. However, Victor does not forget us. He seems to be very gay, though, and rather dissipated, at Paris; knows all the world and goes everywhere; ran a horse last week at Chantilly. You know Chantilly, Sir Harry."

The Baronet's face brightened. He had won a cup, given by Louis Philippe, from all the foreigners there on one occasion, and he liked to be reminded of it.

"Know it," said he, "I should think I do. Why, I trained Flibbertigibbet in the park here myself--I and the old coachman. We never sent him to my own trainer at Newmarket, but took him over ourselves, and beat them all. That was the cup you saw in the centre of the dinner-table yesterday. The two-year-old we tried at Lansdowne was his grandson. Ah! Ropsley, I wish I had taken your advice about him."

Ropsley was, step by step, obtaining great influence over Sir Harry. He returned to the subject of old friendships.

"By-the-bye, Miss Beverley, have you heard anything of poor Egerton? I fear his father's death will be a sad blow to him. I tremble for the consequences."

And here he touched his forehead, with a significant look at Sir Harry.

Constance was a true woman. She was always ready too vigorously to defend an absent friend, but she was no match for her antagonist; she could not keep cool.

"What do you mean?" said she, angrily. "Why should you tremble, as you call it, for Vere?"

Ropsley put on his most provoking air, as he answered, with a sort of playful mock deference--

"I beg your pardon, Miss Beverley, I am continually affronting you, this unlucky morning. First, I bore you about De Rohan, thinking you *do* care for your old friends; then I make you angry with me about Egerton, believing you *don't*. After all, I said no harm about him; nothing more than we all know perfectly well. He always was eccentric as a boy--he is more so than ever, I think, now; and I only meant that I feared any sudden shock or violent affliction might upset his nervous system, and, in short--may I ask you for a little more cream?--end in total derangement. The fact is," he added, *sotto voce*, to Sir Harry, "he is as mad as Bedlam now."

He saw the girl's lip quiver, and her hand shake as she gave him his cup; but he kept his cold grey eye fastened on her. He seemed to read her most secret thoughts, and she feared him now--actually feared him. Well, it was always something gained. He proceeded good-humouredly--

"Do we shoot on the island to-day, Sir Harry?" he asked of his host. "Perhaps Miss Beverley will come over to our luncheon in her boat. How pretty you have made that island, Sir Harry; and what a place for ducks about sundown!"

The island was a pet toy of Sir Harry's; he was pleased, as usual, with his friend's good taste.

"Yes, come over to luncheon, Constance," said he. "You can manage the boat quite well that short way."

"No, thank you, papa," answered Constance, with a glance at Ropsley; "the boat is out of repair, and I had rather not run the risk of an upset."

"You used to be so fond of boating, Miss Beverley," observed Ropsley, with his scarcely perceptible sneer. "You and Egerton used to be always on the water. Perhaps you don't like it without a companion; pray don't think of coming on our account. I quite agree with you, it makes all the difference in a water-party."

Constance began to talk very fast to her father.

"I'll come, papa, after all, I think," said she; "it is such a beautiful day! and the boat will do very well, I dare say--and I'm so fond of the water, papa; and--and I'll go and put my bonnet on now. I've got two or three things to do in the garden before I start."

So she hurried from the room, but not till Ropsley had presented her with a sprig of geranium he had gathered in the conservatory, and thanked her in a sort of mock-heroic speech for her kindness in so readily acceding to his wishes.

Would he have been pleased or not, could he have seen her in the privacy of her own apartment, which she had no sooner reached than she dashed his gift upon the floor, stamping on it with her little foot as though she would crush it into atoms, while her bosom heaved, and her dark eyes filled with tears, shed she scarce knew why? She had a vague consciousness of humiliation, and an undefined feeling of alarm that she could not have accounted for even to herself, but which was very uncomfortable notwithstanding.

The gentlemen put on their belts and shooting apparatus; and Ropsley, with the sneer deepening on his well-cut features, whispered to himself, "*Pour le coup, papillon, je te tiens.*"

Bold and I strolled leisurely along: the dog indulging in his usual vagaries on the way; his master brooding and thoughtful, reflecting on the many happy times he had trod the same pathway when he was yet in ignorance of the fatal secret, and how it was all over now. My life was henceforth to be a blank. I began to speculate, as I had never speculated before, on the objects and aims of existence. What had I done, I thought, that I should be doomed to be *so* miserable?--that I should have neither home nor relatives nor friends?--that, like the poor man whose rich neighbour had flocks and herds and vineyards, I should have but my one pet lamb, and even that should be taken away from me? Then I thought of my father's career--how I had been used to look up to him as the impersonation of all that was admirable and enviable in man. With his personal beauty and his princely air and his popularity and talent, I used to think my father must be perfectly happy. And now to find that he too had been living with a worm at his heart! But then he had done wrong, and he suffered rightly, as he himself confessed, for the sins of his youth. And I tried to think myself unjustly treated; for of what crimes had I been guilty, that I should suffer too? My short life had been blameless, orderly, and dutiful. Little evil had I done; but even then my conscience whispered--Much good had I left undone. I had lived for myself and my own affections; I had not trained my mind for a career of usefulness to my fellow-men. It is not enough that a human being should abstain from gross, palpable evil; he must follow actual good. It is better to go down into the market, and run your chance of the dirt that shall soil it, and the hands it shall pass through, in making your one talent ten talents, than to hide it up in a napkin, and stand aloof from your fellow-creatures, even though it should give you cause, like the Pharisee, to "thank God that you are not as other men are."

"Steady, Bold! Heel, good dog, heel! You hear them shooting, I know, and you would like well to join the sport. Bang! bang! there they go again. It is Sir Harry and his guest at their favourite amusement. We will stay here, old dog, and perhaps we may see her once more, if only at a distance, and we shall not have had our walk for nothing." So Bold and I crouched quietly down amongst the tall fern, on a knoll in the park from whence we could see the Manor House and the mere, and Constance's favourite walk in the shrubbery which I had paced with her so often and so happily in days that seemed now to have belonged to another life.

They were having capital sport in the island; it was a favourite preserve of Sir Harry's; and although artificially stocked with pheasants--as indeed what coverts are not, for that most artificial of all field-sports which we call a *battue*?--it had this advantage, that the game could not possibly stray from its own feeding-place and home. Moreover, as the fine-plumaged old cocks went whirring up out of the copse, there was a great art in knocking them over before they were fairly on the wing, so that the dead birds might not fall into the water, but be picked up on *terra firma*, dry, and in good order to be put into the bag. Many a time had I stood in the middle ride, and brought them down right and left, to the admiration of my old acquaintance, Mr.

Barrells, and the applause of Sir Harry. Many a happy day had I spent there, in the enjoyment of scenery, air, exercise, and sport (not that I cared much for the latter); but, above all, with the prospect of Constance Beverley bringing us our luncheon, or, at the worst, the certainty of seeing her on our return to the Manor House. How my heart ached to think it was all gone and past now!

I watched the smoke from the sportsmen's guns as it curled up into the peaceful autumn sky. I heard the cheery voices of the beaters, and the tap of their sticks in the copse; but I could not see a soul, and was myself completely unseen. I felt I was looking on what had so long been my paradise for the last time, and I lost the consciousness of my own identity in the dreamy abstraction with which I regarded all around. It seemed to me as if another had gone through the experiences of my past life, or rather as if I was no longer Vere Egerton, but one who had known him and pitied him, and would take some little interest in him for the future, but would probably see very little of him again. I know not whether other men experience such strange fancies, or whether it is but the natural effect of continued sorrow, which stuns the mental sense, even as continued pain numbs that of the body; but I have often felt myself retracing my own past or speculating on my own future, almost with the indifference of an uninterested spectator. Something soon recalled me to myself. Bold had the eye of a hawk, but I saw her before Bold did; long ere my dog erected his silken ears and stopped his panting breath, my beating heart and throbbing pulses made me feel too keenly that I was Vere Egerton again.

She seemed to walk more slowly than she used; the step was not so light; the head no longer carried so erect, so naughtily; she had lost the deer-like motion I admired so fondly; but oh! how much better I loved to see her like this. I watched as a man watches all he loves for the *last* time. I strove, so to speak, to print her image on my brain, there to be carried a life-long photograph. She walked slowly down towards the mere, her head drooping, her hands clasped before her, apparently deep, deep in her own thoughts. I would have given all I had in the world could I but have known what those thoughts were. She stopped at the very place where once before she had caressed Bold; she gathered a morsel of fern and placed it in her bosom; then she walked on faster, like one who wakes from a train of profound and not altogether happy reflections.

Meanwhile I had the greatest difficulty in restraining my dog. Good, faithful Bold was all anxiety to scour off at first sight of her, and greet his old friend. He whined piteously when I forbade him. I thought she must have heard him; but no, she walked quietly on towards the water, loosed her little skiff from its moorings, got into it, and pushed off on the smooth surface of the mere.

She spread the tiny sail, and the boat rippled its way slowly through the water. The little skiff was a favourite toy of Constance, and I had taught her to manage it very dexterously. At the most it would hold but two people; and many an hour of ecstasy had I passed on the mere in "The Queen Mab," as we sportively named it, drinking in every look and tone of my idolised companion: poison was in the draught, I knew it well, and yet I drank it to the dregs. Now I watched till my eyes watered, for I should never steer "The Queen Mab" again.

A shout from the shore of the island diverted my attention. Sir Harry had evidently espied her, and was welcoming his daughter. I made out his figure, and that of Barrells, at the water's edge; whilst the report of a gun, and a thin column of white smoke curling upwards from the copse, betokened the presence of Ropsley among the beaters in the covert. When I glanced again at "The Queen Mab," it struck me she had made but little way, though her gossamer-looking sail was filled by the light breeze. She could not now be more than a hundred and fifty yards from her moorings, whilst I was myself perhaps twice that distance from the brink of the mere. Constance rises from her seat, and waves her hand above her head. Is that her voice? Bold hears it too, and starts up to listen. The white sail leans over. God in heaven! it is down! Vivid like lightning the ghastly truth flashes through my brain; the boat is waterlogged--she is sinking--my heart's darling will be drowned in my very sight; it is ecstasy to think I can die with her, if I cannot save her!

"Bold! Bold! Hie, boy; go fetch her; hie, boy; hie!"

The dog is already at the water-side; with his glorious, God-given instinct he has understood it all. I hear the splash as he dashes in; I see the circles thrown behind him as he swims; whilst I am straining every nerve to reach the water's edge. What a long three hundred yards it is! A lifetime passes before me as I speed along. I have even leisure to think of poor Ophelia and her glorious Dane. As I run I fling away coat, waistcoat, watch, and handkerchief. I see a white dress by the side of the white sail. My gallant dog is nearing it even now. The next instant I am overhead in the mere; and as I rise to the surface, shaking the water from my lips and hair, I feel, through all my fear and all my suspense, something akin to triumph in the long, vigorous strokes that are shooting me onwards to my goal. Mute and earnest I thank God for my personal strength, never appreciated till this day; for my hardy education, and my father's swimming lessons in the sluggish, far-away Theiss; for my gallant, faithful dog, who has reached her even now.

"Hold on, Bold! her dress is floating her still. Hold on, good dog. Another ten seconds, and she is saved!"

Once I thought we were gone. My strength was exhausted. I had reached the bank with my rescued love. Her pale face was close to mine; her long, wet hair across my mouth; she was conscious still, she never lost her senses or her courage. Once she whispered, "Bless you, my brave Vere." But the bank was steep, and the water out of our depth to the very edge. A root I caught at gave way. My overtaxed muscles refused to second me. It was hard to fail at the last. I could have saved myself had I abandoned my hold. It was delicious to know this, and then to wind my arm tighter round her waist, and to think we should sleep together for ever down there; but honest Bold grasped her once more in those vigorous jaws--she bore the marks of his teeth on her white neck for many a day. The relief thus afforded enabled me to make one desperate effort, and we were saved.

She fainted away when she was fairly on the bank; and I was so exhausted I could but lie gasping at her side. Bold gave himself a vigorous shake and licked her face. Assistance, however, was near at hand; the accident had been witnessed from the island; Sir Harry and the keeper had shoved off immediately in their boat, and pulled vigorously for the spot. It was a heavy, lumbering craft, and they must have been too late. Oh, selfish heart! I felt that had I not succeeded in saving her, I had rather we had both remained under those peaceful waters; but selfish though it may have been, was it not ecstasy to think that I had rescued *her*--Constance Beverley, my own Constance--from death? I, the ungainly, unattractive man, for whom I used to think no woman could ever care; and she had called me "*her* brave Vere!" HERS! She could not unsay that; come what would, nothing could rob me of *that*. "Fortune, do thy worst," I thought, in my thrill of delight, as I recalled those words, "I am happy for evermore." Blind! blind! *Quem Deus vult perdere prius dementat.*

CHAPTER XVI
PRINCESS VOCQSAL

It was an accommodating *ménage*, that of Prince and Princess Vocqsal, and was carried on upon the same system, whether they were "immured," as Madame la Princesse called it, in the old chateau near Sieberiburgen, or disporting themselves, as now, in the sunshine and gaiety of *her* dear Paris, as the same volatile lady was pleased to term that very lively resort of the gay, the idle, and the good-for-nothing. It was the sort of *ménage* people do not understand in England quite so thoroughly as abroad; the system was simple enough--"live and let live" being in effect the motto of an ill-matched pair, who had better never have come together, but who, having done so, resolved to make the best of that which each found to be a bad bargain, and to see less of each other than they could possibly have done had they remained as formerly, simply an old cousin and a young one, instead of as now, husband and wife.

Prince Vocqsal was the best of fellows, and the most sporting of Hungarians. Time was, "before the Revolution, *mon cher*"--a good while before it, he might have added--that the Prince was the handsomest man of his day, and not indisposed to use his personal advantages for the captivation of the opposite sex. His conquests, as he called them, in France, Spain, Italy, not to mention the Fatherland, were, by his own account, second only to those of Don Juan in the charming opera which bears the name of that libertine; but his greatest triumph was to detail, in strict confidence, of course, how he had met with *un grand succes* amongst *ces belles blondes Anglaises*, whose characters he was good enough to take away with a sweeping liberality calculated to alter a Briton's preconceived notions as to the propriety of those prudish dames whom he had hitherto been proud to call his countrywomen. I cannot say I consider myself bound to believe all an old gentleman, or a young one either, has to say on that score. Men are given to lying, and woman is an enigma better let alone. The Prince, however, clung stoutly to his fascinations, long after time, good living, and field-sports had changed him from a slim, romantic swain to a jolly, roundabout old gentleman. He dyed his moustaches and whiskers, wore a belt patented to check corpulency, and made up for the ravages of decay by the artifices of the toilet. He could ride extremely well (for a foreigner), not in the break-neck style which hunting men in England call "going," and which none except an Englishman ever succeeds in attaining; but gracefully, and like a gentleman. He could shoot with the rifle or the smooth-bore with an accuracy not to be surpassed, and was an "ace-of-diamonds man" with the pistol. Notwithstanding the many times his amours had brought him "on the ground," it was his chief boast that he had never killed his man. "I am sure of my *coup*, my dear," he would say, with an amiable smile, and holding you affectionately by the arm, "and I always take my antagonist just below the knee-pan. I sight a little over the ankle, and the rise of the ball at twelve paces hits the exact spot. There is no occasion to repeat my fire, and he lives to be my friend."

Added to this he was a thorough *bon vivant*, and an excellent linguist. On all matters connected with field-sports he held forth in English, swearing hideously, under the impression that on these topics the use of frightful oaths was national and appropriate. He was past middle age, healthy, good-humoured, full of fun, and he did not care a straw for Princess Vocqsal.

Why did he marry her? The reason was simple enough. Hunting, shooting, horse-racing, gaiety, hospitality, love, life, and libertinism, will make a hole in the finest fortune that ever was inherited, even in Hungary; and Prince Vocqsal found himself at middle age, or what he called the prime of life, with all the tastes of his youth as strong as ever, but none of its ready money left. He looked in the glass, and felt that even he must at length succumb to fate.

"My cousin Rose is rich; she is moreover young and beautiful; *une femme très distinguée et tant soit peu coquette*. I must sacrifice myself, and Comtesse Rose shall become Princess Vocqsal." Such was the fruit of the Prince's reflections, and it is but justice to add he made a most accommodating and good-humoured husband.

Comtesse Rose had no objection to being Princess Vocqsal. A thousand flirtations and at least half-a-dozen *grandes passions*, had a little tarnished the freshness of her youthful beauty; but what she had lost in bloom she had gained in experience. Nobody had such a figure, so round, so shapely, of such exquisite proportions; nobody knew so well how to dress that figure to the greatest advantage. Her gloves were a study; and as for her feet and ankles, their perfection was only equalled by the generosity with which they were displayed. Then what accomplishments, what talents! She could sing, she could ride, she could waltz; she could play billiards, smoke cigarettes, drive four horses, shoot with a pistol, and talk sentiment from the depths of a low *fauteuil* like a very Sappho. Her lovers had compared her at different times to nearly all the heroines of antiquity, except Diana. She had been painted in every costume, flattered in every language, and slandered in every boudoir throughout Europe for a good many years; and still she was bright, and fresh, and sparkling, as if Old Time too could not resist her fascinations, but, like any other elderly gentleman, gave her her own way, and waited patiently for his turn. Thrice happy Princess Vocqsal!--can it be possible that you, too, are bored?

She sits in her own magnificent *salon*, where once every week she "receives" all the most distinguished people in Paris. How blooming she looks with her back to the light, and her little feet crossed upon that low footstool. Last night she had "a reception," and it was gayer and more crowded than usual. Why did she feel a little dull to-day? Pooh! it was only a *migraine*, or the last French novel was so insufferably stupid; or--no, it was the want of excitement. She could not live without that stimulus--excitement she must and would have. She had tried politics, but the strong immovable will at the head of the Government had given her a hint that she must put a stop to *that*; and she knew his inflexible character too well to venture on trifling with *him*. She was tired of all her lovers, too; she began to think, if her husband were only thirty years younger, and less good-humoured, he would be worth a dozen of these modern adorers. *That* Count de Rohan, to be sure, was a good-looking boy, and seemed utterly fancy free. By-the-bye, he was not at the "reception" last night, though she asked him herself the previous evening at "the Tuileries." That was very rude; positively she must teach him better manners. A countryman, too; it was a duty to be civil to him. And a fresh character to study, it would be good sport to subjugate him. Probably he would call to-day to apologise for being so remiss. And she rose and looked in the glass at those eyes whose power needed not to be enhanced by the dexterous touch of rouge; at that long, glossy hair, and shapely neck and bosom, as a sportsman examines the locks and barrels of the weapon on which he depends for his success in the chase. The review was satisfactory, and Princess Vocqsal did not look at all bored now. She had hardly settled herself once more in a becoming attitude, ere Monsieur le Comte de Rohan was announced, and marched in, hat in hand, with all the grace of his natural demeanour, and the frank, happy air that so seldom survives boyhood. Victor was handsomer than ever, brimful of life and spirits, utterly devoid of all conceit or affectation; and moreover, since his father's death, one of the first noblemen of Hungary. It was a conquest worth making.

"I thought you would not go back without wishing me good-bye," said the Princess, with her sweetest smile, and a blush through her rouge that she could summon at command--indeed, this weapon had done more execution than all the rest of her artillery put together. "I missed you last night at my reception; why did you not come?"

Victor blushed too. How could he explain that a little supper-party at which some very fascinating ladies who were not of the Princess's acquaintance had *assisted*, prevented him. He stammered out some excuse about leaving Paris immediately, and having to make preparations for departure.

"And you are really going," said she, in a melancholy, pleading tone of voice,--"going back to my dear Hungary. How I wish I could accompany you."

"Nothing could be easier," answered Victor, laughing gaily; "if madame would but condescend to accept my escort, I would wait her convenience. Say, Princess, when shall it be?"

"Ah, now you are joking," she said, looking at him from under her long eyelashes; "you know I cannot leave Paris, and you know that we poor women cannot do what we like. It is all very well for you men; you get your passports, and you are off to the end of the world, whilst we can but sit over our work and think."

Here a deep sigh smote on Victor's ear. It began to strike him that he had made an impression; the feeling is very pleasant at first, and the young Hungarian was keenly alive to it. He spoke in a much softer tone now, and drew his chair a little nearer that of the Princess.

"I need not go quite yet," he said, in an embarrassed tone, which contrasted strongly with his frank manner a few minutes earlier: "Paris is very pleasant, and--and--there are so many people here one likes."

"And that like you," she interrupted, with an arch smile, that made her look more charming than ever. "One is so seldom happy," she added, relapsing once more into her melancholy air; "one meets so seldom with kindred spirits--people that understand one; it is like a dream to be allowed to associate with those who are really pleasing to us. A happy, happy dream; but then the waking is so bitter, perhaps it is wiser not to dream at all. No! Monsieur de Rohan, you had better go back to Hungary, as you proposed."

"Not if you tell me to stay," exclaimed Victor, his eyes brightening, and his colour rising rapidly; "not if I can be of the slightest use or interest to you. Only tell me what you wish me to do, madame; your word shall be my law. Go or stay, I wait but for your commands."

He was getting on faster than she had calculated; it was time to damp him a little now. She withdrew her chair a foot or so, and answered coldly--

"Who--I, Monsieur le Comte? I cannot possibly give you any command, except to ring that bell. The Prince would like to see you before you go. Let the Prince know Monsieur de Rohan is here," she added, to the servant who answered her summons. "You were always a great favourite of his--of *ours*, I may say;" and she bade him adieu, and gave him her soft white hand with all her former sweetness of manner; and told her servant, loud enough for her victim to hear, "to order the carriage, for she meant to drive in the Bois de Boulogne:" and finally shot a Parthian glance at him over her shoulder as she left the room by one door, whilst he proceeded by another towards the Prince's apartments.

No wonder Victor de Rohan quitted the house not so wise a man as he had entered it; no wonder he was seen that same afternoon caracolling his bay horse in the Bois de Boulogne; no wonder he went to dress moody and out of humour, because, ride where he would, he had failed to catch a single glimpse of the known carriage and liveries of Princess Vocqsal.

They met, however, the following evening at a concert at the Tuileries. The day after--oh, what good luck!--he sat next her at dinner at the English ambassador's, and put her into her carriage at night when she went home. Poor Victor! he dreamed of her white dress and floating hair, and the pressure of her gloved hand. Breakfast next morning was not half so important a meal as it used to be, and he thought the fencing-school would be a bore. She was rapidly getting the upper hand of young Count de Rohan.

Six weeks afterwards he was still in Paris. The gardens of the Tuileries were literally sparkling in the morning sun of a bright Parisian day. The Zouaves on guard at the gate lounged over their firelocks with their usual reckless brigand air, and leered under every bonnet that passed them, as though the latter accomplishment were part and parcel of a Zouave's duty. The Rue de Rivoli was alive with carriages; the sky, the houses, the gilt-topped railings--everything looked in full dress, as it does nowhere but in Paris; the very flowers in the gardens were two shades brighter than in any other part of France. All the children looked clean, all the women well dressed; even the very trees had on their most becoming costume, and the long close alleys smelt fresh and delicious as the gardens of Paradise. Why should Victor de Rohan alone look gloomy and morose when all else is so bright and fair? Why does he puff so savagely at his cigar, and glance so restlessly under the stems of those thick-growing chestnuts? Why does he mutter between his teeth, "False, unfeeling! the third time she has played me this trick? No, it is not she. Oh! I should know her a mile off. She will not come. She has no heart, no pity. She will *not* come. *Sappramento!* there she is!"

In the most becoming of morning toilettes, with the most killing little bonnet at the back of her glossy head, the best-fitting of gloves, and the tiniest of *chaussures*, without a lock out of its place or a fold rumpled, cool, composed, and beautiful, leaving her maid to amuse herself with a penny chair and a *feuilleton*, Princess Vocqsal walks up to the agitated Hungarian, and placing her hand in his, says, in her most bewitching accents, "Forgive me, my friend; I have risked so much to come here; I could not get away a moment sooner. I have passed the last hour in such agony of suspense!" The time to which the lady alludes has been spent, and well spent, in preparing the brilliant and effective appearance which she is now making.

"But you have come at last," exclaims Victor, breathlessly. "I may now speak to you for the first time alone. Oh, what happiness to see you again! All this week I have been so wretched without you; and why were you never at home when I called?"

"*Les convenances*, my dear Count," answers the lady. "Everything I do is watched and known. Only last night I was taxed by Madame d'Alençon about you, and I could not help showing my confusion; and you--you are so foolish. What must people think?"

"Let them think what they will," breaks in Victor, his honest truthful face pale with excitement. "I am yours, and yours alone. Ever since I have known you, Princess, I have felt that you might do with me what you will. Now I am your slave. I offer you----"

What Victor was about to offer never came to light, for at that instant the well-tutored "Jeannette" rose from her chair, and hurriedly approaching her mistress, whispered to her a few agitated words. The Princess dropped her veil, squeezed Victor's hand, and in another instant disappeared amongst the trees, leaving the young Hungarian very much in love, very much bewildered, and not a little disgusted.

One or two more such scenes, one or two more weeks of alternate delight, suspense, and disappointment, made poor Victor half beside himself. He had got into the hands of an accomplished flirt, and for nine men out of ten there would have been no more chance of escape than there is for the moth who has once fluttered within the magic ring of a ground-glass lamp. He may buzz and flap and fume as he will, but the more he flutters the more he singes his wings, the greater his struggles the less his likelihood of liberty. But Victor was at that age when a man most appreciates his own value: a few years earlier we want confidence, a few years later we lack energy, but in the hey-day of youth we do not easily surrender at discretion; besides, we have so many to console us, and we are so easily consoled. De Rohan began to feel hurt, then angry, lastly resolute. One night at the opera decided him. His box had a mirror in it so disposed as to reflect the interior of the adjoining one; a most unfair and reprehensible practice, by-the-bye, and one calculated to lead to an immensity of discord. What he saw he never proclaimed, but as Princess Vocqsal occupied the box adjoining his own, it is fair to suppose that he watched the movements of his mistress.

She bit her lip, and drew her features together as if she had been stung, when on the following afternoon, in the Bois de Boulogne, Vicomte Lascar informed her, with his insipid smile, that he had that morning met De Rohan at the railway station, evidently en route for Hungary, adding, for the Princess was an excellent linguist, and Lascar prided himself much on his English, "'Ome, sweet 'ome, no place like 'ome."

CHAPTER XVII
THE COMMON LOT

"And so, you see, my dear Egerton, it is out of the question. I own to a great liking for your character. I think you behaved yesterday like a trump. I am too old for romance, and all that, but I can understand your feeling, my boy, and I am sorry for you. The objection I have named would alone be sufficient. Let it never be mentioned again. Your father was my oldest friend, and I hope you will not think it necessary to break with us; but marriage is a serious affair, and indeed is not to be thought of."

"No hope, Sir Harry?" I gasped out; "years hence, if I could win fame, distinction, throw a cloak of honour over this accursed brand, give her a name to be proud of, is there no hope?"

"None," replied Sir Harry; "these things are better settled at once. It is far wiser not to delude yourself into the notion that, because you are a disappointed man now, you are destined to become a great one hereafter. Greatness grows, Vere, just like a cabbage or a cauliflower, and must be tended and cultivated with years of labour and perseverance; you cannot pluck it down with one spring, like an apple from a bough. No, no, my lad; you will get over this disappointment, and be all the better for it. I am sorry to refuse you, but I must, Vere, distinctly, and for the last time. Besides, I tell you in confidence, I have other views for Constance, so you see it is totally out of the question. You may see her this afternoon, if you like. She is a good child, and will do nothing in disobedience to her father. Farewell, Vere, I am sorry for you, but the thing's done."

So I walked out of the Baronet's room in the unenviable character of a disappointed suitor, and he went back to his farm book and his trainer's accounts, as coolly as if he had just been dismissing a domestic; whilst I--my misery was greater than I could bear--his last words seemed to scorch me. "I should get over it--I should be the better for it." And I felt all the time that my heart was breaking; and then, "he had other views for Constance;" not only must she never be mine, but I must suffer the additional pang of feeling that she belongs to another. "Would to God," I thought, "that we had sunk together yesterday, never to rise again!"

I went to look for her in the shrubbery: I knew where I should find her; there was an old summer-house that we two had sat in many a time before, and I felt sure Constance would be there. She rose as I approached it: she must have seen by my face that it was all over. She put her hand in mine, and, totally unmanned, I bent my head over it, and burst into a flood of tears, like a child. I remember to this day the very pattern of the gown she wore; even now I seem to hear the soft, gentle accents in which she reasoned and pleaded with me, and strove to mitigate my despair.

"I have long thought it must come to this, Vere," she said, with her dark, melancholy eyes looking into my very soul; "I have long thought we have both been much to blame, you to speak, and I to listen, as we have done: now we have our punishment. Vere, I will not conceal from you I suffer much. More for your sake than my own. I cannot bear to see you so miserable. You to whom I owe so much, so many happy hours, and yesterday my very life. Oh, Vere, try to bear it like a man."

"I cannot, I cannot," I sobbed out; "no hope, nothing to look forward to, but a cheerless, weary life, and then to be forgotten. Oh that I had died with you, Constance, my beloved one, my own!"

She laid her hand gently on my arm--

"Forgotten, Vere," she said; "that is not a kind or a generous speech. I shall never forget you. Always, always I shall think of you, pray for you. Papa knows best what is right. I will never disobey him: he has not forbidden us to see each other; we may be very happy still. Vere, you must be my brother."

"No more," I exclaimed, reproachfully, "no more?"

"No more, Vere," she answered, quite gently, but in a tone that admitted of no further appeal. "Brother and sister, Vere, for the rest of our lives; promise me this," and she put her soft hand in mine, and smiled upon me; pure and sorrowful, like an angel.

I was stung to madness by her seeming coldness, so different from my own wild, passionate misery.

"Be it so," I said; "and as brother and sister must part, so must you and I. Anything now for freedom and repose; anything to drive your image from my mind. I tell you that from henceforth I am a desperate man. Nobody cares for me on earth,--no father, no mother, none for whom to live; and the one I prized most discards me now. Constance, you never can have loved me as I have loved. Cold, heartless, false! I will never see you again."

She was quite bewildered by my vehemence. She looked round wildly at me, and her pale lip quivered, and her eyes filled with tears: even then I remained bitter and unmoved.

"Farewell," I said, "farewell, Constance, and for ever."

Her hand hung passively in mine, her "good-bye" seemed frozen on her lips; but she turned away with more than her usual majesty, and walked towards the house. I remarked that she dropped a white rose--fit emblem of her own dear self--on the gravel path, as she paced slowly along, without once turning her head. I was too proud to follow her and pick it up, but sprang away in an opposite direction, and was soon out of her sight.

That night, when the wild clouds were flying across the moon, and the wind howled through the gloomy yews and the ghostly fir-trees, and all was sad and dreary and desolate, I picked up the white rose from that gravel path, and placed it next my heart. Faded, shrunk, and withered, I have got it still. My home was now no place for me. I arranged my few affairs with small difficulty, pensioned the two old servants my poor father had committed to my charge; set my house in order, packed up my things, and in less than a week I was many hundred miles from Alton Grange and Constance Beverley.

CHAPTER XVIII
OMAR PASHA

It is high noon, and not a sound, save the occasional snort of an impatient steed, is to be heard throughout the lines. Picketed in rows, the gallant little chargers of the Turkish cavalry are dozing away the hours between morning and evening feed. The troopers themselves are smoking and sleeping in their tents; here and there may be seen a devout Mussulman prostrate on his prayer-carpet, his face turned towards Mecca, and his thoughts wholly abstracted from all worldly considerations. Ill-fed and worse paid, they are nevertheless a brawny, powerful race, their broad rounded shoulders, bull necks, and bowed legs denoting strength rather than activity; whilst their high features and marked swarthy countenances betray at once their origin, sprung from generations of warriors who once threatened to overwhelm the whole Western world in a tide that has now been long since at the ebb. Patient are they of hardship, and devoted to the Sultan and their duty, made for soldiers and nothing else, with their fierce, dogged resolution, and their childish obedience and simplicity. Hand-in-hand, two of them are strolling leisurely through the lines to release a restive little horse who has got inexplicably entangled in his own and his neighbour's picket-ropes, and is fighting his way out of his difficulty with teeth and hoofs. They do not hurry themselves, but converse peacefully as they pass along.

"Is is true, Mustapha, that *Giaours* are still coming to join our Bey? The Padisha[#] is indeed gracious to these sons of perdition."

[#] The Sultan.

"It is true, Janum;[#] may Allah confound them!" replies Mustapha, spitting in parenthesis between his teeth: "but they have brave hearts, these Giaours, and cunning heads, moreover, for their own devices. What good Moslem would have thought of sending his commands by wire, faster than they could be borne by the horses of the Prophet?"

[#] "Oh my soul!" a colloquial term equivalent to the French "Mon cher."

"Magic!" argues the other trooper; "black, unholy magic! There is but one Allah!"

"What filth are you eating?" answers Mustapha, who is of a practical turn of mind. "Have not I myself seen the wire and the post, and do I not know that the Padisha sends his commands to the Ferik-Pasha by the letters he writes with his own hand?"

"But you have never seen the letter," urges his comrade, "though you have ridden a hundred times under the lines."

"Oh, mulehead, and son of a jackass!" retorts Mustapha, "do you not know that the letter flies so fast along the wire, that the eye of man cannot perceive it? They are dogs and accursed, these Giaours; but, by my head, they are very foxes in wit."

"I will defile their graves," observes his comrade; and forthwith they proceeded to release the entangled charger, who has by this time nearly eaten his ill-starred neighbour; and I overhear this philosophical disquisition, as I proceed for orders to the Green Tent of Iskender Bey, commandant of the small force of cavalry attached to Omar Pasha's army in Bulgaria.

As I enter the tent, I perceive two men seated in grave discussion, whilst a third stands upright in a respectful attitude. A *chaoosh*, or Serjeant, is walking a magnificently caparisoned bay Arab up and down, just beyond the tent-pegs; while an escort of lancers, with two or three more led horses, and a brace of English pointers, are standing a few paces off. The upright figure, though dressed in a Turkish uniform, with a red fez or skull-cap, I have no difficulty in recognising as Victor de Rohan. He grasps my hand as I pass, and whispers a few words in French, while I salute Iskender Bey, and await his orders.

My chief is more than three parts drunk. He has already finished the best portion of a bottle of brandy, and is all for fighting, right or wrong, as, to do him justice, is his invariable inclination. To and fro he waves his half-grizzled head, and sawing the air with his right hand, mutilated of half its fingers by a blow from a Russian sabre, he repeats in German--

"But the attack! Excellency; the attack! when will you let me loose with my cavalry? The attack! Excellency! the attack!"

The person he addresses looks at him with a half-amused, half-provoked air, and then glancing at Victor, breaks into a covert smile, which he conceals by bending over a map that is stretched before him. I have ample time to study his appearance, and to wonder why I should have a sort of vague impression that I have seen that countenance before.

He is a spare, sinewy man, above the middle height, with his figure developed and toughened by constant exercise. An excellent horseman, a practised shot, an adept at all field-sports, he looks as if no labour would tire him, no hardships affect his vigour or his health. His small head is set on his shoulders in the peculiar manner that always denotes physical strength; and his well-cut features would be handsome, were it not for a severe and somewhat caustic expression which mars the beauty of his countenance. His deep-set eye is very bright and keen; its glance seems accustomed to command, and also to detect falsehood under a threefold mask. He has not dealt half a lifetime with Asiatics to fail in acquiring that useful knack. He wears his beard and moustache short and close; they are

> Grizzled here and there,
>
> But more with toil than age,

and add to his soldierlike exterior. His dress is simple enough; it consists of a close-fitting, dark-green frock, adorned only with the order of the Medjidjie, high riding-boots, and a crimson fez. A curved Turkish sabre hangs from his belt, and a double-barrelled gun of English workmanship is thrown across his knees. As he looks up from his map, his eye rests on me, and he asks Victor in German, "Who is that?"

"An Englishman, who has joined your Excellency's force as an Interpreter," answered my friend, "and who is now attached to Iskender Bey. I believe the Bey can give a good account of his gallantry on more than one occasion."

"The Bey," thus appealed to, musters up a drunken smile, and observes, "A good swordsman, your Excellency, and a man of many languages. Sober too," he adds, shaking his head, "sober as a Mussulman, the first quality in a soldier."

His Excellency smiles again at Victor, who presents me in due form, not forgetting to mention my name.

The great man almost starts. He fixes on me that glittering eye which seems to look through me. "Where did you acquire your knowledge of languages?" he asks. "My aide-de-camp informs me you speak Hungarian even better than you do Turkish."

"I travelled much in Hungary as a boy, Excellency," was my reply. "Victor de Rohan is my earliest friend: I was a child scarcely out of the nursery when I first made his acquaintance at Edeldorf."

A gleam of satisfaction passed over his Excellency's face. "Strange, strange," he muttered, "how the wheel turns;" and then pulling out a small steel purse, but slenderly garnished, he selected from a few other coins an old silver piece, worn quite smooth and bent double. "Do you remember that?" said he, placing it in my hand.

The gipsy troop and the deserter flashed across me at once. I was so confused at my own stupidity in not having recognised him sooner, that I could only stammer out, "Pardon, your Excellency--so long ago--a mere child."

He grasped my hand warmly. "Egerton," said he, "boy as you were, there was heart and honour in your deed. Subordinate as I then was, I swore never to forget it. I have never forgotten it. You have made a friend for life in Omar Pasha."

I could only bow my thanks, and the General added, "Come to me at head-quarters this afternoon. I will see what can be done for you."

"But, Excellency, I cannot spare him," interposed Iskender Bey. "I have here an English officer, the bravest of the brave, but so stupid I cannot understand a word he says. I had rather be without sword or lance than lose my Interpreter. And then, Excellency, the attack to-morrow--the attack."

Omar Pasha rose to depart. "I will send him back this evening with despatches," said he, saluting his host in the Turkish fashion, touching first the heart, then the mouth, then the forehead--a courtesy which the old fire-eater returned with a ludicrous attempt at solemnity.

"De Rohan," he added, "stay here to carry out the orders I have given you. As soon as your friend can be spared from the Bey, bring him over with you, to remain at head-quarters. Salaam!" And the General was on his horse and away long before the Turkish guard could get under arms to pay him the proper compliments, leaving Iskender Bey to return to his brandy-bottle, and my old friend Victor to make himself comfortable in my tent, and smoke a quiet chibouque with me whilst we related all that had passed since we met.

Victor was frank and merry as usual, spoke unreservedly of his *liaison* with Princess Vocqsal, and the reasons which had decided him on seeing a campaign with the Turkish army against his natural enemies, the Russians.

"I like it, *mon cher*," said he, puffing at his chibouque, and talking in the mixture of French and English which seemed his natural language, and in which he always affirmed *he thought*. "There is liberty, there is excitement, there is the chance of distinction; and above all, there are *no women*. It suits my temperament, *mon cher: voyez-vous, je suis philosophe*. I like to change my bivouac day by day, to attach myself to my horses, to have no tie but that which binds me to my sabre, no anxieties but for what I shall get to eat. The General does all the thinking--*parbleu!* he does it *à merveille*; and I--why, I laugh and I ride away. Fill my chibouque again, and hand me that flask;

I think there is a drop left in it. Your health, Vere, *mon enfant*, and *vive la guerre!*"

"*Vive la guerre!*" I repeated; but the words stuck in my throat, for I had already seen something of the miseries brought by war into a peaceful country, and I could not look upon the struggle in which we were engaged with quite as much indifference as my volatile friend.

"And you, Vere," he resumed, after draining the flask, "I heard you were with us weeks ago; but I have been absent from my chief on a reconnaissance, so I never could get an opportunity of beating up your quarters. What on earth brought you out here, my quiet, studious friend?"

I could not have told him the truth to save my life. Any one but *him*, for I always fancied she looked on him with favouring eyes, so I gave two or three false reasons instead of the real one.

"Oh," I replied, "everything was so changed after my poor father's death, and Alton was so dull, and I had no profession, no object in life, so I thought I might see a little soldiering. When they found I could speak Turkish, or rather when I told them so, they gave me every facility at the War Office; so I got a pair of jack-boots and a revolver, and here I am."

"But Omar will make you something better than an Interpreter," urged Victor. "We must get you over to head-quarters, Vere. Men rise rapidly in these days; next campaign you might have a brigade, and the following one a division. This war will last for years; you are fit for something better than a Tergyman."[#]

[#] An Interpreter.

"I think so too," I replied; "though, truth to tell, when I came out here I was quite satisfied with my present position, and only thirsted for the excitement of action. But this soldiering grows upon one, Victor, does it not? Yet I am loth to leave Iskender too; the old Lion stretched me his paw when I had no friends in Turkey, and I believe I am useful to him. At least I must stay with him now, for we shall be engaged before long, I can tell you that."

"*Tant mieux*," retorted Victor, with flashing eyes; "old Brandy-face will ram his cavalry into it if he gets a chance. Don't let him ride too far forward himself, Vere, if you can help it, as he did when he cut his own way through that troop of hussars, and gave them another example of the stuff the Poles are made of. The Muscov nearly had him that time, though. It was then he lost the use of half his fingers, and got that crack over the head which has been an excuse for drunkenness ever since."

"Drunk or sober," I replied, "he is the best cavalry officer we have; but make yourself comfortable, Victor, as well as you can. I recommend you to sleep on my divan for an hour or two; something tells me we shall advance to-night. To-morrow, old friend, you and I may sleep on a harder bed."

"*Vive la guerre!*" replied Victor, gaily as before; but ere I had buckled on my sabre to leave the tent, the chibouque had fallen from his lips, and he was fast asleep.

My grey Arab, "Injour,"[#] was saddled and fastened to a lance; my faithful Bold, who had accompanied me through all my wanderings, and who had taken an extraordinary liking for his equine companion, was ready to be my escort; a revolver was in my holster-pipe, a hunch of black bread in my wallet, and with my sabre by my side, and a pretty accurate idea of my route, I experienced a feeling of light-heartedness and independence to which I had long been a stranger. Poor Bold enjoyed his master's society all the more that, in deference to Moslem prejudices, I had now banished him from my tent, and consigned him to the company of my horses. He gambolled about me, whilst my snorting horse, shaking his delicate head, struck playfully at him with his fore-feet, as the dog bounded in front of him. Bad horseman as I always was, yet in a deep demi-pique Turkish saddle, with broad shovel stirrups and a severe Turkish bit, I felt thoroughly master of the animal I bestrode, and I keenly enjoyed the sensation. "Injour" was indeed a pearl of his race. Beautiful as a star, wiry and graceful as a deer, he looked all over the priceless child of the desert, whose blood had come down to him from the very horses of the Prophet, unstained through a hundred generations. Mettle, courage, and endurance were apparent in the smooth satin skin, the flat sinewy legs, the full muscular neck, broad forehead, shapely muzzle, wide red nostril, quivering ears, and game wild eye. He could gallop on mile after mile, hour after hour, with a stride unvarying and apparently untiring as clockwork; nor though he had a heavy man on his back did his pulses seem to beat higher, or his breath come quicker, when he arrived at the head-quarters of the Turkish army than when he had left my own tent an hour and a half earlier, the intervening time, much to poor Bold's distress, having been spent at a gallop. There was evidently a stir in Omar Pasha's quarters. Turkish officers were going and coming with an eagerness and alacrity by no means natural to those functionaries. An English horse, looking very thin and uncomfortable, was being led away from the tent, smoking from the speed at which he had been ridden. The sentry alone was totally unmoved and apathetic; a devout Mussulman, to him destiny was destiny, and there an end. Had the enemy appeared forty thousand strong, sweeping over his very camp, he would have fired his musket leisurely--in all probability it would not have gone off the first time--and awaited his fate, calmly observing, "Kismet![#] there is but one Allah!"

[#] The Pearl.

[#] Destiny.

More energetic spirits are fortunately within those green canvas walls; for there sits Omar Pasha, surrounded by the gallant little band of foreigners, chiefly Englishmen, who never wavered or hesitated for an instant, however desperate the task to be undertaken, and whom, it is but justice to say, the Turks were always ready to follow to the death. Very different is the expression on each countenance, for a council of war is sitting, and to-day will decide the fate of many a grey-coated Muscov and many a turbaned servant of the Prophet. A Russian prisoner has moreover just been brought in, and my arrival is sufficiently opportune to interpret, with the few words of Russian I have already picked up, between the unfortunate man and his captors. If he prove to be a spy, as is more than suspected, may Heaven have mercy on him, for the Turk will not.

Omar Pasha's brow is contracted and stern. He vouchsafes me no look or sign of recognition as he bids me ask the prisoner certain pertinent questions on which life and death depend.

"What is the strength of the corps to which you belong?"

The man answers doggedly, and with his eyes fixed on the ground, "Twenty thousand bayonets."

Omar Pasha compares his answer with the paper he holds in his hand. I fancy he sets his teeth a little tighter, but otherwise he moves not a muscle of his countenance.

"At what distance from the Danube did you leave your General's head-quarters?"

The prisoner pretends not to understand. My limited knowledge of his language obliges me to put the question in an involved form, and he seems to take time to consider his answer. There is nothing about the man to distinguish him from the common Russian soldier--a mere military serf. He is dressed in the long, shabby, grey coat, the greasy boots, and has a low overhanging brow, a thoroughly Calmuck cast of features, and an intensely stupid expression of countenance; but I remark that his hands, which are nervously pressed together, are white and slender, and his feet are much too small for their huge shapeless coverings.

His eye glitters as he steals a look at the General, whilst he answers, "Not more than an hour and a half."

Again Omar consults his paper, and a gleam passes over his face like that of a chess-player who has checkmated his adversary.

"One more question," he observes, courteously, "and I will trouble you no longer. What force of artillery is attached to your General's *corps d'armée?*"

"Eight batteries of field-cannon and four troops of horse artillery," replies the prisoner, this time without a moment's hesitation; but the sweat breaks out on his forehead, for he is watching Omar Pasha's countenance, and he reads "death" on that impassible surface.

"It is sufficient, gentlemen," observes the General to the officers who surround him. "Let him be taken to the rear of the encampment and shot forthwith."

The prisoner's lip quivers nervously, but he shows extraordinary pluck, and holds himself upright as if on parade.

"Poor devil!" says a hearty voice in English; and turning round, I see a good-looking, broad-shouldered Englishman, in the uniform of a brigadier, who is watching the prisoner with an air of pity and curiosity approaching the ludicrous. "Excellence," says he, in somewhat broken German, "will you not send him to me? I will undertake that he spreads no false reports about the camp. I will answer for his safety in my hands; he must not be permitted to communicate with any one, even by signs; but it is a pity to shoot him, is it not?"

"I would do much to oblige you, Brigadier," replied Omar, with frank courtesy; "but you know the custom of war. I cannot in this instance depart from it--no, not even to oblige a friend;" he smiled as he spoke, and added in Turkish to an officer who stood beside him, "March him out, and see it done immediately. And now, gentlemen," he proceeded, "we will arrange the plan of attack. Mr. Egerton, your despatches are ready; let them reach Iskender Bey without delay. There will be work for us all to-morrow."

At these words a buzz of satisfaction filled the tent; not an officer there but was determined to win his way to distinction *coûte qui coûte*. I felt I had received my dismissal, and bowed myself out. As I left the tent, I encountered the unfortunate Russian prisoner marching doggedly under escort to the place of his doom. When he caught sight of me he made a mechanical motion with his fettered hand, as though to raise it to his cap, and addressed me in French, of which language he had hitherto affected the most profound ignorance.

"Comrade," said he, "order these men to give me five minutes. We are both soldiers; you shall do me a favour."

I spoke to the "mulazim"[#] who commanded the guard. He pointed out an open space on which we were entering, and observed, "The Moscov has reached his resting-place at last. Five minutes are soon gone. What am I that I should disobey the Tergyman? Be it on my head, Effendi."

[#] Lieutenant.

The Russian became perfectly composed. At my desire his arms were liberated, and the first use he made of his freedom was to shake me cordially by the hand.

"Comrade," said he, in excellent French, and with the refined tone of an educated man, "we are enemies, but we are soldiers. We are civilised men among barbarians; above all, we are Christians among infidels. Swear to me by the faith we both worship that you will fulfil my last request."

His coolness at this trying moment brought the tears into my eyes. I promised to comply with his demand so far as my honour as a soldier would permit me.

He had stood unmoved surrounded by enemies, he had heard his death-warrant without shrinking for an instant; but my sympathy unmanned him, and it was with a broken voice and moistened eyes that he proceeded.

"I am not what I seem. I hold a commission in the Russian army. Disguised as a private soldier I crossed the river of my own free will. I have sacrificed myself willingly for my country and my Czar. He will know it, and my brother will be promoted. The favour I ask you is no trifling one." He took a small amulet from his neck as he spoke; it was the image of his patron saint, curiously wrought in gold. "Forward this to my mother, she is the one I love best on earth. *Mother*," he repeated, in a low, heartbreaking voice, "could you but see me now!"

I had fortunately a memorandum-book in my pocket. I tore out a leaf and handed him a pencil. He thanked me with such a look of gratitude as I never saw before on mortal face, wrote a few lines, wrapped the amulet in the paper, and inscribed on it the direction with a hand far steadier than my own. As he gave it me, the mulazim coolly observed, "Effendi! the time has expired," and ordered his men to "fall in." The Russian squeezed my hand, and drew himself up proudly to his full height, whilst his eye kindled, and the colour came once more into his cheek. As I mounted my horse, he saluted me with the grave courteous air with which a man salutes an antagonist in a duel.

I could not bear to see him die. I went off at a gallop, but I had not gone two hundred paces before I heard the rattle of some half-dozen muskets. I pulled up short and turned round. Some inexplicable fascination forced me to look. The white smoke was floating away. I heard the ring of the men's ramrods as they reloaded; and where the Russian had stood erect and chivalrous while he bid me his last farewell, there was nothing now but a wisp of grey cloth upon the ground.

Sick at heart, I rode on at a walk, with the bridle on my horse's neck. But a soldier's feelings must not interfere with duty. My despatches had to be delivered immediately, and soon I was once more speeding away as fast as I had come. An hour's gallop braced my nerves, and warmed the blood about my heart. As I gave Injour a moment's breathing time, I summoned fortitude to read the Russian's letter. My scholarship was more than sufficient to master its brief contents. It was addressed to the Countess D----, and consisted but of these few words: "Console thyself, my mother; I die in the true faith."

He was a gallant man and a good.

"If this is the stuff our enemies are made of," thought I, as I urged Injour once more to his speed, "there is, indeed--as Omar Pasha told us to-day--there is, indeed, 'work cut out for us all.'"

CHAPTER XIX
"'SKENDER BEY"

The old Lion is sober enough now. What a headache he ought to have after all that brandy yesterday: but the prospect of fighting always puts Iskender Bey to rights, and to-day he will have a bellyful, or we are much mistaken. At the head, in the rear, on the flanks of his small force, the fiery Pole seems to have eyes and ears for every trooper under his command. The morning is dark and cloudy; a small drizzling rain is falling, and effectually assists our manoeuvres. We have crossed the Danube in a few flat boats before daybreak, fortunately with no further casualty than the drowning of one horse, whose burial-service has been celebrated in the strongest oaths of the Turkish language. We have landed without opposition; and should we not be surprised by any outpost of the enemy, we are in a highly favourable position for taking our share in the combined attack.

Victor de Rohan has been attached for the occasion to our commander's staff. He is accompanied by a swarthy, powerful man, mounted on a game-looking bay mare, the only charger of that sex present on the field. This worthy goes by the name of Ali Mesrour, and is by birth a Beloochee: fighting has been his trade for more than twenty years, and he has literally fought his way all over the East, till he found himself a sort of henchman to Omar Pasha on the banks of the Danube. He has accompanied De Rohan here from head-quarters, and sits on his mare by the Hungarian's side, grim and unmoved as becomes a veteran warrior. There is charlatanism in all trades. It is the affectation of the young soldier to be excited, keen, volatile, and jocose, while the older hand thinks it right to assume an air of knowing calmness, just dashed with a touch of sardonic humour. We are situated in a hollow, where we are completely hidden from the surrounding district: the river guards our rear and one of our flanks; a strong picket is under arms in our front; and beyond it a few videttes, themselves unseen, are peeping over the eminence before them. Our main body are dismounted, but the men are prepared to "stand to their horses" at a moment's notice, and all noise is strictly forbidden in the ranks. If we are surprised by a sufficiently strong force we shall be cut to pieces, for we have no retreat; if we can remain undiscovered for another hour or so, the game will be in our own hands.

Iskender Bey is in Paradise. This is what he lives for; and to-day, he thinks, will see him a pasha or a corpse.

"Tergyman," he whispers to me, whilst his sides shake, and his eyes kindle with mirth, "how little they think who is their neighbour. And the landing, Tergyman! the landing; the only place for miles where we could have accomplished it, and they had not even a sentry there. Oh, it is the best joke!" And Iskender dismounts from his horse to enjoy his laugh in comfort, while his swollen veins and bloodshot eyes betoken the severity of the internal convulsion, all the more powerful that he must not have it out in louder tones.

"Another hour of this, at least," observes Victor, as he lights a large cigar, and hands another to the commandant, and a third to myself, "one more hour, Egerton, and then comes our chance. You have got a picked body of men to-day, Effendi!" he observes to the Bey; "and not the worst of the horses."

"They are my own children to-day, Count," answers Iskender, with sparkling eyes. "There are not too many of the brood left; but the chickens are game to the backbone. What say you, Ali? These fellows are better stuff than your Arabs that you make such a talk about."

The Beloochee smiles grimly, and pats his mare on the neck.

"When the sun is low," he answers, "I shall say what I think; meanwhile work, and not talk, is before us. The Arab is no bad warrior, Effendi, on the fourth day, when the barley is exhausted, and there is no water in the skins."

Iskender laughs, and points to the Danube. "There is water enough there," he says, "for the whole cavalry of the Padisha, Egyptian guards, and all. Pah! don't talk of water, I hate the very name of it. Brandy is the liquor for a soldier--brandy and blood. Count de Rohan, your Hungarians don't fight upon water, I'll answer for it."

"You know our proverb, Effendi," replies Victor, "'The hussar's horse drinks wine.' But the rain is coming on heavier," he adds, looking up at the clouds; "we shall have water enough to satisfy even a true Mussulman like Ali, presently. How slow the time passes. May I not go forward and reconnoitre?"

The permission is willingly granted; and as my office is to-day a sinecure, I creep forward with Victor beyond our advanced posts to a small knoll, from which, without being seen, we can obtain a commanding view of the surrounding country.

There is a flat extent in front of us, admirably adapted for the operations of cavalry; and a slight eminence covered with brushwood, which will conceal our movements for nearly half-a-mile farther.

"The fools!" whispers Victor; "if they had lined that copse with riflemen, they might have bothered us sadly as we advanced."

"How do you know they have not?" I whisper in reply; "not a man could we see from here; and their grey coats are exactly the colour of the soil of this unhappy country."

Victor points to a flock of bustards feeding in security on the plain. "Not one of those birds would remain a second," says he, "if there were a single man in the copse. Do you not see that they have got the wind of all that brushwood? and the bustard, either by scent or hearing, can detect the presence of a human being as unerringly as a deer. But see; the mist is clearing from the Danube. It cannot but begin soon."

Sure enough the mist was rolling heavily away from the broad, yellow surface of the river; already we could descry the towers and walls of Roustchouk, looming large, like some enchanted keep, above the waters. The rain, too, was clearing off, and a bit of blue sky was visible above our heads. In a few minutes the sun shone forth cheeringly, and a lark rose into the sky from our very feet, with his gladsome, heavenward song, as the boom of a cannon smote heavily on our ears; and we knew that, for to-day, the work of death had at last begun.

The mist rose like a curtain: and the whole attack was now visible from our post. A few flats were putting off from the Bulgarian side of the river, crowded with infantry, whose muskets and accoutrements glittered in the fitful sunlight, loaded to the water's edge. It was frightful to think of the effect a round-shot might have on one of those crazy shallops, with its living freight. The Russian batteries, well and promptly served, were playing furiously on the river; but their range was too high, and the iron shower whizzed harmlessly over the heads of the attacking Moslem. A Turkish steamer, coolly and skilfully handled, was plying to and fro in support of her comrades, and throwing her shells beautifully into the Russian redoubts, where those unwelcome visitors created much annoyance and confusion. Victor's eyes lightened as he puffed at his cigar with an assumed *sang-froid* which it was easy to see he did not feel.

"The old Lion won't stay here long," he whispered to me; "look back at him now, Vere. I told you so: there they go--'boots and saddles.' We, too, shall be at it in ten minutes. *Vive la guerre!*"

As he spoke, the trumpet rang out the order to "mount." Concealment was no longer necessary, and we rushed back to our horses, and placed ourselves on either side of our commander, ready to execute whatever orders he might choose to give.

Iskender Bey was now cool as if on parade; nay, considerably cooler: for the rehearsal was more apt to excite his feelings than the play itself. He moved us forward at a trot. Once more he halted amongst the brushwood, from which the scared bustards were by this time flying in all directions; and whilst every charger's frame quivered with excitement, and even the proud Turkish hearts throbbed quicker under the Sultan's uniform, he alone appeared wholly unmoved by the stake he had to play in the great game. It was but the calm before the hurricane.

From our new position we could see the boats of our comrades rapidly nearing the shore. Iskender, his bridle hanging over his mutilated arm, and his glass pressed to his eye, watched them with eager gaze. It was indeed a glorious sight. With a thrilling cheer, the Turkish infantry sprang ashore, and fixing bayonets as they rushed on, stormed the Russian redoubts at a run, undismayed and totally unchecked by the well-sustained fire of musketry, and the grape and canister liberally showered on them by the enemy. An English officer in the uniform of a brigadier, whom through my glass I recognised as the good-humoured intercessor for the prisoner in Omar Pasha's tent, led them on, waving his sword, several paces in front of his men, and encouraging them with a gallantry and daring that I was proud to feel were truly British.

But the Russian redoubts were well manned, and a strong body of infantry were drawn up in support a few hundred paces in their rear; the guns, too, had been depressed, and the cannonade was terrible. Down went the red fez and the shaven head; Turkish sabre and French musket lay masterless on the sand, and many a haughty child of Osman gasped out his welling life-blood to slake the dry Wallachian soil. Wave your green scarfs, dark-eyed maids of Paradise! for your lovers are thronging to your gates. But the crimson flag is waving in the van, and the Russian eagle even now spreads her wings to fly away. A strong effort is made by the massive grey column which constitutes the enemy's reserve, but the English brigadier has placed himself at the head of a freshly-landed regiment--Albanians are they, wild and lawless robbers of the hills--and he sweeps everything before him. The redoubts are carried with a cheer, the gunners bayoneted, the heavy field-pieces turned on their former masters, and the Russian column shakes, wavers, and gives way. The glass trembles in Iskender's hand; his eye glares, and the veins of his forehead begin to swell: for him too *the* moment has come.

"Count de Rohan," says he, while he shuts up his glass like a man who now sees his way clearly before him, "bring up the rear-guard. Tergyman! I have got them *here* in my hand!" and he clasps the mutilated fingers as he speaks. "Now I can crush them. The column will advance at a trot--'March!'"

Rapidly we clear the space that intervenes between our former position and the retreating columns of the enemy--now to sweep down with our handful of cavalry on their flank, and complete the victory that has been so gallantly begun! For the first time the enemy appears aware of our proximity. A large body of cavalry moves up at a gallop to intercept us. We can see their commander waving his sword and giving his orders to his men; their number is far greater than our own, and Iskender is now indeed in his glory.

"Form line!" he shouts in a voice of thunder, as he draws his glittering sabre and shakes it above his head. "Advance at a gallop!--charge!!"

Victor de Rohan is on one side of him, the Beloochee and myself on the other; the wildest blood and the best horses in Turkey at our backs: and down we go like the whirlwind, with the shout of "*Allah! Allah!*" surging in our ears, lances couched and pennons fluttering, the maddened chargers thundering at their speed, and the life-blood mounting to the brain in the fierce ecstasy of that delirious moment.

I am a man of peace, God knows! What have I to do with the folly of ambition--the tinsel and the glare and the false enthusiasm of war? And yet, with steel in his hand and a good horse between his knees, a man may well be excused for deeming such a moment as this worth many a year of peaceful life and homely duties. Alas! alas! is it all vanity? is *cui bono* the sum and the end of everything? Who knows? And yet it was glorious while it lasted!

Long ere we reach them, the Russian cavalry wavers and hesitates. Their commander gallops nobly to the front. I can see him now, with his high chivalrous features, and long, fair moustache waving in the breeze. He gesticulates wildly to his men, and a squadron or two seem inclined to follow the example of their gallant leader. In vain: we are upon them even now in their confusion, and we roll them over, man and horse, with the very impetus of our charge. Lance-thrust and sabre-cut, stab, blow and ringing pistol-shot, make short work of the enemy. "*Allah! Allah!*" shout our maddened troopers, and they give and take no quarter. The fair-haired Colonel still fights gallantly on. Hopeless as it is he strives to rally his men--a gentleman and a soldier to the last. My comrade, the Beloochee, has his eye on him. They meet in the *mêlée*. The Colonel deals a furious blow at his enemy with his long sabre, but the supple Asiatic crouches on his mare's neck, and wheels the well-trained animal at the same instant with his heel. His curved blade glitters for a moment in the sun. It seems to pass without resistance through the air; then the fair moustache is dabbled all in blood, and the Colonel's horse gallops masterless from the field.

Victor de Rohan fights like a very Paladin, and even I feel the accursed spirit rising in my heart. The Russian cavalry are scattered like chaff before the wind. Their disorganised masses ride in upon their own infantry, who are vainly endeavouring to form with some regularity. The retreat becomes a general rout, and our Turkish troopers fly like hell-hounds to the pursuit.

How might a reserve have turned the tables then! What a bitter lesson might have been taught us by a few squadrons of veteran cavalry, kept in hand by a cool and resolute officer. In vain Iskender rides and curses and gesticulates; he is himself more than half inclined to follow the example of his men. In vain the Beloochee entreats and argues, and even strikes the refractory with the flat of his sabre; our men have tasted blood, and are no longer under control. One regiment of Russian infantry, supported by a few hussars and a field-piece, are still endeavouring to cover the retreat.

"De Rohan," exclaims Iskender, while the foam gathers on his lip and his features work with excitement, "I must have that gun! Forward, and follow me!"

We placed ourselves at the head of two squadrons of the flower of our cavalry; veterans are they, well seasoned in all the artifices of war, and "own children"--so he delights to call them--to their chief. The Beloochee has also succeeded in rallying a few stragglers; and once more we rush to the attack.

The Russian regiment, however, is well commanded, and does its duty admirably. The light field-piece opens on us as we advance, and a well-directed volley, delivered when we are within a few paces, checks us at the instant we are upon them. I can hear the Russian officer encouraging his men.

"Well done, my children," says he, with the utmost *sang-froid*--"once more like that will be enough."

Several of our saddles are emptied, and Iskender begins to curse.

"Dogs!" he shouts, grinding his teeth, and spurring furiously forward--"dogs! I will be amongst you yet. Follow me, soldiers! follow me!"

Meantime, the Russian hussars have been reinforced, and are now capable of showing a front. They threaten our flank, and we are forced to turn our attention to this new foe. The infantry hold their ground manfully, and Iskender, wheeling his men, rushes furiously upon the comparatively fresh regiment of hussars with his tired horses. The Beloochee and myself are still abreast. Despite of a galling fire poured in by the infantry upon our flank, the men advance readily to the attack. We are within six horses' lengths of the hussars. I am setting my teeth and nerving my muscles for the encounter, which must be fought out hand to hand, when--crash!--Injour bounds into the air, falls upon his head, recovers himself, goes down once more, rolls over me, and lies prostrate, shot through the heart. I disentangle myself from the saddle, and rise, looking wildly about me. One leg refuses to support my weight, but I do not know that my ankle-bone is broken by a musket-ball, and that I cannot walk three yards to save my life. A loose charger gallops over me and knocks me down once more. I cannot rise again. The short look I have just had has shown me our cavalry retiring, probably to obtain reinforcements. The Russian hussars are between me and them, whilst the desultory firing on my right tells me that the pursuit is still rolling away far into Wallachia. But all this is dim and indistinct. Again the old feeling comes on that it is not Vere Egerton, but some one else, who is lying there to die. A cold sweat covers my face; a deadly sickness oppresses me; the ground rises and heaves around me, and I grasp the tufts of trodden grass in my hands. The sound of church bells is in my ears. Surely it is the old bell at Alton; but it strikes painfully on my brain. A vision, too, fleets before me, of Constance, with her soft, dark eyes--the white dress makes me giddy--a flash as of fire seems to blind me, and I know and feel no more.

I was brought to my senses by the simple process of a Cossack dropping his lance into the fleshy part of my arm--no pleasant restorative, but in my case a most effectual one. The first sight that greeted my eyes was his little horse's girths and belly, and his own rough, savage countenance, looking grimly down upon me as he raised his arm to repeat the thrust. I muttered the few words of Russian I knew, to beg for mercy, and he looked at his comrades, as though to consult them on the propriety of acceding to so unheard-of a request as that of a wounded man for his life. A few paces off I saw the Beloochee, evidently taken prisoner, disarmed, and his head running with blood, but his whole bearing as dignified and unmoved as usual.

In this awkward predicament I happily bethought me of the Russian prisoner's epistle.

"Quarter, comrade! quarter!" I shouted as loudly as my failing voice would suffer me. "I have a letter from your officer. Here it is."

"Osmanli?" inquired the Cossack, once more raising his arm to strike. I shuddered to think how quickly that steel lance-head might be buried in my body.

"No, Inglis!" I replied, and the man lowered his weapon once more and assisted me to rise.

Fortunately at this juncture an officer rode up, and to him I appealed for mercy and proper treatment as a prisoner of war. I misdoubted considerably the humanity of my first acquaintance, whose eyes I could see wandering over my person, as though he were selecting such accoutrements and articles of clothing as he thought would suit his own taste. The officer, who seemed of high rank, and was accompanied by an escort, fortunately spoke German, and I appealed eloquently to him in that language. He started at the superscription of the deserter's letter, and demanded of me sternly how I obtained it. In a few words I told him the history of the unfortunate spy, and he passed his gloved hand over his face as though to conceal his emotion.

"You are English?" he observed rapidly, and looking uneasily over his shoulder at the same time. "We do not kill our English prisoners, barbarians as you choose to think us; but to the Turk we give no quarter. Put him on a horse," he added, to my original captor, who kept unpleasantly near: "do not ill-treat him, but bring him safely along with you. If he tries to escape, blow his brains out. As for that rascal," pointing to the Beloochee, "put a lance through him forthwith."

A happy thought struck me. I determined to make an effort for Ali. "Excellence," I pleaded, "spare him, he is my servant."

The Russian officer paused. "Is he not a Turk?" he asked, sternly.

"No, I swear he is not," I replied. "He is my servant, and an Englishman."

If ever a lie was justifiable, it was on the present occasion: I trust this *white* one may not be laid to my charge.

"Bring them both on," said the Russian, still glancing anxiously to his rear. "Lieutenant Dolwitz, look to the party. Keep your men together, and move rapidly. This is the devil's own business, and our people are in full retreat." All this, though spoken in Russian, I was able to understand; nor did the hurried manner in which the great man galloped off shake my impression that he still dreaded a vision of Iskender Bey and his band of heroes thundering on his track.

I was placed on a little active Cossack pony. The Beloochee's wrist was tied to mine, and he was forced to walk or rather run by my side; whenever he flagged a poke from the butt-end of a lance admonished him to mend his pace, and a Russian curse fell harmlessly on his ear. Still he preserved his dignity through it all; and so we journeyed onwards into Wallachia, and meditated on the chances of war and the changes that a day may bring forth.

CHAPTER XX
THE BELOOCHEE

The pursuit was fast and furious. After crossing such a river as the Danube, in the teeth of a far superior force and under a heavy fire--after carrying the Russian redoubts with the bayonet, and driving their main body back upon its reserve, the Turkish troops, flushed and wild with victory, were not to be stopped by any soldiers on earth.

Iskender's charge had completely scattered the devoted body that had so gallantly interposed to cover the retreat of their comrades, and a total rout of the Russian forces was the result. The plains of Wallachia were literally strewed with dismounted guns, broken ambulance wagons, tumbrils, ammunition carts, dead and dying, whilst still the fierce Moslem urged his hot pursuit. Straggler after straggler, reeking with haste and all agape with fear, reached the astonished town of Bucharest, and the reports in that pleasure-seeking capital were, as may well be imagined, of the most bewildering and contradictory description.

Many a frightful scene was witnessed by the terrified Wallachian peasant, as fugitive after fugitive was overtaken, struck down and butchered by the dread pursuers. Nay, women and children were not spared in the general slaughter; and the hideous practice of refusing "quarter," which has so long existed between the Turkish and Russian armies, now bore ghastly fruit.

A horse falls exhausted in a cart which contains some Russian wounded, and a woman belonging to their regiment. Its comrade vainly struggles to draw them through the slough in which they are fast. Half-a-dozen Turkish troopers are on their track, urging those game little horses to their speed, and escape is hopeless.

Helpless and mutilated, the poor fellows abandon themselves to their fate. The Turks ride in and make short work of them, the Muscov dying with a stolid grim apathy peculiar to himself and his natural foe. The woman alone shows energy and quickness in her efforts to preserve her child. She covers the baby over with the straw at the bottom of the cart; wounded as she is in the confusion, and with an arm broken, she seeks to divert the attention of her ruthless captors. Satisfied with their butchery, they are about to ride on in search of fresh victims, and the mother's heart leaps to think that she has saved her darling. But the baby cries in its comfortless nest; quick as thought, a Turkish trooper buries his lance amongst the straw, and withdraws the steel head and gaudy pennon, reeking with innocent blood. The mother's shriek flies straight to Heaven. Shall the curse she invokes on that ruthless brute fall back unheard? Ride on, man of blood--ride on, to burn and ravage and slay; and when the charge hath swept over thee, and the field is lost, and thou art gasping out thy life-blood on the plain, think of that murdered child, and die like a dog in thy despair!

By a route nearly parallel with the line of flight, but wandering through an unfrequented district with which the Cossacks seem well acquainted, the Beloochee and myself proceed towards our captivity. We have ample leisure to examine our guards, these far-famed Cossacks of whom warriors hear so much and see so little--the best scouts and foragers known, hardy, rapid, and enduring, the very eyes and ears of an army, and for every purpose except fighting unrivalled by any light cavalry in the world. My original captor, who still clings to me with a most unwelcome fondness, is no bad specimen of his class. He is mounted on a shaggy pony, that at first sight seems completely buried even under the middle-sized man it carries, but with a lean, good head, and wiry limbs that denote speed and endurance, when put to the test. In a snaffle bridle, and with its head up, the little animal goes with a jerking, springing motion, not the least impaired by its day's work, and the fact that it has now been without food for nearly twenty-four hours. Its master, the same who keeps his small bright eye so constantly fastened upon his prisoners, is a man of middle height, spare, strong, and sinewy, with a bushy red beard and huge moustache. His dress consists of enormously loose trousers, a tight-fitting jacket, and high leathern shako; and he sits with his knees up to his chin. His arms are a short sabre, very blunt, and useless, and a long lance, with which he delights to do effective service against a fallen foe. He has placed the Beloochee between himself and me; it seems that he somewhat mistrusts my companion, but considers myself, a wounded man on one of their own horses, safe from any attempt at escape. The Beloochee, notwithstanding that every word calls down a thwack upon his pate (wounded as it is by the sabre-cut which stunned him) from the shaft of a lance, hazards an observation, every now and then, in Turkish. It is satisfactory to find that our guardians are totally ignorant of that language. I remark, too, that Ali listens anxiously at every halt, and apparently satisfied with what he hears, though I for my own part can discern nothing, walks on in a cheerful frame of mind, which I attribute entirely to the Moslem stoicism. His conversation towards dusk consists entirely of curses upon his captors; and these worthies, judging of its tenor by the sound, and sympathising doubtless with the relief thus afforded, cease to belabour him for his remarks.

At nightfall the rain came on again as in the morning; and at length it grew pitch dark, just as we entered a defile, on one side of which was a steep bank covered with short brushwood, and on the other a wood of young oaks nearly impenetrable.

I felt the Beloochee's wrist press mine with an energy that must mean something.

"Are you in pain?" he whispered in Turkish, adding a loud and voluble curse upon the Giaour, much out of unison with his British character, but which was doubtless mistaken for a round English oath.

"Not much," I replied in the same language; "but sick and faint at times."

"Can you roll off your horse, and down the bank on your left?" he added, hurriedly. "If you can, I can save you."

"Save yourself," I replied; "how can I move a step with a ball in my ankle-bone?"

"Silence!" interposed the Cossack, with a bang over the Beloochee's shoulders.

"Both or none," whispered the latter after a few seconds' interval, "do exactly as I tell you."

"Agreed," I replied, and waited anxiously for the result.

Our Cossack was getting wet through. To his hardy frame such a soaking could scarcely be called an inconvenience; nevertheless, it created a longing for a pipe, and the tobacco-bag he had taken from Ali was fortunately not half emptied. As he stopped to fill and light his short silver-mounted meerschaum, the spoil of some fallen foe, the troopers in our rear passed on. We were left some ten paces behind the rest, and the night was as dark as pitch.

Ali handed me a small knife: he had concealed that and one other tiny weapon in the folds of his sash when they searched him on the field of battle. I knew what he meant, and cut the cord that bound our wrists together; his other hand, meanwhile, to lull suspicion, caressed the Cossack's horse. That incautious individual blew upon his match, which refused to strike a good light.

In a twinkling Ali's shawl was unwound from his body and thrown apparently over the Cossack's saddle-bow. The smothered report of a pocket-pistol smote on my ear, but the sound could not penetrate through those close Cashmere folds to the party in front, and they rode unconsciously forward. The Beloochee's hand, too, was on his adversary's throat; and one or two gasps, as they rolled together to the ground, made me doubt whether he had been slain by the ball from that little though effective weapon, or choked in the nervous gripe of the Asiatic.

I had fortunately presence of mind to restrain my own horse, and catch the Cossack's by the bridle; the party in front still rode on.

Ali rose from the ground. "The knife," he whispered hoarsely, "the knife!"

Once, twice, he passed it through that prostrate body. "Throw yourself off," he exclaimed; "let the horses go. Roll down that bank, and we are saved!"

I obeyed him with the energy of a man who knows he has but *one* chance. I scarcely felt the pain as I rolled down amongst the brushwood. I landed in a water-course full of pebbles, but the underwood had served to break my fall; and though sorely bruised and with a broken ankle, I was still alive. The Beloochee, agile as a cat, was by my side.

"Listen," said he; "they are riding back to look for us. No horse on earth but *one* can creep down that precipice; lie still. If the moon does not come out, we are saved."

Moments of dreadful suspense followed. We could hear the Cossacks shouting to each other above, and their savage yell when they discovered their slain comrade smote wildly on our ears. Again I urged the Beloochee to fly--why should he wait to die with me? I could scarcely scrawl, and a cold sickness came on at intervals that unnerved me totally.

To all my entreaties he made but one reply, "Bakaloum" (We shall see), "it is our destiny. There is but one Allah!"

The Cossacks' shouts became fainter and fainter. They seemed to have divided in search of their late prey. The moon, too, struggled out fitfully. It was a wild scene.

The Beloochee whistled--a low, peculiar whistle, like the cry of a night-hawk. He listened attentively; again he repeated that prolonged, wailing note. A faint neigh answered it from the darkness, and we heard the tread of a horse's hoofs approaching at a trot.

"It is Zuleika," he observed, quietly; "there is but one Allah!"

A loose horse, with saddle and bridle, trotted up to my companion, and laid its head against his bosom. Stern as he was, he caressed it as a mother fondles a child. It was his famous bay mare, "the treasure of his heart," "the corner of his liver,"--for by such endearing epithets he addressed her,--and now he felt indeed that he was saved.

"Mount," he said, "in the name of the Prophet. I know exactly where we are. Zuleika has the wings of the wind; she laughs to scorn the heavy steeds of the Giaour; they swallow the dust thrown up by her hoofs, and Zuleika bounds from them like the gazelle. Oh, *jhanum!*--oh, my soul!" Once more he caressed her, and the mare seemed well worthy of his affection; she returned it by rubbing her head against him with a low neigh.

I was soon in the saddle, with the Beloochee walking by my side. His iron frame seemed to acknowledge no fatigue. Once I suggested that the mare should carry double, and hazarded an opinion that by reducing the pace we might fairly increase the burden. The remark well-nigh cost me the loss of my preserver's friendship.

"Zuleika," he exclaimed, with cold dignity, "Zuleika requires no such consideration. She is not like the gross horse of the Frank, who sinks and snorts, and struggles and fails, under his heavy burden. She would step lightly as a deer under three such men as we are. No, light of my eyes," he added, smoothing down the thin silky mane of his favourite, "I will walk by thee and caress thee, and feast my eyes on thy star-like beauty. Should the Giaour be on our track, I will mount thee with the Tergyman, and we will show him the mettle of a real daughter of the desert--my rose, my precious one!"

She was, indeed, a high-bred-looking animal, although from her great strength in small compass she appeared less speedy than she really was. Her colour was a rich dark bay, without a single white hair. Her crest was high and firm as that of a horse; and her lean, long head and expressive countenance showed the ancestry by which her doting master set such store. Though the skin that covered those iron muscles so loosely was soft and supple as satin, she carried no flesh, and her deep ribs might almost be counted by the eye. Long in her quarters, with legs of iron and immense power in her back and loins, she walked with an elastic, springy gait, such as even my own Injour could not have emulated. She was of the highest breed in the desert, and as superior to other horses as the deer is to the donkey. I wondered how my friend had obtained possession of her; and as we plodded on, the Beloochee, who had recovered his good-humour, walking by my side, condescended to inform me of the process by which the invaluable Zuleika had become his own.

"Tergyman!" said he, "I have journeyed through many lands, and with the exception of your country--the island of storms and snows--I have seen the whole world.[#] In my own land the mountains are high and rugged, the winters cold and boisterous; it rears *men* brave and powerful as *Rustam*, but we must look elsewhere for *horses*. Zuleika, you perceive, is from the desert: 'The nearer the sun, the nobler the steed.' She was bred in the tent of a scheik, and as a foal she carried on her back only such children as had a chief's blood in their veins."

[#] This is a common idea amongst Orientals when they
have done Mecca and seen a greater part of Asia Minor.

"From my youth up I have been a man of war, Effendi, and the word of command has been more familiar to my lips than the blessed maxims of the Prophet; but the time will come when I too shall be obliged to cross the narrow bridge that spans the abyss of hell. And if my naked feet have no better protection from its red-hot surface than deeds of arms and blood-stained victories, woe to me for ever! I shall assuredly fall headlong into the depths of fire.

"Therefore I bethought me of a pilgrimage to Mecca, for he is indeed a true believer who has seen with his own eyes the shrine of the Blessed Prophet. Many and long were the days I passed under the burning sun of the desert; wearisome and slow was the march of the caravan. My jaded camel was without water. I said in my soul, 'It is my destiny to die.' Far behind the long array, almost out of hearing of their bells, my beast dragged his weary steps. I quitted his back and led him till he fell. No sooner was he down than the vultures gathered screaming around him, though not a speck had I seen for hours in the burning sky. Then I beheld a small cloud far off on the horizon; it was but of the size of one of these herdsmen's cottages, but black as the raven, and it advanced more rapidly than a body of horsemen. Ere I looked again it seemed to reach the heavens, the skies became dark as night, columns of sand whirled around me, and I knew the simoom was upon us and it was time to die.

"How long I lay there I know not. When I recovered my consciousness, the caravan had disappeared, my camel was already stripped to the bones by the birds of prey, my mouth and nostrils were full of sand. Nearly suffocated, faint and helpless, it was some time ere I was aware of an Arab horseman standing over me, and looking on my pitiable condition with an air of kindness and protection.

"'My brother,' he said, 'Allah has delivered thee into my hand. Mount, and go with me.'

"He gave me water from a skin, he put me on his own horse till we were joined by his tribe; I went with him to his tents, and I became to him as a brother, for he had saved me at my need.

"He was a scheik of the wild Bedouins: a better warrior never drew a sword. Rich was he too, and powerful; but of all his wives and children, camels, horses, and riches, he had two treasures that he valued higher than the pearl of Solomon--his bay mare and his daughter Zuleika."

The Beloochee's voice trembled, and he paused. For a few seconds he listened as if to satisfy himself that the enemy were not on our track, and then nerving himself like a man about to suffer pain, and looking far into the darkness, he proceeded--

"I saw her day after day in her father's tent. Soon I longed for her light step and gentle voice as we long for the evening breeze after the glare and heat of the day. At last I watched her dark eyes as we watch the guiding star by night in the desert. To the scheik I was as a brother. I was free to come and go in his tent, and all his goods were mine. Effendi! I am but a man, and I loved the girl. In less than a year I had become a warrior of their tribe; many a foray had I ridden with them, and many a herd of camels and drove of horses had I helped to obtain. Once I saved the scheik's life with the very sword I lost to-day. Could they not have given me the girl? Oh! it was bitter to see her every hour, and to know she was promised to another!

"A few days more and she was to be espoused to Achmet. He was the scheik's kinsman, and she had been betrothed to him from a child. I could bear it no longer. The maiden looked at me with her dark eyes full of tears. I had eaten the scheik's salt--he had saved me from a lingering death--he was my host, my friend, my benefactor, and I robbed him of his daughter. We fled in the night. I owned a horse that could outstrip every steed in the tribe save one. I took a leathern skin of water, a few handfuls of barley, and my arms. I placed Zuleika on the saddle in front of me, and at daybreak we were alone in the desert, she and I, and we were happy. When the sun had been up an hour, there was a speck in the horizon behind us. I told Zuleika we were pursued; but she bid me take courage, for my steed was the best in the tribe, said she, except her father's bay mare, and he suffered no one to mount that treasure but himself. She had loosed the bay mare the night before from her picket-ropes; it would be morning before they could find her, and there was nothing to fear. I took comfort, and pressed my bride to my heart.

"In the desert, Effendi, it is not as with us. The Arab's life depends upon his horse, and he proves him as you would prove a blade. At two years old he rides him till his back bends,[#] and he never forgets the merits of the colt. Each horse's speed is as well known in the tribe as is each officer's rank in the army of the Padisha. Nothing could overtake my charger save the scheik's bay mare; and, thanks to Zuleika, the bay mare must be hours behind us."

> [#] An Arab maxim, from which they are studious not to depart; their idea being that a horse's worst year is from three to four; during which period they let him run perfectly idle, but feeding him at the same time as if in full work: for, say they, "a horse's goodness goes in at his mouth." At five he is considered mature.

"We galloped steadily on, and once more I looked over my shoulder. The speck had become larger and darker now, and I caught the gleam of a lance in the morning sun. Our pursuer must be nearing us; my horse too began to flag, for I had ridden fiercely, and he carried myself and my bride. Nevertheless, we galloped steadily on.

"Once more I looked back. The object was distinct enough now; it was a horseman going at speed. Allah be praised! there was but one. Zuleika turned pale and trembled--my lily seemed to fade on my bosom. Effendi, I had resolved what to do."

CHAPTER XXI
ZULEIKA

"Man to man, and in the desert, I had but little to fear, yet when I saw Achmet's face, my heart turned to water within me. He was a brave warrior. I had ridden by his side many a time in deadly strife; but I had never seen him look like this before. When I turned to confront him, my horse was jaded and worn out--I felt that my life was in the hand of mine enemy.

"'Achmet,' I said, 'let me go in peace; the maiden has made her choice--she is mine.'

"His only answer was a lance-thrust that passed between Zuleika's body and my own. The girl clung fainting to my bosom, and encumbered my sword-arm. My horse could not withstand the shock of Achmet's charge, and rolled over me on the sand. In endeavouring to preserve Zuleika from injury, my yataghan dropped out of its sheath; my lance was already broken in the fall, and I was undermost, with the gripe of my adversary on my throat. Twice I shook myself free from his hold: and twice I was again overmastered by my rival. His eyes were like living coals, and the foam flew from his white lips. He was mad, and Allah gave him strength. The third time his grasp brought the blood from my mouth and nostrils. I was powerless in his hold. His right arm was raised to strike; I saw the blade quivering dark against the burning sky. I turned my eyes towards Zuleika; for even then I thought of *her*. The girl was a true Arab, faithful to the last. Once, twice, she raised her arm quick and deadly as the lightning. She had seized my yataghan when it dropped from its sheath, and she buried it in Achmet's body. I rose from the ground a living man, and I was saved by her.

"Effendi, we took the bay mare, and left my jaded horse with the dead man. For days we journeyed on, and looked not back, nor thought of the past, for we were all in all to each other; and whilst our barley lasted and we could find water we knew that we were safe: so we reached Cairo, and trusted in Allah for the future. I had a sword, a lovely wife, and the best mare in the world; but I was a soldier, and I could not gain my bread by trade. I loathed the counters and the bazaar, and longed once more to see the horsemen marshalled in the field. So I fed and dressed the bay mare, and cleaned my arms, and leaving Zuleika in the bazaars, placed myself at the gate of the Pasha, and waited for an audience.

"He received me kindly, and treated me as a guest of consideration; but he had a cunning twinkle in his eye that I liked not; and although I knew him to be as brave as a lion, I suspected he was as treacherous as the fox; nevertheless, 'the hungry man knows not dates from bread,' and I accepted service under him willingly, and went forth from his presence well pleased with my fate. 'Zuleika,' I thought, 'will rejoice to hear that I have employment, and I shall find here in Cairo a sweet little garden where I will plant and tend my rose.'

"I thought to rejoin my love where I had left her, in the bazaar; but she was gone. I waited hours for her return; she came not, and the blood thickened round my heart. I made inquiries of the porters and water-carriers, and all the passers-by that I could find: none had seen her. One old woman alone thought she had seen a girl answering my description in conversation with a black, wearing the uniform of the Pasha; but she was convinced the girl had a fawn-coloured robe, or it might have been lilac, or perhaps orange, but it certainly was not green: this could not then be Zuleika, for she wore the colour of the Prophet. She was lost to me--she for whom I had striven and toiled so much; my heart sank within me; but I could not leave the place, and for months I remained at Cairo, and became a Yuz-Bashi in the Guards of the Pasha. But from that time to this I have had no tidings of Zuleika--my Zuleika."

The Beloochee's face was deadly pale, and his features worked with strong emotion: it was evident that this fierce warrior--man of blood though he had been from his youth upward--had been tamed by the Arab girl. She was the one thing on earth he loved, and the love of such wild hearts is fearful in intensity. After a pause, during which he seemed to smother feelings he could not command, he proceeded in a hoarse, broken voice with his tale.

"The days have never been so bright since I lost her, Effendi; but what would you? it was my kismet, and I submitted; as we must all submit when it is fruitless to struggle. Day by day I did my duty, and increased in the good opinion of the Pasha; but I cared for nothing now save only the bay mare, and I gave her the name of one whom I should never see again.

"The Pasha was a haughty old warrior, lavish in his expenses, magnificent in his apparel, and above all, proud of his horses. Some of the swiftest and noblest steeds of the desert had found their way into his stables; and there were three things in the world which it was well known he would not refuse in the shape of a bribe, these were gold, beauty, and horse-flesh. Ere long he cast a wistful look on my bay mare Zuleika.

"It is well known, Effendi, that an Arab mare of pure race is not to be procured. The sons of the desert are true to their principles, and although gold will buy their best horses, they are careful not to part with their mares for any consideration in the world. For long the Pasha would not believe that Zuleika was a daughter of that wonderful line which was blessed so many hundred years ago by the Prophet, nor was I anxious that he should learn her value, for I knew him to be a man who took no denial to his will. But when he saw her outstripping all competitors at the jereed; when he saw her day after day, at work or at rest, in hardship or in plenty, always smooth and sleek and mettlesome as you see her now, he began to covet so good an animal, and with the Pasha to covet was in one way or another to possess.

"Many a hint was given me that I ought to offer him my bay mare as a present, and that I might then ask what I would; but to all these I turned a deaf ear; now that *she* was gone, what had I in the world but Zuleika? and I swore in my soul that death alone should part us. At length the Pasha offered me openly whatever sum I chose to name as the price of my mare, and suggested at the same time that if I continued obdurate, it might be possible that he should obtain the animal for nothing, and that I should never have occasion to get on horseback again. My life was in danger as well as my favourite. I determined, if it were possible, to save both.

"I went to the Pasha's gate and demanded an audience, presenting at the same time a basket of fruit for his acceptance. He received me graciously, and ordered pipes and coffee, bidding me seat myself on the divan by his side.

"'Ali,' said he, after a few unmeaning compliments, 'Ali, there are a hundred steeds in my stable. Take your choice of them and exchange with me your bay mare, three for one."

"'Pasha!' I replied, 'my bay mare is yours and all that I have, but I am under an oath, that never in my life am I to *give* or *sell* her to any one.'

"The Pasha smiled, and the twinkle in his eye betokened mischief. 'It is said,' he answered, 'an oath is an oath. There is but one Allah!'

"'Nevertheless, Highness,' I remarked, 'I am at liberty to LOSE her. She may yet darken the door of your stable if you will match your best horse against her, the winner to have both. But you shall give me a liberal sum to run the race.'

"The Pasha listened eagerly to my proposal. He evidently considered the race was in his own hands, and I was myself somewhat surprised at the readiness with which he agreed to an arrangement which he must have foreseen would end in the discomfiture and loss of his own steed without the gain of mine. I did not know yet the man with whom I had to deal.

"'To-morrow, at sunrise,' said the Pasha, 'I am willing to start my horse for the race; and, moreover, to show my favour and liberality, I am willing to give a thousand piasters for every ten yards' start you may choose to take. If my horse outstrips your mare you return me the money, if you win you take and keep all.'

"I closed with the proposal, and all night long I lay awake, thinking how I should preserve Zuleika in my own possession. That I should win I had no doubt, but this would only expose me to fresh persecutions, and eventually I should lose my life and my mare too. Towards sunrise a thought struck me, and I resolved to act upon it.

"I would hold the Pasha to his word; I would claim a start of fifty yards, and a present of five thousand piasters. I would take the money immediately, and girth my mare for the struggle. With fifty yards of advantage, where was the horse in the world that could come up with Zuleika? I would fly with her once more into the desert, and take my chance. Better death with her, than life and liberty deprived of my treasure. I rose, prayed, went to the bath, and then fed and saddled my favourite, placing a handful of dates and a small bag of barley behind the saddle.

"All Cairo turned out to see the struggle. The Pasha's troops were under arms, and a strong party of his own guards, the very regiment to which I belonged, was marshalled to keep the ground. We were to run a distance of two hours[#] along the sand. Lances pointed out our course, and we were to return and finish in front of a tent pitched for the Pasha himself. His ladies were present, too, in their gilded *arabas*, surrounded by a negro guard. As I led my mare up they waved their handkerchiefs, and one in particular seemed restless and uneasy. I imagined I heard a faint scream from the interior of her *araba*; but the guard closed round it, and ere I had looked a second time it had been driven from the ground. Just then the Pasha summoned myself and my competitor to his tent. I cast my eye over my antagonist. He was considerably lighter than I was, and led a magnificent chestnut stallion, the best in the Pasha's stables; but when I looked at its strong but short form, and thought of Zuleika's elastic gait and lengthy stride, I had no fears for the result."

[#] About seven miles. The Asiatic always counts space by time, and an hour is equivalent to something over a league.

"I saluted the Pasha, and made my request. 'Highness,' I said, 'I claim a start of fifty yards and five thousand piasters. Let the money be paid, that I may take it with me and begin.'

"'It is well,' replied the Pasha; '*Kiātib*,' he added, to his secretary, 'have you prepared the "backshish" for Ali Mesrour? Bestow it on him with a blessing, that he may mount and away,' and again the cruel eye twinkled with its fierce grim humour. Effendi, my heart sank within me when I saw two sturdy slaves bring out a sack, evidently of great weight, and proceed to lay the burden on my pawing mare. 'What is this?' I exclaimed, aghast; 'Highness, this is treachery! I am not to carry all that weight!'

"'Five thousand piasters, oh my soul!' replied the Pasha, with his most ferocious grin; 'and all of it *in copper*, too. Mount, in the name of the Prophet, and away!'

"My adversary was already in his saddle; the sack was fastened in front of mine. I saw that if I made the slightest demur, it would be considered a sufficient excuse to deprive me of my mare, perhaps of my life. With a prayer to Allah, I got into my saddle. Zuleika stepped proudly on, as though she made but little of the weight; and I took my fifty yards of start, and as much more as I could get. The signal-shot was fired, and we were off. Zuleika sniffed the air of the desert, and snorted in her joy. Despite of the piasters, she galloped on. Effendi, from that day to this I have seen neither my antagonist in the race, nor the negro guard, nor the gilded *arabas*, nor the Pasha's angry smile. I won my mare, I won my life and freedom; also I carried off five thousand piasters of the Pasha's money, and doubtless four times a day he curses me in his prayers, but yonder is the dawn, and here is the Danube. Sick and faint you must be, Tergyman! Yet in two hours more we shall reach Omar Pasha's tent, for I myself placed a picket of our soldiers on either bank at yonder spot, and they have a boat; so take courage for a little time longer, and confess that the breath of the morning here is sweeter than the air of a Russian prison. Who can foretell his destiny? There is but one Allah!"

I had not the tough frame of my Beloochee friend; before we reached the waterside I had fainted dead away. I remembered no more till I awoke from my fever in an hospital tent at head-quarters. On that weary time of prostration and suffering it is needless for me to dwell. Ere I could sit upright in bed the winter had commenced, the season for field operations was over, and the army established in cantonments. There was a lull, too, before the storm. The Allies had not yet put forth their strength, and it was far from improbable that the war might even then be near its conclusion.

Victor had determined to return to Hungary, and insisted on my accompanying him. Weak, maimed, and emaciated, I could be of no service to my chief, or to the great General who had so kindly recognised me. I had nothing to keep me in Turkey; I had nothing to take me to England. No, no, anywhere but there. Had I but won a name, I should have rejoiced to return into Somersetshire, to see Constance once again--to repay her coldness with scorn--perhaps to pass her without speaking--or, bitterer still, to greet her with the frankness and ease of a mere acquaintance. But what was I, to dream thus? A mere adventurer, at best a poor soldier of fortune, whose destiny, sooner or later, would be but to fatten a battle-field or encumber a trench, and have his name misspelt in a *Gazette*. No, no, anywhere but England, and why not Hungary? Victor's arguments were unanswerable; and once more--but oh! how changed from the quiet, thoughtful child--I was again at Edeldorf.

CHAPTER XXII
VALÈRIE

"I tell you I saw them led out under my very windows to be shot. Two and two they marched, with their heads erect, and their gait as haughty as if they were leading the assault. Thirteen of them in all, and the oldest not five-and-forty. Oh! woe to the Fatherland!--the best blood in Hungary was shed on that fearful day,--the gallant, the true-hearted, who had risen at the first call, and had been the last to fail. Taken with arms in their hands, forsooth! What should be in a gentleman's hands but arms at such a time? Oh, that I had but been a man!" The girl's dark eyes flashed, and her beautiful chiselled nostril dilated as she threw her head back, and stamped her little foot on the floor. None of your soft-eyed beauties was Valèrie de Rohan, but one who sparkled and blazed, and took your admiration fairly by storm. Those who are experienced in such matters affirm that these are the least dangerous of our natural enemies, and that your regular heart-breaker is the gentle, smiling, womanly woman, who wins her way into the citadel step by step, till she pervades it all, and if she leaves it, leaves desolation and ruin behind her. But of this I am incapable of giving an opinion; all I know is, Valèrie grew soft enough as she went on.

"I knew every man of them intimately; not one but had been my father's guest--my poor father, even then fined and imprisoned in Comorn for the manly part he had played. Not one of them but had been at our 'receptions' in the very room from the windows of which I now saw them marching forth to die; and not one but as he passed me lifted his unfettered hand to his head, and saluted me with a courtly smile. Last of all came Adolphe Zersky, my own second cousin, and the poor boy was but nineteen. I bore it all till I saw him; but when he passed under my very eyes, and smiled his usual light-hearted smile, and waved his handkerchief to me, and pressed it to his lips--a handkerchief I had embroidered for him with my own hands-- and called out blithesomely, as though he were going to a wedding, 'Good-morning, Comtesse Valèrie; I meant to have called to-day, but have got a previous engagement,' I thought my heart would break. He looked prouder than any of them; I hardly think he would have been set free if he could. He was a true Hungarian. God bless him!--I heard the shots that struck them down. I often dream I hear them now. They massacred poor Adolphe last of all--he retained his *sang-froid* to the end. The Austrian officer on guard was an old schoolfellow, and Adolphe remarked to im with a laugh, just before they led him out, 'I say, Fritz, if they mean to keep us here much longer, they really ought to give us some breakfast!'

"Oh, Mr. Egerton, it was a cruel time. I had borne the bombardment well enough. I had seen our beautiful town reduced to ruins; and I never winced, for I am the daughter of a Hungarian; but I gave way when they butchered my friends, and wept--oh, how I wept! What else could I do? We poor weak women have but our tears to give. Had I *but* been born a man!"

Once more Valèrie's eye flashed, and the proud, wild look gleamed over her features; while a vague idea that for same days had pervaded my brain began to assume a certain form, to the effect that Valèrie de Rohan was a very beautiful woman, and that it was by no means disagreeable to have such a nurse when one was wounded in body, or such a friend when one was sick at heart. And she treated me as a *real* friend: she reposed perfect confidence in me; she told me of all her plans and pursuits, her romantic ideas, and visionary schemes for the regeneration of her country, for she was a true patriot; lastly, she confessed to a keen admiration for my profession as a soldier, and a tender pity for my wounds. Who would not have such a friend? Who would not follow with his eyes such a nurse as she glided about his couch?

It is useless to attempt the description of a woman. To say that Valèrie had dark, swimming eyes, and jet-black hair, twisted into a massive crown on her superb head, and round arms and white hands sparkling with jewels, and a graceful floating figure, shaped like a statue, and dressed a little too coquettishly, is merely to say that she was a commonplace handsome person, but conveys no idea of that subtle essence of beauty--that nameless charm which casts its spell equally over the wisest as the weakest, and which can no more be expressed by words than it can be accounted for by reason. Yet Valèrie was a woman who would have found her way straight to the hearts of most men. It seems like a dream to look back to one of those happy days of contented convalescence and languid repose. Every man who has suffered keenly in life must have felt that there is in the human organisation an instinctive reaction and resistance against sorrow, a natural tendency to take advantage of any lull in the storm, and a disposition to deceive ourselves into the belief that we are forgetting for the time that which the very effort proves we too bitterly remember. But even this artificial repose has a good effect. It gives us strength to bear future trials, and affords us also time for reflections which, in the excitement of grief, are powerless to arrest us for a moment.

So I lay on the sofa in the drawing-room at Edeldorf, and rested my wounded leg, and shut my eyes to the future, and drew a curtain (alas, what a transparent one it was!) over the past. There was everything to soothe and charm an invalid. The beautiful room, with its panelled walls and polished floor, inlaid like the costliest marquetry, a perfect mosaic of the forest; the light cane chairs and brocaded ottomans scattered over its surface; the gorgeous cabinets of ebony and gold that filled the spaces between the windows, reflected in long mirrors that ran from floor to ceiling; the gems of Landseer, reproduced by the engraver, sparkling on the walls--for the Hungarian is very English in his tastes, and loves to gaze through the mist at the antlered stag whom Sir Edwin has captured in the corrie, and reproduced in a thousand halls; or to rest with the tired pony and the boy in *sabots* at the halting-place; or to exchange humorous glances with the blacksmith who is shoeing that wondrously-drawn bay horse, foreshortened into nature, till one longs to pat him;--all this created a beautiful interior, and *from* all this I could let my eyes wander away, through the half-opened window at the end, over the undulating park, with its picturesque acacias, far, far athwart the rich Hungarian plain, till it crossed the dim line of trees marking the distant Danube, and reached the bold outline of hills beyond the river, melting into the dun vapours of an afternoon sky.

And there was but one object to intercept the view. In the window sat Comtesse Valérie, her graceful head bent over her work, her pretty hands flitting to and fro, so white against the coloured embroidery, and her soft glance ever and anon stealing to my couch, while she asked, with a foreigner's *empressement*, which was very gratifying, though it might mean nothing, whether I had all I wanted, and if my leg pained me, and if I was not wearying for Victor's return from the *chasse*?

"And you were here years ago, when I was almost a baby, and I was away on a visit to my aunt at Pesth. Do you know, I always felt as if we were old friends, even the first day you arrived with Victor, and were lifted out of the carriage, so pale, so suffering! Oh, how I pitied you! but you are much better now."

"How can I be otherwise," was my unavoidable reply, "with so kind a nurse and such good friends as I find here?"

"And am I *really* useful to you? and do you think that my care *really* makes you better? Oh! you cannot think how glad I am to know this. I cannot be a soldier myself, and bear arms for my beloved country; but I can be useful to those who have done so, and it makes me so proud and so happy!"

The girl's colour rose, and her eyes sparkled and moistened at once.

"But I have not fought for Hungary," I interposed, rather bluntly. "I have no claim on your sympathies--scarcely on your pity."

"Do not say so," she exclaimed, warmly. "Setting apart our regard for you as my brother's friend, it is our enemy with whom you have been fighting--our oppressor who has laid you now on a wounded couch, far from your own country and your friends. Do you think I can tolerate a Russian? he is but one degree better than an Austrian! And I can *hate*--I tell you I can hate to some purpose!"

She looked as if she could. What a strange girl she was!--now so soft and tender, like a gentle ring-dove; anon flashing out into these gleams of fierceness like a tigress. I was beginning to be a little afraid of her. She seemed to divine my thoughts, for she laughed merrily, and resumed, in her usual pleasant voice--

"You do not yet know me, Mr. Egerton. I am a true De Rohan, and we are as strong in our loves as in our hatreds. Beware of either! I warn you," she added archly, "we are a dangerous race to friend or foe."

Was this coquetry, or the mere playful exuberance of a girl's spirits? I began to feel a curious sensation that I had thought I should never feel again--I am not sure that it was altogether unpleasant.

Valèrie looked at me for a moment, as if she expected me to say something; then bent her head resolutely down to her frame, and went on in a low, rapid voice--

"We are a strange family, Mr. Egerton, we 'De Rohans'; and are a true type of the country to which we belong. We are proud to be thought real Hungarians--warm-hearted, excitable, impatient, but, above all, earnest and sincere. We are strong for good and for evil. Our tyrants may break our hearts, but they cannot subdue our spirit. We look forward to the time which *must* come at last. 'Hope on, hope ever!' is our motto: a good principle, Mr. Egerton, is it not?"

As I glanced at her excited face and graceful figure, I could not help thinking that there must be many an aspiring Hungarian who would love well to hear such a sentiment of encouragement from such lips, and who would be ready and willing to hope on, though the ever would be a long word for one of those ardent, impulsive natures. She worked on in silence for a few minutes, and resumed.

"You will help us, you English, we all feel convinced. Are you not the champions of liberty all over the world? And you are so like ourselves in your manners and thoughts and principles. Tell me, Mr. Egerton, and do not be afraid to trust me, *is it not true?*"

"Is not *what* true?" I asked, from the sofa where I lay, apathetic and dejected, a strange contrast to my beautiful companion.

She went to the door, listened, and closed it carefully, then looked out at the open window, and having satisfied herself there was not a soul within ear-shot, she came back close to my couch, and whispered, "An English prince on the throne of Hungary, our constitution and our parliaments once more, and, above all, deliverance from the iron yoke of Austria, which is crushing us down to the very earth!"

"I have never heard of it," said I, with difficulty suppressing a smile at the visionary scheme, which must have had its origin in some brain heated and enthusiastic as that of my beautiful companion; "nor do I think, if that is all you have to look to, that there is much hope for Hungary."

She frowned angrily.

"Oh!" she answered, "you are cautious, Mr. Egerton: you will not trust me, I can see--but you might do so with safety. We are all '*right-thinkers*' here. Though they swarm throughout the land, I do not believe a Government spy has ever yet set foot within the walls of Edeldorf; but I tell you, if *you* will not help us, we are lost. You laugh to see a girl like me interest herself so warmly about politics, but with us it is a question of life and death. Women, as well as men, have all to gain or all to lose. I repeat, if you do not help us we have nothing left to hope for. Russia will take our part, and we shall fall open-eyed into the trap. Why, even as enemies, they succeeded in ingratiating themselves with the inhabitants of a conquered country. Yes, Hungary was a *conquered country*, and the soldiers of the Czar were our masters. They respected our feelings, they spared our property, they treated us with courtesy and consideration, and they lavished gold with both hands, which was supplied to them by their own Government for the purpose. It is easy to foresee the result. The next Russian army that crosses the frontier will march in as deliverers, and Austria *must* give way. They are generous in promises, and unequalled in diplomacy. They will flatter our nobles and give us back our constitution; nay, for a time we shall enjoy more of the outward symbols of freedom than have ever yet fallen to our lot. And *merely* as a compliment, *merely* as a matter of form, a Russian Grand-Duke will occupy the palace at Pesth, and assume the crown of St. Stephen simply as the guardian of our liberties and our rights. Then will be told once more the well-known tale of Russian intrigue and Russian pertinacity. A pretence of fusion and a system of favouritism will gradually sap our nationality and destroy our patriotism, and in two generations it will be Poland over again. Well, even that would be better than what we have to endure now."

"Do you mean to say," I asked, somewhat astonished to find my companion so inveterate a *hater*, notwithstanding that she had warned me of this amiable eccentricity in her character,--"do you mean to say that, with all your German habits and prejudices, nay, with German as your very mother tongue, you would prefer the yoke of the Czar to that of the Kaiser?"

She drew herself up, and her voice quite trembled with anger as she replied--

"The Russians do not beat women. Listen, Mr. Egerton, and then wonder if you can at my bitter hatred of the Austrian yoke. She was my own aunt, my dear mother's only sister. I was sitting with her when she was arrested. We were at supper with a small party of relations and friends. For the moment we had forgotten our danger and our sorrows and the troubles of our unhappy country. She had been singing, and was actually seated at the pianoforte when an Austrian Major of Dragoons was announced. I will do him the justice to say that he was a gentleman, and performed his odious mission kindly and courteously enough. At first she thought there was some bad news of her husband, and she turned deadly pale; but when the officer stammered out that his business was with *her*, and that it was his duty to arrest her upon a charge of treason, the colour came back to her cheek, and she never looked more stately than when she placed her hand in his, with a graceful bow, and told him, as he led her away, that 'she was proud to be thought worthy of suffering for her country.' They took her off to prison that night; and it was not without much difficulty and no little bribery that we were permitted to furnish her with a few of those luxuries that to a lady are almost the necessaries of life. We little knew what was coming. Oh! Mr. Egerton, it makes my blood boil to think of it. Again, I say, were I only a *man*!"

Valèrie covered her face with her hands for a few seconds ere she resumed her tale, speaking in the cold, measured tones of one who forces the tongue to utter calmly and distinctly that which is maddening and tearing at the heart.

"We punish our soldiers by making them run the gauntlet between their comrades, Mr. Egerton, and the process is sufficiently brutal to be a favourite mode of enforcing discipline in the Austrian army. Two hundred troopers form a double line, at arm's-length distance apart, and each man is supplied with a stout cudgel, which he is ordered to wield without mercy. The victim walks slowly down between the lines, stripped to the waist, and at the pace of an ordinary march. I need hardly say that ere the unfortunate reaches the most distant files he is indeed a ghastly object. I tell you, this high-born lady, one of the proudest women in Hungary, was brought out to suffer that degrading punishment--to be beaten like a hound. They had the grace to leave her a shawl to cover her shoulders; and with her head erect and her arms folded on her bosom, she stepped nobly down the tyrant's ranks. The first two men refused to strike; they were men, Mr. Egerton, and they preferred certain punishment to the participation in such an act. They were made examples of forthwith. The other troopers obeyed their orders, and she reached the goal bleeding, bruised, and mangled-- she, that beautiful woman, a wife and a mother. Ah! you may grind your teeth, my friend, and your dog there under the sofa may growl, but it is true, I tell you, *true*, I saw her myself when she returned to prison, and she still walked, *so* nobly, *so* proudly, like a Hungarian, even then. Think of our feelings and of those of her own children; think of her husband's. Mr. Egerton, what would you have done had you been that woman's husband?"

"Done!" I exclaimed furiously, for my blood boiled at the bare recital of such brutality, "I would have shot the Marshal through the heart, wheresoever I met him, were it at the very altar of a church."

Valèrie's pale face gleamed with delight at my violence.

"You say well," she exclaimed, clasping her hands together convulsively; "you say well. Woman as I am, I would have dipped my hands in his blood. But no, no, revenge is not for slaves like us; we must suffer and be still. Hopeless of redress, and unable to survive such dishonour, her husband blew his brains out. What would you have? it was but a victim the more. But it is not forgotten--no, it is not forgotten, and the Marshal lives in the hearts of our Hungarian soldiers, the object of an undying, unrelenting hatred. I will tell you an instance that occurred but the other day. Two Hungarian riflemen, scarcely more than boys, on furlough from the army of Italy, were passing through the town where he resides. Weary, footsore, and hungry, they had not wherewithal to purchase a morsel of food. The Kaiser does not overpay his army, and allows his uniform to cover the man who begs his bread along the road. An old officer with long moustaches saw these two lads eyeing wistfully the hot joints steaming in the windows of a *café*.

"'My lads,' he said, 'you are tired and hungry, why do you not go in and dine?'

"'Excellency,' they replied, 'we come from the army of Italy; we have marched all the way on foot, we have spent our pittance, and we are starving.'

"He gave them a few florins and bade them make merry; he could not see a soldier want, he said, for he was a soldier too. The young men stepped joyfully into the *café*, and summoned the waiter forthwith.

"'Do you know,' said he, 'to whom you have just had the honour of speaking? that venerable old man is Marshal Haynau.'

"The two soldiers rushed from the room; ere the Marshal had reached the end of the street they had overtaken him; they cast his money at his feet, and departed from him with a curse that may have been heard in Heaven, but was happily inaudible at the nearest barrack. So is it with us all; those two soldiers had but heard of his cruelty, whilst I, I had stood by and seen her wounds dressed after her punishment. Judge if I do not *love* him! But, alas! I am but a woman, a poor weak woman; what can I do?"

As she spoke, we heard Victor's step approaching across the lawn, and Valèrie was once more the graceful, high-born lady, with her assured carriage and careless smile. As she took up her embroidery and greeted her brother playfully, with an air from the last new opera, hummed in the richest, sweetest voice, who would have guessed at the volcano of passions concealed beneath that calm and almost frivolous exterior. Are women possessed of a double existence, that they can thus change on the instant from a betrayal of the deepest feelings to a display of apparently utter heartlessness? or are they only accomplished hypocrites, gifted with no *real* character at all, and putting on joy or sorrow, smiles or tears, just as they change their dresses or alter the trimmings of their bonnets, merely for effect? I was beginning to study them now in the person of Valèrie, and to draw comparisons between that lady and my own ideal. It is a dangerous occupation, particularly for a wounded man; and one better indeed for all of us, in sickness or in health, let alone.

CHAPTER XXIII
FOREWARNED

It was a pleasant life that we led in the fine old castle at Edeldorf. Victor was always an enthusiast in field-sports, and since his return from the war he devoted himself to the pursuit of wild animals more assiduously than ever. This was no less a measure of prudence than of inclination on the part of my friend. An inveterate Nimrod seldom busies himself much with politics, and as the antecedents of the De Rohans had somewhat compromised that patriotic family in the eyes of the Government, its present representative was looked on less unfavourably in the character of a young thoughtless sportsman, than he would have been as a disaffected man brooding in solitude, and reserving his energies for more dangerous occupations.

Moreover, to one who loved the fresh breath of morning and the crack of the rifle, Edeldorf was a perfect paradise. Within a ride of two hours its hills furnished many a pair of antlers for the castle hall, and the wild boar whetted his tusks upon the stem of many a fine old forest tree in its deep woodlands. An occasional wolf and a possible bear or two enhanced the interest of the chase; and when the Count quitted his home at early morning, belted and equipped for his work, he could promise himself a day of as varied enjoyment as the keenest sportsman could desire.

I was getting rapidly better, but still unable to accompany my friend on these active expeditions. I am not sure that I longed very eagerly to participate in their delights. As I got stronger, I think I felt less inclined to break my habits of convalescence and helplessness--a helplessness that made me very dependent on Valèrie de Rohan.

I was awaking from a pleasant dream of evening skies and perfumed orange-groves and soft music, with a dim vision of floating hair and muslin dresses, when Victor, with a lighted candle in his hand, entered my apartment--a habit he had acquired in boyhood, and which he continued through life--to bid me "Good-morning," and favour me with his anticipations of his day's amusement.

"I wish you were well enough to come with me, Vere," said he, as he peered out into the dark morning, not yet streaked with the faintest vestige of dawn. "There is nothing like shooting, after all; war is a mistake, Vere, and an uncomfortable process into the bargain; but shooting, I find, gives one quite as much excitement, and has the advantage of being compatible with a comfortable dwelling and plenty to eat every day. I have changed my note, Vere, and I say *Vive la chasse!* now."

"Did you wake me to tell me that?" I yawned out, as I warded the light of the candle from my sleepy eyes, "or do you wish me to get out of my warm bed this cold morning and hold a discussion with you on the comparative attraction of shooting men and beasts? The former is perhaps the more exciting, but the latter the more innocent."

Victor laughed. "You lazy, cold Englander!" he replied; "I woke you as I always do when I anticipate a pleasant day, that I may tell you all I expect to do. In the first place, I shall have a delightful ride up to the hills; I wish you could accompany me. A cigar before dawn, after a cup of coffee, is worth all the smoking of the rest of the twenty-four hours put together. I shall gallop the whole way, and a gallop counts for something in a day's happiness. Confess *that*, at least, you cold, unimpassioned mortal."

I pointed to my wounded leg, and smiled.

"Oh! you will soon be able to get on horseback, and then we two must scamper about across the country once more, as we used to do when we were boys," resumed Victor; "in the meantime, Valèrie will take care of you, and you must get well as quick as you can. What a charming ride it is up to the hills: I shall get there in two hours at the outside, for Caspar goes like the wind; then to-day we mean to beat the woods at the farthest extremity of the Waldenberg, where my poor father shot the famous straight-horned stag years and years ago. There are several wild boar in the ravine at the bottom, and it was only the season before last that Vocqsal shot a bear within twenty yards of the waterfall."

"By the bye," I interrupted him, "are bears and boars and red-deer the only game you have in view? or are there not other attractions as fascinating as shooting, in the direction of the Waldenberg?"

It was a random shaft, but it hit the mark; Victor positively blushed, and I could not help thinking as I watched him, what a handsome fellow he was. A finer specimen of manly beauty you would hardly wish to see than the young Count de Rohan, as he stood there in his green shooting-dress, with his powder-horn slung across his shoulder, and his hunting-knife at his waist. Victor was now in the full glow of youthful manhood, tall, active, and muscular, with a symmetry of frame that, while it was eminently graceful, qualified him admirably for athletic exercises, and a bearing that can best be described by the emphatic term "high-bred." There was a woman's beauty in his soft blue eyes and silky hair of the richest brown, but his marked features, straight, determined eyebrows, and dark, heavy moustaches, redeemed the countenance, notwithstanding its bright winning expression, from the charge of effeminacy. Perhaps, after all, the greatest charm about him was his air of complete enjoyment and utter forgetfulness of self. Every thought of his mind seemed to pass across his handsome face; and to judge by appearances, the thoughts were of the pleasantest description, and now he absolutely blushed as he hurried on without taking any notice of my remark--

"If I can bring Valèrie back a bear-skin for her sledge, I shall be quite satisfied; and I will tell you all about my *chasse* and my day's adventures over a cigar when I return. Meantime, my dear fellow, take care of yourself, order all my carriages and horses, if they are of the slightest use to you, and farewell, or rather *au revoir*."

I heard him humming his favourite waltz as he strode along the gallery (by the way, the very Ghost's Gallery of our childish adventure), and in another minute his horse's hoofs were clattering away at a gallop into the darkness. Whilst I turned round in bed with a weary yawn, and after patting Bold's head--a compliment which that faithful animal returned by a low growl, for the old dog, though true and stanch as ever, was getting very savage now,--I composed myself to cheat a few more hours of convalescence in sleep. What a contrast to my friend! Weary, wounded, and disappointed, I seemed to have lived my life out, and to have nothing more now to hope or to fear. I had failed in ambition, I had made shipwreck in love. I was grey and old in heart, though as yet young in years; whilst Victor, at the same age as myself, had all his future before him, glowing with the sunshine of good health, good spirits, and prosperity. Let us follow the child of fortune as he gallops over the plain, the cool breath of morning fanning his brow and lifting his clustering hair.

To a man who is fond of riding--and what Hungarian is not?--there is no country so fascinating as his own native plains, where he can gallop on mile after mile, hour after hour, over a flat surface, unbroken even by a molehill, and on a light sandy soil, just so soft as to afford his horse a pleasant easy footing, but not deep enough to distress him. Although I could never myself appreciate the ecstatic pleasures of a gallop, or comprehend why there should be a charm about a horse that is not possessed by the cow, the giraffe, the hippopotamus, or any other animal of the larger order of mammalia, I am not so prejudiced as to be unaware that in this respect I am an exception to the general run of my countrymen. Now, I cannot shut my eyes to the fact that there are men whose whole thoughts and wishes centre themselves in this distinguished quadruped; who grudge not to ruin their wives and families for his society; and who, like the Roman Emperor, make the horse the very high-priest of their domestic hearth. To such I would recommend a gallop on a hard-puller over the plains of Hungary. Let him go! There is nothing to stop him for forty miles; and if you cannot bring him to reason in about a minute and a half, you must for ever forfeit your claim to be enrolled amongst the worshipful company of Hippodami to which it seems the noblest ambition of aspiring youth to belong. A deacon of the craft was my friend Victor; and I really believe he enjoyed a pleasure totally unknown to the walking biped, as he urged Caspar along at speed, his fine figure swaying and yielding to every motion of the horse, with a pliancy that, we are informed by those who pique themselves on such matters, can only be acquired by long years of practice superinduced on a natural, or, as they would term it, "heaven-born," aptitude to excel in the godlike art.

So Victor galloped on like Mazeppa, till the dawn "had dappled into day"; and save to light a fresh cigar, gave Caspar no breathing-time till the sun was above the horizon, and the dew-drops on the acacias glittered like diamonds in the morning light. As he quitted the plains at last, and dropped his rein on his horse's neck, while he walked him slowly up the stony road that led to the Waldenberg, he caught sight of a female figure almost in the shadow of the wood, the flutter of whose dress seemed to communicate a corresponding tremor to Victor's heart. The healthy glow paled on his cheek, and his pulses beat fitfully as he urged poor Caspar once more into a gallop against the hill, none the less energetically that for nearly a mile a turn in the road hid the object of interest from his sight. What a crowd of thoughts, hopes, doubts, and fears passed through his mind during that long mile of uncertainty, which, had they resolved themselves into words, would have taken the following form:--"Can she have really come here to meet me, after all? Who else would be on the Waldenberg at this early hour? What can have happened?--is it possible that she has walked all this way on purpose to see me alone, if only for five minutes, before our *chasse* begins? Then she loves me, after all!--and yet she told me herself she was so volatile, so capricious. No, it is impossible!--she won't risk so much for me. And yet it is--it must be! It is just her figure, her walk,--how well I know them. I have mistrusted, I have misjudged her; she is, after all, true, loving, and devoted. Oh! I will make her such amends." Alas! poor Victor; the lady to whom you are vowing so deep a fidelity--to whom you are so happy to think you owe so much for her presence on the wild Waldenberg--is at this moment drinking chocolate in a comfortable dressing-room by a warm stove at least ten miles off; and though you might, and doubtless would, think her extremely lovely in that snowy *robe de chambre*, with its cherry-coloured ribbons, I question whether you would approve of the utter indifference which her countenance displays to all sublunary things, yourself included, with the exception of that very dubious French novel on her knee, which she is perusing or rather devouring with more than masculine avidity. Better draw rein at once, and ride back to Edeldorf, for one hundred yards more will undeceive you at the turn round that old oak-tree; and it is no wonder that you pull up in utter discomfiture, and exclaim aloud in your own Hungarian, and in tones of bitter disgust--"Psha! it's only a Zingynie, after all."

"*Only* a Zingynie, Count de Rohan!" replied a dark majestic old woman, with a frown on her fine countenance and a flash in her dark eye, as she placed herself across the road and confronted the astonished horseman; "*only* your father's friend and your own; *only* an interpreter of futurity, who has come to warn you ere it be too late. Turn back, Victor de Rohan, to your own halls at Edeldorf. I have read your horoscope, and it is not good for you to go on."

Victor had by this time recovered his good-humour; he forced a few florins into the woman's unwilling hand. "Promise me a good day's sport, mother!" he said, laughingly, "and let me go. I ought to be there already."

"Turn back, my child, turn back," said the gipsy; "I will save you if I can. Do you know that there is danger for you on the Waldenberg? Do you know that I--I, who have held you in my arms when you were a baby, have walked a-foot all the way from the Banat on purpose to warn you? Do you think I know not why you ride here day after day, that you may shoot God's wild animals with that bad old man? Is it purely for love of sport, Victor de Rohan? Answer me that!"

He waxed impatient, and drew his reins rudely from the woman's grasp.

"Give your advice when it is asked, mother," said he, "and do not delay me any longer. If you want food and shelter, go down to Edeldorf. I can waste no more time with a chattering old woman here."

She was furious; she flung the money he had given her down beneath his horse's feet. Tears rose to her eyes, and her hand shook with passion as she pointed with outstretched arm in the direction of the Waldenberg.

"Ay, go on," said she, "go on, and neglect the gipsy's warning till it is too late. Oh! you are a nobleman and a soldier, and you know best; a man of honour, too, and you will go *there*. Listen to me once for all, Victor de Rohan, for I loved you as a baby, and I would save you even now, if I could. I slept by the waters of the Danube, and I saw in a vision the child I had fondled in my arms full-grown and handsome, and arrived at man's estate. He was dressed as you are now, with powder-horn and hunting-knife slung over his broad shoulders, and the rifle that he set such store by was in his hand. He spoke kindly and smilingly as was his wont, not angrily as you did now. He was mounted on a good horse, and I was proud to watch him ride gallantly away with St. Hubert's blessing and my own. Again I saw him, but this time not alone. There was a fair and lovely woman by his side, dressed in white, and he hung his head, and walked listlessly and slowly, as though his limbs were fettered and he was sore and sick at heart. I could not bear to think the boy I had loved was no longer free; and when he turned his face towards me it was pale and sorrowful, and there was suffering on his brow. Then my dream changed, and I saw the Waldenberg, with its rugged peaks and its waving woods, and the roar of the waterfall sounded strange and ominous in my ears; and there were clouds gathering in the sky, and the eagle screamed as he swept by on the blast, and the rain plashed down in large heavy drops, and every drop seemed to fall chill upon my heart. Then I sat me down, weary and sorrowful, and I heard the measured tread of men, and four noble-looking foresters passed by me, bearing a body covered with a cloak upon their shoulders, and one said to the other, 'Alas for our master! is it not St. Hubert's day?' But a corner of the cloak fell from the face of him they carried, and I knew the pale features, damp with death, and the rich brown hair falling limp across the brow--it was the corpse of him whom I had loved as a baby and watched over as a man, and I groaned in my misery and awoke. Oh, my boy, my young handsome De Rohan, turn, then, back from the Waldenberg, for the old Zingynie's sake."

"Nonsense, mother," replied Victor, impatiently; "St. Hubert's day is past; I cannot help your bad dreams, or stay here to prate about them all day. Farewell! and let me go." He turned his horse's head from her as he spoke, and went off at a gallop.

The old gipsy woman looked after him long and wistfully, as the clatter of his horse's hoofs died away on the stony causeway; she sat down by the roadside, buried her face in her cloak, and wept bitterly and passionately; then she rose, picked up the money that lay neglected on the ground, and took her way down the hill, walking slow and dejected, like one who is hopelessly and grievously disappointed, and ever and anon muttering to herself, in words that seemed to form something between a curse and a prayer.

CHAPTER XXIV
"ARCADES AMBO"

Prince Vocqsal possessed a delightful shooting-box in the immediate vicinity of the Waldenberg; and, as a portion of those magnificent woodlands was on his property, he and the De Rohans, father and son, had long established a joint guardianship and right of sporting over that far-famed locality. Perhaps what the Prince called a shooting-box, an Englishman's less magnificent notions would have caused him to term a country-house; for the "chalet," as Madame la Princesse delighted to name it, was a roomy, commodious dwelling, with all the appliances of a comfortable mansion, furnished in the most exquisite taste. She herself had never been induced to visit it till within the last few weeks--a circumstance which had not seemed to diminish its attractions in the eyes of the Prince; now, however, a suite of apartments was fitted up expressly for "Madame," and this return to primitive tastes and rural pleasures, on the part of that fastidious lady, was hailed by her domestics with astonishment, and by her husband with a good-humoured and ludicrous expression of dismay. To account for the change in Madame's habits, we must follow Victor on his solitary ride, the pace of which was once more reduced to a walk as soon as he was beyond the gipsy's ken. Who does not know the nervous anxiety with which we have all of us sometimes hurried over the beginning of a journey, only to dawdle out its termination, in absolute dread of the very moment which yet we long for so painfully.

Now, it was strange that so keen a sportsman as Victor, one, moreover, whose ear was as practised as his eye was quick, should have been deceived in the direction from which he heard the reports of at least half-a-dozen shots, that could only have been fired from the gun of his friend the Prince, whom he had promised faithfully to meet that morning at a certain well-known pass on the Waldenberg. It was strange that, instead of riding at once towards the spot where he must have seen the smoke from a gun actually curling up amongst the trees, he should have cantered off in an exactly opposite direction, and never drawn rein till he arrived at the gate of a white house surrounded by acacias, at least five miles from the familiar and appointed trysting-place, and in a part of the Waldenberg by no means the best stocked with game.

It was strange, too, that he should have thought it necessary to inform the grim hussar who opened the door how he had unaccountably missed the Prince in the forest, and had ridden all this distance out of his way to inquire about him, and should have asked that military-looking individual, in a casual manner, whether it was probable Madame la Princesse could put him in the right way of finding his companion, so as not to lose his day's sport. It might have occurred to the hussar, if not too much taken up with his moustaches, that the simplest method for so intimate a friend would have been to have asked at once if "Madame was at home," and then gone in and prosecuted his inquiries in person. If a shrewd hussar, too, he may have bethought him that the human biped is something akin to the ostrich, and is persuaded, like that foolish bird, that if he can only hide his head, no one can detect his great long legs. Be this how it may, the official never moved a muscle of his countenance, and in about half-a-minute Victor found himself, he did not exactly know how, alone with "Madame" in her boudoir.

She gave him her hand, with one of those sunny smiles that used to go straight to the Hungarian's heart. Madame was never demonstrative; although her companion would joyfully have cast himself at her feet and worshipped her, she wilfully ignored his devotion; and while she knew from his own lips that he was her lover, nor had the slightest objection to the avowal, she persisted in treating him as a commonplace friend. It was part of her system, and it seemed to answer. Princess Vocqsal's lovers were always wilder about her than those of any other dame half her age and possessed of thrice her beauty. She had the knack of managing that strange compound of vanity, recklessness, and warm affections which constitutes a man's heart; and she took a great delight in playing on an instrument of which she had sounded all the chords, and evoked all the tones, till she knew it thoroughly, and undervalued it accordingly.

Victor had very little to say! he who was generally so gay and unabashed and agreeable. His colour went and came, and his hand positively shook as he took hers--so cold, and soft, and steady--and carried it to his lips.

"What, lost again in the Waldenberg?" said she, with a laugh, "and within five leagues of Edeldorf. Count de Rohan, you are really not fit to be trusted by yourself; we must get you some one to take care of you."

Victor looked reproachfully at her.

"Rose," he stammered, "you laugh at me; you despise me. Again I have succeeded in seeing you without creating suspicion and remark; but I have had to do that which is foreign to my nature, and you know not what it costs me. I have had to act, if not to speak, a lie. I was to have met the Prince at the waterfall, and I wilfully missed him that I might come down here to inquire which way he had gone; I felt like a coward before the eye of the very servant who opened your door; and all to look on you for five minutes--to carry back with me the tones of your beloved voice, and live upon them for weeks in my dreary home, till I can see you again. Rose! Rose! you little know how I adore you."

"But I cannot pity you in this instance, Monsieur le Comte," replied the lady; "I cannot, indeed. Here you are, in my comfortable boudoir, with a warm stove, and a polished floor, and your choice of every arm-chair and sofa in the room, instead of stamping about on that bleak and dreary Waldenberg, with your hands cold and your feet wet, and a heavy rifle to carry, and in all probability nothing to shoot. Besides, sir, does my company count for nothing, instead of that of *Monsieur le Prince*? It may be bad taste, but I confess that, myself, I very much prefer my own society to his." And the Princess laughed her cheerful ringing laugh, that seemed to come straight from the heart.

Victor sighed. "You will never be serious, Rose, for a minute together."

"Serious!" she replied, "no! why should I? Have I not cause to be merry? I own I might have felt *triste* and cross to-day if I had been disappointed; but you are come, *mon cher Comte*, and everything is *couleur de rose*."

This was encouraging; and Victor opened the siege once more. He loved her with all the enthusiasm and ardour of his warm Hungarian heart. Wilfully shutting his eyes to ruin, misery, and crime, he urged her to be his--to fly with him--to leave all for his sake. He vowed to devote himself to her, and her alone. He swore he would obey her lightest word, and move heaven and earth to fulfil her faintest wish for the rest of his life, would she but confide her happiness to him. He was mad--he was miserable without her: life was not worth having unless gilded by her smiles; he would fly his country if she did not consent: he would hate her, he would never see her more, and a great deal to the same purpose, the outpouring of an eager, generous nature, warped by circumstances to evil; but in vain; the lady was immovable; she knew too well the value of her position to sacrifice it for so empty an illusion as love. Prudence, with the Princess, stood instead of principle; and Prudence whispered, "Keep all you have got, there is no need to sacrifice anything. You have all the advantage, take care to retain it. He may break his chains to-day, but he will come back voluntarily and put them on again to-morrow! it is more blessed to *receive* than to *give*." Such was the Princess's reasoning, and she remained firm and cold as a rock. At last his temper gave way, and he reproached her bitterly and ungenerously.

"You do not love me," he said; "cold, false, and heartless, you have sacrificed me to your vanity; but you shall not enjoy your triumph long; from henceforth I renounce you and your favour--from this day I will never set eyes on you again. Rose! for the last time I call you by that dear name; Rose! for the last time, Farewell!"

She tried the old conquering glance once more, but it failed. She even pressed his hand, and bade him wait and see the Prince on his return, but in vain. For the time, her power was gone. With lips compressed, and face as white as ashes, Victor strode from the room. In less than five minutes he was mounted, and galloping furiously off in the direction of Edeldorf.

Princess Vocqsal was a sad coquette, but she was a woman after all. She went to the window, and gazed wistfully after the horseman's figure as it disappeared amongst the acacias.

"Alas!" she thought, "poor Victor, it is too late now! So gallant, so loving, and so devoted. Ten years ago I had a heart to give, and you should have had it then, wholly and unreservedly; but now--what am I now? Oh that I could but be as I was then! Too late! too late!"

Her *femme-de-chambre* attributed Madame's *migraine* entirely to the weather and the dulness of the country, so different from Paris, or even Vienna; for that domestic at once perceived her mistress's eyes were red with weeping, when she went to dress. But sal volatile and rouge, judiciously applied, can work wonders. The Princess never looked more brilliant than when she descended to dinner, and she sat up and finished her French novel that night before she went to bed.

Victor must have been half-way home when, leaning on his sister's arm, I crept out into the garden to enjoy an hour of fresh air and sunshine in the company of my sedulous nurse and charming companion. Valèrie and I had spent the morning together, and it had passed like a dream. She had made my breakfast, which she insisted on giving me in truly British fashion, and poured out my tea herself, as she laughingly observed, "*comme une meess Anglaise.*" She had played me her wild Hungarian airs on the pianoforte, and sung me her plaintive national songs, with sweetness and good-humour. She had even taught me a new and intricate stitch in her embroidery, and bent my stubborn fingers to the task with her own pretty hands; and now, untiring in her care and kindness, she was ready to walk out with me in the garden, and wait upon all my whims and fancies as a nurse does for a sick child. I could walk at last with no pain, and but little difficulty. Had I not been so well taken care of, I think I should have declared myself quite recovered; but when you have a fair round arm to guide your steps, and a pair of soft eyes to look thrillingly into yours--as day after day a gentle voice entreats you not to hurry your convalescence and "attempt to do too much," it is a great temptation to put off as long as possible the evil hour when you must declare yourself quite sound again, and begin once more to walk alone.

So Valèrie and I paced up and down the garden, and drank in new life at every pore in the glad sunshine and the soft balmy air.

It was one of those days which summer seems to have forgotten, and which we so gladly welcome when we find it at the close of autumn. A warm, mellow sunshine brightened the landscape, melting in the distance into that golden haze which is so peculiarly the charm of this time of year: while the fleecy clouds, that seemed to stand still against the clear sky, enhanced the depth and purity of that wondrous, matchless blue. Not a breath stirred the rich yellow leaves dying in masses on the trees; and the last rose of the garden, though in all the bloom of maturity, had shed her first petal, and paid her first tribute to decay. Valèrie plucked it, and gave it me with a smile, as we sat down upon a low garden seat at one extremity of the walk. I thanked her, and, I know not why, put it to my lips before I transferred it to the buttonhole of my coat. There was a silence of several minutes.

I broke it at last by remarking "that I should soon be well now, and must ere long bid adieu to Edeldorf."

She started as though I had interrupted a train of pleasant thoughts, and answered, with some commonplace expression of regret and hope, that "I would not hurry myself;" but I thought her voice was more constrained than usual, and she turned her head away as she spoke.

"Valèrie," I said--and this was the first time I had ever called her by her Christian name--"it is no use disguising from oneself an unpleasant truth: my duty, my character, everything bids me leave my happy life here as soon as I am well enough. You may imagine how much I shall regret it, but you cannot imagine how grateful I feel for all your kindness to me. Had you been my sister, you could not have indulged me more. It is not my nature to express half I feel, but believe me, that wherever I go, at any distance of time or place, the brightest jewel in my memory will be the name of the Comtesse de Rohan."

"You called me Valèrie just now," said she, quickly.

"Well, of Valèrie, then," I replied. "Your brother is the oldest friend I have--older even than poor Bold." That sagacious dog had lain down at our feet, and was looking from one to the other with a ludicrous expression of wistful gravity, as if he could not make it all out. Why should he have reminded me at that instant so painfully of the glorious struggle for life and death in Beverley mere? That face! that face! would it never cease to haunt me with its sweet, sad smile? "Yes, Valèrie," I proceeded, "that he should have received me as a brother is only what I expected, but your unwearying kindness overpowers me. Believe me, I feel it very deeply, and I shall leave you, oh! with such regret!"

"And we too shall regret you very much," answered Valèrie, with flushed cheeks and not very steady tones. "But can you not stay a little longer? your health is hardly re-established, though your wound is healed, and--and--it will be very lonely when you are gone."

"Not for you," I replied; "not for the young Comtesse de Rohan (well, Valèrie, then), admired and sought after by all. Beautiful and distinguished, go where you will, you are sure to command homage and affection. No, it is all the other way, I shall be lonely, if you like."

"Oh, but men are so different," said she, with a glance from under those long, dark eyelashes. "Wherever they go they find so much to interest, so much to occupy them, so much to do, so many to love."

"Not in my case," I answered, rather pursuing my own train of thoughts than in reply to my companion. "Look at the difference between us. You have your home, your brother, your friends, your dependants, all who can appreciate and return your affection; whilst I, I have nothing in the world but my horses and my sword."

She looked straight into my face, a cloud seemed to pass over her features, and she burst into tears. In another moment she was sobbing on my breast as if her heart would break.

A horse's hoofs were heard clattering in the stable yard, and as Victor, pale and excited, strode up the garden, Valèrie rushed swiftly into the house.

CHAPTER XXV
"DARK AND DREARY"

The pea-soup thickness of a London fog is melting into drizzling rain. The lamp-posts and area railings in Mayfair are dripping with wet, like the bare copses and leafless hedges miles off in the country. It is a raw, miserable day, and particularly detestable in this odious town, as a tall old gentleman seems to think who has just emerged from his hotel into the chill, moist atmosphere; and whose well-wrapped-up exterior, faultless goloshes, and neat umbrella denote one of that class who are seldom to be met with in the streets during the winter season. As he picks his way along the sloppy pavement, he turns to scan the action of every horse that splashes by, and ventures, moreover, on sundry peeps under passing bonnets with a pertinacity, and, at the same time, an air of unconsciousness that prove how habit can become second nature. The process generally terminates in disappointment, not to say disgust, and Sir Harry Beverley--for it is no less a person than the Somersetshire Baronet--walks on, apparently more and more dissatisfied with the world in general at every step he takes. As he paces through Grosvenor-square he looks wistfully about him, as though for some means of escape. He seems bound on an errand for which he has no great fancy, and once or twice he is evidently on the point of turning back. Judging by his increase of pace in South Audley-street, his courage would appear to be failing him rapidly; but the aspect of Chesterfield House, the glories of which he remembers well in its golden time, reassures him; and with an inward ejaculation of "poor D'Orsay!" and a mental vision of that extraordinary man, who conquered the world with the aid only of his whiskers and his cab-horse, Sir Harry walks on. "They are pleasant to look back upon," thinks the worn old "man of the world"--"those days of Crocky's and Newmarket, and cheerful Melton, with its brilliant gallops, and cozy little dinners, and snug parties of whist. London, too, was very different in my time. Society was not so large, and *we*" (meaning the soliloquist and his intimate friends) "could do what we liked. Ah! if I had my time to come over again!" and something seems to knock at Sir Harry's heart, as he thinks, if indeed he could live life over once more, how differently he would spend it. So thinks every man who lives for aught but doing good. It is dreadful at last to look along the valley that was once spread before us so glad and sunny, teeming with corn, and wine, and oil, and to see how barren we have left it. Count your good actions on your fingers, as the wayfarer counts the miles he has passed, or the trader his gains, or the sportsman his successes-- can you reckon one a day? a week? a month? a year? And yet you will want a large stock to balance those in the other scale. Man is a reasoning being and a free agent: he makes a strange use of both privileges.

At last Sir Harry stops in front of a neat little house with the brightest of knockers and the rosiest of muslin curtains, and flowers in its windows, and an air of cheerful prettiness even in this dull dark day.

A French servant, clean and sunshiny as French servants always are, answers the visitor's knock, and announces that "Monsieur" has been "de Service"; or in other words, that Captain Ropsley has that morning come "off guard." Whilst the Baronet divests himself of his superfluous clothing in an outer room, let us take a peep at the Guardsman in his luxurious little den.

Ropsley understands comfort thoroughly, and his rooms are as tastefully furnished and as nicely arranged as though there were present the genius of feminine order to preside over his retreat. Not that such is by any means the case. Ropsley is well aware that he owes much of his success in life to the hardness of his heart, and he is not a man to throw away a single point in the game for the sake of the sunniest smile that ever wreathed a fair false face. He is no more a man of pleasure than he is a man of business, though with him pleasure is business, and business is pleasure. He has a sound calculating head, a cool resolute spirit, an abundance of nerve, no sentiment, and hardly any feeling whatever. Just the man to succeed, and he does succeed in his own career, such as it is. He has established a reputation for fashion, a position in the world; with a slender income he lives in the highest society, and on the best of everything; and he has no one to thank for all these advantages but himself. As he lies back in the depths of his luxurious armchair, smoking a cigar, and revelling in the coarse witticisms of Rabelais, whose strong pungent satire and utter want of refinement are admirably in accordance with his own turn of mind, a phrenologist would at once read his character in his broad but not prominent forehead, his cold, cat-like, grey eye, and the habitual sneer playing round the corners of an otherwise faultless mouth. Handsome though it be, it is not a face the eye loves to look upon. During the short interval that elapses between his servant's announcement and his visitor's entrance, Ropsley has time to dismiss Rabelais completely from his mind, to run over the salient points of the conversation which he is determined to have with Sir Harry, and to work out "in the rough" two or three intricate calculations, which are likely somewhat to astonish that hitherto unconscious individual. He throws away his cigar, for he defers to the prejudices of the "old school," and shaking his friend cordially by the hand, welcomes him to town, stirs the fire, and looks, as indeed he feels, delighted to see him.

Sir Harry admires his young friend much, there is something akin in their two natures; but the acquired shrewdness of the elder man is no match for the strong intellect and determined will of his junior.

"I have come up as you desired, my dear fellow," said the Baronet, "and brought Constance with me. We are at ----'s Hotel, where, by the way, they've got a deuced bad cook: and having arrived last night, here I am this morning."

Ropsley bowed, as he always did, at the mention of Miss Beverley's name; it was a queer sort of half-malicious little bow. Then looking her father straight in the face with his cold bright eye, he said, abruptly--"We've got into a devil of a mess, and I required to see you immediately."

Sir Harry started, and turned pale. It was not the first "devil of a mess" by a good many that he had been in, but he felt he was getting too old for the process, and was beginning to be tired of it.

"Those bills, I suppose," he observed, nervously; "I expected as much."

Ropsley nodded. "We could have met the two," said he, "and renewed the third, had it not been for Green's rascality and Bolter's failure. However, it is too late to talk of all that now; read that letter, Sir Harry, and then tell me whether you do not think we are what Jonathan calls 'slightly up a tree.'"

He handed the Baronet a lawyer's letter as he spoke. The latter grew paler and paler as he proceeded in its perusal; at its conclusion he crushed it in his hand, and swore a great oath.

"I can do nothing more," he said, in a hoarse voice; "I am dipped now till I cannot get another farthing. The estate is so tied up with those accursed marriage-settlements, that I must not cut a stick of timber at my own door. If Bolter had paid we could have gone on. The villain! what right had he to incur liabilities he could not meet, and put honest men in the hole?"

"What right, indeed?" answered the Guardsman, with a quiet smile, that seemed to say he thought the argument might apply to other cases than that of poor Bolter. "I am a man of no position, Sir Harry, and no property; if I go I shall scarcely be missed. Now with you it is different: your fall would make a noise in the world, and a positive crash down in Somersetshire" (the Baronet winced). "However, we should neither of us like to lose caste and character without an effort. Is there *nothing* can be done?"

Sir Harry looked more and more perplexed. "Time," he muttered, "time; if we could only get a little time. Can't you see these fellows, my dear Ropsley, and talk to them a little, and show them their own interests? I give you carte blanche to act for me. I must trust all to you. I don't see my way."

Ropsley pushed a wide red volume, something like an enlarged betting-book, across the table. It was his regimental order-book, and on its veracious columns was inscribed the appalling fact that "leave of absence had been granted to Lieutenant and Captain Ropsley for an indefinite period, on *urgent private affairs*." Sir Harry's hand trembled as he returned it. He had been so accustomed to consult his friend and confederate on all occasions, he had so completely acquired the habit of deferring to his judgment and depending on his energy, that he felt now completely at a loss as he thought of the difficulties he should have to face unassisted and alone. It was with unconcealed anxiety that he gasped out, "D---- it, Ropsley, you don't mean to leave the ship just at the instant she gets aground!"

"I have only secured my retreat, like a good general," answered Ropsley, with a smile; "but never fear, Sir Harry, I have no intention of leaving you in the lurch. Nevertheless, you are a man of more experience than myself, you have been at this sort of thing for a good many years: before we go any further, I should like to ask you once more, is there no plan you can hit upon, have you nothing to propose?"

"Nothing, on my honour," answered Sir Harry. "I am at my wits' end. The money must be got, and paid too, for these fellows won't hear of a compromise. I can't raise another farthing. You must have been cleared out long ago. Ropsley, it strikes me we are both beaten out of the field."

"Not yet, Sir Harry," observed Ropsley, quietly; "I have a plan, if you approve of it, and think it can be done."

"By Jove! I always said you were the cleverest fellow in England," burst out poor Sir Harry, eagerly grasping at the shadow of a chance. "Let us have it, by all means. Approve of it! I'll approve of anything that will only get us clear of this scrape. Come, out with it, Ropsley. What is it?"

"Sit down, Sir Harry," said Ropsley, for the Baronet was pacing nervously up and down the room; "let us talk things over quietly, and in a business-like manner. Ever since the day that I came over to Beverley from Everdon--(by the way, that was the first good bottle of claret I drank in Somersetshire)--ever since that day you and I have been intimate friends. I have profited by your experience and great knowledge of the world; and you, I think, have derived some advantage from my energy and painstaking in the many matters with which we have been concerned. I take all the credit of that affair about the mines in Argyllshire, and it would be affectation on my part to pretend I did not know I had been of great use to you in the business."

"True enough, my dear fellow," answered the Baronet, looking somewhat alarmed; "if I had not sold, as you advised, I should have been 'done' that time, and I confess in all probability--" "ruined," the Baronet was going to say, but he checked himself, and substituted the expression, "much hampered now."

"Well, Sir Harry," resumed his friend, "you and I are men of the world; we all know the humbug fellows talk about friendship and all that. It would be absurd for us to converse in such a strain, but yet a man has his likes and dislikes. You are one of the few people I care for, and I will do for you what I would not do for any other man on earth."

Sir Harry stared. Though by no means a person of much natural penetration, he had yet an acquired shrewdness, the effect of long intercourse with his fellow-creatures, which bade him as a general rule to mistrust a kindness; and he looked now as if he scented a *quid pro quo* in the generous expressions of his associate.

Ropsley kept his cold grey eye fixed on him, and proceeded--"I have already said, I am a 'man of straw,' and if I *go* it matters little to any one but myself. They will ask after me for two days in the bow-window at White's, and there will be an end of it. I sell out, which will not break my heart, as I hate soldiering; and I start quietly for the Continent, where I go to the devil my own way, and at my own pace. *Festina lente*; I am a reasonable man, and easily satisfied. You will allow that this is not your case."

Poor Sir Harry could only shuffle uneasily in his chair, and bow his acquiescence.

"Such being the state of affairs," proceeded Ropsley, and the hard grey eye grew harder than ever, and seemed to screw itself like a gimlet into the Baronet's working physiognomy; "such being the state of affairs, of course any sacrifice I make is offered out of pure friendship, regard, and esteem for yourself. Psha! it's nonsense talking like that! My dear fellow, I like you; I always have liked you; the pleasantest hours of my life have been spent in your house, and I'll see you out of this scrape, if I ruin myself, stock, lock, and barrel, for it!"

Sir Harry flushed crimson with delight and surprise; yet the latter feeling predominated more than was pleasant, as he recollected the old-established principle of himself and his clique, "Nothing for nothing, and very little for a halfpenny."

"Now, Sir Harry, I'll tell you what I will do. Five thousand will clear us for the present. With five thousand we could pay off the necessary debts, take up that bill of Sharon's, and get a fresh start. When they saw we were not completely floored, we could always renew, and the turn of the tide would in all probability set us afloat again. Now the question is, *how* to get at the five thousand? It will not come out of Somersetshire, I *think*?"

Sir Harry shook his head, and laughed a hard, bitter laugh. "Not five thousand pence," he said, "if it was to save me from hanging to-morrow!"

"And you really do not know which way to turn?"

"No more than a child," answered Sir Harry. "If you fail me, I must give in. If you can help me, and *yourself too*, out of this scrape, why, I shall say what I always did--that you are the cleverest of fellows and the best of friends."

"I think it can be done," said the younger man, but he no longer looked his friend in the face; and a faint blush, that faded almost on the instant, passed over his features. He had one card left in his hand; he had kept it to the last; he thought he ought to play it now. "I have never told you, Sir Harry, that I have a few acres in Ireland, strictly tied up in the hands of trustees, but with their consent I have power to sell. It is all the property I have left in the world; it will raise the sum we require, and--it shall follow the rest."

This was true enough. Gambler, libertine, man of pleasure as he was, Ropsley had always kept an eye to the main chance. It was part of his system to know all sorts of people, and to be concerned in a small way with several speculative and money-making schemes. After the passing of the Irish Encumbered Estates Bill, it so happened that a fortunate investment at Newmarket had placed a few loose thousands to the credit side of our Guardsman's account at Cox and Co.'s. He heard casually of a capital investment for the same, within a day's journey of Dublin, as he was dining with a party of stock-jobbing friends in the City. Six hours afterwards Ropsley was in the train, and in less than six weeks had become the proprietor of sundry remunerative Irish acres, the same which he was now prepared unhesitatingly to sacrifice in the cause of gratitude, which with this philosopher, more than most men, might be fairly termed "a lively sense of benefits to come."

"Yes, it shall follow the rest," he repeated, stirring the fire vigorously, and now looking studiously *away* from the man he was addressing,--"Sir Harry, you are a man of the world--you know me thoroughly, we cannot humbug each other. Although I would do much for your sake, you cannot think that a fellow sacrifices his last farthing simply because he and his confederate have made a mistake in their calculations. No, Sir Harry, your honour is dear to me as my own--nay, dearer, for I now wish to express a hope that we may become more nearly connected than we have ever been before, and that the ties of relationship may give me a right, as those of friendship have already made it a pleasure, to assist you to the best of my abilities."

Sir Harry opened his mouth and pushed his chair back from the fire. Hampered, distressed, ruined as he was, it *did* seem a strong measure thus to sell Constance Beverley, so to speak, for "a mess of pottage"; and the bare idea of such a contract for the moment took away the Baronet's breath. Not that the notion was by any means a strange one to his mind; for the last two or three years, during which he had associated so much with the Guardsman, and had so many opportunities of appreciating his talents, shrewdness, and attractive qualities, the latter had been gradually gaining a complete ascendancy over his mind and character. Sir Harry was like a child in leading-strings in the hands of his confederate; and it had often occurred to him that it would be very pleasant, as as well as advantageous, always to have this mainstay on which to rely--this "ready-reckoner," and man of inexhaustible resources, to consult on every emergency. Vague ideas had sometimes crossed the Baronet's brain, that it was just possible his daughter might be brought to *like* well enough to marry (for *loving* was not a word in her father's vocabulary) an agreeable man, into whose society she was constantly thrown; and then, as Constance was an heiress, and the Baronet himself would be relieved from divers pecuniary embarrassments on her marriage, by the terms of a certain settlement with which we have nothing to do--why, it would be a delightful arrangement for all parties, and Ropsley could come and live at Beverley, and all be happy together.

Such were the ideas that vaguely floated across the Baronet's mind in those moments of reflection of which he allowed himself so few; but he was a father, and a kind one, with all his faults; and it had never yet entered his head either to force his daughter's inclinations, or even to encourage with his own influence any suitor who was not agreeable to the young lady. He was fond of Constance, in his own way--fonder than of anything in the world, save his own comfort, and a very stirring and closely-contested race at Newmarket. So he looked, as indeed he felt, somewhat taken aback by Ropsley's proposal, which his own instinct as a gentleman told him was peculiarly ill-timed.

He laughed nervously, and thanked his friend for his kindness.

"With regard to--Miss Beverley," he stammered; "why--you know, my dear Ropsley,--business is business, and pleasure is pleasure. I--I--had no wish,--at least I had not made up my mind--or rather, I had no absolute intention that my daughter should settle so early in life. You are aware she is an heiress--a very great heiress" (Ropsley was indeed, or they would not have been at this point of discussion now), "and she might look to making a great match; in fact, Constance Beverley might marry anybody. Still, I never would thwart her inclinations; and if you think, my dear fellow, you can make yourself agreeable to her, why, I should make no objections, as you know there is no man that I should individually like better for a son-in-law than yourself."

Ropsley rose, shook his new papa cordially by the hand, rang for luncheon, and rather to the Baronet's discomfiture, seemed to look upon it at once as a settled thing.

"My business will not take long," said he, helping his guest to a large glassful of sherry. "You do not go abroad for another week; I can make all my arrangements, *our* arrangements, I should say, by that time. Why should we not travel together? My servant is the best courier in Europe; you will have no trouble whatever, only leave it all to me."

Sir Harry hated trouble. Sir Harry liked the Continent. The scheme was exactly suited to his tastes and habits; so it was settled they should all start at once--a family party.

And where is the young lady all this time? the prime origin of so much scheming, the motive power of all this mechanism? In the front drawing-room of the gloomy hotel she sits over the fire, buried deep in thought--to judge by her saddened countenance--not of the most cheering description. Above the fire-place hangs a large engraving of Landseer's famous Newfoundland dog, that "Member of the Humane Society" whom he has immortalised with his pencil. The lady sighs as she gazes on the broad, honest forehead, the truthful, intelligent face, the majestic attitude denoting strength in repose. Either the light is very bad in this room, or the glass over that engraving is dim and blurred, and the dog seems crouching in a mist, or are Constance Beverley's dark eyes dimmed with tears?

CHAPTER XXVI
"SURVEILLANCE"

I did not question my friend as to his success in the *chasse*. Victor was evidently ill at ease, and after a few commonplace remarks returned to his apartments, from whence he did not reappear till dinner-time. Valèrie, too, was nowhere to be found, and I spent the afternoon in the *salon* with a strange visitor, who was announced by the groom of the chambers as Monsieur Stein, and whose business at Edeldorf I confess I was at a loss to discover.

The time passed agreeably enough. I was indisposed for reflection, a process which, under existing circumstances, could only have involved me in a labyrinth of perplexities; and my new acquaintance was possessed of a fund of information and small talk which must have been acquired by much intercourse with the world.

He seemed perfectly familiar with English habits and English politics, professing great admiration for the one and interest in the other. He had *served* too, he said, although I did not make out exactly in what grade; and altogether he was evidently a man of varied experience and considerable acquirements.

Silent as I naturally am, and especially reserved with strangers, there was something about my new acquaintance that led me to be communicative in spite of myself. His whole address and exterior were so thoroughly *confidential*, his manner so easy and unaffected; there was so much good-humour and *bonhommie* in his quiet smile and subdued enunciation, that I found myself almost unconsciously detailing events and imparting information with a facility of which I should have once thought I was incapable. Monsieur Stein listened, and bowed, and smiled, and put in a slight query here, or hazarded an observation there, which proved that he too was well acquainted with the topics on which I was enlarging; nor did he fail to compliment me on the lucid manner in which he was good enough to say I had explained to him the whole system of Turkish politics, and the relations of that tottering country with our own. As we went to make our toilets before dinner, I could not help asking my friend, the groom of the chambers, whose arm assisted me upstairs (ah! it was Valèrie's the night before!), "who he was, this Monsieur Stein, who had arrived so unexpectedly, and had not yet seen the Count?" The man's face assumed a comical expression of mingled terror and disgust as he professed an utter ignorance of the guest; but when I added an inquiry as to whether he was a friend of Count Victor, his disclaimer was far more vigorous than the occasion seemed to demand. "Well," thought I, "I shall know all about it from Valérie this evening;" and proceeded with my toilet--shall I confess it?--with more pains than I had ever taken in my life before.

But when we met at dinner a chill seemed to have fallen on our party, hitherto so merry and vivacious. Victor, though polite and courteous as ever, was reserved, absent, and out of spirits. Valérie turned red and white by turns, answered only by monosyllables, and never once allowed her eyes to wander in my direction. I, too, felt sad and preoccupied. My coming departure seemed to cast a damp over my spirits; and yet when I thought of Valérie's unconcealed regret, and frank avowal of interest in my future, my heart leapt with a strange, startling thrill, half of pleasure, half of pain. Monsieur Stein, however, appeared to suffer from none of these uncomfortable sensations. He ate, he drank, he talked, he made the agreeable, and amidst it all he seemed to note with a lynx-eye the gorgeous furniture, the glittering plate, the host of servants attired in their gaudy hussar uniforms, the choice wine, and excellent cookery, for which the *ménage* of Edeldorf had always been remarkable. In the brilliant light that shed its glare over the dining-table I was able to examine my new acquaintance more minutely than I had previously done before we went to dress. He seemed to me, without exception, the *least* remarkable man I had ever met. He was neither young nor old, neither dark nor fair, neither short nor tall, stout nor thin; his dress, that of a civilian, was plain and unstudied in the extreme; his demeanour, quiet and unaffected, was in admirable keeping with his whole exterior. There was nothing military about the man save a closely-clipped and carefully-trained moustache; but this warlike appendage was again contradicted by a slight stoop, and a somewhat hesitating gait, by no means that of a soldier. His eye, too, of a cold, dead grey, with light eyelashes, was soft and sleepy. Once I fancied I caught a lightning glance directed at Valérie; but the orbs were so quickly veiled by their drooping lids that I could not be satisfied it was more than a trick of my own imagination. Altogether M. Stein was a man that in England would have been described emphatically as "very gentlemanlike," for want of any more characteristic qualifications; in France he would have been passed over as an undemonstrative cipher; my friends the Turks would have conferred a silent approval on his quiet, unassuming demeanour. Why was it that in Hungary his presence should act as what we call at home "a wet blanket"?

Dinner progressed slowly. Monsieur Stein addressed himself chiefly to Count de Rohan; and I could not help remarking that the latter's answers to his guest were marked by a caution and reserve totally foreign to his usual straightforward manner and off-hand way of saying whatever came uppermost. His air gave me the idea of a man who was determined not to be *pumped*. He drank less wine also than usual; and altogether was certainly not at his ease. Valèrie, too, whenever she raised her eyes from the tablecloth, glanced uneasily towards Monsieur Stein; and when I made a casual remark to her, answered so absently and stiffly as to cause me for my part to feel uncomfortable and *de trop* in this small ill-organised party. It was a relief to all of us when coffee made its appearance, and the newly-arrived guest, giving his hand to Valèrie with a courtly bow, led her back to the drawing-room, whilst I followed with Victor, and took the opportunity of whispering to my old friend, in English--

"Who is this gentleman, Victor, that seems to know a little of everything and everybody, and whose thirst for information seems so unquenchable?"

"Hush!" replied Victor, with an uneasy look at the couple in front of us; "he speaks English as well as you do, though I dare say he told you not. My dear Vere, for Heaven's sake, to-night sit still and hold your tongue!"

At this instant Valèrie turned round, and addressed some trifling observation to her brother, but with a warning expression of countenance that seemed to tell him he had been overheard. The next moment we were seated round her work-table, chatting as gaily upon the merits of her embroidery as though we were all the most intimate friends in the world. Certainly ladies' work promotes conversation of the most harmless and least suspicious description; and I think it would indeed have been difficult to affix a definite meaning to the remarks made by any one of us on the intricacies of Countess Valèrie's stitching, or the skill displayed by that lady in her graceful and feminine employment.

The evening dragged on. Monsieur Stein conversed freely on the state of the country, the condition of the peasantry, the plans of the Government, and a projected railroad, for the construction of which he did not seem to think it possible the Austrian exchequer would ever be able to pay. Victor listened, and scarcely spoke; Valèrie seemed interested in the railway, and determined to pursue that subject as long as possible; whilst I sat, out of spirits, and, truth to tell, out of humour, a silent observer of all three. I was deprived of my habitual occupations, and missed the care and interest to which I was accustomed as an invalid. Valèrie did not make my tea for me as usual, nor explain to me, for the hundredth time, the cunning splendour of her embroidery, nor ask for my assistance in the thousand trifling ways with which a woman makes you fancy you are essential to her comfort; and I was childish enough to feel sad, if not a little sulky, in consequence. At last I lost patience, and throwing down abruptly the paper which I had been reading, I asked Countess Valèrie to "give us a little music," adding in perfect innocence, "Do play that beautiful march out of 'The Honijàdy'--it is so inspiriting and so thoroughly national!"

If a shell had fallen into the room, and commenced its whizzing operations under Valèrie's work-table, it could not have created greater consternation than did my very natural request. The Countess turned deadly pale, and her hand trembled so that she could scarcely hold her needle. Victor rose from his chair with a tremendous oath, and walking off to the fire-place (for he was sufficiently an Englishman to prefer a grate to a stove), commenced stirring an already huge fire with much unnecessary energy, talking the whole time as if to drown my unlucky observation. Monsieur Stein flashed one of his lightning glances--there was no mistaking it this time--upon the whole of us, and then relapsed into his previous composure; whilst I felt that I had committed some unpardonable *gaucherie*, but could not, for the life of me, discover how or why.

It was hopeless that evening to make any more attempts at conversation. Even the guest seemed to think he had exerted himself sufficiently, and at an earlier hour than usual we retired for the night. When I came down next morning he was gone.

Victor did not appear at breakfast, and Valèrie's excuses for her brother were delivered with a degree of restraint and formality which made me feel very uncomfortable.

"Victor was busy," she said, "with the steward and the land-agent. He had a great deal to do; he would not be at leisure for hours, but he would see me before he started on his journey."

"Journey!" said I; "what journey does he mean to take? and what is all this mystery and confusion? Pardon me, Countess Valèrie, I am a straightforward man, Victor is my oldest friend, and I do claim to be in the secret, if I can be of any assistance or comfort to you in anything."

She looked at me once more with the frank, confiding look that reminded me so of *another*; and putting her hand in mine, she said--

"I know we can trust you; I know *I* can trust you. Victor is *compromised*; he must go to Vienna to clear himself. He has yesterday received a hint that amounts indeed to an order. We are not even free to live on our own lands," she added bitterly, and with the old gleam of defiance flashing over her features; "the proudest noble in Hungary is but a serf after all."

"And Monsieur Stein?" I asked, for I was beginning to penetrate the mystery.

"Is an agent of police," she replied, "and one of the cleverest in the Emperor's service. Did you remark how *civil* we were forced to be to him? Did you not notice Victor's constrained and uncomfortable manner? Whilst he remained, that man was our master--that low-born spy our master! This is what we have come to. His mission was understood plainly enough by both of us. He came with a hint from the Emperor that we were very remiss in our attendance at Court; that his Imperial Majesty valued our loyalty too much to doubt its sincerity; and that it would be better, *all things considered*, if we were to spend the winter at Vienna. Also, I doubt not, information was required as to what our English friend was about; and when it is reported-- as reported it will be--that his musical taste leads him to admire 'the march in the Honijàdy,' why we shall probably be put under 'surveillance' for six months, and be obliged to reside in the capital for a year or two, till we have got thoroughly Austrianised, when we shall return here, feeling our degradation more bitterly than ever."

"And why may I not consult my own taste in music?" I inquired; "or what is there so deadly in that beautiful march which you play with such brilliancy and spirit?"

Valèrie laughed.

"Do you not know," said she, "that the Honijàdys were nearly connected with our ancestors--that the De Rohans, originally Norman, only became Hungarian through their alliance with that princely family--a race who were never found wanting when it was necessary to assert the independence of their country? It was a Honijàdy that rolled the Turks back from the very gates of Vienna. It was a Honijàdy that first resisted the oppression of Austrian despotism. It was a Honijàdy that shed the last drop of noble blood spilt in our late struggle for independence. The finest of our operas is founded on the history of this devoted family, and the Honijàdy march is the very gathering tune of all who hate the iron yoke under which we groan. Only look at the faces of a Hungarian audience as they listen to its forbidden tones--for it must now only be played in secret--and you comprehend why, of all the airs that ever were composed, the last you should have asked for in the presence of Monsieur Stein was the march in 'The Honijàdy.'"

"I do truly regret my indiscretion," was my reply; "but if Victor is compelled to go to Vienna, I shall certainly accompany him. It is not my practice to abandon a friend, and *such* a friend, in his distress. Though I can be of little use, my presence may be some comfort and amusement to him; besides, the very fact of my proceeding straight into the lion's mouth will show that I have not been staying here with any ulterior views."

"You are, indeed, true as steel," replied Valèrie, with a frank, honest smile, that went straight to my heart. "We will all start together this very afternoon; and I am glad--at least it is far better--that you should not be parted from your nurse till you are quite strong again. Your presence will be a great comfort to my brother, who is----" Valèrie hesitated, blushed up to her forehead, and added, abruptly, "Mr. Egerton, have you not remarked any difference in Victor lately?"

I replied, that "I thought his spirits were less mercurial than formerly, but that probably he had the anticipation of yesterday's domiciliary visit hanging over him, which would at once account for any amount of discontent and depression."

"No, it is not that," answered Valèrie, with increasing embarrassment. "It is worse even than that. My poor Victor! I know him so well--I love him so much! and he is breaking his noble heart for one who is totally unworthy of him. If there is one being on earth that I hate and despise more than another, it is a *coquette*," added the girl, with flashing eyes; "a woman who is so wanting in womanly pride as to lay herself out for admiration--so false to her own nature as to despise it when it is won."

"All women like admiration," I ventured to interpose very humbly, for it struck me that the young Countess herself was in this respect no abnormal variety of her species; "and I conclude that in this, as in everything else, difficulty enhances the pleasure of success."

She darted a reproachful look at me from under her dark eyelashes, but she had her say out notwithstanding.

"No woman," she exclaimed, "has a right any more than a man, to trifle with the affections of another. Why should any one human being, for the sake of an hour's amusement, or the gratification of a mere passing vanity, inflict on another the greatest pain which mortal heart can suffer? You would be thought a monster so to torture the body; and are not the pangs of the soul infinitely worse to bear? No! I repeat it, she has deceived my brother with her silver accents and her false, false smiles; she is torturing the noblest, truest, kindest heart that ever brave man bore, and I hate her for it with a deadly, quenchless hatred!"

I never found Valèrie so charming as when she thus played the termagant. There was something so *piquante* in her wild, reckless manner on these occasions--in the flash of her bright eyes, the play of her chiselled features, and the attitude of her lithe, graceful figure, when she said she *hated*, that I could have found it in my heart to make her say she hated me rather than not hear the well-known word. I replied accordingly, rather mischievously I own--

"Do you not think, Valèrie, you are throwing away a great deal of indignation unnecessarily? Men are not so sensitive as you seem to think. We do not break our hearts very readily, I assure you; and even when we do, we mend them again nearly as good as new. Besides, the rest of you take compassion on us when we are ill-treated by one. They console us, and we accept their consolation. If the rose is not in bloom, what shall prevent us from gathering the violet? Decidedly, Countess Valèrie, we are more philosophers than you."

"You do not know Victor, if you say so," she burst forth. "You do not think as you speak. You are a dishonest reasoner, and you try to impose upon *me*! I tell you, *you* are the last man in the world to hold such opinions. You are wrong, and you know you are wrong, and you only speak thus to provoke me. I judge of others by myself. I believe that all of us are more or less alike, and I know that *I* could never forgive such an injury. What! to be led on day by day, to feel if not to confess a preference, to find it bit by bit eating into one's being, till at length one belongs no longer to oneself, but knows one's whole existence to be wrapped up in another, and then at the last moment to discover that one has been deceived! that one has been giving gold for silver! that the world is empty, and the heart dead for ever! I know what I should do."

"What *would* you do?" I asked, half amused and half alarmed at her excited gestures.

"Take a De Rohan's revenge, if I broke my heart for it the next instant," she replied: and then, as if ashamed of her enthusiasm, and the passion into which she had very unnecessarily put herself, rushed from the room.

"What a dangerous lady to have anything to do with," I remarked to Bold, as he rose from the hearthrug, with a stretch and a yawn. "Well, old dog, so you and I are bound for Vienna this afternoon; I wonder what will come of it all?"

Yet there was a certain pleasant excitement about my position, too. It was evident that Valèrie took more than a common interest in her brother's friend. Her temper had become very variable of late; and I had remarked that although, until the scene in the garden, she had never shunned my society, she had often appeared provoked at any expression of opinion which I chanced to hazard contrary to her own. She had also of late been constantly absent, *distraite*, and preoccupied, sometimes causelessly satirical, bitter, and even rude, in her remarks. What could it all mean? was I playing with edged tools? It might be so. Never mind, never mind, Bold; anything, *anything* for excitement and forgetfulness of the days gone by.

CHAPTER XXVII
GHOSTS OF THE PAST

Every one has heard of the gentleman who went to spend a fortnight at Vienna in the prime of his youth, and died there at a ripe old age, having never afterwards been beyond the walls of the town. Though the climate is allowed to be detestable, the heat of summer being aggravated by a paucity of shade and a superabundance of dust, whilst the rigorous cold of winter is enhanced by the absence of fire-places and the scarcity of fuel; though the streets are narrow and the carriages numerous, the hotels always full, and the shops very dear; though the police is strict and officious to a degree, and its regulations tyrannical in the extreme; though every house, private as well as public, must be closed at ten o'clock, and a ball-giver or lady who "receives" must have a special permission from the Government,--yet, with all these drawbacks, no city in the world, not even lively Paris itself, seems so popular with pleasure-seekers as Vienna. There is a gaiety in the very air of the town: a smiling, prosperous good-humour visible on the countenances of its inhabitants, a picturesque beauty in the houses, a splendid comfort in the shops, and a taste and magnificence in the public buildings, which form a most attractive *tout ensemble*.

Then you lead a pleasant, cheerful, do-nothing sort of life. You have your coffee in bed, where you can also read a novel in perfect comfort, for German beds have no curtains to intercept the morning light, or make a bonfire of the nocturnal student. You perform an elaborate toilet (are not Vienna gloves the only good fits in the world?), and you breakfast about noon in the *salon* of some luxurious hotel, where you may sit peradventure between an Austrian Field-Marshal, decorated with a dozen or so of orders, and a Polish beauty, who counts captives by the hundred, and breaks hearts by the score. Neither will think it necessary to avoid your neighbourhood as if you had confluent small-pox, and your eye as if you were a basilisk, simply because you have not had the advantage of their previous acquaintance. On the contrary, should the courtesies of the table or any chance occurrence lead you to hazard a remark, you will find the warrior mild and benevolent, the beauty frank and unaffected. Even should you wrap yourself up in your truly British reserve, they will salute you when they depart; and people may say what they will about the humbug and insincerity of mere politeness, but there can be no doubt that such graceful amenities help to oil the wheels of life. Then if you like to walk, have you not the Prater, with its fine old trees and magnificent red deer, and its endless range of woodland scenery, reminding you of your own Windsor forest at home; if you wish to drive, there is much beautiful country in the immediate vicinity of the town; or would you prefer a quiet chat in the friendly intimacy of a morning visit, the Viennese ladies are the most conversational and the most hospitable in the world. Then you dine at half-past five, because the opera begins at seven, and with such a band who would miss the overture? Again, you enter a brilliant, well-lighted apartment, gay with well-dressed women and Austrian officers in their handsome uniforms, all full of politeness, *bonhommie*, and real kindness towards a stranger. Perhaps you occupy the next table to Meyerbeer, and you are more resolved than ever not to be too late. At seven you enjoy the harmony of the blessed, at a moderate outlay that would hardly pay for your entrance half-price to a farce in a London theatre, and at ten o'clock your day is over, and you may seek your couch.

I confess I liked Vienna very much. My intimacy with Victor gave me at once an introduction into society, and my old acquaintance with the German language made me feel thoroughly at home amongst these frank and warm-hearted people. It has always appeared to me that there is more homely kindliness, more *heart*, and less straining after effect in German society than in any other with which I am acquainted. People are less artificial in Vienna than in Paris or in London, better satisfied to be taken for what they really are, and not what they wish to be, more tolerant of strangers, and less occupied about themselves.

I spent my days very happily. Victor had recovered his spirits, those constitutional good spirits that in the young it requires so much suffering to damp, that once lost never return again. Valèrie was charming as ever, it may be a little more reserved than formerly, but all the more kind and considerate on that account; then when I wearied of society and longed for solitude and the indulgence of my own reflections, could I not pace those glorious galleries of ancient art, and feast my eyes upon the masterpieces of Rubens or Franceschini, in the Hotel Liechtenstein and the Belvedere? My father's blood ran in my veins, and although I had always lacked execution to become a painter, keenly and dearly could I appreciate the excellencies of the divine art. Ah! those Rubenses, I can see them now! the glorious athletic proportions of the men, heroes and champions every one; the soft, sensuous beauty of the women,--none of your angels, or goddesses, or idealities, but, better still, warm, breathing, loving, palpable women, the energy of action, the majesty of repose, the drawing, the colouring, but above all the honest manly sentiment that pervades every picture. The direct intention so truthfully carried out to bid the human form and the human face express the passions and the feelings of the human heart. I could look at them for hours.

Valèrie used to laugh at me for what she called my new passion--my devotion to art; the goddess whom I had so neglected in my childhood, when with my father's assistance I might have wooed and won from her some scraps of favour and encouragement. One morning I prevailed on Victor and his sister to accompany me to the Hotel Liechtenstein, there to inspect for the hundredth time what the Countess termed my "last and fatal attachment," a Venus and Adonis of Franceschini, before which I could have spent many a long day, quenching the thirst of the eye. It was in my opinion the *chef-d'oeuvre* of the master; and yet, taking it as a whole, there was no doubt it was far from a faultlessly-painted picture. The Adonis appeared to me stiffly and unskilfully drawn, as he lay stretched in slumber, with his leash of hounds, undisturbed by the nymphs peering at him from behind a tree, or the fat golden-haired Cupids playing on the turf at his feet. All this part of the picture I fancied cold and hard; but it was the Venus herself that seemed to me the impersonation of womanly beauty and womanly love. Emerging from a cloud, with her blue draperies defining the rounded symmetry of her form, and leaving one exquisite foot bare, she is gazing on the prostrate hunter with an expression of unspeakable tenderness and self-abandonment, such as comes but once in a lifetime over woman's face. One drooping hand carelessly lets an arrow slip through its fingers, the other fondling a rosy Cupid on her knee, presses his cheek against her own, as though the love overflowing at her heart must needs find relief in the caresses of her child.

"It is my favourite picture of all I ever saw, except one," I remarked to my two companions as we stopped to examine its merits; I to point out its beauties, they maliciously to enumerate its defects.

"And that other?" asked Valèrie, with her quick, sharp glance.

"Is one you never saw," was my reply, as I thought of the "Dido" in the old dining-room at Beverley. "It is an Italian painting with many faults, and probably you would not admire it as much as I do."

Valèrie was not listening; her attention was fixed on a party of strangers at the other end of the room. "*Tenez, ce sont des Anglais,*" said she, with that intuitive perception of an islander which seems born in all continental nations. I knew it before she spoke. The party stopped and turned round--two gentlemen and a lady. I only saw *her*; of all the faces, animate and inanimate, that looked downward with smiles, or upward with admiration, in that crowded gallery, there was but one to me, and that one, was Constance Beverley's.

I have a confused recollection of much hand-shaking and "How-do-you-do's?" and many expressions of wonder at our meeting *there*, of all places in the world, which did not strike me as so *very* extraordinary after all. And Valèrie was *so* enchanted to make Miss Beverley's acquaintance; she had heard so much of her from Victor, and it was so delightful they should all be together in Vienna just at this gay time; and was as affectionate and demonstrative as woman always is with her sister; and at the same time scanned her with a comprehensive glance, which seemed to take in at once the charms of mind and body, the graces of nature and art, that constituted the weapons of her competitor. For women are always more or less rivals; and with all her keenness of affections and natural softness of disposition, there is an unerring instinct implanted in the breast of every one of the gentler sex, which teaches her that her normal state is one of warfare with her kind--that "her hand is against every woman, and every woman's hand against her."

I dared not look in Miss Beverley's face as I shook her hand; I fancied her voice was *harder* than it used to be. I was sure her manner to *me* was as cold as the merest forms of politeness would admit. She took Victor's arm, however, with an air of *empressement* very foreign to the reserve which I remembered was so distinguishing a characteristic in her demeanour. I heard her laughing at his remarks, and recalling to him scenes in London and elsewhere, which seemed to afford great amusement to themselves alone. Even Ropsley looked graver than usual, but masked his astonishment, or whatever it was, under a great show of civility to Valèrie, who received his attentions, as she did those of every stranger, with a degree of pleasure which it was not in her nature to conceal. Sir Harry fell to my share, and I have a vague recollection of his being more than ever patronising and paternal, and full of good advice and good wishes; but the treasures of his wisdom and his little worldly sarcasms were wasted on a sadly heedless ear.

I put him into his carriage, where *she* was already seated. I ventured on one stolen look at the face that had been in my dreams, sleeping and waking, for many a long day. It was pale and sad; but there was a hard, fixed expression that I did not recognise, and she never allowed her eyes to meet mine.

How cold the snowy streets looked; and the dull grey sky, as we walked home to our hotel--Victor and Ropsley on either side of Valèrie, whilst I followed, soberly and silently, in the rear.

CHAPTER XXVIII
LA DAME AUX CAMELLIAS

"My dear, you *must* go to this ball," said Sir Harry to his daughter, as they sat over their morning chocolate in a spacious room with a small glazed stove, very handsome, very luxurious, and *very cold*. "You have seen everything else here; you have been a good deal in society. I have taken you everywhere, although you know how 'going out' bores me; and now you refuse to go to the best thing of the year. My dear, you *must!*"

"But a masked ball, papa," urged Constance. "I never went to one in my life; indeed, if you please, I had rather not."

"Nonsense, child, everybody goes; there's your friend Countess Valèrie wild about it, and Victor, and even sober Vere Egerton, but of course *he* goes in attendance on the young Countess--besides, Ropsley wishes it."

Constance flushed crimson, then grew white, and bit her lip. "Captain Ropsley's wishes have nothing to do with me, papa," said she, with more than her usual stateliness; "I do not see what right he has to express a wish at all."

Sir Harry rose from his chair; he was getting very feeble in his limbs, though he stoutly repudiated the notion that he grew a day older in strength and spirits. He walked twice across the room, went to his daughter's chair, and took her hand in his. She knew what was coming, and trembled all over.

"My dear child," said he, with a shaky attempt at calmness, and a nervous quivering of his under lip--for loving, obedient, devoted as she was; Sir Harry stood in awe of his daughter--"you remind me I wish to speak to you on the subject of Captain Ropsley, and his intimacy with ourselves. Constance, has it never occurred to you what all this must eventually lead to?"

She looked up at him with her clear, shining eyes, and replied--

"It has, papa, and I quite dread the end of it."

"You know, dear, how I have encouraged him," continued her father, without noticing the unpropitious remark; "you can guess my wishes without my speaking more plainly. He is an excellent fellow--clever, popular, agreeable, and good-looking. There can be no objection, of course, on *your* side. I think your old father has not done so badly for you after all--eh, Constance?" and Sir Harry made a feeble attempt at a laugh, which stopped, and, as it were, "went out" all of a sudden.

She looked him full in the face. Truth shone brightly in the depths of those clear eyes.

"Papa," said she, slowly and steadily, "do you really mean you wish me to--to marry Captain Ropsley?"

"You ladies jump at conclusions very fast," answered the Baronet, still striving, shakingly, to be jocose. "*Rem acu tetigisti.* Ha, ha! I have not forgotten my Latin, or that I was young once, my dear. You have run your needle into the very heart of the matter, you little witch! That is indeed my earnest wish and intention."

He changed at once into a tone of majestic and uncompromising decision, but he only looked at her askance, and once more left his place to amble up and down the room. She never took her eye off his face.

"And suppose I should tell you, papa, that I cannot comply with your wish; that I hate and loathe the very sight of the man whom you would make my husband; that I fear and distrust his intimacy with you more than anything in the world; that I implore you, papa, dear papa, to give up this dreadful idea; that for this once, and once only, you would listen to me, be guided by me, and, at any sacrifice, that you would break immediately and for ever with that bad, reckless, unprincipled man--what should you say then?"

She looked at him for an instant with a vague sort of half-hope in her truthful, shining eyes; but it was more resignation than disappointment that clouded her face over immediately afterwards.

"Say, my dear," answered the Baronet, gaily, but his teeth were set tight as he spoke; "why I should say that my girl was a romantic little fool, instead of one of the cleverest women of my acquaintance; or, more likely still, I should say she was joking, in order to try her father's patience and indulgence to the utmost. Listen to me, Constance. I have reasons of my own for wishing to see you married--of course I mean well married, and safely settled in life--never mind what they are; it may be that I am getting old, and feel that I have not much time to lose. Well, I have promised you to Ropsley--of course with your own consent. In these days we don't lock up our refractory children, or use force when persuasion alone is necessary. Heaven forbid!" Sir Harry said it with an expression of countenance somewhat contradictory of his language. "But I feel sure I need only point out to you what my wishes are to have your sincere co-operation. You behaved so well once before, you will behave well this time. Constance, I am not used to entreat; you cannot surely refuse me now?"

She burst into tears

"Oh, papa," she said, "anything--anything but this."

He thought to try the old sarcastic mood that had done him good service with many a woman before.

"What, we are premature, are we, Miss Beverley? We cannot forget old days and childish absurdities. We must, of course, be more sensitive than our boyish adorer. Psha! my dear, it's perfectly absurd; why, you can see with your own eyes that Vere Egerton is hopelessly entangled with that bold Hungarian girl, and I can tell you, to my certain knowledge, that he is to marry her forthwith. What she can see in his ugly face is more than I can make out; but this I suppose is prejudice on my part. Good Heaven! Constance, are you really afraid of seeing them together to-night? You! *my* daughter! the proud Miss Beverley?"

The old reprobate knew how to manage a woman still. He had served a long apprenticeship to the trade, and paid pretty dearly for his lessons in his time.

She did not cry now.

"Papa, I will go to the ball," was all she said; and Sir Harry thought it wiser to push matters no further for the present.

Our little party had been established in Vienna for several weeks when the above-mentioned conversation took place; and the De Rohans were living on terms of close intimacy with the Beverleys. Ropsley made no secret of his engagement to Constance, and bestowed all the attentions of a future husband on the unwilling girl with a tact which made escape impossible. Victor took his place as an old friend by her side, and she seemed to find the more pleasure in his society that it relieved her from the Guardsman's sarcastic though amusing conversation, and, as I once overheard her remark, with a deep sigh, "reminded her of old times." Valèrie and I were, as usual, inseparable; but there was something of late in the manner of the young Countess which grated on my feelings. She was gay, volatile, demonstrative as ever; but I missed those fits of abstraction, that restless, preoccupied air which seems so charming when we fancy we can guess the cause; and altogether I never was so much in danger of falling in love with Valèrie as now, when, piqued, hopeless, and miserable, I felt I was uncared for by every one on earth--even by her. I was one too many in the party. Sir Harry seemed worldly, sharp, and in good spirits, as usual. Ropsley scheming, composed, self-contained, and successful. Victor lively, careless, and like his former self again. Constance haughty and reserved, habitually silent, and preserving an exterior of icy calmness. Valèrie sparkling, triumphant, and *coquette* as possible. Only Bold and I were out of spirits; the old dog resenting with truly British energy the indignity of an enforced muzzle, without which no animal of his species was allowed to go at large in the streets of Vienna; whilst his master was wearied and ill at ease, tired of an aimless, hopeless life, and longing for the excitement of action, or the apathy of repose.

Such were the ingredients of the party that dined together at that well-known hotel rejoicing in the appellation of "Munsch," on the day of the masked ball, to which all Vienna meant to go, to be mystified for pleasure, and have its secrets told and its weaknesses published for amusement.

Many were the glances of admiration cast at our table, and many, I doubt not, were the comparisons made between the stately beauty of the Englishwoman and the brilliant charms of her Hungarian friend. I sat next to Valèrie, and opposite Miss Beverley--the latter scarcely ever spoke to me now, and, save a formal greeting when we met and parted, seemed completely to ignore my existence; but she tolerated Bold, and the dog lay curled up under the table at her feet, keeping watch and ward over her--faithful Bold!--as he used to do long, long ago. Ropsley held forth upon the political state of Europe; and although Victor and Sir Harry expressed loudly their admiration of his sentiments, and the lucid manner in which he expressed them, I have yet reason to believe that, as he spoke in English, a very garbled and eccentric translation of his remarks reached the imperial and kingly bureau of police. Constance and Valèrie seemed to have some secret understanding which called forth a smile even on the pale face of the former, whilst the latter was exuberant in mirth and spirits, and was ardently anticipating the pleasures of the ball. I was roused from my dreamy state of abstraction by her lively voice.

"Vere," she exclaimed, with a sly glance across the table at her friend, "we are engaged for the first dance, you know."

She always called me "Vere," now, in imitation of her brother.

"Are we?" was my somewhat ungallant reply. "I was not aware of it, I do not think I shall go to the ball."

"Not go to the ball!" exclaimed Valèrie; "and I have told you the colour of my dress and everything. Not go to the ball! do you hear him, Victor? do you hear him, Sir Harry? do you hear him, Captain Ropsley?"

"We can hardly believe it," replied the latter, with a quiet smile; "but, Countess Valèrie, he does not deserve your confidence: will you not tell *us* what your dress is to be?"

"Nobody but Vere," persisted the Countess, with another arch smile at Constance; "you know he is engaged to me, at least for this evening. But he is cross and rude, and deserves to be mystified and made unhappy. But seriously, Vere, you *will* go? Ask him, Miss Beverley; he won't refuse *you*, although he is so ungallant towards *me*."

Constance looked up for a moment, and in a dry, measured voice, like a child repeating a lesson, said, "I hope you will go, Mr. Egerton;" and then resumed the study of her plate, paler and more reserved than ever.

I heard Bold's tail wagging against the floor. "What have I done to offend her," I thought, "that she will thus scarcely even deign to speak to me?" I bowed constrainedly, and said nothing; but the torture was beginning to get more severe than I could bear, and making an excuse that I should be late for the opera, whither none of my companions were going, I hurried from the table, Valèrie giving me as I rose a camellia from her bouquet, and charging me to return it to her at the ball. "I shall count upon you, Vere," she said, as I adjusted it in my coat, "and keep myself disengaged."

I threaded my way through the dirty streets to the opera. I ensconced myself in the corner of the De Rohans' box; and resting my head on my hand, I began to reflect for the first time for many weeks on my position and my prospects. I could not conceal from myself that I was no longer justified in living on the terms of intimacy with Victor and his sister which had so long constituted such an agreeable distraction in my life. It was evident that Valèrie considered me in the light of something more than a friend, and it was due to the lady, to her brother, and to myself, that such a misconception should be rectified at once and for ever. I was well aware in my heart of hearts that Constance Beverley was still, as she would always be, the idol of my life, but I was too proud to confess this even to myself. It was evident that she cared no longer for the friend of her childhood, that she was totally indifferent as to what became of the nameless, ill-starred adventurer who had once presumed to ask her to be his; and I ground my teeth as I told myself I was too proud, far too proud, to care for any woman that did not care for me. But I could not lead this life of inaction and duplicity any longer. No, I was well now, I was able to walk again (and I thought of my gentle nurse with a sigh). I would not go to the ball to-night; I would leave Vienna to-morrow; it was far better not to see Miss Beverley again, better for me at least, and ought I not to consult my own interest first? Others were selfish. I would be selfish too! Even Valèrie, I had no doubt, was just like all other women; she wouldn't care, not she! And yet she was a frank, open-hearted girl, too. Poor Valèrie! And mechanically I placed the camellia she had given me to my lips, and raised my eyes to examine the house for the first time since my entrance.

What was my surprise to remark the action I have just described imitated exactly by a lady in a box opposite mine, but whose face was so turned away from me, and so masked, moreover, by a bouquet she held in her hand, that I could not identify her features, or even make out whether she was young or old, handsome or plain! All I could see was a profusion of rich brown hair, and a well-turned arm holding the bouquet aforesaid, with the odours of which she seemed much gratified, so perseveringly did she apply it to her face. After a short interval, I adjusted my opera-glass and took a long survey of the flower-loving dame. As soon as she was sure she had attracted my attention, she once more applied the white camellia to her lips with much energy and fervour, still, however, keeping her face as far as possible turned away from me, and shaded by the curtains of her box. Three times this absurd pantomime was enacted. So strong a partiality for so scentless a flower as the camellia could not be accidental; and at last I made up my mind that, in all probability, she mistook me for somebody else, and would soon find out her error without my giving myself any further trouble on the subject. I had too much to occupy my own mind to distress myself very long about the *Dame aux Camellias*; and I turned my attention to the stage, to seek relief, if only for half-an-hour, from the thoughts that were worrying at my heart.

The ballet of *Sattinella* was being enacted, and a man must have been indeed miserable who could entirely withdraw his attention from the magnificent figure of Marie Taglioni, as she bounded about in the character of that fire-born Temptress, a very impersonation of grace, symmetry, beauty, and *diablerie*. The moral of the piece is very properly not developed till the end, and it is too much to expect of a human heart that it shall sympathise with the unfortunate victim of Satan's charming daughter as long as his tortures are confined to performing wondrous bounds towards the footlights in her fiendish company, and resting her diabolical form upon his knee in the most graceful and bewitching attitude that was ever invented below, and sent up expressly for the delectation of a Viennese audience. Neither did I think the "first male dancer" very much to be pitied when he was inveigled into a beautiful garden by moonlight, where he discovered the whole *corps de ballet* arranged in imitation of statues, in the most fascinating of *poses plastiques*, and so well drilled as scarcely even to wink more than the very marble it was their part to represent. Soft music playing the whole time, and fountains, real fountains, spouting and splashing the entire depth of the stage, constituted the voluptuous accessories of the scene, and it was not till the senses of the spectators had been thoroughly entranced by beauty and melody--by all that could fascinate the eye and charm the ear, that the whole spectacle changed to one of infernal splendour; the fountains becoming fireworks, the pure and snowy statues turning to gorgeous she-devils of the most diabolical beauty and fierceness, whilst Sattinella herself, appearing in a bewitching costume of crimson and flames, carried off the bewildered victim of her blandishments, to remain bound to her for ever in the dominions of her satanic father.

Having once got him, it is understood that she will never let him go again, and I could not pity him very sincerely notwithstanding.

The opera was over, the company rapidly departing, and I stood alone at the stove in the crush-room, wondering why the house was not burnt down every time this beautiful ballet was performed, and speculating lazily between whiles as to whether I was ever likely to witness an opera again. I was one of the last spectators left in the house, and was preparing to depart, when a female figure, cloaked and hooded, passed rapidly under my very nose, and as she did so, pressed a camellia to her lips in a manner which admitted of no misconception as to her motive. I could not see her face, for a black satin hood almost covered it, but I recognised the rounded arm and the handsome bouquet which I had before remarked in the opposite box. Of course I gave instantaneous chase, and equally of course came up with the lady before she reached her carriage. She turned round as she placed her foot on the step, and dropped her fan upon the muddy pavement; I picked it up, and returned it to her with a bow. She thanked me in French, and whispered hurriedly, "Monsieur will be at the Redouten-Saal to-night?" I was in no humour for an adventure, and answered "No." She repeated in a marked manner, "Yes, monsieur will be at the ball; monsieur will find himself under the gallery of the Emperor's band at midnight. *De grâce*, monsieur will not refuse this *rendezvous*."

"I had not intended to go," was my unavoidable reply, "but of course to please Madame it was my duty to make any sacrifice. I would be at the appointed place at the appointed time."

She thanked me warmly and earnestly. "She had travelled night and day for a week, the roads were impassable, frightful, the fatigue unheard of. She had a *migraine*, she had not slept for nights, and yet she was going to this ball. I would not fail her, I would be sure to be there. *Adieu*--no, *au revoir*."

So the carriage drove off, splashing no small quantity of mud over my face and toilet. As I returned to my hotel to dress, I wondered what was going to happen *now*.

CHAPTER XXIX
"A MERRY MASQUE"

It was a beautiful sight, one calculated to inspire feelings of mirth and gaiety, even in a heart ill at ease with itself. Such a ball-room as the Redouten-Saal is perhaps hardly to be seen elsewhere in Europe. Such music I will venture to say can only be heard in Vienna, where the whole population, from the highest to the lowest, seem to live only that they may dance. Everybody knows the effect of brilliant light on the animal spirits; the walls of these magnificent rooms are of a pale fawn colour, almost approaching to white--the very shade that best refracts and enhances the effect of hundreds of wax candles, shedding their soft radiance on the votaries of pleasure below. No wonder people are in good spirits; no wonder they throng the spacious halls, or parade the long galleries above, and looking down from their elevated position, pass many a pointed jest and humorous sally on the varied scene that crowds the floor below. No wonder they frequent the refreshment-rooms that skirt these galleries, and flirt and talk nonsense, and quiz each other with the cumbrous vivacity of the Saxon race. When I entered from the quiet street I was dazzled by the glare, and almost stupefied by the hum of many voices, and the pealing notes of one of those waltzes which Strauss seems to have composed expressly to remind the fallen children of Adam of their lost Paradise. From a boy music has made me melancholy--the sweeter the sadder; and although it is a morbid unmanly feeling, which I have striven hard to overcome, it has always conquered me, it will always conquer me to the last. I felt bitterly out of place amongst these pleasure-worshippers. What had I to do here, where all were merry and full of enjoyment? My very dress was out of keeping with the scene, for I was one of a very small minority in civil attire. Gorgeous uniforms, white, blue, and green, glittered all over the ball-room; for in Austria no officer nowadays ever appears out of uniform; and as an army of six hundred thousand men is officered almost exclusively from the aristocracy, the fair ball-goers of Vienna find no lack of partners in gaudy and warlike attire. The ladies were all masked; not so their respective cavaliers, it being part of the amusement of these balls that the gentler sex alone should appear *incognito*, and so torment their natural prey at more than their usual advantage; thus many a poisoned dart is planted, many a thrust driven securely home, without a chance of a parry or fear of a return. Though Pity is represented in a female garb, it seems to me that woman, when she does strike, strikes harder, straighter, swifter, more unsparingly than man. Perhaps she suffers as much as she inflicts, and this makes her ruthless and reckless--who knows? if so, she would rather die than acknowledge it. These are not thoughts for a ball, and yet they crowded on me more and more as I stood under the musicians' gallery, gazing vacantly at the throng.

Victor and his party had not yet arrived. I was sure to distinguish them by Ropsley's scarlet uniform, and I was also sure that in such an assemblage of military connoisseurs the costume of Queen Victoria's body-guard would attract observation and remark that could not pass unnoticed even by so preoccupied a spectator as myself. Besides, I knew the colour of Valèrie's dress; it was to be pink, and of some fabric, beautiful exceedingly, of which I had forgotten the name as soon as told. I was consequently sure of finding them whenever I wished, so I stood quietly in my corner, and watched the crowd go by, without caring to mingle in the stream or partake of the amusements every one else seemed to find so delightful. How poor and vapid sounded the conversation of the passers-by; how strained the efforts at wit; how forced and unnatural the attempts at mystification! The Germans are too like ourselves to sustain for any length of time the artificial pace of badinage and repartee. It is not the genius of the nation, and they soon come to a humble jog-trot of old trite jokes, or, worse still, break down completely, and stop once for all. The only man that seemed in his element was a French *attaché*, and he indeed entered into the spirit of the thing with a zest and enthusiasm of truly Parisian origin. Surrounded by masks, he kept up a fire of witticism, which never failed or diminished for an instant; like the juggler who plays with half-a-dozen balls, now one, now another, now all up in air at once. The Frenchman seemed to ask no respite, to shrink from no emergency; he was little, he was ugly, he was not even gentleman-like, but he was "the right man in the right place," and the ladies were enchanted with him accordingly. Surrounded by his admirers, he was at a sufficient distance for me to watch his proceedings without the risk of appearing impertinent, and so I looked on, half amused at his readiness, half disgusted with his flippancy, till I found my attention wandering once more to my own unprofitable and discontented thoughts.

"*Mouton gui rêve,*" said a voice at my elbow, so close that it made me start.

I turned rapidly round, and saw a lady standing so near that her dress touched mine, masked, of course, and thoroughly disguised in figure and appearance. Had it not been for the handsome arm and the camellia she held to her lips, I should not have recognised her as the lady I had spoken to at the door of the Opera, and who had appointed to meet me at this very spot--a *rendezvous* which, truth to tell, I had nearly forgotten.

"*Mouton gui rêve*," she repeated, and added, in the same language, "Your dreams must be very pleasant if they can thus abstract you from all earthly considerations, even music and dancing, and your duty towards the fair sex."

"Now what *can* this woman want with me? I wish she would let me alone," was my inward thought: but my outward expression thereof was couched in more polite language.

"Dreaming! of course I was dreaming--and of Madame; so bright a vision, that I could hardly hope ever to see it realised. I place myself at Madame's feet as the humblest of her slaves."

She laughed in my face. "Do not attempt compliments," she said, "it is not your *métier*. The only thing I like about you English is your frankness and straight-forward character. Take me upstairs. I want to speak seriously to you. Don't look so preoccupied."

At this instant I recognised Ropsley's scarlet uniform showing to great advantage on his tall person in the distance; I could not help glancing towards the part of the room in which I knew the pink dress was to be found, for the pink dress would of course have entered with Ropsley, and where the pink dress was there would be *another*, whom, after to-night, I had resolved *never, never* to see again.

My mysterious acquaintance had now hooked herself on to my arm, and as we toiled up the stairs it was necessary to say something. I said the first thing that occurred to me. "How did you know I was an Englishman?" She laughed again.

"*Not* by your French," she answered; "for without compliment, you speak it as well as I do; but who except an Englishman would go to sleep with his eyes open in such a place as this? who else would forget such a *rendezvous* as I gave you here? who else, with a pretty woman on his arm (I *am* a pretty woman, though I don't mean to unmask), would be longing to get away, and hankering after a pink dress and a black domino at the other end of the room? You needn't wince, my friend; I know all your secrets. You were in the seventh heaven when I interrupted you. I wish you would come down to earth again."

I will not say where I wished *she* would go down to, but I answered gravely and politely enough--"It was not to tell me this you stopped your carriage after the opera to-night; tell me how I can serve you--I am at the disposition of Madame, though I am at a loss to discover what she means by her pink dresses and black dominoes."

"I will not laugh at you for being serious," she replied. "I am serious myself now, and I shall be for the next ten minutes. Frankly, I know you; I know all about you. I know the drawing-room at Edeldorf, and I know Valèrie de Rohan--don't look so frightened, your secret is safe with me. Be equally frank, Monsieur l'Interprète, and interpret something for me, under promise of secrecy. You are an Englishman," she added, hurriedly, her manner changing suddenly to one of earnestness, not unmixed with agitation; "can I depend upon you?"

"Implicitly, Madame," was my reply.

"Then tell me why Victor de Rohan is constantly at the Hôtel Munsch with his foreign friends; tell me why he is always in attendance on that proud young lady, that frigid specimen of an English 'meess'? Is it true, I only ask you--tell me, is it true?"

Agitated as was the questioner, her words smote home to her listener's heart. How blind I had been, living with them every day, and never to see it! while here was a comparative stranger, one at least who, by her own account, had been absent from Vienna for weeks, and she was mistress of the details of our every-day life; she had been watching like a lynx, whilst I was sleeping or dreaming at my post; well, it mattered little which, now. The hand that held her bouquet was shaking visibly, but her voice was steady and even slightly sarcastic as she read her answer in my face, and resumed--

"What I have heard, then, is true, and Count de Rohan is indeed an enviable man. You need not say another word, Monsieur l'Interprète, I am satisfied. I thank you for your kindness. I thank you for your patience; you may kiss my hand;" and she gave it me with the air of a queen. "I am an old friend of his and of his family; I shall go and congratulate him; you need not accompany me. Adieu! good sleep and pleasant dreams to you."

I followed her with my eyes as she moved away. I saw her walk up to Victor, who had a lady in blue, Constance, of course, upon his arm. She passed close by him and whispered in his ear. He started, and I could see that he turned deadly pale. For an instant he hesitated as if he would follow her, but in a twinkling she was lost amongst the crowd, and I saw her no more that night.

I threaded my way to where Ropsley in his scarlet uniform was conversing with a knot of distinguished Austrian officers; they were listening to his remarks with attention, and here, as elsewhere, in the ball-room at Vienna as in the playground at Everdon, it seemed natural that my old school-fellow should take the lead. Sir Harry was by his side occasionally putting in his word, somewhat *mal-à-propos*, for though a shrewd capable man, foreign politics were a little out of Sir Harry's depth. Behind him stood the much-talked-of pink dress; its wearer was closely masked, but I knew the flowers she held in her hand, and I thought now was the time to bid Valèrie a long farewell. She was a little detached from her party, and I do not think expected me so soon, for she started when I spoke to her, but bowed in acquiescence, and put her arm within mine when I proposed to make the tour of the room with her, although, true to the spirit of a masquerade, not a word escaped her lips. I led her up to the galleries, and placed a seat for her apart from the crowd. I did not quite know how to begin, and contrary to her wont, Valèrie seemed as silently disposed as myself. At last I took courage, and made my plunge.

"I have asked to speak to you, to wish you good-bye," I said. "I am going away to-morrow. For my own sake I must stay here no longer. I am going back to the East. I am well now, and anxious to be on service again. I have stayed in the Fatherland far too long as it is. To-morrow at daybreak Bold and I must be *en route* for Trieste." I paused; she winced, and drew in her breath quickly, but bowed her head without speaking, and I went on--"Mine has been a strange lot, and not a very happy one; and this must account to you for my reserved, unsociable conduct, my seeming ingratitude to my best and kindest friends. Believe me, I am not ungrateful, only unhappy. I might have been, I ought to have been a very different man. I shall to-night bid you farewell, perhaps for ever. You are a true friend; you have always borne and sympathised with me. I will tell you my history; bear and sympathise with me now. I have been a fool and an idolater all my life; but I have been at least consistent in my folly, and true in my idolatry. From my earliest boyhood there has been but one face on earth to me, and that one face will haunt me till I die. Was it my fault, that seeing her every day I could not choose but love her? that loving her I would have striven heart and soul, life and limb, to win her? And I failed. I failed, though I would have poured out my heart's blood at her feet. I failed, and yet I loved her fondly, painfully, madly as ever. Why am I an exile from my country--a wanderer on the face of the earth--a ruined, desperate man? Why, because of her. And yet I would not have it otherwise, if I could. It is dearer to me to sorrow for her sake, than it could ever have been to be happy with another. Valèrie, God forbid you should ever know what it is to love as I have done. God forbid that the feeling which ought to be the blessing and the sunshine of a life should turn to its blight and its curse! Valèrie!"

She was shaking all over; she was weeping convulsively under her mask: I could hear her sobs, and yet I was pitiless. I went on. It was such a relief in the selfishness of my sorrow, to pour out the pent-up grief of years, to tell any one, even that merry, light-hearted girl, how bitterly I had suffered--how hopeless was my lot. It was not that I asked for sympathy, it was not that I required pity; but it seemed a necessity of my being, that I should establish in the ears of one living witness the fact of my great sorrow, ere I carried it away with me, perhaps to my grave. And all this time the melody of the "Weintrauben" was pealing on, as if in mockery. Oh, that waltz! How often she had played it to me in the drawing-room at Beverley! Surely, surely, it must smite that cold heart even now.

My companion's sobs were less violent, but she grasped the bouquet in her hand till every flower drooped and withered with the pressure.

"Valèrie," I continued, "do not think me vain or presumptuous. I speak to you as a man who has death looking him in the face. I am resolved never to return. I am no braver than my neighbours, but I have nothing on earth to live for, and I pray to die. I can speak to you now as I would not dare to speak if I thought ever to look in your face again. You have been my consoler, my sister, my friend. Oh, I could have dared to love you, Valèrie; to strive for you, to win you, had I but been free. You are, perhaps, far worthier than that proud, unfeeling girl, and yet--and yet--it cannot be. Farewell, Valèrie, dear Valèrie; we shall never meet again. You will be happy, and prosperous, and beloved; and you will think sometimes of the poor wounded bird whose broken wing you healed, only that it might fly away once more into the storm. As for me, I have had no future for years. I live only in the past. Bold and I must begin our wanderings again to-morrow--Bold whom she used to fondle, whom I love for her sake. It is not every man, Countess Valèrie, that will sacrifice his all to an idea, and that idea a false one!"

"Stop, Vere!" she gasped out wildly; "hush, for mercy's sake, hush!"

Oh! that voice, that voice! was I dreaming? was it possible? was I mad? Still the wild tones of the "Weintrauben" swelled and sank upon mine ear; still the motley crowd down below were whirling before my sight; and as surely as I saw and heard, so surely was it Constance Beverley who laid her hand in mine, and tearing down her mask, turned upon me a look so wild, so mournful, so unearthly, that, through all my astonishment, all my confusion, it chilled me to the heart. Many a day afterwards--ay, in the very jaws of death, that look haunted me still.

"So true," she muttered; "oh, misery, misery! too late."

"Forgive me, Miss Beverley," I resumed, bitterly, and with cold politeness; "this communication was not intended for you. I meant to bid Countess Valèrie farewell. You have accidentally heard that which I would have died sooner than have told you. It would be affectation to deny it now. I shall not annoy you any further. I congratulate you on your many conquests, and wish you good-bye."

She was weeping once more, and wrung my hand convulsively.

"Vere, Vere," she pleaded, "do not be so hard upon me; so bitter, so mocking, so unlike yourself. Spare me, I entreat you, for I am very miserable. You do nob know how I am situated. You do not know how I have struggled. But I must not talk thus *now*."

She recovered her self-command with a strong effort, and pale as death, she spoke steadily on.

"Vere, we may not make our own lot in life; whatever is, is for the best. It is too late to think of what might have been. Vere, dear Vere, you are my brother--you never can be more to me than a dear, *dear* brother."

"Why not?" I gasped, for her words, her voice, her trembling frame, her soft, sweet, mournful looks, had raised once more a legion of hopes that I thought were buried for ever in my breast; and despite my cruel taunts, I loved her, even whilst I smote, as the fierce human heart can love, and tear, and rend, and suffer the while, far, far more keenly than its victim.

"Because I am the promised wife of another. Your friend, Count de Rohan, proposed for me this very day, and I accepted him."

She was standing up as she said it, and she spoke in a steady measured voice; but she sat down when she had finished, and tried to put her mask on again. Her fingers trembled so that she could not tie the strings.

I offered her my arm, and we went downstairs. Not a word did we exchange till we had nearly reached the place where Sir Harry was still standing talking to Victor de Rohan. Ropsley, in his scarlet uniform, was whirling away with a lady in a blue dress, whose figure I recognised at once for that of the Countess Valèrie. It was easy to discover that the young ladies, who resembled each other in size and stature, had changed dresses; and the Countess, to enhance the deception, had lent her bouquet to her friend. I was giddy and confused, like a man with his death-hurt, but pride whispered in my ear to bear it in silence and seeming unconcern.

Three paces more would bring us to Sir Harry. I should never see her again. In a short time she might perhaps read my name in the *Gazette*, and then hard, haughty, false as she was, she would like to know that I had been true to her to the last. No, I would not part with her in anger; my better angel conquered, and I wrung her hand, and whispered, "God bless you, Constance." "God bless you, Vere," she replied; and the pressure of those soft trembling fingers thrilled on mine for many a day.

I recollect but little more of that ball in the Redouten-Saal. I believe I congratulated Victor on his approaching marriage. I believe I wished Valèrie good-bye, and was a little disappointed at the resignation with which she accepted my departure. I have a vague impression that even Ropsley, usually so calm, so selfish, so unsympathising, accompanied me home, under the impression that I was ill. My mind had been overstrung, and I walked about like a man in a dream. But morning came at last, and with my cased sword under my arm, and Bold in a leash at my feet, I stood on the platform of the railway-station, waiting for the departure of my train. An English servant, in the well-known livery, touched his hat as he put a letter into my hand. Miser that I was! I would not read it till I was fairly settled in the carriage. Little thought the faded belle, with her false front, opposite me, or the fat man, with a seal-ring on his fore-finger, by my side, how that scrap of paper was all my wealth on earth; but they were honest Germans, and possessed that truest of all politeness, which does as it would be done by. No inquisitive regards annoyed me during its perusal; no impertinent sympathy remarked on the tears which I am ashamed to say fell thick and fast upon it ere it closed. I have it by me now, that yellow well-worn paper. I have read those delicate womanly characters by scorching sunlight, by the faint glimmer of a picket's lantern, far away on the boundless sea, cramped and close in the stifling tent. If indeed "every bullet has its billet," and any one of them had been destined to lodge in my bosom, it must have found its way right through that fragile shield--ay, carried in with it the very words which were ineffaceably engraven on my heart. No wonder I can remember it all. Here it is:--

"Vere, you must not judge me as men are so prone to judge women-- harshly, hastily, uncharitably. We are not all frivolous, selfish, and fond of change, caring only for our amusements, our *conquests*, as you call them, and our enmities. You were bitter and cruel to me last night. Indeed, indeed, I feel you had a right to be so, Vere. I am so, *so* sorry for you. But you must not think I have treated you unkindly, or with want of confidence. Remember how you have avoided me ever since we came to Vienna; remember how you have behaved to me as a stranger, or at most a mere acquaintance; how you have never once inquired about my prospects, or alluded to old times. Perhaps you were right; perhaps you felt hurt, proud, and angry; and yet, Vere, I had expected better things from *you*. Had I been in your place I think I could have forgiven, I think I could have cared for, sympathised with, and respected one whom I was forbidden to love. If I were a man, it seems to me that I should not place happiness, however great, as the one sole aim of my existence; that I should strive to win honour and distinction, to benefit my fellow-men, and above all, to fulfil my duty, even with no higher reward here below than my own approval. Vere, when a man feels he is doing right, others think so too. I could be proud, oh! so proud, of my brother. Yes, Vere, it is my turn to implore now, and I entreat you let me be a sister, a very dear sister to you. As such I will tell you all my griefs, all my doings; as such I can confide in you, write to you, think of you, pray for you, as indeed I do, Vere, every morning and evening of my life. And now let us dismiss at once and for ever the thoughts of what might have been. The past is beyond recall--the present, as you used to say, does not exist. The future none can call their own. There is but one reality in life, and that is Right. Vere, I have done right. I have followed the path of duty. Brother, I call upon you for your help along the rough steep way; you have never failed me yet, you will not fail me now.

"You know my mother died when I was very young. Since then my father has fulfilled the duties of both parents towards his child. As I have grown older and seen more of the world, I have been better able to appreciate his affection and devotion to myself. A little girl must have been a sad clog upon a man like my dear father, a high-spirited gentleman, fond of the world, fond of society, fond of pleasure. Besides, had it not been for me, he would have married again, and he preferred to sacrifice his happiness to his child. Can I ever repay him? No. Whatever may have been his faults, he has been a kind, kind father to me. I will tell you all frankly, Vere, as this is the last time the subject can ever be mentioned between us. Had I been free to choose, I would have been yours. I am not ashamed--nay, I am *proud* to own it. But you know how impossible it was, how absolutely my father forbade it. To have disobeyed him would have been wicked and ungrateful. I feel that even you would not have respected me had I done so. But of late he has become most anxious to see me settled in life. From his own hints, and Captain Ropsley's open assertions, it seems this alone can stave off some dreadful evil. I do not understand it. I only know I am bound to do all in my power for papa; and that he is entangled with that bad, unprincipled man I feel convinced. Oh, Vere, it might have been far, far worse. In accepting Count de Rohan I have escaped a great and frightful danger. Besides, I esteem him highly, I like his society, I admire his open, honourable character. I have known him all my life; he is your oldest friend--I need not enlarge upon his merits to you. His sister, too, is a charming, frank-hearted girl. From all I heard, from all I saw, I had hoped, Vere, that she had effaced in your mind the unhappy recollections of former days. She is beautiful, accomplished, and attractive; can you wonder that I believed what I was told, and judged, besides, by what I saw? Even now we might be related. You seem to like her, and she would make any one happy. Forgive me, Vere, forgive me for the suggestion. It seems so unfeeling now, whilst I have your tones of misery ringing in my ears; and yet, Heaven knows, *your* happiness is the wish nearest my heart. Consult only *that*, and I shall be satisfied. To hear of your welfare, your success, will make me happy. I cannot, I must not write to you again. You yourself would not wish it. I ought to write no more now. I feel for you, Vere; I know how you must suffer, but the steel must be tempered in the fire, and it is through suffering that men learn to be great and good. There are other prizes in life besides happiness. There is an hour coming for us all, when even the dearest and closest will have to part. May we both be ready when that hour arrives. And now it is time to bid the long farewell; our paths in life must henceforth be separate. Do not think unkindly of me, Vere; I may not be with you, but I may be proud of you, and wish you every happiness. Forget me--yet not altogether. Dear, *dear* brother, God bless you! and farewell!

"Take care of poor Bold."

So it was really over at last. Well, and what then? Had it not been over, to all intents and purposes, long ago? Yes, there was something worth living for, after all. There was no bitterness now, for there was nothing to hope; the cup had been drained to the dregs, and the very intoxication of the draught had passed away, but it had invigorated the system and given new life to the heart. It was much to feel that I had been valued and appreciated by such a woman--much to know that my name would never fall unmeaningly on her ear. And I would be worthy, I would never fail. The sacrifice should be perfected. And though I might never see her again on earth, I would preserve her image pure and unsullied in my heart of hearts. Constance Beverley should henceforth and for ever be my ideal of all that was purest and noblest and best beloved in woman.

CHAPTER XXX
THE GOLDEN HORN

"Johnny, want to see the bazaar?" The speaker was a Greek of the lowest class, depraved and dirty, with a flexibility of limb and cunning of countenance only to be seen in the present representatives of that race who once furnished the sculptor with his glorious ideal of godlike strength and intellectual beauty. I longed to kick him--the climate of Constantinople is provocative of irritation, and I felt that with my bushy beard, my Oriental demeanour, my acquaintance with Turkish habits and proficiency in the language, it was irritating to be called "Johnny," and asked to "see the bazaar," as though I had been the smoothest and ruddiest ensign, disembarked for a day's leave from yonder crowded troop-ship, an innocent lamb frisking in the sun on my way up to the shambles before Sebastopol.

Yes, I was pretty well acclimatised in Turkey now. A year and more had passed over my head since I had left Vienna, the morning after that memorable ball at the Redouten-Saal, and what changes had that year brought forth! Sir Harry Beverley was gathered to his fathers, and an investigation into that worthy gentleman's affairs had explained much that was hitherto incomprehensible in his conduct as to his daughter's marriage and his connection with Ropsley. The latter had played his game scientifically throughout. He was aware that on a proper settlement being made, by marriage or otherwise, for his daughter, Sir Harry would obtain the fee-simple of certain property which, until such an event, he only held in trust for the young lady's benefit; and as these were the sole funds to which the far-seeing Guardsman could look to liquidate Sir Harry's debts to himself, incurred no one knew exactly how, it was his object to expedite as speedily as possible the marriage of my early love. As she was an heiress he would have had no objection to wed her himself, and indeed, as we have already seen, had entered into terms with her father for the furtherance of this object. That scheme was, however, defeated by her own determination, and it had long been apparent to my mind that Constance had only married my old friend Victor to escape from the dreadful alternative of becoming Ropsley's wife: that such an alliance promised but ill for the future happiness of both I could not conceal from myself, and yet so selfish is the human heart, so difficult is it to shake the "trail of the serpent" from off the flowerets of our earthly love, I could not regret as I ought to have done that the two people whom most I cared for in the world, should not be as devoted to each other as is essential to the happiness of those whom the tie of marriage has bound indissolubly together.

Ah! she was Countess de Rohan now, living at Edeldorf in all that state and luxury which she was so well calculated to adorn; and I, what had I done since we parted for ever at the masquerade? Well, I had striven to fulfil her wishes--to rise to honour and distinction, to be worthy of her friendship and esteem. Fame I had gained none, but I had done my duty. Omar Pasha, my kind patron, who had never forgotten the child that sympathised with him at Edeldorf, had expressed himself satisfied with my services; and 'Skender Bey, drunk or sober, never passed me without a cordial grasp of the hand. For more than a year I had shared the fortunes of the Turkish commander and the Turkish army. I had seen the merits of those poor, patient, stanch, unflinching troops, and the shortcomings of their corrupt and venal officers. I knew, none better, how the Turkish soldier will bear hunger, thirst, privation, ill-usage, and arrears of pay without a murmur; how, with his implicit faith in destiny, and his noble self-sacrifice in the cause of God and the Sultan, he is capable of endurance and effort such as put the ancient Spartan to the blush--witness the wan faces, the spectral forms, gaunt, famine-stricken and hollow-eyed, that so doggedly carried out the behests of the tameless defender of Kars. I had seen him starved and cheated that his colonel might gormandise--ay! and, in defiance of the Prophet, drink to intoxication of the forbidden liquid--and I wondered not, as none who knew the nation need wonder, that Russian gold will work its way to the defeat of a Turkish army far more swiftly than all the steel that bristles over the thronging columns of the Muscovite. Keep the Pasha's hands clean, or make it worth his while to be faithful to his country--forbid the northern eagle from spreading his wing over the Black Sea, and you may trust the Turkish soldier that not a Russian regiment ever reaches the gates of Constantinople. All this I had seen, and for long I was content to cast in my lot with this brave people, struggling against the invader; but my own countrymen were in arms scarce two hundred miles off, the siege of Sebastopol was dragging wearily on from day to day--I felt that I would fain be under the dear old English flag, would fain strike one blow surrounded by the kindly English faces, cheered by the homely English tongues. She was more likely to hear of me, too, if I could gain some employment with the English army; and this last argument proved to me too painfully what I had vainly striven to conceal from myself, how little these long months of trials, privations, and excitement had altered the real feelings of my heart. Would it be always so? Alas, alas! it was a weary lot!

"Johnny, want to see the bazaar?" He woke me from my day-dream, but I felt more kindly towards him now, more cosmopolitan, more charitable. In such a scene as that, how could any man, a unit in such a throng, think only of his own individual interests or sufferings?

Never since the days of the Crusaders--ay, scarcely even in that romantic time, was there seen such a motley assemblage as now crowded the wooden bridge that traverses the Golden Horn between bustling, dirty, dissonant Pera, and stately, quiet, dignified Stamboul, those two suggestive quarters that constitute the Turkish capital. On that bridge might be seen a specimen of nearly every nation under the sun--the English soldier with his burly, upright figure, and staid, well-disciplined air; the rakish Zouave, with his rollicking gait, and professed libertinism of demeanour, foreign to the real character of the man. Jauntily he sways and swaggers along, his hands thrust into the pockets of his enormous red petticoat trousers, his blonde hair shaved close *à la Khabyle*, and his fair complexion burnt red by an African sun long before he came here, "en route, voyez-vous," to fill the ditch of the Malakhoff. "Pardon," he observes to a tall, stately Persian, fresh from Astracan, whom he jostles unwittingly, for a Frenchman is never impolite, save when he really *intends* insult; the fire-worshipper, in his long sad-coloured robes and high-pointed cap, wreathes his aquiline nose into an expression of stately astonishment--for a Persian, too, has his notions of good breeding, and is extremely punctilious in acting up to them. His picturesque costume, however, and dignified bearing, are lost upon the Zouave, for a gilded *araba* is at the moment passing, with its well-guarded freight, and the accursed Giaour ogles these flowers of the harem with an impudent pertinacity of truly Parisian growth. The beauties, fresh from their bath, attempt, with henna-tinted fingers, to draw their thin veils higher over their radiant features, their bed-gown-looking dresses tighter round their plump forms; an arrangement which by some fatality invariably discloses the beauties of face and figure more liberally than before. Here a Jew, in his black dress and solemn turban, is counting his gains attentively on his fingers; there an Armenian priest, with square cap and long dusky draperies, tells his prayers upon his sandal-wood beads. A mad dervish, naked to the loins, his hair knotted in elf-locks, his limbs macerated by starvation, howls out his unearthly dirge, to which nobody seems to pay attention, save that Yankee skipper in a round hat, fresh from Halifax to Balaklava, who is much astonished, if he would only confess it, and who sets down in his mental log-book all that he sees and hears in this strange country as an "almighty start." Italian sailors, speaking as much with their fingers as their tongues, call perpetually on the Virgin; whilst Greeks, Maltese, and Ionian Islanders scream and gesticulate, and jabber and cheat whenever and however they can. Yonder an Arab from the desert stalks grim and haughty, as though he trod the burning sands of his free, boundless home. Armed to the teeth, the costly shawl around his waist bristling with pistols and sword and deadly yataghan, he looks every inch the tameless war-hawk whose hand is against every man, and every man's hand against him. Preoccupied as he is, though, and ill at ease, for he has left his steed in a stable from whence he feels no certainty that priceless animal may not be stolen ere he returns; and should he lose his horse, what will his very life avail him then? Nevertheless he can sneer bitterly on that gigantic Ethiopian--a slave, of course--who struts past him in all the borrowed importance of a great man's favourite. At Constantinople, as at New Orleans,--in the City of the Sultan as in the Land of the Free--the swarthy skin, the flattened features, and the woolly hair of the negro denote the slave. That is a tall, stalwart fellow, though, and would fetch his price in South Carolina fast enough, were he put up for sale to the highest bidder. Such a lot he need not dread here, and he leads some half-dozen of his comrades, like himself, splendidly dressed and armed, with a confident, not to say bellicose air, that seems to threaten all bystanders with annihilation if they do not speedily make way for his master the Pasha. And now the Pasha himself comes swinging by at the fast easy walk of his magnificent Turkish charger, not many crosses removed from the pure blood of the desert. The animal seems proud of its costly accoutrements, its head-stall embossed with gold, and housings sown with pearls, nor seems inclined to flag or waver under the goodly weight it carries so jauntily. A gentleman of substantial proportions is the Pasha; broad, strong, and corpulent, with the quiet, contented air of one whose habitual life is spent amongst subordinates and inferiors. He is a true Turk, and it is easy to trace in his gestures and demeanour--haughty, grave and courteous--the bearing of the dominant race. His stout person is buttoned into a tight blue frock-coat, on the breast of which glitters the diamond order of the Medjidjie, and a fez or crimson skull-cap, with a brass button in the crown, surmounts his broad, placid face, clean and close shaved, all but the carefully trimmed black moustache. A plain scimitar hangs at his side, and the long chibouques, with their costly amber mouthpieces, are carried by the pipe-bearer in his rear. The cripple asking for alms at his horse's feet narrowly escapes being crushed beneath its hoofs; but in Turkey nobody takes any trouble about anybody else, and the danger being past, the cripple seems well satisfied to lie basking in the sun on those warm boards, and wait for his destiny like a true Mussulman as he is. Loud are the outcries of this Babel-like throng; and the porters of Galata stagger by under enormous loads, shouting the while with stentorian lungs, well adapted to their Herculean frames. Water-carriers and sweetmeat-venders vie with each other in proclaiming the nature of their business in discordant tones;

a line of donkeys, bearing on their patient backs long planks swaying to and fro, are violently addressed by their half-naked drivers in language of which the poetic force is equalled only by the energetic enunciation; and a string of Turkish firemen, holloaing as if for their lives, are hurrying--if an Osmanli can ever be said to hurry--to extinguish one of those conflagrations which periodically depopulate Pera and Stamboul.

The blue sparkling water, too, is alive with traffic, and is indeed anything but a "silent highway." Graceful caïques, rowed by their lightly-clad watermen--by far the most picturesque of all the dwellers by the Bosphorus--shoot out in all directions from behind vessels of every rig and every tonnage; the boatmen screaming, of course, on every occasion, at the very top of their voices. All is bustle, confusion, and noise; but the tall black cedars in the gardens of the Seraglio-palace tower, solemn and immovable, into the blue cloudless sky, for there is not a breath of air stirring to fan the scorching noon, and the domes and minarets of Stamboul's countless mosques glitter white and dazzling in the glare. It is refreshing to watch the ripple yonder on the radiant Bosphorus, where the breeze sighs gently up from the sea of Marmora--alas! we have not a chance of it elsewhere; and it is curious to observe the restless white sea-fowl, whom the Turks believe to be the lost souls of the wicked, scouring ever along the surface of the waters, seemingly without stay or intermission, during the livelong day. It is ominous, too; mark that enormous vulture poised aloft on his broad wing, like a shadow of evil impending over the devoted city. There are few places in the world so characteristic as the bridge between Galata[#] and Stamboul.

> [#] The suburb of Pera lying next the Bosphorus, a locality combining the peculiarities of our own Smithfield, St. Giles's, and Billingsgate in their worst days. There is another bridge across the Golden Horn, higher up; but its traffic, compared to that of its neighbour, is as that of Waterloo to London Bridge.

And now the traffic is brought to a stand-still, for the huge fabric has to be opened, and swings back on its hinges for the passage of some mighty craft moving slowly on to the inner harbour to refit. It is a work of time and labour: the former article is of considerably less value to our Moslem friends than the latter, and is lavished accordingly; but though business may be suspended for the nonce, noise increases tenfold, every item of the throng deeming the present an opportune moment at which to deliver his, her, or its opinion on things in general. Nimble fingers roll the fragrant cigarette, and dissonant voices rise above the white spiral smoke into the clear bright air. Close behind me I recognise the well-known Saxon expletive adjuring *Johnny* to "drive on,"--said "Johnny" invariably returning a blessing for a curse, but "driving on," if by that expression is meant activity and progress, as little as may be. Turning round, I confront a florid Saxon face, with bushy beard and whiskers, surmounting a square form that somehow I think I have seen before. "Scant greeting serves in time of strife," and taking my chance of a mistake, I salute my neighbour politely.

"Mr. Manners, I believe? I am afraid you do not recollect me."

"*Major* Manners, sir; *Major* Manners--very much at your service," is the reply, in a tone of mild correction. "No; I confess you have the advantage of me. And yet--can it be? Yes, it is--Vere Egerton!"

"The same," I answered, with a cordial grasp of the hand; "but it is strange we should meet here, of all places in the world."

"I always told you I was born to be a soldier, Egerton," said the usher, with his former jaunty air of good-humoured bravado; "and here I am amongst the rest of you. Bless me, how you're grown! I should not have known you had you not spoken to me. And I--don't you think I am altered, eh? improved perhaps, but certainly altered--what?"

I glanced over my friend's dress, and agreed with him most cordially as to the *alteration* that had taken place in his appearance. The eye gets so accustomed to difference of costume at Constantinople, that it is hardly attracted by any eccentricity of habit, however uncommon; but when my attention was called by Manners himself to his exterior, I could not but confess that he was apparelled in a style of gorgeous magnificence, such as I had never seen before. High black riding-boots of illustrious polish, with heavy steel spurs that would have become Prince Rupert; crimson pantaloons under a bright green tunic, single-breasted, and with a collar *à la guillotine*, that showed off to great advantage the manly neck and huge bushy beard, but at the same time suggested uncomfortable ideas of sore throats and gashing sabre-strokes; a sash of golden tissue, and a sword-belt, new and richly embroidered, sustaining a cavalry sabre nearly four feet long,--all this was more provocative of admiration than envy; but when such a *tout ensemble* was surmounted by a white beaver helmet with a red plume, something of a compromise between the head-dress of the champion at Astley's and that which is much affected by the Prince Consort, the general effect, I am bound to confess, became striking in the extreme.

"I see," said I; "I admire you very much; but what is it?--the uniform, I mean. Staff corps? Land Transport? What?"

"Land Transport, indeed!" replied Manners, indignantly. "Not a bit of it--nothing half so low. The Bashi-Bazouks--Beatson's Horse--whatever you like to call them. Capital service--excellent pay--the officers a jovial set of fellows; and really--eh now? confess, a magnificent uniform. Come and join us, Egerton--we have lots of vacancies; it's the best thing out."

"And your men?" I asked, for I had heard of these Bashi-Bazouks and their dashing leader. "What sort of soldiers are they?--can you depend upon them?"

"I'd lead them anywhere," replied my enthusiastic friend, whose experience of warfare was as yet purely theoretical. "The finest fellows you ever saw; full of confidence in their officers, and such horsemen! Talk of your English dragoons! why, *our* fellows will ride up to a brick wall at a gallop, and pull up dead short; pick a glove off the ground from the saddle, or put a bullet in it when going by as hard as they can lay legs to the ground. You should really see them under arms. *My opinion is*, they are the finest cavalry in the world."

"And their discipline?" I continued, knowing as I did something of these wild Asiatics and their predatory and irregular habits.

"Oh, discipline!" answered my embryo warrior; "bother the discipline! we mustn't begin by giving them too much of that; besides, it's nonsense to drill those fellows, it would only spoil their *dash*. They behave very well in camp. I have been with them now six weeks, and we have only had one row yet."

"And was that serious?" I asked, anxious to obtain the benefit of such long experience as my friend's.

"Serious"--replied Manners, thoughtfully; "well, it was serious; pistols kept popping off, and I thought at one time things were beginning to look very ugly, but the chief soon put them to rights. They positively adore him. I don't know whether he punished the ringleaders. However," added he, brightening up, "you must expect these sort of things with Irregulars. It was the first time I ever was shot at, Egerton; it's not half so bad as I expected: we are all dying to get into the field. Hollo! they have shut the bridge again, and I must be getting on. Which way are you going?--to the Seraskerât? Come and dine with me to-day at Messirie's--Salaam!"

And Manners strutted off, apparently on the best of terms with himself, his uniform, and his Bashi-Bazouks. Well! he, too, had embarked on the stormy career of war. It was wonderful how men turned up at Constantinople, on their way to or from the Front. It seemed as if society in general had determined on making an expedition to the East. Dandies from St. James's-street were amusing themselves by amateur soldiering before Sebastopol, and London fine ladies were to be seen mincing about on the rugged stones of Pera, talking bad French to the astonished Turks with a confidence that was truly touching. It was Europe invading Asia once more, and I could not always think Europe showed to advantage in the contrast. A native Turk, calm, dignified, kindly, and polite, is a nobler specimen of the human race than a bustling French barber or a greedy German Jew; and of the two latter classes Pera was unfortunately full even to overflowing. Well, it was refreshing to have crossed the bridge at last--to have left behind one the miserable attempt at Europeanism, the dirt, the turmoil, and the discomfort of Pera, for the quiet calm, the stately seclusion, and the venerable magnificence of Stamboul.

CHAPTER XXXI
THE SERASKERÂT

True believers were thronging in and out of the great mosque of St. Sophia, pious in the consciousness of their many prostrations, rigorous in their observance of the hour of prayer. A *mollah* was shouting from one of the minarets, calling north, south, east, and west on all the faithful servants of the Prophet to offer up their daily orisons; and the infidel, as we term him, responded zealously to the call. Business was drowsily nodding in the bazaar; and the tradesman, sitting cross-legged on his counter, pointed feebly with his pipe towards the rich wares which his customer seemed barely to have energy to select. Slipshod Turkish ladies, accompanied by their negro damsels, were tripping slowly home from the bath, peeping at the Giaour through the thin folds of their *yashmaks* with curiosity not untempered by scorn. Pot-bellied children, pashas in miniature, holding up their garments with one hand, whilst they extended the henna-dyed fingers of the other, waddled after the stranger, now spitting at him with precocious fanaticism, now screaming out something about "Bono Johnny" and "Para," in unseemly cupidity for an alms. Dogs, gorged and sleepy, the recognised scavengers of the streets, lay coiled up in each shady corner and recess. Everything betokened somnolence and repose. The very sentry at the gate of the Seraskerât had laid his musket carefully aside, and was himself leaning against the wall in an attitude of helpless resignation and imbecility. My Turkish uniform, and his knowledge of my person as attached to the staff of Omar Pasha, served somewhat to arouse him; but ere he was fairly under arms I was already in the inner court of the Seraskerât, and beyond reach of his challenge or salute. What a contrast did it present to our own Horse-Guards, to which office it is a corresponding institution! Notwithstanding our boasted superiority, notwithstanding the proverbial supineness and indolence of the Sultan's officials, the comparison was hardly in favour of our London head-quarters for the hindrance of military affairs. Here was no helpless messenger, whose business it seems to be to *know nothing*, and who, answering every question with the unfailing "I will go and inquire," disappears and is seen no more. Here was no supercilious clerk, whose duty would appear to enjoin concealment of all he *does* know, and an imperative necessity of throwing difficulties in everybody's way. Here was no lingering for hours in an ante-room, to obtain a five minutes' interview of authoritative disapprobation on the one hand, and submissive disappointment on the other. On the contrary, at the foot of the stairs leading to the Seraskier's apartments were collected a posse of bustling, smart attendants, all alive and willing to assist in whatever was going on. Foreign officers, chiefly Hungarians, passed to and fro in eager conclave or thoughtful meditation. Interpreters were on the alert to solve a difficulty, and well-bred, active horses stood saddled and bridled, ready to start at a moment's notice with an order or a despatch. A knavish dragoman was jabbering bad Italian to a Jewish-looking individual, who I concluded must be a contractor; and a tall colonel of Turkish cavalry rolling a cigarette in his brown, well-shaped fingers, stood looking on in dignified indifference, as if he understood every word of their conversation, but considered it immeasurably beneath his haughty notice.

I sent up my name by a slim-waisted young officer, a Turk of the modern school, with long hair and varnished boots, over which, however, he was forced to wear indiarubber goloshes, that on going into the presence of a superior he might pay the indispensable compliment of uncovering his feet; and almost ere I had followed him three steps upstairs he had returned, and informing me that I was expected, held aside the curtain, under which I passed into the presence of the Seraskier.

Again, how unlike the Horse-Guards! the room, though somewhat bare of furniture, was gorgeously papered, painted, and decorated, in the florid style of French art; a cut-glass chandelier hung from the centre of the ceiling, and richly-framed mirrors adorned the walls. From the windows the eye travelled over the glorious Bosphorus, with its myriads of shipping, to the Asiatic shore, where beautiful Scutari, with its background of hills and cypresses, smiled down upon the waters now gleaming like a sheet of burnished gold. A low divan, covered with velvet cushions and costly shawls, stretched round three sides of the apartment, and on this divan were seated in solemn conclave the greatest general of the day and the Seraskier or Commander-in-Chief of the Turkish army.

Some knotty point must have been under discussion before I entered, for Omar Pasha's brow was perplexed and clouded, and a dead silence, interrupted only by the bubble of the Seraskier's *narghileh*, reigned between the two. The latter motioned me courteously to seat myself by the side of my chief; an attendant brought me a spoonful of sweetmeat, a tiny cup of strong, thick coffee, and an amber-tipped chibouque adorned with priceless diamonds, and filled with tobacco such as the houris will offer to the true believer in Paradise. I knew my assistance would soon be required; for although Omar Pasha is a good Turkish scholar, few men save those to whom it is almost a mother-tongue can converse fluently for any length of time with a Turk in his own language: so I smoked in silence and waited patiently till I was wanted.

True to the custom of the country, Omar Pasha resumed the conversation in an indifferent tone, by a polite inquiry after his Excellency's health, "which must have suffered from his exertions in business during the late heats."

To this his Excellency replied, "that he had been bled, and derived great benefit from it; but that the sight of his Highness, Omar Pasha, had done him more good than all the prescriptions of the *Hakim*."

A long silence, broken only as before; Omar Pasha, who does not smoke, waxing impatient, but keeping it down manfully.

The Seraskier at length remarked, without fear of contradiction, that "his Highness was exceedingly welcome at Constantinople," and that "God is great."

Such self-evident truths scarcely furnished an opening for further comment, but Omar Pasha saw his opportunity, and took advantage of it.

"Tell the Seraskier," said he to me, as being a more formal manner of acknowledging his courtesy, "that his welcome is like rain on a parched soil; that Constantinople is the paradise of the earth, but the soldier ought not to leave his post, and I must return to the army, taking with me those supplies and arrears of pay of which I stand in need."

All this I propounded in the florid hyperbole of the East.

"Assuredly," answered the Seraskier, a stout, sedate, handsome personage, who looked as if nothing could ruffle or discompose him, and was therefore the very man for the place,--"Assuredly, the beard of his Highness overflows with wisdom; there is but one God."

This was undeniable, but hardly conclusive; Omar Pasha came again to the attack.

"I have made a statement of my wants, and the supplies of arms, ammunition, and money, that I require. The army is brave, patient, and faithful; they are the children of the Sultan, and they look to their father to be fed and clothed. That statement has been forwarded to your Excellency through the proper channels. When the children ask for bread and powder to fight the accursed 'Moscov,' what is their general to reply?"

"Bakaloum" (we shall see), answered the Seraskier, perfectly unmoved. "If your Highness's statement has been duly forwarded, doubtless it has reached our father the Sultan, with the blessing of God. Our father is all-powerful; may he live for a thousand years."

Omar Pasha began to lose patience.

"But have you not seen and read it yourself?" he exclaimed, with rising colour; "do you not acknowledge the details? do you not know the urgency of our wants? have you not taken measures for supplying them?"

The Seraskier was driven into a corner, but his *sang-froid* did not desert him for a moment.

"I have seen the statement," said he, "and it was cleverly and fairly drawn up. The war is a great war, and it has great requirements. By the blessing of God, the armies of the faithful will raze the walls of Sebastopol, and drive the 'Moscov' into the sea. Kismet--it is destiny, praise be to Allah!"

"Before I set foot on board ship, before I leave the quay at Tophana, I must have those supplies shipped and ready to sail," urged Omar Pasha, now thoroughly roused, and showing his European energy in strong contrast to the Oriental apathy of the other; "I cannot proceed without them, I must have them by the end of the month. Orders must be sent out to-night--will you promise me this?"

"Bakaloum" (we shall see), replied the Seraskier, and after a few unmeaning compliments the audience ended, and I accompanied my chief downstairs into the courtyard of the Seraskerât.

"And this, my dear Egerton," said he, as he mounted his horse to proceed to his own quarters, "is one of the many difficulties with which I have to contend. Nobody knows anything--nobody cares for anything--nobody *does* anything. If we had but a Government, if we were not paralysed, why, with such an army as mine I could have done much. As it is, we are worse than useless. If the men have no shoes, no powder, no bread, and I apply to the authorities, as I have done to-day, it is 'Bakaloum'" (we shall see). "We shall indeed see some fine morning when the troops have all deserted, or are starved to death in their tents. Every official, high and low, seems only to look out for himself; what is there for us but to follow the example? And yet what chances lost! what an army thrown away!"

"But the Allies will soon take the place," I remarked, wishing to look on the bright side of things if possible, "and then our plan of a campaign is feasible enough. We shall sweep the whole of the Crimea, and strike him such a blow in Asia as will cripple our old friend the 'Rusky' for many a long day."

Omar smiled and shook his head. "Too many masters, friend Egerton," he replied; "too many masters. The strings are pulled in Paris, and London--ay, and in Vienna too. Diplomatists who do not know their own business are brought forward to teach us ours, and what is a general to do? There should be but one head to two hands. Here we have it all the other way. No, no, it is all 'Bakaloum' together, and we must make the best of it! I will send for you to-morrow if I want you."

As he rode away in his long dark overcoat and crimson fez, I looked after his manly, nervous figure, and thought to myself what a commander would that have been in any other service in the world. Had he but chanced to be born a Pole instead of a Croat, would the Danube still form a line of demarcation between the eagle and its prey? Would the Sultan be even now basking in beauty and revelling in champagne amongst the enervating delights of the Seraglio gardens? Would the balance of power in Europe be still held in equipoise? and the red flag, with its star and crescent, still flaunt over the thronging masts of the Golden Horn?

Several of my old acquaintances crowded round me ere I left the courtyard of the Seraskerât, welcoming me back to Constantinople, and eager to learn all the thrilling news of the day; every man believing every other to be better informed than himself as to all that was going on in front. I could gratify them but little, as my duty had now for some considerable period removed me from the scene of active operations. Truth to tell, I longed ardently to be in the field once more.

Amongst others, my old comrade, Ali Mesrour, the Beloochee, touched me on the shoulder, and greeted me with the heartfelt cordiality that no Asiatic ever assumes save with a fast and well-tried friend. The last time I had seen him he was engaged with some half-dozen Cossacks on the heights above Baidar, in the most romantic portion of the Crimea. He had kept them gallantly at lance's length for more than ten minutes, and made his escape after all, wounded in two places, and leaving three of his enemies dismounted on the field. Then he was ragged, jaded, dirty, and half-starved, for we were all on short rations about that time; now I should hardly have recognised him, sleek, handsome, and debonair, dressed, moreover, with unparalleled magnificence, and carrying, as is the custom of these warriors, all his worldly wealth in the jewelled hilt of his dagger, the mounting of his pistols, and the costly shawls that protected his head and wound about his middle. He seized my right hand, and pressed it to his heart, his eyes, and his forehead; then poured forth a volume of welcomes in the picturesque language of the East.

Could I do less than ask after the welfare of Zuleika, the gallant animal to whom I owed liberty and life?

"Allah has preserved her," replied the Beloochee, "and she is now in a stable not far from this spot. Her skin is sleek and fair; she is still my soul, and the corner of my heart."

"May she live a thousand years," was my comment; "to her and her master I am indebted for being here now. She is one of the best friends I ever had."

The Beloochee's eyes sparkled at the recollection.

"It was a favourable night," he answered, "and destiny was on our side. The dog of a Cossack! What filth I made him devour! How he rolled in the dust, and gasped at the kisses of my sharp knife! The Effendi rode in pain and weakness, but Allah strengthened him. The Effendi can walk now as well as when he left his mother's side."

We were strolling together down one of the shady narrow streets that lead to the water's edge, for I was on my return to Pera, and the Beloochee, in his delight at meeting his old comrade, would not suffer me to proceed alone. It was about five o'clock in the afternoon, and the scorching heat which had reigned all day was at last tempered with the breeze from the Black Sea. Oh! blessings on that breeze from the north! Without it how could we have endured the stifling atmosphere of Roumelia in the dog-days? By one of those wonderful arrangements of nature, which, after all (being accounted for on natural principles), would be far more wonderful were they not so, this welcome air began to blow every day at the same hour. I used to look for it as for the coming of a friend. If he was not with me at half-past three, he was sure not to be later than five-and-twenty minutes to four; and when he did come, I received him with bare brow and open arms. Ere we reached the bridge, the climate, from being well-nigh unbearable had become delightful, and all the inhabitants of Constantinople seemed to have turned out to drink in new life at every pore, and enjoy the unspeakable refreshment of a lowered temperature, till the dews should fall and the sun go down.

CHAPTER XXXII
A TURK'S HAREM

As we neared the water's edge, my companion started and turned perfectly livid, as if labouring under some fearfully strong emotion. True to his self-command, however, he allowed no other outward sign to betray his feelings. In front of us walked a Turkish lady, closely veiled, of course, and accompanied by a female negro slave. Following the Beloochee's gaze, I observed by the lady's dress and demeanour that she was of high rank, and in all probability the property of some great man, a Pasha at least. At that time a black attendant argued no inferiority on the part of the mistress as it does now. It is only since the peace of '56 that the negro woman has been at such a discount in Stamboul as to fill every corner of the streets with her lamentations, looking in vain for a purchaser, a master, and a home.

The cause of this sudden fall in the value of a strong, serviceable article, which had hitherto commanded a fair and remunerative price, is to be found as usual in the enterprise of speculators, and the luxurious tendencies of an unfeeling public. The far-seeing slave-dealers who provide the Turkish market with Circassian wares had no difficulty in foretelling that the Treaty of Paris would abandon to their fate those gallant mountaineers of the Caucasus who have so long and so manfully struggled for independence from the Russian yoke, and that soon they must bid an eternal farewell to their lucrative traffic in Circassian beauty, and their judicious supply of wives for the Pashas of Constantinople. Accordingly, ere the treaty came into operation, and the Government of the Czar was authorised to forbid the export of its new subjects, they proceeded to buy up, far and near, every eligible young lady of Circassian origin, and forward her as speedily as possible to the Emporium of Matrimony at Constantinople. Nor was this so hard a lot for these mountain-daisies as it may at first sight appear. They are taught to look upon the slave-market of the Turkish capital as the arena in which they are to contend for the prizes of life--namely, comfortable quarters, luxurious baths, a house full of slaves, and a rich master. To be deprived of her season at Stamboul is a bitter disappointment to a Circassian belle. We in England cannot understand this. Our fair Anglo-Saxons broil in London through the dog-days simply and entirely for the exquisite delights of its amusements and its society. Who ever heard of an English girl going to a ball with any ulterior view but that of dancing? Who ever detected her paying her modest court to an elderly Pasha (of the Upper House) for the sake of having jewels and amber, and gilded arabas and slaves, at her disposal? Who ever knew a blooming rose of June, that would have made the treasure of his life to Lazarus, and changed his gloomy dwelling to a bower of Paradise, transplanted by her own desire to the hothouses of Dives, there to queen it for a day among all his plants and exotics, and then pine neglected and withering away? No, no, we know nothing of such doings, but the trade flourishes handsomely in the East, and consequently the spring and summer of '56 saw Constantinople literally *smothered* in beauty. I use the word advisedly, for an Oriental enslaver, in the language of Burns, is "a lass who has acres of charms," and a Pasha purchases his wife as he does his mutton, by the pound. Now, demand and supply, like action and reaction, are "equal and contrary," nor is woman more than any other marketable commodity exempt from the immutable law; so when this invasion of beauty came pouring into Constantinople, the value even of a Circassian decreased steadily in an alarming ratio, till a damsel that, in the golden days of gallantry, would have fetched a hundred and fifty pounds sterling, was now to be bought "warranted" for five! Mark the sequel. Luxury crept in amongst the lower classes. The poor Turkish artisan, ambitioning a Circassian bride, sold his tools, his all--nay, his faithful black wives--to purchase the unheard-of blessing. The poor negro women were turned adrift into the streets. Who was to bid for them? During the worst period of the panic, black women were selling in Constantinople at a shilling a dozen!

The Beloochee griped my arm hard. "It is Zuleika!" he whispered between his set teeth. "She has not seen me--she does not know I am here. Perhaps she has forgotten me!"

"Let us follow her," said I, for in truth I sympathised with poor Ali, and my English blood boiled at the manner in which he had been deprived of his bride.

The Beloochee loosened his dagger in its sheath, and drew the folds of his shawl tighter round his waist. "Effendi," said he, "you are a true comrade--Bismillah! the end is yet to come."

The lady and her attendant walked provokingly slow, looking at every object of curiosity on their way, and making it exceedingly difficult for us to adapt our pace to theirs without exciting observation in the passers-by. At length they reached the waterside, and summoning a caïque, pushed out into the Bosphorus. We were speedily embarked in another, and following in their wake, our caïgee, or boatman, at once penetrating our intentions, and entering into the spirit of the thing with all the fondness for mischief and intrigue so characteristic of his class. As we glided along over the rippling waters we had ample time to dispose our plans, the object of which was to give the Beloochee an opportunity of communicating with his lost love, to learn, and, if possible, to rescue her from her fate. "Keep close to that caïque," said I to our sympathising waterman, "and when we are secure from observation go up alongside." The rascal showed all his white teeth, as he grinned intelligence and approval.

So we glided down the beautiful Bosphorus, past marble palaces and glittering kiosks, till we came under the very walls of a building, more magnificent than any we had yet passed, with a wide frontage towards the water, supported on shafts as of smoothest alabaster, the closed lattices of which, with its air of carefully-guarded seclusion, denoted the harem of some great dignitary of the empire, who was in the habit of retiring hither to solace himself after the labours of government and the cares of state. Through a gate of iron trellis-work, beautifully designed and wrought, we caught a glimpse of a lovely garden, rich in gorgeous hues, and sparkling with fountains murmuring soothingly on the ear, whilst from the lofty doors, securely clamped and barred, wide steps of marble reached down to the water's edge, lipped and polished by the lazy ripple of the waves.

Here we brought our bark alongside the object of our chase, but we had reckoned without our host in counting on the imperturbability of a lady's nerves, for no sooner had the Beloochee turned his face towards Zuleika, and whispered a few short syllables straight from his heart, than with a loud shriek she tossed her hands wildly above her head, and fainted dead away in the bottom of the caïque.

At that instant the boat's nose touched the lower step of the palace, and the negro woman, almost as helpless as her mistress, began screaming loudly for assistance, whilst a guard of blacks opening the huge double doors came swarming down to the water's edge, scowling ominously at the Beloochee and myself, who with our mischievous boatman had now shoved off and remained at some distance from the shore.

There was but one thing to be done, and that quickly. "Hakim!" I shouted to the blacks, who were bearing the lifeless form of the girl up the palace steps; "I am a doctor, do you want my assistance?" and at the same time I handed my pencil-case and the back of a letter to my comrade. Alas! he could not write, but in a hurried whisper entreated me, if possible, to communicate with Zuleika, and bear her the message which he confided to me from his old and faithful love.

By dint of threats and a kick or two, I prevailed on my friend the caïgee, who began to think the fun was getting too hot for him, to pull ashore;

and boldly mounting the steps, I informed the chief of the harem-guard authoritatively that I was a physician, and that if the Khanum's (lady's) life was to be saved, not a moment must be lost. She was evidently a favourite wife of her lord, for her fainting-fit seemed to have caused much commotion in the household, and during his absence the major-domo of the harem took upon himself, not without many misgivings and much hesitation, to admit me, a Giaour and a *man*, within the sacred and forbidden precincts.

The Turks have a superstitious reverence for the science of medicine, which they believe, and not without reason, to be practised by the Franks more successfully than by themselves. To my adoption of the character of a *Hakim* I owed my present immunity and my entrance into that sanctum of a Turk's house, which it is considered indecorous even to *mention* in conversation with its master.

I do not lay claim to more courage than my neighbours, and I confess it was with a beating heart that I followed the helpless form of Zuleika borne by her swarthy attendants up the palace steps, through the massive doors which swung and closed behind me, as if to shut out all chance of escape, to find myself at the top of a handsome staircase, on the very threshold of the women's apartment. What confusion my entrance created! Shrieks and jeers and stifled laughter resounded on all sides, whilst black eyes flashed inquiring glances at the Frankish doctor, veiled, indeed, but scarcely dimmed by the transparent folds of the *yashmak*, and loosely-clad forms, in all the colours of the rainbow, flitted hither and thither, with more demonstration of activity than the occasion seemed to warrant.

I had heard much of the discipline of these caged birds, and pictured to myself, with sympathising pity, their isolated condition, cut off from friends and relatives, weighed down by all the fetters of wedlock, but denied the consolations of domestic happiness, and had imagined that the Turkish woman was probably the most unhappy of all the daughters of Eve. What a deal of commiseration thrown away! Perhaps no woman in the world is more completely her own mistress in her own way than is the wife of a Turkish dignitary. Habit reconciles her to the veil, which indeed is of the thinnest material, and is almost her only restriction. She can walk abroad for business or pleasure, attended by only one female slave, and with such a convoy comes and goes unquestioned. It is only of very late years that an English lady could walk through the streets of London without at least as efficient a guard. The Oriental beauty, too, has her own hours, and her own apartments. Even her lord himself, he whom we picture as a turbaned Blue-beard, despotic in his own household, the terror of his wives and servants, preserves a chivalrous etiquette towards the lady that adorns his harem. He does not venture to cross the threshold of her apartment should he find her slippers placed outside. It is a signal that he is not wanted, and nothing would induce him to be guilty of such an act of rudeness as to go in. He comes at stated times, and his visits are always preceded by due notice. He lavishes handsome presents on his departure, and when he is unable to sun himself in the sight of her beauty, in consequence of his other engagements, and the rest of the suns in whose rays it is his duty to bask, he provides her with caïques and *arabas* to take her abroad, and furnishes her with plenty of pin-money to spend in the delightful occupation of shopping.

The chief of the negro-guard looked wistfully at me as I accompanied him, rolling the whites of his eyes in evident uncertainty and perturbation. As, however, Zuleika was still senseless, it seemed absolutely necessary that I should prescribe for her before my departure, and, accordingly, he motioned me to follow the stout blacks who were carrying her into the very inner recesses of the harem.

As I passed through those luxuriously-furnished apartments, I could not refrain from casting many a curious glance around at the diverse implements and accessories of the Turkish toilette, the many devices practised here, as in all lands, by the ladies, to "keep them beautiful or leave them neat." Costly shawls, silks from India, muslins like the web of a gossamer, and brocades stiff and gorgeous as cloth of gold, were scattered about in unlimited profusion, mixed with amber beads, massive gold chains, necklaces, bracelets, and anklets, French watches set to Turkish time, precious stones of every value and hue, sandal-wood fans, and other rare knick-knacks, mixed up with the most insignificant articles one can imagine, such as card-racks, envelope-cases of papier-maché, small brushes with oval mirrors at the back, and all sorts of trifles sent out from Paris, and bought in Pera, to amuse those grown-up children. The rooms were lofty and spacious, but the casements, even those that overlooked the gardens, jealously closed, and the lattices almost impervious even to the cool northern breeze. Bath-rooms opened from either side of the apartments, and every appliance for that Turkish luxury was of the most complete kind. At length we reached the room appropriated to Zuleika's especial use, and as her bearers laid her on the divan I observed that in this, more than in any other apartment of the palace, luxury reigned supreme. I argued Zuleika must be, at least for the present, the reigning favourite and queen of the seraglio.

CHAPTER XXXIII
MY PATIENT

"With the blessing of Allah! rub the palms of her hands with saffron!"

"Allah-Illah! Allah-Illah!--tickle the soles of her feet with feathers!"

"It is destiny! In the name of the Prophet pour cold water down her back!" "Room for the Frankish *Hakim!*" "May dogs defile the grave of the Giaour!"

Such were the exclamations that followed me into the apartment of Zuleika; for the Moslem daughters of Eve are not exempt from the curiosity attributed by tradition to the common mother; and have, moreover, superinduced on that pardonable failing certain prejudices of their own against the Christian unbeliever, whom, even when availing themselves of his assistance, they do not scruple to curse fluently, spitting the while between their teeth with considerable energy and effect.

Pending the application of their customary remedies, which in my ignorance of fainting-fits I judged to be the professional course of treatment, the ladies of the harem crowded and chatted at the door, peering over each other's shoulders, advancing a step into the apartment, retiring in confusion with a giggle and a scream, flirting atrociously with their negro guards--men of ebony without and ice within, as indeed they had need be--and otherwise to the best of their abilities increasing the general confusion.

One alone came boldly forward to my assistance; venerable she was, but a dame whom age, though it had deprived her of charms, had not robbed of the enchanting timidity of youth.

In her efforts to assist the sufferer she had cast her veil aside, but true to Oriental modesty she scrupulously covered her mouth[#] (and a very black set of teeth) with her hand even while she addressed me. Authoritative in her manner, and evidently accustomed to despotic sway in this part of the establishment, I confess I sincerely pitied the Pasha to whom this energetic lady must for several years have belonged. She came close up to me, tore the *yashmak* from Zuleika's face, and exclaimed in tones which admitted of no dispute—

[#] A curious custom peculiar to the sex all over the East. The veil, indeed, seems only adopted as a screen for the mouth, since the eyes are suffered to flash undimmed by its transparent folds. Should a Turkish woman be surprised by chance without her *yashmak*, she immediately claps her hand to her lips, and so remains till the male stranger has passed by.

"Bring otto of roses to anoint our dove; strip her at once from head to foot; and kick the Giaour downstairs!"

It was now time to assume a certain amount of dignified authority. I waved away the uncompromising old lady with the air of a magician dismissing his familiar; I ordered the lattice to be immediately thrown open--fortunately it looked towards the east, which was considered much to enhance the virtue of the breeze that stole through its aperture--and taking advantage of the returning animation which dawned on Zuleika's countenance, I repeated an incantation in English--if I remember right it was the negro melody of *"Oh, Susannah!"* accompanying the monotonous tones with appropriate gestures, until my patient opened her languishing black eyes, glanced heavily around her, and sitting upright on her couch, announced herself completely recovered.

My popularity was now at the flood. Had I administered the simple remedies which I have since been informed are beneficial in such cases, I should, however successful, have been looked upon merely in the light of a common practitioner; but that the lady should recover to the tones of a popular air, accompanied by a deportment of ludicrous solemnity, constituted a success which stamped me at once as a proficient in the Black Art, and won for me unqualified obedience and respect, not wholly devoid of fear.

To take advantage of the happy moment, I pulled my watch from my pocket, and placing my finger on the patient's wrist, bid the imperious dame aforesaid remark how the pulsations corresponded with the ticks of that instrument. This, too, was a great discovery, and the watch was handed round for examination to all the curious inmates of the harem in turn.

I then ordered the room to be cleared, and insisted that I should be left alone with my patient until the minute-hand of my watch had reached the favourable hour.

This I knew would give me five minutes' conversation with Zuleika, and as I expected the Pasha home at every instant, I could not afford more than this short space of time to give my friend the Beloochee's message and plead his cause. The room was speedily cleared, not, however, without much laughing, screaming, and scuffling in the passage. As soon as I was alone with Zuleika, I whispered gently in her ear not to be afraid, but to trust me, as I came from him she loved best in the world.

The girl started, and began to tremble violently; she was so pale that I dreaded another fainting-fit, and the consequent destruction of my reputation as a doctor. Though an Arab, she was a *woman*; and at this crisis of her destiny was of course paralysed by fear and totally incapable of acting for herself. Had her emotion mastered her once more, the golden opportunity would have been lost; there was nothing for it but to work upon her feelings, and I proceeded in a tone of indifference--

"You have forgotten him. He bids me say that 'the rose has been transplanted into a garden of purer air and cooler streams; he has seen with his own eyes that she is blooming and fragrant, and he is satisfied. He rejoices in your happiness, and bids you farewell!'"

She burst into a flood of tears; her woman's heart was touched, as I hoped it would be, by the sentiment I had put into her lover's mouth, and the relief thus afforded brought her composure and self-command. She came of a race, too, that never lacked courage or fortitude, and the wild desert-blood soon mantled once more in her rich, soft cheek--the tameless spirit of the Bedouin soon flashed again from her large dark eyes.

"Effendi!" she replied, in a firm though mournful voice, "my father's daughter can never forget. Bid him think no more of the rose he cherished so fondly. She has been plucked from the stem, and now she is drooping and withering away."

"But Allah suffers not the flowers to perish," I proceeded in Oriental metaphor, while she clasped her slender hands and seemed to look through me with her glittering eyes. "He sends the dews from heaven to refresh them at night. A wild bird will sing to the rose before dawn, and she will open her petals and bloom once more fresh and glistening in the morning sun. Zuleika, have you completely forgotten Ali Mesrour?"

At the sound of his name a soft, saddened expression stole over her eager face, large drops gathered in her drooping eyelashes, and it was with a thrilling voice that she replied--"Never! never! once more to see him, only once more to hear his voice, and so to die! so to die!" she repeated, looking dreamily as if into the hopeless future.

"It is destiny," was my answer. "There is but one Allah! An hour before dawn there will be a caïque at the garden gate. Zuleika must contrive the rest. The risk is great, but 'the diver cannot fetch pearls without wetting his hair.' Will Zuleika promise?"

"I promise!" was all she had time to reply, for at this instant no slight commotion was heard in the household, and looking from the casement I perceived an eight-oared caïque brought alongside of the palace steps, from which a pipe-bearer springing rapidly ashore, followed by a more sedate personage, evidently a *kiâtib*, or secretary, heralded the great man of the party, who, emerging from the shade of a white silk umbrella, hitherto held carefully over him by a third official, now laboured majestically up the marble steps, pausing occasionally to draw a long breath, and looking around him the while with an air of corpulent satisfaction that no one but a Turk could imitate with the slightest prospect of success.

It was indeed the Pasha himself--the fortunate possessor of the magnificent dwelling, the owner of all these negro slaves, this gorgeous retinue, these beautiful women--and more still, the lord and master of poor Zuleika. I thought it better to meet him on the threshold than to risk his astonishment and displeasure by awaiting his entrance into the harem; accordingly I hurried down to the court-yard of his palace, and presented myself before him with a mixture of Eastern courtesy and European self-respect, such as never fails to impress a Turk with the feeling that in the presence of a Frank he is himself but of an inferior order of mankind.

"Salaam, Effendi!" was the observation of the proprietor, as polite and unmoved as if he had expected me all day. "You are welcome! My house with all it contains is at your disposal!" He motioned me courteously into a large, handsome apartment on the ground-floor of the palace, bid me to be seated, and clapping his palms together, called for pipes and coffee; then placing himself comfortably on the divan, he crossed his hands over his stomach, and repeated, "You are welcome!" after which he sat perfectly silent, nodding his head from side to side, and peering curiously at me out of his small, twinkling grey eyes.

He was an enormously fat man, buttoned up of course into the usual single-breasted frock-coat, on the outside of which glittered the diamond order of the Medjidjie. His huge, shapeless legs were encased in European trousers of the widest dimensions, and terminated in varnished Wellington boots, from which he had just cast off a pair of india-rubber goloshes. It was the modern Turkish costume, affected by the Sultan himself, and a dress so ill-adapted for the dog-days at Constantinople can hardly be imagined; yet every official, every dignitary, every military man, is now clad in these untoward habiliments, for which they have discarded the picturesque draperies of their ancestors; so that the fine old Turk, "shawled to the eyes, and bearded to the nose," is only to be seen in Stamboul amongst the learned professions and the inferior orders of tradesmen and mechanics. A red fez was the single characteristic article of clothing worn by the

Pasha; and a more villainous expression of countenance than that which it overshadowed, it has seldom been my lot to confront. We stared at each other without speaking. It would have been ill-bred on the part of my host to ask me what I wanted, and I should have been guilty of an equal solecism in entering on my business until I had partaken of the customary refreshment.

Coffee was ere long brought in by negro slaves armed to the teeth, and of savage, scowling aspect. It was served in delicate filigree cups, set with priceless diamonds. Long chibouques were then filled and lighted. As I pressed the pure amber to my lips, and inhaled the fragrant aroma of the narcotic weed, I resolved to brazen it out manfully; but never, never again to find myself in such another scrape, no, not for all the warriors in Beloochistan, nor all the "Zuleikas" that ever eloped with them from the desert.

I thought I would say nothing of my visit to the harem. I judged, and rightly, that neither the ladies themselves, nor the negro-guard, whose duty it was to watch over those caged birds, would be over anxious to communicate the breach of discipline which had just been enacted, and that, although the secret was sure to ooze out in the course of a day or two, it was needless to anticipate the turmoil and disturbance which would attend its discovery.

But what excuse to make for my ill-timed visit? How to account for my intrusion on the leisure of so great a man as Papoosh Pasha, one of the half-dozen highest dignitaries of the empire, the friend and counsellor of the Sultan himself, even then fresh from the sacred precincts of the Seraglio Palace, where he had been helping sundry other ponderous Pashas to mismanage the affairs of his country, and to throw dust in the eyes of the enervated voluptuary who held the reins of power in a sadly palsied grasp. I too must take a leaf out of the book of Asiatic duplicity. I had seen a ship full of wounded dropping her anchor as I came along; there must have been another attack on the stronghold at Sebastopol--I was pretty safe in surmising, with no satisfactory result. I would pretend then that I had been sent to inform his Excellency of the particulars, and accordingly I puffed forth a volume of pure white smoke towards the ceiling, and advanced under cover of the discharge.

"His Highness has sent me hither in haste to inform your Excellency of the great news from the front. Am I too late to be the fortunate bearer, or has your Excellency already heard the particulars from the Elshie?"[#]

[#] The ambassador.

He darted a keen, suspicious glance at me, and replied gravely enough, "The war goes on prosperously in the front. We shall yet sweep 'the Moscov' from the face of the earth!"

"I am desired to inform your Excellency," I resumed, determined to persevere at all hazards, "that the Allies have again attacked the place. The Moscov came out in great numbers to repel the assault; the French have suffered severely; the Turkish troops covered the retreat with great gallantry and steadiness; fifteen hundred Russians remained dead upon the field; many more are disabled; Sebastopol must surrender within ten days."

"Mashallah!" replied the Pasha, laying his pipe down by his side; but for the life of me I could not make out whether or not he believed a word I had been telling him.

"Have I fulfilled my duty to your Excellency?" I continued, becoming every moment more and more anxious to make my escape. "I am at your Excellency's disposal; I am the humblest of your slaves. Have I your permission to depart?"

He looked uneasily around, but there seemed no apparent excuse for delay. It was evident to me that he wished to communicate with his retainers, but that his politeness forbade him to do so in my presence, and a Turk never allows any emergency to make him forget the exigencies of etiquette. He bade me farewell with much cordiality, ordered a horse to be got ready to carry me home, and dismissed me with many expressions of affection, but with the same fierce twinkle in that cunning leaden eye that had already more than once warned me to beware.

Many and devoted were the Pasha's retainers; hundreds slept on his mats, and followed at his heels, but I question whether I, the poor nameless Interpreter, could not command a greater amount of affection, courage, and fidelity, in the breast of my one trusty four-footed slave and companion, than existed in the whole retinue, black and white, of the Oriental dignitary.

Bold had followed me through my wanderings, faced with me many of the dangers of warfare, and shared in all its privations. The old dog was getting very time-worn now, quite grizzled about the muzzle, and ludicrously solemn, both in countenance and demeanour. To the world in general his temper was anything but conciliatory, and it required little provocation to make him set his mark on man or beast that affronted him; but with me he was always the same, obedient, devoted, and affectionate. He accompanied me everywhere, and would wait for hours in the courtyards of the Seraskerât or the Embassy, till his master emerged from the long-watched portal, when he would rise, give himself a lazy shake, and stalk on gravely by my side, occasionally thrusting his wet cold nose into my hand, and scowling at all strangers, even of his own species, with a very ominous "*noli me tangere*" expression, that forbade the slightest approach to familiarity.

Now the dog is an unclean animal to the Mussulman, and although his life is spared, as being the authorised scavenger of the streets, the true disciple of the Prophet scrupulously shuns all contact with the brute that the Christian loves to train as a servant and cherish as a friend. There is a curious old Arabic legend, which, although not to be found in the Koran, is recognised by the faithful as a trustworthy tradition, and to believe in which is esteemed an essential point of doctrine by the devout, that accounts for this unkindly superstition. Freely translated, it runs much in the following fashion:--

"When Allah had created the land and the sea, the mountains, the forests, the flowers, and the precious stones, he looked, and behold there was beauty and silence all over the earth.

"Then Allah created the birds and the beasts and the fishes; all things that swim, and creep, and fly, and run, and every living thing rejoiced in the sunshine.

"So Allah rested from his work in the Garden of Eden, by the Four Rivers, and looked around him, and behold the whole earth was astir in the forepart of the day.

"Then the breeze blew, and the waters laughed and rippled, and the birds sang, and the blossoms fell.

"So the angels smiled, and said, Praise be to Allah. It is very good--Allah! Bismillah!

"Then Allah saw that there were none of the inhabitants of earth that could smile as the angels smiled, or walk erect and praise him with the face to heaven.

"For the steed was grazing downward, and the lion lay couched in his lair, and the eagle, though she turned her eye to the sun, had neither praise nor smile.

"Then Allah took clay, and moistened it, and fashioned it till the sun went down.

"And Allah rested from his work, and left it in the Garden of Eden, by the Great Tree, where the Four Rivers spring.

"Now Gabriel walked in the garden, and he stopped where the work of Allah lay plastic on the sward, and the star shone bright on his forehead, for he praised Allah in his heart.

"And Shaitán came to walk in the garden, to cool his brow, and he stopped over against Gabriel and mocked.

"And Shaitán said, 'What is this, that I may know it, and name it, and claim my share in it for my own?'

"And Gabriel answered, 'Praise be to Allah; who has made all things well. This is Allah's work, and it shall be the perfection of all. Bismillah!'

"Then Shaitán laughed once more, and he turned the image over with his foot, so that it stood on all fours, with its face to the dust, and spat upon it, and said, 'It is empty! On my eyes be it!'

"And in the morning there was silence in Eden, for the work of Allah had been defiled.

"And Allah said, 'This is the doing of Shaitán. Behold, I will make of it yet another brute, and it shall be called the Dog, and be accursed.

"'And I will take other clay, and fashion another image that shall smile as the angels smile, and walk erect with its face to heaven, and I will call it Man.'

"And Shaitán cowered behind the Great Tree and listened to the voice of Allah, and though he trembled, he smiled.

"For Shaitán knew that he would have his share in the Man as in the beast."

Poor Bold, unconscious of his excommunication, hurried up to me in the court-yard of the Pasha's palace, where a fine horse, richly caparisoned, was being brought alongside the mounting-block for my use. In doing so the dog's tail, waving to greet his master, touched the hand of a tall forbidding-looking negro that stood by, grinning from ear to ear, as is the custom of his countrymen. The black swore a great oath, and kicked my dog savagely in the jaws. As Bold pinned him by the leg, I caught him such a buffet under the ear as knocked him fairly into the dust; from which abject position he embraced my feet and called me "his father." With some little difficulty I rated Bold off his prostrate foe, and mounting my horse, or rather the Pasha's, rode quietly to my hotel, where I dismissed the steed, and the groom who had accompanied him on foot, with a "*baksheesh*," and thought nothing more of the transaction. "A word and a blow" is as common a proceeding in Constantinople as at Donnybrook fair, though it leads to far different results; inasmuch as in the former abode of despotic authority and slavish submission it is very generally the only argument that is capable of enforcing proper subordination and respect.

It is seldom that a man loses his temper, even under the greatest provocation, without having cause, sooner or later, to regret his want of self-command. There are few of our fellow-creatures so unimportant that it is not worth while to conciliate them, none that may not some time have it in their power to inflict on us an injury; besides, an angry man is only less contemptible than a frightened one. And, like everything else that is unchristianlike, it is surely ungentlemanlike to put oneself in a passion. There was not much in knocking down a negro slave for his brutality towards my favourite, yet, ere long, I had cause bitterly to rue that I had not let him alone.

CHAPTER XXXIV
"MESSIRIE'S"

A narrow street, paved with the roughest and sharpest of flints, debouching into three other streets even less commodious than itself; a Turkish sentry dozing torpid at his post--half-a-dozen *hamauls*[#] clad in rough frieze jackets, and wide pantaloons of the same material, gathered in at the knee, scratching their brown herculean legs, and examining their broad flat feet, as they recline against a dirty dead wall, and interchange their jests with a degree of humour foreign to our English ideas of Turkish gravity--a rascally-looking dragoman in a black frock-coat and a fez, rolling a cigarette, prepared to cheat, rob, swindle, or lie at the shortest notice, a slave to every sensual vice except drunkenness, and speaking all the languages on earth in bad Italian--a brace of English Jack-tars, afire with raki, trolling out "Cheer, boys, cheer," and a stray Zouave, equally exhilarated, joining in chorus; a T.G., or travelling gent, with nascent beard, and towel wound turban-wise around his straw-hat, wishing himself in Pall Mall, and indignant at the natives, who call him *"Johnny."*

[#] Porters.

The REAL thing from the Crimea, in a curiously worn-out shell jacket, patched and darned, stained and tarnished, with a bronzed face, a bushy beard of two years' growth, and a slight limp that for the rest of his life will bid him "remember the fifth of November," and the turning of the tide upon the declivity of Inkermann.

Two or three English merchants, like crows, to be seen all over the world, and everywhere in the same dress, with white shirts, and honest broad-cloth coats, that remind one of home; a Queen's messenger, with tweed shooting-jacket and official forage-cap, clean shaved and clear-looking, after the bad passage and gale of wind he is sure at all seasons to encounter in the Mediterranean, a miracle to us *habitués* of the place, being actually as fresh from London as yonder copy of *The Times* newspaper, which came with him by the same mail, the only unfeathered biped in creation that thoroughly carries out the idea of "Here to-day, gone to-morrow." Such are the concomitants of the scene upon which I enter at the door of Messirie's hotel, that well-known rendezvous in Pera where congregate all that have any connection with the mother country; a place where every rumour is to be heard with its latest embellishments, and where, for the sum of seventeen francs a day, I can command a moderate breakfast, a dinner into the components of which it is better not to inquire, and a murky bedroom, where the fierce mosquito shall drain my life-blood all the weary night.

"Is Major Manners in the hotel?" I inquire, as I throw myself off the Pasha's horse, and, glancing at a face in the street very like that of the man I knocked down some three-quarters of an hour ago, reflect what a family resemblance reigns amongst the wretched sons of Ham. Bold is in his worst of humours, and growls ominously. "Is Major Manners here?" I repeat, and three Greek servants, with an abortive attempt to pronounce the Frankish name, shrug their shoulders and open their hands to express the hopeless imbecility in which they rejoice. I perceive a stout man in a white hat, picking his teeth unconcernedly in the passage, and, recognising him for the master, I apply at once for the information I require. He looks contemptuously at me in reply, and, turning his broad back upon me, walks off without deigning to take any further notice of a customer; but I have been here before, and I know there is balm in Gilead. I know that in a certain little room on the left I shall find the hostess, and that she, the mainstay and prop of the establishment, will spare no pains to assist a countryman. Kindly Madame Messirie! always ready to aid one in a difficulty, always busy, always good-humoured, always so thoroughly English, it was quite refreshing to hear the tones of your homely voice, and fancy oneself in the "White Lion," or the "Blue Bear," or some other pleasant hostelry, with post-horses and a bar, and an ostler's bell, far away in merry England.

"Vere Egerton! can that be you?" said a voice that I thought I recognised, as I entered the sanctum in which the hostess reigned supreme. "Little Egerton, as I'm alive, growed out of knowledge, and doubtless by this time a Pasha with three tails, and a true believer. Tell me all about the process of conversion and the tenets of your faith."

It was indeed Ropsley,--Ropsley the Guardsman--Ropsley the dandy, but how altered! The attenuated *roué* of former days had grown large and muscular, his face was brown and healthy, his forehead frank and open, the clear grey eye was brighter and quicker than it used to be; it had caught the ready, eager glance of those who look death habitually in the face, but had lost much of the cruel, calculating, leaden expression I remembered so well. Despite his worn-out uniform, the rents in which showed here and there a red flannel shirt,--despite his close-cropped hair and flowing beard,--I could not but confess to myself, as I grasped his hand, that Ropsley looked ten years younger and ten times handsomer than when I saw him last.

Yes, I met him cordially, and as an old friend. 'Tis true he had been my greatest enemy, 'tis true he had inflicted on me a wound, the scar of which I felt I should carry to my grave; but months had passed away since then; months which, crowding events upon events, had seemed like years; months of danger, labour, hardship, and tribulation. Of what avail is suffering if it does not soften and purify the heart? Why are those that mourn blessed, if it is not that they learn the bitter lesson grief alone can teach? My task had been a hard one--how hard none knew save the poor humbled scholar who conned it day by day, and blistered the page with his tears; but I had conquered it at last, and so I freely forgave Ropsley, and clasped him by the hand.

"You dine here, of course," he said, in his old half-humorous, half-sarcastic voice. "Madame Messirie, princess of Pera, and queen of my soul, order a place to be set for my friend the Pasha, and lots of champagne to be put in ice. I have only just come down from the front; I have scarcely had a decent dinner, or seen a silver fork, for a year and a half. It's an endless business, this, Egerton; hammer, hammer, hammer, yet nothing comes of it, and the old place looks whiter and more inviting than ever, but we *can't get in!*"

"And the Mamelon?" said I, eager for the last news from the spot to which millions of hearts were reaching, all athirst for hope.

"Got it at last," was his reply, "at least, our neighbours have; I hope they'll keep it. We made a sad mess last week, Egerton; lost no end of men, and half our best officers. Whew! I say nothing, only mark my words, if ever--but there's the bell! Never mind the siege now. War's a mistake, but dinner (if you can get it) never deceives you." And so saying, the *ci-devant* dandy patted me on the back, and pushed me before him into the well-lighted and now crowded *salon*.

In that strange country, so thoroughly Asiatic, which we call Turkey in Europe, there were so few links to connect us with the life of civilisation which seemed to have passed from us like a dream, that it was no wonder we clung to Messirie's hotel and thronged its *table d'hôte* with a constancy and devotion less to be attributed to its own intrinsic merits than to the associations and reminiscences it called forth. Here were to be met all the gallant fellows who were going to, or coming from, the front. Heroes, whose names were destined to gild the page of history, might here be seen drinking bad tea and complaining of the butter like ordinary mortals; but always in the highest spirits, as men seem invariably to be during the short lulls of a campaign. When you are likely to be shot next Monday week, if you have small hopes, you have few anxieties. Here, too, you might sit opposite a diplomatist, who was supposed to know the innermost secrets of the court at Vienna, and to be advised of what "the Austrians meant to do," whilst rubbing shoulders with you as he helped himself to fish; and confronting the man of ciphers, some heroic refugee, Pole, Croat, or Hungarian, whose name was in every journal in Europe, as it was inscribed on every military post in Austria or Russia, munched away with a capital appetite, and appeared only conspicuous for the extreme modesty and gentleness of his demeanour. Contractors of every nation jabbered in every language, nor was the supple Armenian, grafting the bold spirit of European speculation on his own Oriental duplicity, wanting to grasp his share of the plunder, which John Bull was so magnanimously offering as a premium to every description of fraud. Even the softer sex was not without its representatives. Two or three high-born English ladies, whose loving hearts had brought them hovering as near the seat of war as it was possible for a non-combatant to venture, daily shed the light of their presence at the dinner-table, and were silently welcomed by many a bold spirit with a degree of chivalrous enthusiasm, of which, anxious and pre-occupied, they were but little aware. A man must have been living for months among men, must have felt his nature gradually brutalising amidst the hardships, the sufferings, and the horrors of war, thoroughly to appreciate the softening influence of a woman's, and especially of a *countrywoman's*, society. Even to look on those waving white dresses, those gentle English faces, with their blooming cheeks and rich brown hair, was like a draught of water to a pilgrim in a weary land. It reminded us of home--of those we loved--and we went our way back into the desert a thought saddened, perhaps, yet, for all that, kindlier and happier men.

"What a meeting!" exclaimed Manners, as, gorgeously arrayed in the splendours of a full-dress uniform, he took his seat by my side and shook hands with Ropsley, who returned his greeting with a cordial pressure and a look of quiet amusement in his eye that almost upset my gravity: "Everdon at Constantinople!" continued our former usher; "we only want De Rohan to make our gathering quite perfect!"

I winced, and for the first time in my life I saw Ropsley colour, but Manners was too much occupied to notice the emotion of either of us; for, during his many visits to Constantinople, the dashing officer of Bashi-Bazouks had made such numerous acquaintances, and become so necessary an ingredient in the society of Pera, that there seemed to be hardly an individual at table, from the *attaché* of the Embassy down to the last-joined officer of the Commissariat, with whom he was not on terms of intimate familiarity. He had scarcely taken his seat and unfolded his dinner-napkin, ere the cross-fire of greetings and inquiries began. Manners, too, in the sunshine of all his popularity, had expanded into a wag; and although his witticisms were of a somewhat profound order, and not always very apparent to the superficial observer, they were generally well received; for a wag was a scarcer article in Constantinople than at the front.

So Manners proceeds with his dinner in great satisfaction and glory. After a couple of glasses of champagne he becomes overpoweringly brilliant. He is good enough, too, to take upon himself the onerous task of drilling the waiters, which he affects in bad French, and of abusing the deficiencies of the *cuisine*; a topic affording, indeed, ample scope for declamation. The waiters, especially a cunning old Greek, with a most villainous expression of countenance, betray an immense respect for Manners, tinged with an amused sort of amazement, and always help him first.

They bring him a dish of hare, large of limb and venerable in point of years. Our Bashi-Bazouk exclaims indignantly, *"Qu'est que ça?"*

"C'est un lièvre, M'sieur," replies the waiter, with a forced smile, as of one who expects a jest he will not comprehend.

"C'est un chat!" gasps out Manners, glaring indignantly on the official.

"Pardon, M'sieur," says the waiter, *"c'est trop gros pour un chat."*

"Chat," repeats Manners; *"Chat* THOMAS!" he adds, in a sepulchral voice, and with a frowning brow. The waiter shrinks abashed, the company laugh, and Manners's observation counts for a joke.

By this time conversation begins to buzz pretty freely around. Everybody drinks champagne, and tongues soon become loosened by the exhilarating fluid. Various topics are discussed, including a new beauty that has just arrived from Smyrna, of French extraction, and supposed to possess a fortune that sounds perfectly fabulous when calculated in francs. Manners listens attentively, for he has not totally abandoned the idea of combining the excitement of war with the pursuit of beauty--properly gilded, of course--and his maxim is that "None but the brave deserve the fair." Her praises, however, as also her name and address, are intercepted by the voluble comments of two stout gentlemen, his neighbours, on the utter incapacity of the Turkish Government, and the hopeless imbecility of "the people of this unhappy country, Sir,--a people without a notion of progress---destined to decay, Sir, from the face of the earth," as the stouter of the two, a British merchant, who is about investing in land here, remarks to his neighbour, a jovial Frenchman, who has already bought many a fertile acre in the neighbourhood of Constantinople, under the new Hatti-Sheriff;[#] and who replies, fixing his napkin securely in his button-hole--

[#] An act empowering foreigners to hold land in Turkey.

"Pourri, voyez-vous, mon cher. Crac! ça ne durera pas trois ans."

Opposite these worthies, an ensign in the Guards, and the Queen's messenger, who is of a theatrical turn, are busy with the character, private as well as professional, of a certain star of the Opera, whom the latter has already criticised in the execution of his duty at Vienna, and an ardent desire to hear whom haunts the former enthusiast to such a degree, even in the very trenches, that he longs to attack and take Sebastopol single-handed, in order to get home again before she leaves London for the winter. The Turkish Ministry, changing as it does about once a week; the policy of Austria; the Emperor Napoleon's energy; the inefficiency of our own Commissariat; the ludicrous blunders of the War Office, and the last retort courteous of Lord Stratford, all come in for their share of remark from prejudiced observers of every party and every opinion; but by degrees one voice rises louder than the rest, one individual attracts the notice of the whole dinner-table, and nowise abashed, but rather encouraged by the attention he commands, details volubly his own account of the capture of the Mamelon. He is a Frenchman, and a civilian, but somehow he has a red ribbon on his breast, and belongs to the Legion of Honour, so he "assisted," as he calls it, at the attack; and if he speaks truth, it must indeed have been an awful sight, and one in which his countrymen outdid themselves for valour, and that quality peculiar to the soldiers of France which they term *élan*, a word it is hopeless to think of translating. His opinions are decided, if not satisfactory; his plan of storming the place an excellent one, if it could only be carried out.

"We have taken the Mamelon!" says he, "and what remains? Bah! The Malakhoff Tower is the key to the whole position. What would you have? Every simple soldier in the army knows it as well as you and I do. I tell you I 'assisted' at the capture of the *Mamelon Vert*. They received us with a fire, well sustained, of grape and small arms. Our ammunition failed us at the critical moment. I was in the ditch--*me!*--when the Zouaves came on with their yell--the 152nd of the line were in front of them. It must be carried with the bayonet!--*Pflan!*--our little red pantaloons were swarming up the work and over the parapet ere you could count ten--the tricolor was hoisted and the guns spiked in a twinkling--that is the only way to arrange these affairs. Now, see here--you have your Redan, you others--you have sapped up to it, as near as you can get. There must be a combined attack. You cannot hold it till we have silenced that little rogue of a Malakhoff. What to do? One of these *'four mornings,'* as it was with the Mamelon so will it be with the Malakhoff! Give me a thick column, with the Zouaves in front and rear. These are not follies. I advance my column under cover--I pour in a volley!--I rush on with the bayonet! At the same moment the Redan falls. Your Guards and Scotchmen run in with their heads, a thousand cannon support you with their fire, the Allies hold the two most important defences, the Garden Batteries are silenced. Chut! the place is ours! France and England are looking on. I do not say that this will be done; but this is how it ought to be done. If your generals are fools, what is that to me? I am not a general--I!--but a simple civilian!--Waiter, a cigar! *Qui vivra, verra.*"

It is all *pipe-clay*, as the soldiers call it, now. The one engrossing topic silences every other. Alma, Inkermann, Lord Raglan's flank march, and the earlier incidents of the siege, are related by the very men who took an active share in those deeds of glory. Two cavalry officers, both wounded on the fatal day, recapitulate once more the *pros* and *cons* of the immortal charge at Balaklava--a question that has been vexed and argued till the very actors themselves in that most brilliant of disasters scarcely know how they got in, and still less how they ever got out. Though struck down by the same shell, and within ten yards of one another, each takes a diametrically opposite view of the whole transaction from his comrade. They differ materially as to time, position, pace, and results; above all, as to the merits of the leader whose wreath of laurels faded as undeservedly as it bloomed prematurely.

"I was close behind him the whole way," says the one; "I never saw a fellow so cool in my life, or so well 'got up.' He regulated every stride of that good chestnut horse like clock-work. When we came into fire, our line was dressed as if on parade. I know it by my own squadron. Will you tell me *that* man lost his head?"

"But where was he after we rode through the guns?" replied the other. "Answer me that! I grant you he took us in like a *brick*. But why didn't he bring us out? I never saw him after I was hit, and I *must* have seen him if he had rallied the first line, and been in his proper place to look out for his support. You were close to me, old fellow! I never knew before that bob-tailed Irish horse of yours could gallop a mile and a half. You were sickish, my boy, for I saw your face; but your eyesight was unimpaired. Tell me, did *you* see him, and what was he doing?"

"I *did*, I'll swear!" answers the partisan, as fine a specimen of a young hussar as ever drew a sword. "And I'll tell you what he was doing. Mind, I don't say it because I *like him*, for I don't. Confound him! he put me under arrest once in Dublin, and I believe it was only because my boots weren't well blacked. But I saw him, with my own eyes, striking at three Cossacks, who were prodding him with their long lances; and if poor old Champion had not dropped under me just at that moment, I'd have gone in and had a shy to help him, if I lost my stick. No, no! he's game as a pebble, let them say what they will; and if it wasn't for those cursed papers, he'd have had all the credit he deserves. It was the quickest thing I ever rode to, my boy," adds the young one, rather flushed, and drinking off his champagne at a gulp in his excitement. "He had a *lead*, and he kept it right well, and I won't hear him run down."

"I don't care," replies his friend. "I maintain it's a general's duty to know everything that's going on. I maintain he ought to have stood still and looked about him (to be sure, we couldn't see much in that smoke); ay! and, if necessary, waited there for the Heavies to come up. Now, I'll prove it to you in five minutes, if you'll only listen, you obstinate young beggar! Do you remember, just before we were both hit, your saying to me, 'What a go this is!' and my answering, 'Whatever we do, we must keep the men together, but half my horses are blown.' Do you remember that?"

"I *admit* nothing," answers the young man, laughing, "but I do remember that. It was just before we saw that strong body of Russian cavalry in rear of the guns, and I don't make out now why they weren't down upon us."

"Never mind that," pursues his opponent. "They behaved very steadily, and retired in good order; but you remember the circumstance. Well, he was then about six horses' lengths from us on our fight."

"On our left," interposes the younger man--"on our left; for I remember poor Blades was knocked over between me and him."

"On our *right*," persists the other. "I am certain of it, my dear fellow, for I remarked at the time----"

"I am positive he was on our left! I remember it as well as if it was yesterday."

"I could take my oath he was on our right; for I recollect seeing his sabretasche swinging."

"Left!" says one, "Right!" says the other; and they never advance one step farther in the discussion, which will be prolonged far into the night, to the consumption of much brandy and water, together with countless cigars, but with no further result.

If no two men see any one action of common life in the same light, how hopeless must it be to endeavour to get at the true statement of an event which takes place in the presence of a crowd of witnesses, all excited, all in peril of their lives, all enveloped in the dense smoke of a hundred guns, all maddening with the fierce, blood-stirring turmoil of such a deed of arms as the death-ride at Balaklava.

The instant dinner is finished, and coffee served, cigars are lit. It is a signal for the ladies to retire, and our handsome countrywomen sail out of the room, with that stately walk that none but an English lady ever succeeds in effecting. Many a glance follows them as they disappear; many a stout heart tightens under its scarlet covering, to think of the ideal at home--her gloves, her dress, her fragrant hair, her graceful gestures, and the gentle smile that may never gladden him again. Men are strange mixtures! the roughest and the coldest exteriors sometimes hide the most sensitive feelings; and when I hear a man professing audacious libertinism, and a supreme contempt for women, I always mistrust the bravado that is but a covering for his weakness, and set him down at once as a puppet, that a pair of white hands--if one only knew where to find them--can turn and twist and set aside at will.

Ropsley was much softer in his manner than he used to be. Had he, too, experienced the common fate? Was the dandy Guardsman no longer impervious, *nulli penetrabilis astro*? Painful as was the subject, he talked much of the De Rohans. He had seen Constance married; he had heard repeatedly from Victor during the past year; and though he evidently knew my hopes and their disappointment, by the tenderness with which he handled the subject, he could not resist enlarging on the topic, and talking to me of that family, in which I could never cease to take the warmest interest. I winced, and yet I listened, for I longed to know and hear of her even now. I would have lain quietly on the rack only to be told of her welfare. It *was* painful too. Perhaps there is no moment at which the heart feels so empty--at which the hopelessness of a loss is so completely realised, as when we hear the idol of our lives talked of in a matter-of-course way, as being totally unconnected with, and independent of, ourselves.

I remarked that, of his own accord, Ropsley never mentioned Valèrie. To an inquiry of mine as to the welfare of my kind and handsome nurse, he gave, I thought, rather an abrupt reply; and, turning suddenly round to Manners, asked him "if there was nothing to be done in the evening in this stupid place?" To which our gallant Bashi-Bazouk, who considered himself responsible for our amusement, answered delightedly, "No opera yet, Ropsley, though we shall have one in six weeks; no evening parties either, except a few amongst the French inhabitants--delightful people, you know, and very select. I am invited to-night to a little music, not far from here. I could take you both, if you like, with *me*. As friends of mine you would be most welcome. You speak French, Ropsley, if I remember right?"

"A little," replied the latter, much amused, "but *not* with *your accent;*" which, indeed, was true enough; for he had lived a good deal at Paris, and knew Chantilly as well as Newmarket. "Am I well enough dressed, though, for your fastidious friends?" he added, glancing, not without a gleam of inward satisfaction, from his own war-worn, threadbare uniform, to Manners's brilliant and somewhat startling costume.

"Couldn't be better!" replied the latter; "looks workmanlike, and all that. This time next year I only hope mine will be half as good. Meanwhile, come along, you and Egerton; never mind your cigars, they all smoke here."

"What! ladies and all, at these *select* parties?" laughed Ropsley. "I thought we were going amongst a lot of duchesses: but I hope they don't drink as well?"

"Custom of the country, my dear sir," replied Manners, gravely--"only cigarettes, of course. If a young lady offers to roll you one, don't refuse it. These little things are matters of etiquette, and it is as well to know beforehand." So, drilling us on the proper behaviour to be observed at a Pera party, our cicerone swaggered out into the night air, clanking his spurs, and rattling his sabre, with a degree of jingling vigour which seemed to afford him unlimited satisfaction. It was rather good to see Ropsley of the Guards--the man who had the *entrée* to all the best houses in London, the arbiter of White's, the quoted of diners-out, the favourite of fine ladies--listening with an air of the greatest attention to our former usher's lectures on the proper deportment to be assumed in the company to which he was taking us, and thanking him with the utmost gravity for his judicious hints and kind introduction to the *élite* of Pera society.

"Go home, Bold, go home." The old dog *would* accompany me out of the hotel, *would* persist in following close at my heel along the narrow street. Not a soul but our three selves seemed to be wandering about this beautiful starlight night. The Turkish sentry was sound asleep on his post; a dark figure, probably some houseless *hamaul*, crouched near the sentry-box. Savage Bold wanted to fly at it as he passed.

"How cantankerous the old dog grows," remarked Ropsley, as Bold stalked behind us, ears erect, and bristling all over with defiance. Ere we were fifty yards from the hotel he stopped short and barked loudly; a footstep was rapidly approaching up the street. Murders and robberies were at this time so frequent in Constantinople, that every passenger was an object of mistrust in the dark. We, however, were three strong men, all armed, and had nothing to fear. Bold, too, seemed to recognise the step. In another moment the Beloochee overtakes us, and with even a more imperturbable air than usual salutes me gravely, and whispers a few words in my ear. On my reply, he places my hand against his forehead, and says, "The brothers of the sword are brothers indeed. Effendi, you know Ali Mesrour, the son of Abdul. From henceforth my life is at the disposal of my Frankish brother."

A hurried consultation between the three Englishmen succeeds. Manners makes a great virtue of sacrificing sundry waltzes on which he seems to have set his heart, and is pathetic about the disappointment his absence will too surely inflict on Josephine, and Philippine, and Seraphine, but is amazingly keen and full of spirits notwithstanding. Ropsley, no longer the unimpressionable, apathetic dandy, whom nothing can excite or amuse, enters with zest into our project, and betrays a depth of feeling,-- nay, a touch of romance--of which I had believed him incapable. Bold is ordered peremptorily to "go home," and obeys, though most unwillingly, stopping some twenty paces off, and growling furiously in the darkness. Two and two we thread the narrow streets that lead down to the water's edge. The Beloochee is very silent, as is his wont, but ever and anon draws his shawl tighter round his waist, and loosens his dagger in its sheath. It is evident that he means *real business*. Manners and Ropsley chat and laugh like boys out of school. The latter never seemed half so boyish as now; the former will be a boy all his life--so much the better for him. At the bridge Ali gives a low shrill whistle. It reminds me of the night we escaped from the Cossacks in Wallachia; but the good mare this time is safe in her stable, and little thinks of the errand on which her master is bound. The whistle is answered from the water, and a double-oared caïque, with its white-robed watermen, looms through the darkness to take us on board. As we glide silently up the Bosphorus, listening to the unearthly chorus of the baying wild-dogs answering each other from Pera to Stamboul, Manners produces a revolver from his breast-pocket, and passing his finger along the barrel shining in the starlight, observes, "Four of us, and five *here*, make nine. If the gate is only unlocked, we can carry the place by storm."

CHAPTER XXXV
"THE WOLF AND THE LAMB"

Papoosh Pasha is taking his *kief*[#] in his harem. Two softly shaded lamps, burning perfumed oil, shed a voluptuous light over the apartment. Rich carpets from the looms of Persia are spread upon the floor; costly shawls from Northern India fall in graceful folds over the low divan on which he reclines. Jewel-hilted sabres, silver-sheathed daggers, and firearms inlaid with gold, glitter above his head, disposed tastefully against the walls, and marking the warlike character of the owner; for Papoosh Pasha, cruel, sensual, and corrupt to the very marrow, is nevertheless as brave as a lion.

[#] Repose.

Two *nautch-girls* belonging to his seraglio have been dancing their voluptuous measure for his gratification. As they stand now unveiled, panting and glowing with their exertions, the rich Eastern blood crimsoning their soft cheeks, and coursing wildly through their shapely, pliant limbs, the old man's face assumes a placid expression of content only belied by the gleam in that wicked eye, and he is good enough to wave his amber-tipped pipe-stick in token of dismissal, and to express his approbation by the single word "*Peki*" (very well). The girls prostrate themselves before their lord, their silver armlets and anklets ringing as they touch the floor, and bounding away like two young antelopes, flit from the presence, apparently not unwilling to escape so easily. Papoosh Pasha is left alone with the favourite; but the favourite looks restless and preoccupied, and glances ever and anon towards the casement which opens out into the garden of the seraglio, now beginning to glisten in the light of the rising moon, and breathing the odours of a thousand flowers, heavy and fragrant with the dews of night. This part of the harem is on the ground floor, and is a retreat much affected by his Highness for the facility with which the breeze steals into it from the Bosphorus.

Zuleika is dressed in all the magnificence of her richest Oriental costume. Her tiny feet, arched in true Arabian symmetry, are bare to the ankle, where her voluminous muslin trousers are gathered in by a bracelet, or more correctly an anklet, set with rubies and emeralds. A string of beads of the purest lemon-coloured amber marks the outlines of her slender waist, and terminates a short, close-fitting jacket of pink satin, embroidered with seed-pearls, open at the bosom, and with long sleeves fringed by lace of European manufacture. This again is covered by a large loose mantle of *green* silk, carelessly thrown over the whole figure. Zuleika has not forgotten that she is lineally descended from the Prophet, and wears his colour accordingly. Her hands, in compliance with Eastern custom, are dyed with *henna*, but even this horrid practice cannot disguise the symmetry of her tapered fingers; and although the hair is cut short on her left temple, the long raven locks from the other side are gathered and plaited into a lustrous diadem around her brows. She has pencilled her lower eyelashes with some dark substance that enhances their natural beauty, but even this effort of the toilette has not succeeded in imparting the languishing expression which a Turkish beauty deems so irresistible. No; the gleam in Zuleika's eye is more that of some wild animal, caught but not tamed glancing eagerly around for a chance of escape, and ready to tear the hand that would caress it and endeavour to reconcile it to its fetters.

She does not look as if she loved you, Papoosh Pasha, when you order her to your feet, and stroke her hair with your fat hand, and gloat on that mournful, eager face with your little twinkling eye. Better be a bachelor, Papoosh Pasha, and confine yourself to the solace of coffee and pipes, and busy your cunning intellect with those puzzling European politics, and look after the interests of your dissipated master the Sultan, than take a wild bird to your bosom that will never know you or care for you, or cease to pine and fret, and beat her breast against the bars of the cage in which you have shut her up.

The old man sinks back upon his cushions with a sigh of corporeal contentment. His fat person is enveloped in a flowing shawl-gown, which admits of his breathing far more freely than does that miserable tight frock-coat he wore all day. He has gorged himself with an enormous meal, chiefly composed of fat substances, vegetables, and sweetmeats. He has had his tiny measure of hot strong coffee, and is puffing forth volumes of smoke from a long cherry-stick pipe. He bids Zuleika kneel at his feet and sing him to his rest. The girl glances eagerly towards the window, and seems to listen; she dare not move at once to the casement and look out, for her lord is mistrustful and suspicious, and woe to her if she excites his jealousy to such a pitch that she cannot lull it to sleep again. She would give him an opiate if she dared, or something stronger still, that should settle all accounts; but there is a dark story in the harem of a former favourite--a Circassian--who tried to strike the same path for freedom, and failed in the attempt. She has long slept peacefully some forty fathom deep in the sparkling Bosphorus, and the caïques that take her former comrades to the Sweet-Waters glide along over her head without disturbing her repose. Since then, whenever Papoosh Pasha drinks in the women's apartment, he has the gallantry to insist on a lady pledging him first before he puts his own fat lips to the bowl.

"Come hither, Zuleika, little dove," says the old man, drawing her towards him; "light of my eyes and pearl of my heart, come hither that I may lay my head on thy bosom, and sleep to the soft murmurings of thy gentle voice."

The girl obeys, but glances once more uneasily towards the window, and takes her place with compressed lips, and cheeks as pale as death. A long Albanian dagger, the spoil of some lawless chief, hangs temptingly within arm's length. Another such caress as that, Papoosh Pasha, and who shall ensure you that she does not bury it in your heart!

But a more feminine weapon is in her hand--a three-stringed lute or gittern, incapable of producing much harmony, but nevertheless affording a plaintive and not inappropriate accompaniment to the measured chant with which the reigning Odalisque lulls her master to his rest. The tones of her voice are very wild and sad. Ever and anon she stops in her music and listens to the breathing of the Pasha; so surely he opens his eyes, and raising his head from her lap bids her go on,--not angrily nor petulantly, but with a quiet overbearing malice that irritates the free spirit of the girl to the quick. She strikes the gittern with no unskilful hand; and although her voice is mournful, it is sweet and musical as she sings; but the glance of her eye denotes mischief, and I had rather be sleeping over a powder magazine with my lighted chibouque in my mouth, than pillow my head, as you are doing, Papoosh Pasha, on the lap of a woman maddened by tyranny and imprisonment,--her whole being filled with but two feelings--Love stronger than death; Hatred fiercer than hell. And this is the caged bird's song:--

Down in the valley where the Sweet-Waters meet--where the Sweet-Waters meet under the chestnut trees,--

There Hamed had a garden; and the wild bird sang to the Rose.

In the garden were many flowers, and the pomegranate grew in the midst. Fair and stately she grew, and the fruit from her branches dropped like dew upon the sward.

And Hamed watered the tree and pruned her, and lay down in the cool freshness of her shade.

Beautiful was the pomegranate, yet the wild bird sang to the Rose.

The Lily bent lowly to the earth, and drooped for very shame, because the breeze courted the Lily and kissed her as he swept by to meet the Sweet-Waters under the chestnut trees.

For the Lily was the fairest of flowers; yet the wild bird sang to the Rose.

Then there came a blast from the desert, and the garden of Hamed was scorched and withered up;

And the pomegranate sickened and died; and Hamed cut her down by the roots, and sowed corn over the place of her shade.

And the breeze swept on, and stayed not, though the Lily lay trampled into the earth.

Every flower sickened and died; yet the wild bird sang to the Rose.

In the dawn of early morning, when the sky is green with longing, and the day is at hand,

When the winds are hushed, and the waters sleep smiling, and the stars are dim in the sky:

When she pines for his coming, and spreads her petals to meet him, and droops to hear his note;

When the garden gate is open, and the watchers are asleep, and the last, *last* hope is dying,--will the wild bird come to the Rose?

The concluding lines she sang in a marked voice there was no mistaking, and I doubt if they did not thrill to the heart's core of more than one listener.

The moon had now fairly risen, and silvered the trees and shrubs in the harem garden with her light, leaving, however, dense masses of shade athwart the smooth lawn and under the walls of the building. Cypress and cedar quivered in her beams. Not a breath of air stirred the feathery leaves of the tall acacia, with its glistening stem; and the swelling ripple of the Bosphorus plashed drowsily against the marble steps. All was peace and silence and repose. Far enough off to elude observation, yet within hail, lay our caïque, poised buoyantly on the waters, and cutting with its dark outline right athwart a glittering pathway as of molten gold. Close under the harem window, concealed by the thick foliage of a broad-leaved creeper, Ali Mesrour and myself crouched, silent and anxious, scarce daring to breathe, counting with sickening eagerness the precious moments that were fleeting by, so tedious yet so soon past. Twenty paces farther off, under a dark group of cypresses, lay Ropsley and Manners ready for action, the latter with his hand in his bosom caressing the trusty revolver by which he set such store.

Everything had as yet gone off prosperously. We had landed noiseless and unobserved. The garden gate, thanks to woman's foresight and woman's cunning, had been left open. The sentry on guard, like all other Turkish sentries when not before an enemy, had lain down, enveloped in his great-coat, with his musket by his side, and was snoring as only a true son of Osman can snore after a bellyful of *pilaff*. If his lord would but follow his example, it might be done; yet never was old man so restless, so ill at ease, so wakefully disposed as seemed Papoosh Pasha.

We could see right into the apartment, and the rich soft lamplight brought out in full relief the faces and figures of its two occupants. Zuleika sat with her feet gathered under her on the divan: one hand still held the lute; the other was unwillingly consigned to the caresses of her lord. The old man's head reclined against her bosom; his parted lips betokened rest and enjoyment; his eyes were half closed, yet there was a gleam of vigilant malice upon his features that denoted anything but sleep. The poor girl's face alternated from a scowl of withering hatred to a plaintive expression of heart-broken disappointment. Doubtless she was thinking "the last, *last* hope is dying, and the wild bird is not coming to the rose."

Ali Mesrour gazed on her he loved. If ever there was a trying situation, it was his--to see her even now in the very embrace of his enemy--so near, yet so apart. Few men could have enough preserved their self-command not to betray even by the workings of the countenance what a storm of feelings must be wasting the heart; yet the Beloochee moved not a muscle; his profile, turned towards me, was calm and grim as that of a statue. Once only the right hand crept stealthily towards his dagger, but the next moment he was again as still as death. The Pasha whispered something in the girl's ear, and a gleam of wild delight sparkled on her face as she listened. She rose cheerfully, left the room with a rapid, springing step, and returned almost immediately with a flask under her arm, and a huge goblet set with precious stones in her hand. Papoosh Pasha, true believer and faithful servant of the Prophet, it needs not the aid of a metal-covered cork, secured with wire, to enable us to guess at the contents of that Frankish flask. No sherbet of roses is poured into your brimming goblet--no harmless, unfermented liquor, flavoured with cinnamon or other lawful condiment; but the creaming flood of amber-coloured champagne whirls up to the very margin, and the Pasha's eye brightens with satisfaction as he stretches forth his hand to grasp its taper stem. Cunning and careful though, even in his debauches, he proffers the cup to Zuleika ere he tastes.

"Drink, my child," says the old hypocrite, "drink of the liquid such as the houris are keeping in Paradise for the souls of the true believers; drink and fear not--it is lawful. *Allah Kerim!*"

Zuleika wets her lips on the edge, and hands the cup to her lord, who drains it to the dregs, and sets it down with a sigh of intense satisfaction.

"It is lawful," he continues, wiping his moustaches. "It is not forbidden by the blessed Prophet. Wine indeed is prohibited to the true believer, but the Prophet knew not the flavour of champagne, and had he tasted it, he would have enjoined his servants to drink it four times a day. Fill again, Zuleika, oh my soul! Fill again! There is but one Allah!"

The girl needs no second bidding; once and again she fills to the brim; once and again the Pasha drains the tempting draught; and now the little twinkling eye dims, the cherry-stick falls from the opening fingers, the Pasha's head sinks upon Zuleika's bosom, and at last he is fast asleep. Gently, tenderly, like a mother soothing a child, she hushes him to his rest. Stealthily, slowly she transfers his head from her own breast to the embroidered cushions. Dexterously, noiselessly, see extricates herself from his embrace. A low whistle, scarcely perceptible, reaches her ear from the garden, and calls the blood into her cheek; and yet, a very woman even now, she turns to take one last look at him whom she is leaving for ever. A cool air steals in from the window, and plays upon the sleeper's open neck and throat. She draws a shawl carefully, nay, caressingly, around him. Brute, tyrant, enemy though he is, yet there have been moments when he was kindly and indulgent towards her, for she was his favourite; and she will not leave him in anger at the last. Fatal delay! mistaken tenderness! true woman! always influenced by her feelings at the wrong time! What did that moment's weakness cost us all? She had crossed the room--we were ready to receive her--her foot was on the very window-sill; another moment and she would have been in Ali's arms, when a footstep was heard rapidly approaching up the street, a black figure came bounding over the garden wall, closely followed by a large English retriever, and shouting an alarm wildly at the top of his voice. As the confused sentry fired off his musket in the air; as the Pasha's guards and retainers woke and sprang to their arms; as the Beloochee glared wildly around him; as Ropsley, no longer uninterested, swore volubly in English, and Manners drew the revolver from his bosom, Bold, for the second time that day, pinned a tall negro slave by the throat, and rolling him over and over on the sward, made as though he would have worried him to death in the garden.

It was, however, too late; the alarm was given, and all was discovered. The man I had struck in the afternoon of that very day had dogged me ever since, in hopes of an opportunity to revenge himself. He had followed me from place to place, overheard my conversation, and watched all those to whom I spoke. He had crouched under the sentry-box at the door of Messirie's hotel, had tracked us at a safe distance down to the very water's edge, and had seen us embark on our mysterious expedition. With the cunning of his race, he guessed at once at our object, and determined to frustrate it. Unable, I conclude, at that late hour to get a caïque, he had hastened by land to his master's house, and, as the event turned out, had arrived in time to overthrow all our plans. He was followed in his turn by my faithful Bold, who, when so peremptorily ordered to leave us, had been convinced there was something in the wind, and accordingly transferred his attentions to the figure that had been his object of distrust the live-long day. How he worried and tore at him, and refused to relinquish his hold. Alas! alas! it was too late--too late!

The Pasha sprang like a lion from his lair. At the same instant, Ali Mesrour and myself bounded lightly through the open window into the apartment. Zuleika flung herself with a loud shriek into her lover's arms. Manners and Ropsley came crowding in behind us, the former's revolver gleaming ominously in the light. The Pasha was surrounded by his enemies, but he never faltered for an instant. Hurrying feet and the clash of arms resounded along the passages; lights were already twinkling in the garden; aid was at hand, and, Turk, tyrant, voluptuary though he was, he lacked not the courage, the promptitude which aids itself. At a glance he must have recognised Ali; or it might have been but the instinct of his nation which bid him defend his women. Quick as thought, he seized a pistol that hung above his couch, and discharged it point-blank at the Beloochee's body. The bullet sped past Zuleika's head and lodged deep in her lover's bosom. At the same instant that Ropsley, always cool and collected in an emergency, dashed down both the lamps, Ali's body lurched heavily into my arms, and poor Zuleika fell senseless on the floor.

The next moment a glare of light filled the apartment. Crowds of slaves, black and white, all armed to the teeth, rushed in to the rescue. The Pasha, perfectly composed, ordered them to seize and make us prisoners. Encumbered by the Beloochee's weight, and outnumbered ten to one, we were put to it to make good our retreat, and ere we could close round her and carry her off, two stout negroes had borne the still senseless Zuleika through the open doorway into the inner chambers of the palace. Placing the Beloochee between myself and Ropsley, we backed leisurely into the garden, the poor fellow groaning heavily as we handed him through the casement, and so made our way, still fronting the Pasha and his myrmidons, towards our caïque, which at the first signal of disturbance had been pulled rapidly in shore. Manners covered our retreat with great steadiness and gallantry, keeping the enemy at bay with his revolver, a weapon with which one and all showed much disinclination to make further acquaintance. By this time shrieks of women pervaded the palace. The blacks, too, jabbered and gesticulated with considerably more energy than purpose, half-a-dozen pistol shots fired at random served to increase the general confusion, which even their lord's presence and authority were completely powerless to quell, and thus we were enabled to reach our boat, and shove off with our ghastly freight into the comparative safety of the Bosphorus.

"He will never want a doctor more," said Ropsley, in answer to an observation from Manners, as, turning down the edge of the Beloochee's jacket, he showed us the round livid mark that, to a practised eye, told too surely of the irremediable death-wound. "Poor fellow, poor fellow," he added, "he is bleeding inwardly now, he will be dead before we reach the bridge."

Ali opened his eyes, and raising his head, looked around as though in search of some missing face.

"Zuleika," he whispered, "Zuleika!" and sank back again with a piteous expression of hopeless, helpless misery on his wan and ghastly features. The end was obviously near at hand, his cheeks seemed to have fallen in the last few minutes, dark circles gathered round his eyes, his forehead was damp and clammy, and there was a light froth upon his ashy lips. Yet as death approached he seemed to recover strength and consciousness; a true Mussulman, the grave had for him but few terrors, and he had confronted the grim monarch so often as not to wince from him at last when really within his grasp.

He reared himself in the boat, and supported by my arm, which was wound round his body, made shift to sit upright and look about him, wildly, dreamily, as one who looks for the last time. "Effendi," he gasped, pressing my hand, "Effendi, it is destiny. The good mare--she is my brother's! Oh, Zuleika! Zuleika!"

A strong shudder convulsed his frame, his jaw dropped, I thought he was gone, but he recovered consciousness once more, snatched wildly at his sword, which he half drew, and whispering faintly, "Turn me to the East! There is but one Allah!" his limbs collapsed--his head sunk upon my shoulder--and so he died.

Row gently, brawny watermen, though your freight is indeed but the shell which contained even now a gallant, faithful spirit. One short hour ago, who so determined, so brave, so sagacious as the Beloochee warrior? and where is he now? That is not Ali Mesrour whom you are wafting so sadly, so smoothly towards the shore. Ali Mesrour is far away in space, in the material Paradise of your own creed, with its inexhaustible sherbets, and its cool gardens, and its dark-eyed maidens waving their green scarfs to greet the long-expected lover; or to the unknown region, the shadowy spirit-land of a loftier, nobler faith, the mystical world on which Religion herself dare hardly speculate, where "the tree shall be known by its fruits," "where the wicked cease from troubling, and the weary are at rest."

So we carried him reverently and mournfully to the house he had occupied; and we laid him out in his warrior dress, with his arms by his side and his lance in his hand, and ere the morrow's sun was midway in the heavens, the earth had closed over him in his last resting-place, where the dark cypresses are nodding and whispering over his tomb, and the breeze steals gently up from the golden Bosphorus, smiling and radiant, within a hundred paces of his grave.

The good bay mare has never left my possession. For months she was restless and uncomfortable, neighing at every strange step, and refusing her food, as if she pined truly and faithfully for her master. He came not, and after a time she forgot him; and another hand fed and cared for her, and she grew sleek and fat and light-hearted. What would you? It is a world of change. Men and women, friends and favourites, lovers and beloved, all must forget and float with the stream and hurry on; if there be an exception- -if some pale-eyed mourner, clinging to the bank, yearns hopelessly for the irrevocable Past, what matter, so the stream can eddy round him, and laugh and ripple by? Let him alone! he is not one of us. God forbid!

Of Zuleika's fate I shudder to think. Though I might well guess she could never expect to be forgiven, it was long before surmise approached certainty, and even now I strive to hope against hope, to persuade myself that there may still be a chance. At least I am thankful Ali was spared the ghastly tidings that eventually came to my ears--a tale that escaped the lips of a drunken caïgee, and in which I fear there is too much truth.

Of course the attack on the Pasha's palace created much scandal throughout Constantinople; and equally of course, a thousand rumours gained credence as to the origin and object of the disturbance. The English officers concerned received a hint that it would be advisable to get out of the way as speedily as possible; and I was compelled to absent myself for a time from my kind friend and patron, Omar Pasha. One person set the whole thing down as a drunken frolic; another voted it an attempt at burglary of the most ruffian-like description; and the Turks themselves seemed inclined to resent it as a gratuitous insult to their prejudices and customs. A stalwart caïgee, however, being, contrary to his religion and his practice, inebriated with strong drink, let out in his cups that, if he dared, he could tell more than others knew about the attack on the palace of Papoosh Pasha, and its sequel. Influenced by a large bribe, and intimidated by threats, he at length made the following statement:--"That the evening after the attack, about sun-down, he was plying off the steps of Papoosh Pasha's palace; that he was hailed by a negro guard, who bade him approach the landing-place; that two other negroes then appeared, bearing between them a sack, carefully secured, and obviously containing something weighty; that they placed it carefully in the bottom of his caïque, and that more than once he distinctly saw it move; that they desired him to pull out into mid-stream, and when there, dropped the sack overboard; that it sunk immediately, but that he fancied he heard a faint shriek as it went down, and saw the bubbles plainly coming up for several seconds at the place where it disappeared; further, that the negro gave him fifty piastres over his proper fare for the job, and that he himself had been uncomfortable and troubled with bad dreams ever since."

Alas, poor Zuleika! there is but little hope that you survived your lover four-and-twenty hours. The wild bird came, indeed, as he had promised, in the early morning, to the rose, but the wild bird got his death-wound; and the rose, I fear, lies many a fathom deep in the clear, cold waters of the silent Bosphorus.

CHAPTER XXXVI
"THE FRONT"

Man has been variously defined by philosophers as a cooking animal (the truth of this definition, unless when applied to our Gallic neighbours, I stoutly contest), as a reasoning animal (this likewise will hardly hold water), as a self-clothing animal, as an omnivorous one, as an unfeathered biped, and as an improved specimen of the order of Simiæ without the tail! None of these definitions will I accept as expressing exactly the conditions and necessities of our species. I believe man to be an animal fed on excitement-- the only one in creation that without that pabulum, in some shape or another, languishes, becomes torpid, and loses its noblest energies both of mind and body. Why do men drink, quarrel, gamble, and waste their substance in riotous living? Why does Satan, according to good Dr. Watts, always provide work "for idle hands to do"? Why, but because man *must* have excitement. If he have no safety-valve for his surplus energies in the labour which earns his daily bread, they will find vent through some other channel, either for good or evil, according to his bias one way or the other. There is no such thing as repose on the face of the earth; "push on--keep moving," such is the motto of humanity. If we are not making we must be marring, but we cannot sit still. How else do we account for the proverbial restlessness of the sailor when he has been a few weeks ashore? How else can we conceive it possible for a rational being, whilst enjoying the luxuries and liberty of a landsman's existence, to pine for the hardships, the restraint, the utter discomfort which every one must necessarily experience on board ship? How, except upon this principle, can we understand the charm of a soldier's life, the cheering influence of a campaign? It is most unnatural to like rigid discipline, short rations, constant anxiety, and unremitting toil. A wet great-coat on the damp earth is a bad substitute for a four-post bed, with thick blankets, and clean sheets not innocent of the warming-pan. A tent is a miserable dwelling-place at the best of times, and is only just preferable to the canopy of heaven in very hot or very cold, or very windy or very wet weather. There is small amusement in spending the livelong night in sleepless watching for an enemy, and little satisfaction in being surprised by the same about an hour before dawn. It is annoying to be starved, it is irritating to be frightened, it is uncomfortable to be shot,--yet are all these casualties more or less incidental to the profession of arms; and still the recruiting sergeant flaunts his bunch of ribbons in every market town throughout merry England, and still the bumpkin takes the shilling, and sings in beery strains, "Huzza for the life of a soldier!"

And I too had tasted of the fierce excitement of strife--had drunk of the stimulating draught which, like some bitter tonic, creates a constant craving for more--had been taught by the influence of custom and companionship to loathe the quiet dreamy existence which was my normal state, and to long for the thrill of danger, the variety and unholy revelry of war.

So I returned with Ropsley to the Crimea. I had small difficulty in obtaining leave from Omar Pasha to resign, at least for a time, my appointment on his personal staff.

"They are queer fellows, my adopted countrymen," said his Highness, in his dry, humorous manner, and with his quaint smile, "and the sooner you get out of the way, friend Egerton, the better. I shall be asked all sorts of questions about you myself; and if you stay here, why, the nights are dark and the streets are narrow. Some fine morning it might be difficult to wake you, and nobody would be a bit the wiser. Our Turk has his peculiar notions about the laws of honour, and he cannot be made to comprehend why he should risk his own life in taking yours. Besides, he is ridiculously sensitive about his women, particularly with a Christian. Had you been a good Mussulman, now, Egerton, it could have been easily arranged. You might have bought the lady, got drunk on champagne with old Papoosh Pasha, and set up a harem of your own. Why don't you become a convert, as I did? The process is short, the faith simple, the practice satisfactory. Think it over, my good Interpreter, think it over. Bah! in ten minutes you would be as good a Mussulman as I am, and better." And his Highness laughed, and bid me "Good-bye," for he had a good deal upon his hands just then, being on the eve of marriage with his *fifth* wife, a young lady twelve years of age, daughter to his Imperial Majesty the Sultan, and bringing her husband a magnificent dowry of jewels, gold, and horses, in addition to many broad and fertile acres in Anatolia, not to mention a beautiful kiosk near Scutari and a stately palace on the Bosphorus, without which adventitious advantages she might perhaps have hardly succeeded in winning the heart of so experienced a warrior as Omar Pasha.

Thus it was that I found myself one broiling sunny morning leaning over the side of a transport, just then dropping her anchor in Balaklava Bay.

The scorching rocks frowned down on the scorching sea; the very planks on the deck glistened with the heat. There was no shade on land, and not a breath of air ruffled the shining bosom of the water. The harbour was full, ay, choked with craft of every rig and every tonnage; whilst long, wicked-looking steamers and huge, unwieldy troop-ships dotted the surface of the land-locked bay. The union-jack trailed idly over our stern, the men were all on deck, gazing with eager faces on that shore which combined for *them* the realities of history with the fascinations of romance. Young soldiers were they, mostly striplings of eighteen and twenty summers, with the smooth cheeks, fresh colour, and stalwart limbs of the Anglo-Saxon race--too good to fill a trench! And yet what would be the fate of at least two-thirds of that keen, light-hearted draft? *Vestigia nulla retrorsum.* Many a time has it made my heart ache to see a troop-ship ploughing relentlessly onward with her living freight to "the front,"--many a time have I recalled Æsop's fable, and the foot-prints that were all *towards* the lion's den,--many a time have I thought how every unit there in red was himself the centre of a little world at home; and of the grey heads that would tremble, and the loving faces that would pale in peaceful villages far away in England, when no news came from foreign parts of "our John," or when the unrelenting *Gazette* arrived at last and proclaimed, as too surely it would, that he was coming back "never, never no more."

Boom!--there it is again! Every eye lightens at that dull, distant sound. Every man's pulse beats quicker, and his head towers more erect, for he feels that he has arrived at the *real thing* at last. No sham fighting is going on over yonder, not two short leagues from where he stands--no mock bivouac at Chobham, nor practice in Woolwich Marshes, nor meaningless pageant in the Park: that iron voice carries *death* upon its every accent. For those in the trenches it is a mere echo--the unregarded consequence that necessarily succeeds the fierce rush of a round-shot or the wicked whistle of a shell; but for us here at Balaklava it is one of the pulsations of England's life-blood--one of the ticks, so to speak, of that great Clock of Doom which points ominously to the downfall of the beleaguered town.

Boom! Yes, there it is again; you cannot forget why you are here. Day and night, sunshine and storm, scarce five minutes elapse in the twenty-four hours without reminding you of the work in hand. You ride out from the camp for your afternoon exercise, you go down to Balaklava to buy provisions, or you canter over to the monastery at St. George's to visit a sick comrade--the iron voice tolls on. In the glare of noon, when everything else seems drowsy in the heat, and the men lie down exhausted in the suffocating trenches--the iron voice tolls on. In the calm of evening, when the breeze is hushed and still, and the violet sea is sleeping in the twilight--the iron voice tolls on. So when the flowers are opening in the morning, and the birds begin to sing, and reviving nature, fresh and dewy, seems to scatter health and peace and good-will over the earth--the iron voice tolls on. Nay, when you wake at midnight in your tent from a dream of your far-away home-- oh! what a different scene to this!--tired as you may be, ere you have turned to sleep once more, you hear it again. Yes, at midnight as at noon, at morn as at evening, every day and all day long, Death is gathering his harvest--and the iron voice tolls on.

"Very slack fire they seem to be keeping up in the front," yawns out Ropsley, who has just joined me on deck, and to whom the siege and all its accessories are indeed nothing new. Many a long and weary month has he been listening to that sound; and what with his own ideas on the subject, and the information a naturally acute intellect has acquired touching the proceedings of the besiegers, his is indeed a familiarity which "breeds contempt."

"Any news from the camp?" he shouts out to a middy in a man-of-war's boat passing under our stern. The middy, a thorough specimen of an English boy, with his round laughing face and short jacket, stands up to reply.

"Another sortie! No end of fellows killed; and *they say* the Malakhoff is blown up."

Our young soldiers listen eagerly to the news. They have heard and read of the Malakhoff for many a day, and though their ideas of the nature and appearance of that work are probably of a somewhat confused description, they are all athirst for intelligence, and prepared to swallow everything connected with the destruction of that or any other of the defences with a faith that is, to say the least of it, a sad temptation to the laughter-loving informant.

A middy, though from some organic cause of which I am ignorant, is always restless and impatient towards the hour of noon; and our friend plumps down once more in the stern of his gig, and bids his men "give way"; for the sun is by this time high in the heavens; so we take our places in the ship's boat which our own captain politely provides for us, and avoiding the confusion of a disembarkation of men and stores, Ropsley, Bold, and I leap ashore at Balaklava, unencumbered save by the slender allowance of luggage which a campaign teaches the most luxurious to deem sufficient.

Ashore at Balaklava! What a scene of hurry and crowding and general confusion it is! Were it not that every second individual is in uniform and bearded to the waist, it would appear more like the mart of some peaceful and commercial sea-port, than the threshold of a stage on which is being fought out to the death one of the fiercest and most obstinate struggles which History has to record on her blood-stained pages. There are no women, yet the din of tongues is perfectly deafening. Hurrying to and fro, doing as little work with as much labour as possible, making immense haste with small speed, and vociferating incessantly at the top of their voices, Turks and Tartars, Armenians, Greeks, and Ionians, all accosted by the burly English soldier under the generic name of "Johnny," are flitting aimlessly about, and wasting her Majesty's stores in a manner that would have driven the late Mr. Hume frantic. Here a trim sergeant of infantry, clean and orderly, despite his war-worn looks and patched garments, drives before him a couple of swarthy nondescripts, clad in frieze, and with wild elf-locks protruding over their jutting foreheads, and twinkling Tartar eyes. They stagger under huge sacks of meal, which they are carrying to yonder storehouse, with a sentry pacing his short walk at the door. The sacks have been furnished by contract, so the seams are badly sewn; and the meal, likewise furnished by contract, and of inferior quality, is rapidly escaping, to leave a white track in the mud, also a contract article, and of the deepest, stickiest, and most enduring quality. The labours of the two porters will be much lightened ere they reach their destination; but this is of less moment, inasmuch as the storehouse to which they are proceeding is by no means watertight, and the first thunderstorm that sweeps in from the Black Sea is likely much to damage its contents. It is needless to add that this edifice of thin deal planks has been constructed by contract for the use of her Majesty's Government.

A little farther on, a train of mules, guided by a motley crowd of every nation under heaven, and commanded by an officer in the workmanlike uniform of the Land Transport, is winding slowly up the hill. They have emerged from a perfect sea of mud, which even at this dry season shows not the least tendency to harden into consistency, and they will probably arrive at the front in about four hours, with the loss of a third only of their cargo, consisting of sundry munitions which were indispensable last week, and might have been of service the day before yesterday, but the occasion for which has now passed away for ever.

A staff officer on a short sturdy pony gallops hastily by, exchanging a nod as he passes with a beardless cornet of dragoons, whose English charger presents a curious study of the anatomy of a horse. He pulls up for an instant to speak to Ropsley, and the latter turns to me and says--

"Not so bad as I feared, Vere. It was a mere sortie, after all, and we drove them back very handsomely, with small loss on our side. The only officer killed was young ----, and he was dying, poor fellow! at any rate, of dysentery."

This is the news of the day here, and the trenches form just such a subject of conversation before Sebastopol as does the weather in a country-house in England--a topic never new, but never entirely worn out.

Side by side, Ropsley and myself are journeying up the hill towards the front. A sturdy batman has been in daily expectation of his master's return, and has brought his horses down to meet him. It is indeed a comfort to be again in an English saddle--to have the lengthy, powerful frame of an English horse under one--and to hear the homely, honest accents of a *provincial* English tongue. When a man has been long amongst foreigners, and especially serving with foreign troops, it is like being at home again to be once more within the lines of a British army; and to add to the pleasure of our ride, although the day is cloudless and insufferably hot in the valleys, there is a fresh breeze up here, and a pure bracing air that reaches us from the heights on which the army is encamped.

It is a wild, picturesque scene, not beautiful, yet full of interest and incident. Behind us lies Balaklava, with its thronging harbour and its busy crowds, whose hum reaches us even here, high above the din. It is like looking down on an ant-hill to watch the movements of the shifting swarm.

On our right, the plain, stretching far and wide, is dotted with the Land Transport--that necessary evil so essential to the very existence of an army; and their clustering wagons and scattered beasts carry the eye onwards to a dim white line formed by the neat tents and orderly encampment of the flower of French cavalry, the gallant and dashing Chasseurs d'Afrique.

On our left, the stable call of an English regiment of Light Dragoons reaches us from the valley of Kadikoi, that Crimean Newmarket, the doings of which are actually chronicled in *Bell's Life*! Certainly an Englishman's nationality is not to be rooted out of him even in the jaws of death. But we have little time to visit the race-course or the lines--to pass our comments on the condition of the troopers, or gaze open-mouthed at the wondrous field-batteries that occupy an adjoining encampment--moved by teams of twelve horses each, perhaps the finest animals of the class to be seen in Europe, with every accessory of carriage, harness, and appointments, so perfect as not to admit of improvement, yet, I believe, not found to answer in actual warfare. Our interest is more awakened by another scene. We are on classic ground now, for we have reached the spot whence

> Into the valley of death
>
> Rode the six hundred!

Yes, stretching down from our very feet lies that mile-and-a-half gallop which witnessed the boldest deed of chivalry performed in ancient or modern times. Well might the French general exclaim, *"C'est magnifique!"* although he added, significantly, *"mais ce n'est pas la guerre."* The latter part of his observation is a subject for discussion, but of the former there is and there can be but one opinion. *Magnifique* indeed it must have been to see six hundred horsemen ride gallantly down to almost certain death--every heart beating equally high, every sword striking equally hard and true.

> Groom fought like noble, squire like knight,
>
> As fearlessly and well.

Not a child in England at this day but knows, as if he had been there, the immortal battle of Balaklava. It is needless to describe its situation, to dwell upon the position they were ordered to carry, or the fire that poured in upon front, flanks, ay, and rear, of the attacking force. This is all matter of history; but as the valley stretched beneath us, fresh, green, and smiling peacefully in the sun, it required but little imagination to call up the stirring scene of which it had been the stage. Here was the very ground on which the Light Brigade were drawn up; every charger quivering with excitement, every eye flashing, every lip compressed with the sense of coming danger. A staff officer rides up to the leader, and communicates an order. There is an instant's pause. Question and reply pass like lightning, and the aide-de-camp points to a dark, grim mass of artillery bristling far away down yonder in the front. Men's hearts stop beating, and many a bold cheek turns pale, for there is more excitement in uncertainty than in actual danger. The leader draws his sword, and faces flush, and hearts beat high once more. Clear and sonorous is his voice as he gives the well-known word; gallant and chivalrous his bearing as he takes his place--that place of privilege--*in front-* -*"Noblesse oblige"* and can he be otherwise than gallant and chivalrous and devoted, for is he not a *gentleman?* and yet, to the honour of our countrymen be it spoken, not a man of that six hundred, of any rank, but was as gallant and chivalrous and devoted as he--he has said so himself a hundred times.

So the word is given, and the squadron leaders take it up, and the Light Brigade advances at a gallop; and a deadly grasp is on the sword, and the charger feels his rider's energy as he grips him with his knees, and holding him hard by the head urges him resolutely forward--to death!

And now they cross the line of fire: shot through the heart, an aide-de-camp falls headlong from the saddle, and his loose horse gallops on, wild and masterless, and wheels in upon the flank, and joins the squadron once more. It has begun now. Man upon man, horse upon horse, are shot down and rolled over; yet the survivors close in, sterner, bolder, fiercer than before, and still the death-ride sweeps on.

"Steady, men--forward!" shouts a chivalrous squadron leader, as he waves his glittering sword above his head, and points towards the foe.

Clear and cheerful rings his voice above the tramp of horses and the rattle of small-arms and the deadly roar of artillery. He is a model of beauty, youth, and gallantry--the admired of men, the darling of women, the hope of his house.--Do not look again.--A round-shot has taken man and horse; he is lying rolled up with his charger, a confused and ghastly mass. Forward! the squadron has passed over him, and still the death-ride sweeps on.

The gaps are awful now, the men told off by threes look in vain for the familiar face at right or left; every trooper feels that he must depend on himself and the good horse under him, but there is no wavering. Officers begin to have misgivings as to the result, but there is no hesitation. All know they are galloping to destruction, yet not a heart fails, not a rein is turned. Few, very few are they by this time, and still the death-ride sweeps on. They disappear in that rolling sulphurous cloud, the portal of another world; begrimed with smoke, ghastly with wounds, comrade cannot recognise comrade, and officers look wildly round for their men; but the guns are still before them--the object is not yet attained--the enemy awaits them steadily behind his gabions, and the fire from his batteries is mowing them down like grass. If but one man is left, that one will still press forward: and now they are on their prey. A tremendous roar of artillery shakes the air. Mingled with the clash of swords and the plunge of horses, oath, prayer, and death-shriek fly to heaven. The batteries are reached and carried. The death-ride sweeps over them, and it is time to return.

"The batteries are reached and carried." The Interpreter

In twos, and threes, and single files, the few survivors stagger back to the ground, from whence, a few short minutes ago, a gallant band had advanced in so trim, so orderly, so soldier-like a line.

The object has been attained, but at what a sacrifice? Look at yon stalwart trooper sinking on his saddle-bow, sick with his death-hurt, his head drooping on his bosom, his sword hanging idly in his paralysed right hand, his failing charger, wounded and feeble, nobly bearing his master to safety ere he falls to rise no more. The soldier's eye brightens for an instant as he hears the cheer of the Heavy Brigade completing the work he has pawned his life to begin. Soon that eye will glaze and close for ever. Men look round for those they knew and loved, and fear to ask for the comrade who is down, stiff and stark, under those dismounted guns and devastated batteries; horses come galloping in without riders; here and there a dismounted dragoon crawls feebly back to join the remnants of what was once his squadron, and by degrees the few survivors get together and form something like an ordered body once more. It is better not to count them, they are so few, so *very* few. Weep, England, for thy chivalry! mourn and wring thy hands for that disastrous day; but smile with pride through thy tears, thrill with exultation in thy sorrow, to think of the sons thou canst boast, of the deed of arms done by them in that valley before the eyes of gathered nations--of the immortal six hundred--thy children, every man of them, that rode the glorious death-ride of Balaklava!

"That was a stupid business," observed Ropsley, as he brought his horse alongside of mine, and pointed down the valley; "quite a mistake from beginning to end. What a licking we deserved to get, and what a licking we *should* have got if our dragoons were not the only cavalry in the world that will *ride straight!*"

"And yet what a glorious day!" I exclaimed, for the wild cheer of a charge seemed even now to be thrilling in my ears. "What a chance for a man to have! even if he did not survive it. What a proud sight for the army! Oh, Ropsley, what would I give to have been there!"

"*Not whist*, my dear fellow," replied my less enthusiastic friend; "that is not the way to *play the game*, and no man who makes mistakes deserves to win. I have a theory of my own about cavalry, they should never be offered too freely. I would almost go so far as to say they should not be used till a battle is won. At least they should be kept in hand till the last moment, and then let loose like lightning. What said the Duke? 'There are no cavalry on earth like mine, but I can only use them *once;*' and no man knew so well as he did the merits and the failings of each particular arm. Nor should you bring the same men out again too soon after a brilliant charge; let them have a little time to get over it, they will *come* again all the better. Never *waste* anything in war, and never run a chance when you can stand on a certainty. But here we are at the camp of the First Division. Yonder you may catch a glimpse of the harbour and a few houses of the town of Sebastopol. How quiet it looks this fine day! quite the sort of place to take the children to for sea-bathing at this time of the year! I am getting tired of the *outside*, though, Egerton; I sometimes think we shall *never* get in. There they go again," he added, as a white volume of smoke rose slowly into the clear air, and a heavy report broke dully on our ears; "there they go again, but what a slack fire they seem to be keeping up; we shall never do any good till we try a *coup de main*, and take the place by assault;" so speaking, Ropsley picked his way carefully amongst tent-ropes and tent-pegs, and all the impediments of a camp, to reach the main street, so to speak, of that canvas town, and I followed him, gazing around me with a curiosity rather sharpened than damped by the actual warfare I had already seen on so much smaller a scale.

There must have been at least two hundred thousand men at that time disposed around the beleaguered town, this without counting the Land Transport and followers of an army, or the crowds of non-combatants that thronged the ports of Kamiesch and Balaklava. The white town of tents stretched away for miles, divided and subdivided into streets and alleys; you had only to know the number of his regiment to find a private soldier, with as great a certainty as you could find an individual in London if you knew the number of his house and the name of the street where he resided--always pre-supposing that the soldier had not been killed the night before in the trenches, a casualty by no means to be overlooked. We rode down the main street of the Guards' division, admired the mountaineer on sentry at the adjoining camp of the Highland brigade, and pulled up to find ourselves at home at the door of Ropsley's tent, to which humble abode my friend welcomed me with as courteous an air and as much concern for my comfort as he would have done in his own luxurious lodgings in the heart of May-fair. A soldier's life had certainly much altered Ropsley for the better. I could see he was popular in his regiment. The men seemed to welcome back the Colonel (a captain in the Guards holds the rank of lieutenant-colonel in the army), and his brother officers thronged into the tent ere we had well entered it ourselves, to tell him the latest particulars of the siege, and the ghastly news that every morning brought fresh and bloody from the trenches.

As a stranger, or rather as a guest, I was provided with the seat of honour, an old, shrivelled bullock-trunk that had escaped the general loss of baggage on the landing of the army, previous to the battle of the Alma, and which, set against the tent-pole for a "back," formed a commodious and delightful resting-place; the said tent-pole, besides being literally the main-stay and prop of the establishment, fulfilling all the functions of a wardrobe, a chest of drawers, and a dressing-table; for from certain nails artfully disposed on its slender circumference, depended the few articles of costume and necessaries of the toilet which formed the whole worldly wealth of the *ci-devant* London dandy.

The dandy aforesaid, sitting on his camp-bedstead in his ragged flannel-shirt, and sharing that seat with two other dandies more ragged than himself, pledged his guest in a silver-gilt measure of pale ale, brought up from Balaklava at a cost of about half-a-guinea a bottle, and drank with a gusto such as the best-flavoured champagne had never wooed from a palate formerly too delicate and fastidious to be pleased with the nectar of the immortals themselves, now appreciating with exquisite enjoyment the strongest liquids, the most acrid tobacco, nay, the Irish stew itself, cooked by a private soldier at a camp-fire, savoury and delicious, if glutinous with grease and reeking of onions.

"Heavy business the night before last," said a young Guardsman with a beautiful girlish face, and a pair of uncommonly dirty hands garnished with costly rings--a lad that looked as if he ought to be still at school, but uniting the cool courage of a man with the mischievous light-hearted spirits of a boy. "Couldn't get a wink of sleep for them at any time--never knew 'em so restless. Tell you what, Colonel, 'rats leave a falling house,' it's my belief there's *something up* now, else why were we all relieved at twelve o'clock instead of our regular twenty-four hours in the trenches? Good job for me, for I breakfasted with the General, and a precious blow-out he gave me. Turkey, my boys! and cherry-brandy out of a shaving-pot! Do you call that nothing?"

"Were you in the advanced trenches?" inquired Ropsley, stopping our young friend's gastronomic recollections; "and did you see poor ---- killed?"

The lad's face fell in an instant; it was with a saddened and altered voice that he replied--

"Poor Charlie! yes, I was close to him when he was hit. You know it was his first night in the trenches, and he was like a boy out of school. Well, the beggars made a sortie, you know, on the left of our right attack: they couldn't have chosen a worse place; and he and I were with the light company when we drove them back. The men behaved admirably, Colonel; and poor Charlie was so delighted, not being used to it, you know," proceeded the urchin, with the gravity of a veteran, "that it was impossible to keep him within bounds. He had a revolver (that wouldn't go off, by the way), and he had filled a soda-water bottle with powder and bullets and odd bits of iron, like a sort of mimic shell. Well, this thing burst in his hand, and deuced near blew his arm off, but it only made him keener. When the Russians retired, he actually ran out in front and threw stones at them. I tried all I could to stop him." (The lad's voice was getting husky now.) "Well, Colonel, it was bright moonlight, and I saw a Russian private take a regular 'pot-shot' at poor Charlie. He hit him just below the waist-belt; and we dragged him into the trenches, and there he--he died. Colonel, this 'baccy of yours is very strong; I'll--I'll just walk into the air for a moment, if you'll excuse me. I'll be back directly."

So he rose and walked out, with his face turned from us all; and though there was nothing to be ashamed of in the weakness, I think not one of us but knew he had gone away to have his "cry" out, and liked him all the better for his mock manliness and his feeling heart.

Ere he came back again the bugles were sounding for afternoon parade. Orderly corporals were running about with small slips of paper in their hands, the men were falling in, and the fresh relief, so diminished every four-and-twenty hours, was again being got ready for the work of death in the trenches.

CHAPTER XXXVII
"A QUIET NIGHT"

On an elevated plateau, sloping downward to a ravine absolutely paved with iron, in the remains of shot and shell fired from the town during its protracted and vigorous defence, are formed in open column "the duties" from the different regiments destined to carry on the siege for the next four-and-twenty hours. Those who are only accustomed to see British soldiers marshalled neat and orderly in Hyde Park, or manoeuvring like clock-work in "the Phoanix," would hardly recognise in that motley, war-worn band the staid and uniform figures which they are accustomed to contemplate with pride and satisfaction as the "money's-worth" of a somewhat oppressive taxation. The Highlanders--partly from the fortune of war, partly from the nature of their dress--are less altered from their normal exterior than the rest of the army, and the Guardsman's tall figure and bear-skin cap still stamp him a Guardsman, notwithstanding patched clothing and much-worn accoutrements; but some of the line regiments, which have suffered considerably during the siege, present the appearance of regular troops only in their martial bearing and the scrupulous discipline observed within their ranks. To the eye of a soldier, however, there is something very pleasing and "workmanlike" in the healthy, confident air of the men, and the "matter-of-course" manner in which they seem to contemplate the duty before them. Though their coats may be out at elbows, their firelocks are bright and in good order, while the havresacks and canteens slung at their sides seem to have been carefully replenished with a view to keeping up that physical vigour and stamina for which the British soldier is so celebrated, and which, with his firm reliance on his officers, and determined bull-dog courage, render him so irresistible an enemy.

There are no troops who are so little liable to panic--whose _morale_, so to speak, it is so difficult to impair, as our own. Napoleon said they "never knew when they were beaten." And how often has this generous ignorance saved them from defeat! Long may it be ere they learn the humiliating lesson! But that they are not easily disheartened may be gathered from the following anecdote, for the truth of which many a Crimean officer will readily vouch:--

Two days after the disastrous attack of the 18th of June, 1855, a private soldier on fatigue duty was cleaning the door-step in front of Lord Raglan's quarters; but his thoughts were running on far other matters than holystone and whitewash, for on a staff officer of high rank emerging from the sacred portal, he stopped the astonished functionary with an abrupt request to procure him an immediate interview with the Commander-in-Chief.

"If you please, Colonel," said the man, standing at "attention," and speaking as if it was the most natural thing in the world, "if it's not too great a liberty, I wants to see the General immediate and particular!"

"Impossible! my good fellow," replied the Colonel--who, like most brave men, was as good-natured as he was fearless--"if you have any complaint to make, tell it me; you may be sure it will reach Lord Raglan, and if it is just, it will be attended to."

"Well, sir, it's not exactly a complaint," replied the soldier, now utterly neglecting the door-step, "but more a request, like; and I wanted to see his lordship special, if so be as it's not contrary to orders."

The Colonel could hardly help laughing at the coolness with which so flagrant a military solecism was urged, but repeated that Lord Raglan was even then engaged with General Pelissier, and that the most he could do for his importunate friend was to receive his message and deliver it to the Commander-in-Chief at a favourable opportunity.

The man reflected an instant, and seemed satisfied. "Well, Colonel," he said, "we *knows you*, and we *trusts* you. I speak for myself and comrades, and what I've got to say to the General is this here. We made a bad business o' Monday, and we knows the reason why. You let *us* alone. There's plenty of us to do it; only you give us leave, and issue an order that not an officer nor a non-commissioned officer is to interfere, and *we*, the private soldiers of the British army, will have that place for you if we pull the works down with our fingers, and crack the stones with our teeth!"

"And what," said the Colonel, utterly aghast at this unheard-of proposal, "what----"

"What time will we be under arms to do it?" interrupted the delighted delegate, never doubting but that his request was now as good as granted,--"why, at three o'clock to-morrow morning; and you see, Colonel, when the thing's done, if me and my company *wasn't the first lads in!*"

Such is the material of which these troops are made who are now waiting patiently to be marched down to the nightly butchery of the trenches.

"It reminds one of the cover-side at home," remarked Ropsley, as we cantered up to the parade, and dismounted; "one meets fellows from all parts of the camp, and one hears all the news before the sport begins. There goes the French relief," he added, as our allies went slinging by, their jaunty, disordered step, and somewhat straggling line of march, forming as strong a contrast to the measured tramp and regular movements of our own soldiers, as did their blue frock-coats and crimson trousers to the *véritable rouge* for which they had conceived so high a veneration. Ere they have quite disappeared, our own column is formed. The brigade-major on duty has galloped to and fro, and seen to everything with his own eyes. Company officers, in rags and tatters, with swords hung sheathless in worn white belts, and wicker-covered bottles slung in a cord over the hip, to balance the revolver on the other side,--and brave, gentle hearts beating under those tarnished uniforms, and sad experiences of death, and danger, and hardship behind those frank faces, and honest, kindly smiles,--have inspected their men and made their reports, and "fallen in" in their proper places; and the word is given, and its head moves off--"By the left; quick march!"--and the column winds quietly down into the valley of the shadow of death.

Ropsley is field-officer of the night, and I accompany him on his responsible duty, for I would fain see more of the town that has been in all our thoughts for so long, and learn how a siege is urged on so gigantic a scale.

The sun is just setting, and gilds the men's faces, and the tufts of arid grass above their heads in the deepening ravine, with a tawny orange hue, peculiar to a sunset in the East. The evening is beautifully soft and still, but the dust is suffocating, rising as it does in clouds from the measured tread of so many feet; and there is a feeling of depression, a weight in the atmosphere, such as I have often observed to accompany the close of day on the shores of the Black Sea. Even the men seem to feel its influence-- the whispered jest, the ready smile which usually accompanies a march, is wanting; the youngest ensign looks thoughtful, and as if he were brooding on his far-off home; and the lines deepen on many a bearded countenance as we wind lower and lower down the ravine, and reach the first parallel, which to some now present must be so forcible a reminder of disappointed hopes, fruitless sacrifices, and many a true and hearty comrade who shall be friend and comrade no more.

Ropsley has a plan of the works in his hand, which he studies with eager attention. He hates soldiering--so he avows--yet is he an intelligent and trustworthy officer. With his own ideas on many points at variance with the authorities, and which he never scruples to avow, he yet rigidly carries out every duty entrusted to him, and if the war should last, promises to ascend the ladder as rapidly as any of his comrades. It is not the path he would have chosen to distinction, nor are the privations and discomforts of a soldier's life at all in harmony with his refined perceptions and luxurious habits; but he has embarked on the career, and, true to his principle, he is determined to "make the most of it." I think, too, that I can now perceive in Ropsley a spice of romance foreign to his earlier character. It is a quality without which, in some shape or other, nothing great was ever yet achieved on earth. Yet how angry would he be if he knew that I had thought he had a grain of it in his strong practical character, which he flatters himself is the very essence of philosophy and common-sense.

As we wind slowly up the now well-trodden covered way of the first parallel, from the shelter of which nothing can be seen of the attack or defence, I am forcibly reminded of the passages in a theatre, which one threads with blindfold confidence, in anticipation of the blaze of light and excitement on which one will presently emerge. Ropsley smiles at the conceit as I whisper it in his ear.

"What odd fancies you have!" says he, looking up from the plan on which he has been bending his earnest attention. "Well, you won't have long to wait for the opera; there's the first bar of the overture already!" As he speaks he pulls me down under the embankment, while a shower of dust and gravel, and a startling explosion immediately in front, warn us that the enemy has thrown a shell into the open angle of the trench, with a precision that is the less remarkable when we reflect how many months he has been practising to attain it.

"Very neatly done," observes Ropsley, rising from his crouching attitude with the greatest coolness; "they seldom trouble one much so soon as this. Probably a compliment to you, Egerton," he adds, laughing. "Now let us see what the damage is."

Stiff and upright as the ramrod in his firelock, which rattles to his salute, a sergeant of the Guards marches up and makes his report:--"Privates Wood and Jones wounded slightly, sir; Lance-corporal Smithers killed."

They pass us as they are taken to the rear; the lance-corporal has been shot through the heart, and must have died instantaneously. His face is calm and peaceful, his limbs are disposed on the stretcher as if he slept. Poor fellow! 'Tis quick work, and in ten minutes he is forgotten. My first feeling is one of astonishment, at my own hardness of heart in not being more shocked at his fate.

So we reach the advanced trenches without more loss. It is now getting quite dark, for the twilight in these latitudes is but of short duration. A brisk fire seems to be kept up on the works of our allies, responded to by the

French gunners with ceaseless activity; but our own attack is comparatively unmolested, and Ropsley makes his arrangements and plants his sentries in a calm, leisurely way that inspires the youngest soldier with confidence, and wins golden opinions from the veterans who have spent so many bleak and weary nights before Sebastopol.

We are now in the advanced trenches. Not three hundred paces to our front are yawning the deadly batteries of the Redan. The night is dark as pitch. Between the intervals of the cannonade, kept up so vigorously far away on our right, we listen breathlessly as the night-breeze sweeps down to us from the town, until we can almost fancy we hear the Russians talking within their works. But the "pick, pick" of our own men's tools, as they enlarge the trench, and their stifled whispers and cautious tread, deaden all other sounds. Each man works with his firelock in his hand; he knows how soon it may be needed. Yet the soldier's ready jest and quaint conceit is ever on the lip, and many a burst of laughter is smothered as it rises, and enjoyed all the more keenly for the constraint.

"Not so much noise there," says Ropsley, in his quiet, authoritative tone, as the professed buffoon of the light company indulges in a more lively sally than usual; "I'll punish any man that speaks above a whisper. Come, my lads," he adds good-humouredly, "keep quiet now, and perhaps it will be OUR turn before the night is over!" The men return to their work with a will, and not another word is heard in the ranks.

The officers have established a sort of head-quarters as a *place d'armes*, or re-assembling spot, near the centre of their own "attack." Three or four are coiled up in different attitudes, beguiling the long, dark hours with whispered jests and grave speculations as to the intentions of the enemy. Here a stalwart captain of Highlanders stretches his huge frame across the path, puffing forth volumes of smoke from the short black pipe that has accompanied him through the whole war--the much-prized "cutty" that was presented to him by his father's forester when he shot the royal stag in the "pass abune Craig-Owar"; there a slim and dandy rifleman passes a wicker-covered flask of brandy-and-water to a tall, sedate personage who has worked his way through half-a-dozen Indian actions to be senior captain in a line regiment, and who, should he be fortunate enough to survive the present siege, may possibly arrive at the distinguished rank of a Brevet-Major. He prefers his own bottle of cold tea; as it gurgles into his lips the Highlander pulls a face of disgust.

"Take those long, indecent legs of yours out of the way, Sandy," says a merry voice, the owner of which, stumbling over these brawny limbs in the darkness, makes his way up to Ropsley, and whispers a few words in his ear which seem to afford our Colonel much satisfaction.

"You couldn't have done it better," says he to the new arrival, a young officer of engineers, the "bravest of the brave," and the "gayest of the gay;" "I could have spared you a few more men, but it is better as it is. I hate harassing our fellows, if we can help it. What will you have to drink?"

"A drain at the flask first, Colonel," answers the light-hearted soldier; "I've been on duty now, one way or another, for eight-and-forty hours, and I'm about beat. Sandy, my boy, give us a whiff out of 'the cutty.' I'll sit by you. You remind me of an opera-dancer in that dress. Mind you dine with me to-morrow, if you're not killed."

The Highlander growls out a gruff affirmative. He delights in his volatile friend; but he is a man of few words, although his arm is weighty and his brain is clear.

A shell shrieks and whistles over our heads. We mark it revolving, bright and beautiful, like a firework through the darkness. It lights far away to our rear, and bounds once more from the earth ere it explodes with a loud report.

"Not much mischief done by that gentleman," observes Ropsley, taking the cigar from his mouth; "he must have landed clear of all our people. We shall soon have another from the same battery. I wish I knew what they are doing over yonder," he adds, pointing significantly in the direction of the Redan.

"I think I can find out for you, Colonel," says the engineer; "I am going forward to the last 'sap,' and I shall not be very far from them there. Your sharpshooters are just at the corner, Green," he adds to the rifleman, "won't you come with me?" The latter consents willingly, and as they rise from their dusty lair I ask leave to accompany them, for my curiosity is fearfully excited, and I am painfully anxious to know what the enemy is about. The last "sap" is a narrow and shallow trench, the termination of which is but a short distance from the Russian work. It is discontinued at the precipitous declivity which here forms one side of the well-known Woronzoff ravine; and from this spot, dark as it is, the sentry can be discerned moving to and fro--a dusky, indistinct figure--above the parapet of the Redan.

The engineer officer and Green of the Rifles seat themselves on the very edge of the ravine; the former plucks a blade or two of grass and flings them into the air.

"They can't hear us with this wind," says he. "What say you, Green; wouldn't it be a good lark to creep in under there, and make out what they're doing?"

"I'm game!" says Green, one of those dare-devil young gentlemen to be found amongst the subalterns of the British army, who would make the same reply were it a question of crossing that glacis in the full glare of day to take the work by assault single-handed. "Put your sword off, that's all, otherwise you'll make such a row that our own fellows will think they're attacked, and fire on us like blazes. Mind you, my chaps have had lots of practice, and can hit a haystack as well as their neighbours. Now then, are you ready? Come on."

The engineer laughed, and unbuckled his sabre.

"Good-afternoon, Mr. Egerton, in case I shouldn't see you again," said he; and so the two crept silently away upon their somewhat hazardous expedition.

I watched their dark figures with breathless interest. The sky had lifted a little, and there was a ray or two of moonlight struggling fitfully through the clouds. I could just distinguish the two English officers as they crawled on hands and knees amongst the slabs of rock and inequalities of ground which now formed their only safety. I shuddered to think that if I could thus distinguish their forms, why not the Russian riflemen?--and what chance for them then, with twenty or thirty "Miniés" sighted on them at point-blank distance? However, "Fortune favours the brave;" the light breeze died away, and the moon was again obscured. I could see them no longer, and I knew that by this time they must have got within a very few paces of the enemy's batteries, and that discovery was now certain death. The ground, too, immediately under the Russian work was smoother and less favourable to concealment than under our own. The moments seemed to pass very slowly. I scarcely dared to move, and the tension of my nerves was absolutely painful, every faculty seeming absorbed in one concentrated effort of listening.

Suddenly a short, sharp stream of light, followed by the quick, angry report of the Minié--then another and another--they illumine the night for an instant; and during that instant I strain my eyes in vain to discover the two dark creeping forms. And now a blinding glare fills our trenches--the figures of the men coming out like phantoms in their different attitudes of labour and repose. The enemy has thrown a fire-ball into our works to ascertain what we are about. Like the pilot-fish before the shark, that brilliant messenger is soon succeeded by its deadly followers, and ere I can hurry back to the rallying-point of the attack, where I have left Ropsley and his comrades, a couple of shells have already burst amongst our soldiers, dealing around them their quantum of wounds and death, whilst a couple more are winging their way like meteors over our heads, to carry the alarm far to the rear, where the gallant blue-jackets have established a tremendous battery, and are at this moment in all probability chafing and fretting that they are not nearer the point of danger.

"Stand to your arms! Steady, men, steady!" is the word passed from soldier to soldier along the ranks, and the men spring like lions to the parapet, every heart beating high with courage, every firelock held firmly at the charge. They are tired of "long bowls" now, and would fain have it out with the bayonet.

The fire from the Redan lights up the intervening glacis, and as I rush hurriedly along the trench, stooping my head with instinctive precaution, I steal a glance or two over the low parapet, which shows me the figure of a man running as hard as his legs can carry him towards our own rallying-point. He is a mark for fifty Russian rifles, but he speeds on nevertheless. His cheery voice rings through all the noise and confusion, as he holloas to our men not to fire at him.

"Hold on, my lads," he says, leaping breathlessly into the trench; "I've had a precious good run for it. Where's the Colonel?"

His report is soon made. It is the young officer of engineers who thus returns in haste from his reconnoitring expedition. His companion, Green, has reached his own regiment by another track, for they wisely separated when they found themselves observed, and strange to say, notwithstanding the deadly fire through which they have "run the gauntlet," both are unwounded. The engineer confers with Ropsley in a low voice.

"They only want to draw off our attention, Colonel," says he; "I am quite sure of it. When I was under the Redan I could hear large bodies of men moving towards their left. That is the point of attack, depend upon it. There they go on our right! I told you so. Now we shall have it, hot and heavy, or I'm mistaken."

Even while he speaks a brisk fire is heard to open on our right flank. The clouds clear off, too, and the moon, now high in the heavens, shines forth unveiled. By her soft light we can just discern a dark, indistinct mass winding slowly along across an open space of ground between the Russian works. The rush of a round-shot from one of our own batteries whizzes over our heads. That dusky column wavers, separates, comes together again, and presses on. Ropsley gets cooler and cooler, for it is coming at last.

"Captain McDougal," says he to that brawny warrior, who does not look the least like an opera-dancer now, as he rears his six feet of vigour on those stalwart supporters, "I can spare all the Highlanders; form them directly, and move to your right flank. Do not halt till you reach the ground I told you of. The Rifles and our own light company will stand fast! Remainder, right, form four deep--march!"

There is an alarm along the whole line. Our allies are engaged in a brisk cannonade for their share, and many an ugly missile hisses past our ears from the foe, or whistles over our heads from our own supports. Is it to be a general attack?--a second Inkermann, fought out by moonlight? Who knows? The uncertainty is harassing, yet attended with its own thrilling excitement--half a pleasure, half a pain.

A few of our own people (we cannot in the failing light discover to what regiment they belong) are giving way before a dense mass of Russian infantry that outnumber them a hundred to one. They have shown a determined front for a time, but they are sorely pressed and overpowered, and by degrees they give back more and more. The truth must out--they are on the point of turning tail and running away. A little fiery Irishman stands out in front of them; a simple private is he in the regiment, and never likely to reach a more exalted rank, for, like all great men, he has a darling weakness, and the temptation to which he cannot but succumb is inebriety--the pages of the Defaulters' Book call it "habitual drunkenness." Nevertheless, he has the heart of a hero. Gesticulating furiously, and swearing, I regret to say, with blasphemous volubility, he tears the coat from his back, flings his cap on the ground, and tossing his arms wildly above his head, thus rebukes, like some Homeric hero, his more prudent comrades--

"Och, bad luck to ye, rank cowards and shufflers that ye are! and bad luck to the day I listed! and bad luck to the rig'ment that's disgracin' me! Would I wear the uniform, and parade like a soldier again, when it's been dirtied by the likes of you? 'Faith, not I, ye thunderin' villains. I'll tread and I'll trample the coat, and the cap, and the facin's, and the rest of it; and I'll fight in my shirt, so I will, if they come on fifty to one. Hurroo!"

Off goes his musket in the very faces of the enemy; with a rush and a yell he runs at them with the bayonet. His comrades turn, and strike in vigorously with the hero. Even that little handful of men serves for an instant to check the onward progress of the Russians. By this time the supports-- Guards, Highlanders, and the flower of the British infantry--are pouring from their entrenchments; a tremendous fire of musketry opens from the whole line; staff officers are galloping down hurry-skurry from the camp. Far away above us, on those dark heights, the whole army will be under arms in ten minutes. The Russian column wavers once more--breaks like some wave against a sunken rock; dark, flitting figures are seen to come out, and stagger, and fall; and then the whole body goes to the right-about and returns within its defences, just as a mass of heavy clouds rising from the Black Sea sweeps across the moon, and darkness covers once more besiegers and besieged.

We may lie down in peace now till the first blush of dawn rouses the riflemen on each side to that sharp-shooting practice of which it is their custom to take at least a couple of hours before breakfast. We may choose the softest spots in those dusty, covered ways, and lean our backs against gabions that are getting sadly worn out, and in their half-emptied inefficiency afford but an insecure protection even from the conical ball of the wicked "Minié." We may finish our flasks of brandy-and-water and our bottles of cold tea, and get a few winks of sleep, and dream of home and the loved ones that, except in the hours of sleep, some of us will never see more. All these luxuries we may enjoy undisturbed. We shall not be attacked again, for this is what the soldiers term "A *quiet* night in the trenches."

CHAPTER XXXVIII
THE GROTTO

It is not *all* fighting, though, before Sebastopol. Without coinciding entirely with the somewhat Sancho Panza-like philosophy which affirms that the "latter end of a feast is better than the beginning of a fray," there is many a gallant fellow who has not the slightest objection to take his share of both; and from the days of Homer's heavy-handed heroes, down to those of the doughty Major Dugald Dalgetty himself, a good commissariat has always been considered essential to the success of all warlike enterprise. Every campaigner knows what a subject of speculation and excitement is afforded by the prospect of "what he will have for dinner," and the scantiness of that meal, together with the difficulty of providing for it, seems but to add to the zest with which it is enjoyed. Many a quaint incident and laughable anecdote is related of the foraging propensities of our allies, particularly the Zouaves, who had learned their trade in Algeria, and profited by the lessons of their Khabyle foe. The Frenchman, moreover, knows how to *cook* a dinner *when* he has filched it, which is more than can be said for our own gallant countrymen.

Had it not been for Fortnum and Mason--names which deserve to be immortalised, and which will ever be remembered with gratitude by the British army--our heroes would indeed have been badly off for luxurious living on that bracing and appetite-giving plateau. Yet, thanks to the energy of this enterprising firm, Amphitryons were enabled to indulge their taste for hospitality, and guests to admire and criticise the merits of the very commendable delicacies placed before them.

A dinner-party at Sebastopol, just out of cannon-shot, had something inexpressibly enlivening in its composition. There was no lack of news, no lack of laughter, no lack of eatables and drinkables, above all, no lack of hunger and thirst. The same faces were to be seen around the board that might have been met with at any dinner-table in London, but white neckcloths and broadcloth had given place to tawny beards and tarnished uniforms, whilst the bronzed countenances and high spirits of the party formed an exhilarating contrast to the weary looks and vapid conversation which makes London society, in its own intrinsic attractions, the stupidest in the world.

The sun's last rays are lighting up that well-known hill where sleeps "the bravest of the brave," he whose name will go down to our children's children coupled with Inkermann, as that of Leonidas with Thermopylæ. He whose fall evoked a deed of chivalry such as minstrel and troubadour snatched from oblivion in the olden time, and handed down to us for a beacon along the pathway of honour. Had they ever a nobler theme than this? A chief falls, surrounded and overpowered, in his desperate attempt to retrieve the fortunes of a day that he deems all but lost. His friend and comrade, faint and mangled, turns once more into the battle, and bestrides the form of the prostrate hero. One to ten, the breathless and the wounded against the fresh and strong, but the heart of an English gentleman behind that failing sword, beat down and shattered by the thirsty bayonets. An instant the advance is checked. An instant and they might both have been saved. Oh, for but one half-dozen of the towering forms that are even now mustering to the rescue! They are coming through the smoke! Too late--too late! the lion-hearted chieftain and the gentle, chivalrous warrior are down, slain, trampled, and defaced, but side by side on the bed of honour; and though the tide sweeps back, and the broken columns of the Muscovite are driven, routed and shattered, to the rear, *their* ears are deaf to the shout of victory, *their* laurel wreaths shall hang vacant and unworn, for they shall rise to claim them no more.

The setting sun is gilding their graves--the white buildings of Sebastopol smile peacefully in his declining rays--the sea is blushing violet under the rich purple of the evening sky. The allied fleets are dotted like sleeping wild-fowl over the bosom of the deep; one solitary steamer leaves its long dusky track of smoke to form a stationary cloud, so smooth is the water that the ripple caused by the sunken ships can be plainly discerned in the harbour, and the Russian men-of-war still afloat look like children's toys in the distance of that clear, calm atmosphere. The bleak and arid foreground, denuded of vegetation, and trampled by a thousand footmarks, yet glows with the warm orange hues of sunset, and the white tents contrast pleasingly with here and there the richer colouring of some more stationary hut or storehouse. It is an evening for peace, reflection, and repose; but the dull report of a 68-pounder smites heavily on the ear from the town, and a smart soldier-servant, standing respectfully at "attention," observes, "The General is ready, sir, and dinner is upon the table."

In a grotto dug by some Tartar hermit out of the cool earth are assembled a party of choice spirits, who are indeed anchorites in nothing but the delight with which they greet the refreshing atmosphere of their banqueting-hall. A flight of stone steps leads down into this well-contrived vault, in so hot a climate no contemptible exchange for the stifling interior of a tent, or even the comparative comfort of a wooden hut thoroughly baked through by the sun. A halting figure on crutches is toiling painfully down that staircase, assisted, with many a jest at their joint deficiencies, by a stalwart, handsome Guardsman, a model of manly strength and symmetry, but lacking what he is pleased to term his "liver wing." They are neither of them likely to forget the Crimea whilst they live. Ere they reach the bottom they are overtaken by a cavalry officer with jingling spurs and noisy scabbard, who, having had a taste of fighting, such as ought to have satisfied most men, at Balaklava, is now perpetually hovering about the front, disgusted with his enforced idleness at Kadikoi, and with a strong impression on his mind-- which he supports by many weighty arguments--that a few squadrons of Dragoons would be valuable auxiliaries to a storming party, and that a good swordsman on a good horse can "go anywhere and do anything."

"I think we are all here now," says the host; "Monsieur le Général, shall we go to dinner?"

The individual addressed gives a hearty affirmative. He is a stout, good-humoured-looking personage, with an eagle eye, and an extremely tight uniform covered with orders and decorations. He is not yet too fat to get on horseback, though the privations of campaigning seem to increase his rotundity day by day, and he expects ere long to go to battle, like an ancient Scythian, in his war-chariot. By that time he will be a marshal of France, but meanwhile he pines a little for the opera, and enjoys his dinner extremely. He occupies the seat of honour on the right hand of his host. The latter bids his guests welcome in frank, soldier-like style; and whilst the soup is handed round, and those bearded lips are occupied with its merits, let us take a look round the table at the dozen or so of guests, some of whom are destined ere long to have their likenesses in every print-shop in merry England. First of all the dinner-giver himself--a square, middle-sized man, with a kindling eye, and a full, determined voice that suggests at once the habit of command--a kindly though energetic manner, and a countenance indicative of great resolution and clear-headedness; perhaps the best drill in the British army, and delighting much in a neat touch of parade tactics even before an enemy. Many a Guardsman nudged his comrade with a grin of humorous delight when, on a certain 20th of September, his old colonel coolly doubled a flank company in upon the rear of its battalion, and smiled to see the ground it would otherwise have occupied ploughed and riddled by the round-shot that was pouring from the enemy's batteries in position on the heights above the Alma. The British soldier likes coolness above all things; and where in command of foreign troops an officer should rave and gesticulate and tear his hair to elicit a corresponding enthusiasm from his men, our own phlegmatic Anglo-Saxons prefer the quiet smile and the good-humoured "*Now*, my lads!" which means so much.

On the left, and facing the Frenchman, sits a middle-aged decided-looking man, somewhat thoughtful and abstracted, yet giving his opinions in a clear and concise manner, and with a forcible tone and articulation that denote great energy and firmness of character. His name, too, is destined to fill the page of history--his future is bright and glowing before him, and none will grudge his honours and promotion, for he is endeared to the army by many a kindly action, and it has been exertion for their welfare and watching on their behalf, that have wasted his strong frame with fever, and turned his hair so grey in so short a time. Soldier as he is to his heart's core, he would fain be outside in the sunset with his colours and his sketch-book, arresting on its pages the glorious panorama which is even now passing away; but he is listening attentively to his neighbour, a handsome young man in the uniform of a simple private of Zouaves, and is earnestly occupied in "getting a wrinkle," as it is termed, concerning the interior economy and discipline of that far-famed corps. The Zouave gives him all the information he can desire with that peculiarly frank and fascinating manner which is fast dying out with the *ancien régime*, for though a private of Zouaves he is a marquis of France, the representative of one of the oldest families in the Empire, and a worthy scion of his chivalrous race. Rather than not draw the sword for his country, he has resigned his commission in that body of household cavalry termed "The Guides," and entered as a trooper in the Chasseurs d'Afrique: a display of martial enthusiasm for which he has been called out from the ranks of his original corps and publicly complimented by the Empress Eugénie herself. Arrived in the Crimea, he found his new comrades placed in enforced idleness at far too great a distance from active operations to suit his taste, and he forthwith exchanged once more into the Zouaves, with whom he took his regular share of duty in the trenches, and he is now enjoying a furlough of some six hours from his quarters, to dine with an English general, and cultivate the *entente cordiale* which flourishes so vigorously on this Crimean soil. Alas for the gallant spirit, the graceful form, the warm noble heart! no bird of ill omen flew across his path as he came to-day to dinner, no warning note of impending death rang in his ears to give him notice of his doom. To-night he is as gay, as lively, as cheerful as usual; to-morrow he will be but a form of senseless clay, shot through the head in the trenches.

Meanwhile the champagne goes round, and is none the less appreciated that although there is an abundance of bottles, there is a sad deficiency of glasses. A light-hearted aide-de-camp, well accustomed to every emergency, great or small, darts off to his adjoining tent, from which he presently returns, bearing two tin cups and the broken remains of a coffee-pot; with these auxiliaries dinner progresses merrily, and a fat turkey--how obtained it is needless to inquire--is soon reduced to a skeleton. A little wit goes a long way when men are before an enemy; and as the aide-de-camp strongly repudiates the accusation of having purloined this hapless bird, jokes are bandied about from one to another, every one wishing to fasten on his neighbour the accusation of knowing how to "make war support war."

The English officers are a long way behind their allies in this useful accomplishment; and the French general shakes his jolly sides as he relates with much gusto sundry Algerian experiences of what we should term larceny and rapine, but which his more liberal ideas seem to consider excusable, if not positively meritorious.

"The best foragers I had in Algeria," says he, "were my best soldiers too. If I wanted fresh milk for my coffee, I trusted to the same men that formed my storming parties, and I was never disappointed in one case or the other. In effect, they were droll fellows, my Zouaves Indigènes--cunning too, as the cat that steals cream; the Khabyles could keep nothing from them. If we entered their tents, everything of value was taken away before you could look round. To be sure we could carry nothing with us, but that made no difference. I have seen the men wind shawls round their waists that were worth a hundred louis apiece, and throw them aside on a hot day on the march. There was one Khabyle chief who was very conspicuous for the magnificent scarlet cashmere which he wore as a turban. On foot or on horseback, there he was, always fighting and always in the front. Heaven knows why, but the men called him Bobouton, and wherever there was a skirmish Bobouton was sure to be in the thick of it. One day I happened to remark 'that I was tired of Bobouton and his red shawl, and I wished some one would bring me the turban and rid me of the wearer.' A little swarthy Zouave, named Pépé, overheard my observation. 'Mon Colonel,' said he, with a most ceremonious bow,' to-morrow is your jour de fête--will you permit me to celebrate it by presenting you with the scarlet turban of Bobouton?' I laughed, thanked him, and thought no more about it.

"The following morning, at sunrise, I rode out to make a reconnaissance. A party, of whom Pépé was one, moved forward to clear the ground. Contrary to all discipline and ordonnance, my droll little friend had mounted a magnificent pair of epaulettes. Worn on his Zouave uniform, the effect was the least thing ridiculous. As I knew of no epaulettes in the camp besides my own, I confess I was rather angry, but the enemy having opened a sharp fire upon my skirmishers, I did not choose to sacrifice an aide-de-camp by bidding him ride on and visit Pépé with condign punishment; so, reserving to myself that duty on his return, I watched him meanwhile through my glass with an interest proportioned to my regard for my epaulettes, an article not too easily replaced in Algeria. Nor were mine the only eyes that looked so eagerly on the flashing bullion. Bobouton soon made his appearance from behind a rock, and by the manner in which he and Pépé watched, and, so to speak, 'stalked' each other, I saw that a regular duel was pending between the two. In fine, after very many manoeuvres on both sides, the Zouave incautiously exposed himself at a distance of eighty or ninety paces, and was instantaneously covered by his watchful enemy. As the smoke cleared away from the Khabyle's rifle, poor Pépé sprang convulsively in the air, and fell headlong on his face. 'Tenez!' said I to myself, 'there is Pépé shot through the heart, and I shall never see my epaulettes again.'

"The Khabyle rushed from his hiding-place to strip his fallen antagonist. Already his eyes glittered with delight at the idea of possessing those tempting ornaments--already he was within a few feet of the prostrate body, when 'crack!' once more I heard the sharp report of a rifle, and presto, like some scene at a carnival, it was Bobouton that lay slain upon the rocks, and Pépé that stood over him and stripped him of the spoils of war. In another minute he unrolled the red turban at my horse's feet. 'Mon Colonel,' said he, 'accept my congratulations for yourself and your amiable family. Accept also this trifling token of remembrance taken from that incautious individual who, like the mouse in the fable, thinks the cat must be dead because she lies prostrate without moving. And accept, moreover, my thanks for the loan of these handsome ornaments, without the aid of which I could not have procured myself the pleasure of presenting my worthy colonel with the shawl of ce malheureux Bobouton.' The rascal had stolen them out of my tent the night before, though my aide-de-camp slept within two paces of me, and my head rested on the very box in which they were contained."

"Alas! we have no experiences like yours, General," says a tall, handsome colonel of infantry, with the Cape and Crimean ribbons on his breast; "wherever we have made war with savages, they have had nothing worth taking. A Kaffre chief goes to battle with very little on besides his skin, and that is indeed scarce worth the trouble of stripping. When we captured Sandilli, I give you my word he had no earthly article upon his person but a string of blue beads, and yet he fought like a wildcat to make his escape."

"Your health, my friend," replies the General, clinking his glass with that of his new acquaintance. "You have been in Caffraria? Ah! I should have known it by your decorations. Are they not a fierce and formidable enemy? Is it not a good school for war? Tell me, now"--looking round the table for an explanation--"why do you not reserve South Africa, you others, as we do the northern shore, to make of it a drill-ground for your soldiers and a school for your officers? It would cost but little--a few hundred men a year would be the only loss. Bah!--a mere trifle to the richest and most populous country in the world. I do not understand your English *sang-froid*. Why do you not establish *your* Algeria at the Cape?"

Many voices are immediately raised in explanation; but it is difficult to make the thorough soldier--the man who has all his life been the military servant of a military Government--understand how repugnant would be such a proceeding to the feelings of the British people--how contrary to the whole spirit of their constitution. At length, with another glass of champagne, a new light seems to break in upon him. "Ah!" says he, "it would not be approved of by *Le Times*; now I understand perfectly. We manage these matters better with us. *Peste!* if we go to war, there it is. We employ our *Gazettes* to celebrate our victories. Your health, *mon Général*; this is indeed a wearisome business in which we are engaged--a life totally brutalising. Without change, without manoeuvring, and without pleasure: what would you? I trust the next campaign in which we shall meet may be in a civilised country--the borders of the Rhine, for instance; what think you?--where, instead of this barbarian desert, you find a village every mile, and a good house in every village, with a bottle of wine in the cellar, a smoked ham in the chimney, and a handsome Saxon *blonde* in the kitchen. '*A la guerre, comme à la guerre, n'est ce pas, mon Général?*'"

The company are getting merry and talkative; cigars are lit, and coffee is handed round; the small hours are approaching, and what Falstaff calls the "sweet of the night" is coming on, when the tramp and snort of a horse are heard at the entrance of the grotto, a steel scabbard rings upon the stone steps, and although the new-comer's place at one end of the table has been vacant the whole of dinner-time, he does not sit down to eat till he has whispered a few words in the ear of the English general, who receives the intelligence with as much coolness as it is imparted.

In five minutes the grotto is cleared of all save its customary occupants. The French general has galloped off to his head-quarters; the English officers are hurrying to their men; each as he leaves the grotto casts a look at an ingenious arrangement at its mouth, which, by means of a diagram formed of white shells, each line pointing to a particular portion of the attack, enables the observer to ascertain at once in which direction the fire is most severe. The originator of this simple and ingenious indicator meanwhile sits down for a mouthful of food. He has brought intelligence of the sortie already described, and which will turn out the troops of all arms in about ten minutes; but in the meantime he has five to spare, and, being very hungry, he makes the best use of his time. As the light from the solitary lamp brings into relief that square, powerful form--that statue-like head, with its fearless beauty and its classical features--above all, the frank, kindly smile, that never fades under difficulties, and the clear, unwavering eye that never quails in danger,--any physiognomist worthy of the name would declare "that man was born to be a hero!" And the physiognomist would not be mistaken.

CHAPTER XXXIX
THE REDAN

The days dragged on in the camp. Sometimes wearily enough, sometimes enlivened by a party of pleasure to Baidar, an expedition to the monastery of St. George, a general action at the Tchernaya, a hurdle-race at Kadikoi, or some trifling excitement of the same kind. Already the great heat was beginning to be tempered by the bracing air of autumn, and the army was more than half inclined to speculate on the possibility of another long dreary winter before Sebastopol.

But the time had come at last. The blow so long withheld was to be launched in earnest, and for a day or two before the final and successful assault, men's minds seemed to tell them--they scarce knew why--that a great change was impending, and that every night might now be the last on which the dogged valour of the besieged would man those formidable defences that, under the names of the Malakhoff, the Redan, etc., had for so long occupied the attention of France, England, and indeed the whole of Europe.

I was sitting outside Ropsley's tent, sharing my breakfast of hard biscuit with Bold, at daybreak of a fine September morning. The old dog seemed on this occasion to have renewed his youth, and was so demonstrative and affectionate as to call down a strong reproof from Ropsley, with whom he was never on very friendly terms, for laying his broad paw on the well-brushed uniform of the Colonel. "Tie the brute up, Vere," said he, carefully removing the dirt from his threadbare sleeve, "or he will follow us on parade. Are you ready? if so, come along. I would not be late to-day of all days, for a thousand a year."

I remained in his rear, as he completed the inspection of his company. I had never seen the men so brisk or so smartly turned out, and there was an exhilarated yet earnest look on their countenances that denoted their own opinion of the coming day. Ropsley himself was more of the *bon camarade*, and less of the "fine gentleman" than usual. As we marched down to the trenches side by side, he talked freely of old times,--our school-days at Everdon, our later meeting at Beverley, and, by a natural transition, turned the subject of conversation to Victor de Rohan and his sister Valèrie. I had never known him allude to the latter of his own accord before. He seemed to have something on his mind which pride or mistrust, or both, would not permit him to bring out. At last, apparently with a strong effort, he whispered hurriedly--

"Vere, I've a favour to ask you--if I should be *hit* to-day by chance, and badly, you know, I should like you to write and remember me to the De Rohans, and--and--particularly to Countess Valèrie. If ever you should see her again, you might tell her so."

I pressed his hand in answer, and I thought his voice was hoarser as he resumed.

"Vere, it is not often I confess myself wrong, but I have wronged you fearfully. If I'm alive to-morrow I'll tell you all; if not, Vere, can you--*can* you forgive me?"

"From my heart," was all I had time to reply, for at that instant up rode the leader of the assault, and Ropsley's voice was calm and measured, his manner cold and cynical as ever, while he answered the short and military catechism usual on such occasions.

"Then it's all right," was the remark of the mounted officer, in as good-humoured and jovial a tone as if the affair in hand were a mere question of one of his own Norfolk battues; "and what a fine morning we've got for the business," he added, dismounting, and patting his horse as it was led away, ere he turned round to put himself at the head of the storming party.

I watched him as one watches a man whose experiences of danger have given him a fascination perfectly irresistible to inferior minds. It was the same officer whom I have already mentioned as the latest arrival to disturb the dinner-party in the grotto, but to-day he looked, if possible, more cheerful, and in better spirits than his wont. I thought of his antecedents, as they had often been related to me by one of his oldest friends,--of his unfailing good-humour and kindliness of disposition--of his popularity in his regiment--of his skill and prowess at all sports and pastimes, with the gloves, the foils, the sharp-rowelled spurs of the hunting-field, or the velvet cap that fails to protect the steeplechaser from a broken neck--of his wanderings in the desert amongst the Bedouin Arabs, and his cold bivouacs on the prairie with the Red Indians--of his lonely ride after the Alma, when, steering by the stars through a country with which he was totally unacquainted, he arrived at the fleet with the news of the famous flank march to Balaklava--of his daring *sang-froid* when "the thickest of war's tempest lowered" at Inkermann, and of the daily dangers and privations of the weary siege, always borne and faced out with the same merry light-hearted smile; and now he was to *lead the assault*.

None but a soldier knows all that is comprised in those three simple words--the coolness, the daring, the lightning glance, the ready resource, the wary tactics, and the headlong gallantry which must all be combined successfully to fill that post of honour; and then to think that the odds are ten to one he never comes back alive!

As I looked at his athletic frame and handsome, manly face, as I returned his cordial, off-hand greeting, as courteous to the nameless Interpreter as it would have been to General Pelissier himself, my heart tightened to think of what might--nay, what *must* surely happen on that fire-swept glacis, unless he bore indeed a life charmed with immunity from shot and steel.

Man by man he inspected the Forlorn Hope,--their arms, their ammunition pouches, their scaling-ladders, all the tackle and paraphernalia of death. For each he had a word of encouragement, a jest, or a smile. Ropsley and his company were to remain in support in the advanced trenches. All was at length reported "ready," and then came the awful hush that ever ushers in the most desperate deeds--the minutes of pale and breathless suspense, that fly so quickly and yet seem to pass like lead--when the boldest cheek is blanched, and the stoutest heart beats painfully, and the change to action and real peril is felt to be an unspeakable relief to all.

A cold wet nose was poked into my hand. Bold had tracked me from the camp, and had followed me even here; nothing would induce him now to quit my side, for even the dog seemed to think something awful was impending, and watched with red, angry eyes and lowered tail and bristling neck, as if he too had been "told off" for the attack.

A roar of artillery shakes the air; our allies have opened their fire on the Malakhoff, and their columns are swarming like bees to the assault. Battalion after battalion, regiment after regiment, come surging through the ditch, to break like waves on the sea-shore, as the depressed guns of the enemy hew awful gaps in their ranks--to break indeed but to re-form, and as fresh supports keep pressing them on from the rear, to dash upwards against the earthwork, and to overflow and fling themselves from the parapet in the face of the Russian gunners below.

The Muscovite fights doggedly, and without dream of surrender or retreat. Hand to hand the conflict must be decided with the bayonet, and the little Zouaves shout, and yell, and stab, and press onward, and revel, so to speak, in the wild orgy of battle.

But the Northman is a grim, uncompromising foe, and more than once the "red pantaloons" waver and give back, and rally, and press on again to death. Instances of gallantry and self-devotion are rife amongst the officers. Here, a young captain of infantry flings himself alone upon the bayonets of the enemy, and falls pierced with a hundred wounds; there, an old white-headed colonel, *décoré* up to his chin, draws an ominous revolver, and threatens to shoot any one of his own men through the head that shows the slightest disinclination to rush on. "*Ma foi*," says he, "*c'est pour encourager les autres!*" The southern blood boils up under the influence of example, and if French troops are once a little flushed with success, their *élan*, as they call that quality for which we have no corresponding expression, is irresistible. The Russians cannot face the impetuosity of their charge; already many of the guns are spiked, and the gunners bayoneted; the grey-coated columns are yielding ground foot by foot; fresh troops pour in over the parapet, for the living are now able to pass unscathed over the dead, with whom the ditch is filled. The fire of the Russians is slackening, and their yell dies away fainter on the breeze. A French cheer, wild, joyous, and unearthly, fills the air,--it thrills in the ears of Pelissier, sitting immovable on his horse at no great distance from the conflict; his telescope is pressed to his eye, and he is watching eagerly for the well-known signal. And now he sees it! A gleam of fierce joy lights up his features, and as the tricolor of France is run up to the crest of the Malakhoff, he shuts his glass with a snap, dismounts from his horse, and rolling himself round in his cloak, lies down for a few minutes' repose, and observes, with a zest of which none but a Frenchman is capable, "*Tenez! voilà mon bâton de Maréchal!*"

His are not the only eyes eagerly watching the progress of the attack; many a veteran of both armies is busied recalling all his own experiences and all his knowledge of warfare, to calculate the probabilities of their success whose task it is to cross that wide and deadly glacis which is swept by the batteries of the Redan.

The men are formed for the assault, and the word is given to advance.

"Now, my lads," says the leader, "keep cool--keep steady--and keep together--we'll do it handsomely when we're about it. Forward!"

It is related of him whom Napoleon called "the bravest of the brave," the famous Ney, that he was the only officer of that day who could preserve his *sang-froid* totally unmoved when standing with *his back* to a heavy fire. Many a gallant fellow facing the enemy would pay no more regard to the missiles whistling about his ears, than to the hailstones of an April shower; but it was quite a different sensation to *front* his own advancing troops, and never look round at the grim archer whose every shaft might be the last. What the French Marshal, however, piqued himself upon as the acme of personal courage and conduct, our English leader seems to consider a mere matter-of-course in the performance of an every-day duty. Step by step, calm, collected, and good-humoured, he regulates the movements of the attacking force. Fronting their ranks, as if he were on parade, he brings them out of their sheltering defences into the iron storm, now pouring forth its deadly wrath upon that rocky plateau which *must* be crossed in defiance of everything.

"Steady, men," he observes once more, as he forms them for the desperate effort; "we'll have them *out of that* in ten minutes. Now, my lads! Forward, and follow me!"

The cocked hat is waving amongst the smoke--the daring Colonel is forward under the very guns--with a British cheer, the Forlorn Hope dash eagerly on, comrade encouraging comrade, side by side, shoulder to shoulder--hearts throbbing wild and high, and a grip of iron on good "Brown Bess." Men live a lifetime in a few such moments. There are two brothers in that doomed band who have not met for years--they quarrelled in their hot youth over their father's grave, about the quiet orchard and the peaceful homestead that each had since longed so painfully to see once more; and now they have served, with half the globe between them, and each believes the other to have forgotten him, and the orchard and the homestead have passed away from their name for ever. They would weep and be friends if they could meet again. There are but four men between them at this moment, and two are down, stark and dead, and two are dragging their mangled bodies slowly to the rear, and the brothers are face to face under the fatal batteries of the Redan.

"Is't thou, my lad?" is all the greeting that passes in that wild moment; but the blackened hands meet with a convulsive clasp, and they are brothers once more, as when, long ago, they hid their sturdy little faces in their mother's gown. Thank God for that! In another minute it would have been too late, for Bill is down, shot through the lungs, his white belts limp and crimson with blood; and John, with a tear in his eye, and something betwixt an oath and a prayer upon his lips, is rushing madly on, for the cocked hat is still waving forward amongst the smoke. and the Colonel is still cheering them after him into the jaws of death.

But soldiers, even British soldiers, are but men, and the fire grows so deadly that the attacking force cannot but be checked in its headlong charge. The line breaks--wavers--gives way--the awful glacis is strewed with dead and dying--groans and curses, and shrieks for "*water! water!*" mingle painfully with the wild cheers, and the trampling feet, and the thunder of the guns; but volumes of smoke, curling low and white over the ground, veil half the horrors of that ghastly scene; yet through the smoke can be discerned some three or four figures under the very parapet of the

Redan, and the cocked hat and square frame of the Colonel are conspicuous amongst the group.

It must have been a strange sight for the few actors that reached it alive. A handful of men, an officer or two, a retiring enemy, a place half taken, and an eager longing for reinforcements to complete the victory.

An aide-de-camp is despatched to the rear; he starts upon his mission to traverse that long three hundred yards, swept by a deadly cross-fire, that blackens and scorches the very turf beneath his feet. Down he goes headlong, shot through the body ere he has "run the gauntlet" for a third of the way. Another and another share the same fate! What is to be done? The case is urgent, yet doubtful; it demands promptitude, yet requires consideration. Our Colonel is a man who never hesitates or wavers for an instant. He calls up a young officer of the line, one of the few survivors on the spot; even as he addresses him, the rifleman on his right lurches heavily against him, shot through the loins, and a red-coated comrade on his left falls dead at his feet, yet the Colonel is, if possible, cooler and more colloquial than ever.

"What's your name, my young friend?" says he, shaking the ashes from a short black pipe with which he has been refreshing himself at intervals with much apparent zest. The officer replies, somewhat astonished, yet cool and composed as his commander. The Colonel repeats it twice over, to make sure he has got it right, glances once more at the enemy, then looking his new acquaintance steadily in the face, observes--

"Do I seem to be in a *funk*, young man?"

"No," replies the young officer, determined not to be outdone, "not the least bit of one, any more than myself."

The Colonel laughs heartily. "Very well," says he; "now, if I'm shot, I trust to you to do me justice. I'll tell you what I'm going to do. I must communicate with my supports. Every aide-de-camp I send gets knocked over. I'm no use here alone--I can't take the Redan single-handed--so I'm going back myself. It's only three hundred yards, but I can't run quite so fast as I used, so if I'm killed, I shall expect you to bear witness that I didn't go voluntarily into that cross-fire because *I was afraid*."

The young officer promised, and the Colonel started on his perilous errand. On the success of his mission or the tactics of that attack it is not my province to enlarge. Amongst all the conflicting opinions of the public, there is but one as to the daring gallantry and cool promptitude displayed on that memorable day by the leader of the assault.

Every man, however, moves in his own little world, even at the taking of Sebastopol. It was not for a nameless stranger, holding no rank in the service, to run into needless danger, and I was merely in the trenches as a looker-on, therefore did I keep sedulously under cover and out of fire. It is only the novice who exposes himself unnecessarily, and I had served too long with Omar Pasha not to appreciate the difference between the cool, calculating daring that willingly accepts a certain risk to attain a certain object, and the vainglorious foolhardiness that runs its head blindly against a wall for the mere display of its own intrinsic absurdity.

That great general himself was never known to expose his life unnecessarily. He would direct the manoeuvres of his regiments, and display the tactics for which he was so superior, at a safe distance from the fire of an enemy, as long as he believed himself sufficiently near to watch every movement, and to anticipate every stratagem of the adversary; but if it was advisable to encourage his own troops with his presence, to head a charge, or rally a repulse, who so daring and so reckless as the fortunate Croatian adventurer?

And yet, with all my care and all my self-denial--for indeed, on occasions such as these, curiosity is a powerful motive, and there is a strange instinct in man's wilful heart that urges him into a fray--I had a narrow escape of my own life, and lost my oldest friend and comrade during the progress of the attack.

I was gazing eagerly through my double glasses--the very same that had often done me good service in such different scenes--to watch the forms of those devoted heroes who were staggering and falling in the smoke, when a stray shell, bursting in the trench behind me, blew my forage-cap from my head, and sent it spinning over the parapet on to the glacis beyond. Involuntarily I stretched my hand to catch at it as it flew away, and Bold, who had been crouching quietly at my heel, seeing the motion, started off in pursuit. Ere I could check him, the old dog was over the embankment, and in less than a minute returned to my side with the cap in his mouth. The men laughed, and cheered him as he laid it at my feet.

Poor Bold! poor Bold! he waved his handsome tail, and reared his great square head as proudly as ever; but there was a wistful expression in his eye as he looked up in my face, and when I patted him the old dog winced and moaned as if in pain. He lay down, though quite gently, at my feet, and let me turn him over and examine him. I thought so--there it was, the small round mark in his glossy coat, and the dark stain down his thick foreleg--my poor old friend and comrade, must I lose you too? Is everything to be taken from me by degrees? My eyes were blinded with tears--the rough soldiers felt for me, and spared my favourite some water from their canteens; but he growled when any one offered to touch him but myself, and he died licking my hand.

Even in the turmoil and confusion of that wild scene I could mourn for Bold. He was the one link with my peaceful boyhood, the one creature that she and I had both loved and fondled, and now *she* was lost to me for ever, and Bold lay dead at my feet. Besides, I was fond of him for his own sake--so faithful, so true, so attached, so brave and devoted--in truth, I was very, *very* sorry for poor Bold.

CHAPTER XL
THE WAR-MINISTER AT HOME

Except at the crisis of great convulsions, when the man with the bayonet is the only individual that clearly knows what he has got to do and how to do it, the soldier is but the puppet upon the stage, while the diplomatist pulls the strings from behind the scenes. Before Sebastopol the armies of England, France, and Sardinia keep watch and ward, ever ready for action; at Vienna, the spruce *attaché* deciphers and makes his *précis* of those despatches which decide the soldier's fate. Is it to be peace or war? Has Russia entered into a league with the Austrian Government, or is the Kaiser, in his youthful enthusiasm, eager for an appeal to arms, and forgetful of his defenceless capital, not thirty leagues from the Polish frontier, and innocent of a single fortified place between its walls and the enemy, prepared to join heart and hand with France and England against the common foe? These are questions everybody asks, but nobody seems able to answer. On the Bourse they cause a deal of gambling, and a considerable fluctuation in the value of the florin as computed with reference to English gold. Minor capitalists rise and fall, and Rothschild keeps on adding heap to heap. Money makes money, in Austria as in England; nor are those moustached and spectacled merchants smoking cigars on the Bourse one whit less eager or less rapacious than our own smooth speculators on the Stock Exchange. The crowd is a little more motley, perhaps, and a little more demonstrative, but the object is the same.

"And what news have you here this morning, my dear sir?" observes a quiet-looking, well-dressed bystander who has just strolled in, to a plethoric individual, with a double chin, a double eye-glass, and a red umbrella, who is making voluminous entries in a huge pocket-book. The plethoric man bows to the ground, and becomes exceedingly purple in the face.

"None, honourable sir, none," he replies, with a circular sweep of his hat that touches his toes; "the market is flat, honourable sir, flat, and money, if possible, scarcer than usual."

Whereat the stout man laughs, but breaks off abruptly, as if much alarmed at the liberty he has taken. The well-dressed gentleman turns to some one else with the same inquiry, and, receiving a less cautious answer, glances at his fat friend, who pales visibly under his eye. They are all afraid of him here, for he is no other than our old acquaintance, Monsieur Stein, clean, quiet, and undemonstrative as when we saw him last in the drawing-room at Edeldorf. Let us follow him as he walks out and glides gently along the street in his dark, civil attire, relieved only by a bit of ribbon at the button-hole.

All great men have their weaknesses. Hercules, resting from his labours, spun yarns with Omphale; Antony combined fishing and flirtation; Person loved pale ale, and refreshed himself copiously therewith; and shall not Monsieur Stein, whose Protean genius can assume the characters of all these heroes, display his taste for the fine arts in so picturesque a capital as his own native Vienna? He stops accordingly at a huge stone basin ornamenting one of its squares, and, producing his note-book, proceeds to sketch with masterly touches the magnificent back and limbs of that bronze Triton preparing to launch his harpoon into the depths below. Sly Monsieur Stein! is it thus you spread your nets for the captivation of unwary damsels, and are you always rewarded by so ready a prey as that well-dressed *soubrette* who is peeping on tiptoe over your shoulder, and expressing her artless admiration of your talent in the superlative exclamations of her Teutonic idiom?

"Pardon me, honourable sir, that I so bold am, as so to overlook your wondrously-beautiful design, permit me to see it a little nearer. I thank you, love-worthy sir."

Monsieur Stein is too thoroughly Austrian not to be the pink of politeness. He doffs his hat, and hands her the note-book with a bow. As she returns it to him an open letter peeps between the leaves, and they part and march off on their several ways with many expressions of gratitude and politeness, such as two utter strangers make use of at the termination of a chance acquaintanceship; yet is the *soubrette* strangely like Jeannette, Princess Vocqsal's *femme de chambre*; and the letter which Monsieur Stein reads so attentively as he paces along the sunny side of the street, is certainly addressed to that lady in characters bearing a strong resemblance to the handwriting of Victor, Count de Rohan.

Monsieur Stein pockets the epistle--it might be a receipt for *sour-krout* for all the effect its perusal has on his impassible features--and proceeds, still at his equable, leisurely pace, to the residence of the War-Minister.

While he mounts the steps to the second floor, on which are situated the apartments of that functionary, and combs out his smooth moustaches, waiting the convenience of the porter who answers the bell, let us take a peep inside.

The War-Minister is at his wit's end. His morning has been a sadly troubled one, for he has been auditing accounts, to which pursuit he cherishes a strong disinclination, and he has received a letter from the Minister of the Interior, conveying contradictory orders from the Emperor, of which he cannot make head or tail. Besides this, he has private annoyances of his own. His intendant has failed to send him the usual supplies from his estates in Galicia; he is in debt to his tailor and his coach-maker, but he must have new liveries and an English carriage against the next Court ball; his favourite charger is lame, and he does not care to trust himself on any of his other horses; and, above all, he has sustained an hour's lecture this very morning, when drinking coffee in his dressing-gown, from Madame la Baronne, his austere and excellent spouse, commenting in severe terms on his backslidings and general conduct, the shortcomings of which, as that virtuous dame affirms, have not failed to elicit the censure of the young Emperor himself. So the War-Minister has drunk three large tumblers of *schwartz-bier*, and smoked as many cigars stuck up on end in the bowl of a meerschaum pipe, the combined effects of which have failed to simplify the accounts, or to reconcile the contradictory instructions of the Court.

He is a large, fine-looking man, considerably above six feet in height. His grey-blue uniform is buttoned tightly over a capacious chest, covered with orders, clasps, and medals; his blue eyes and florid complexion denote health and good-humour, not out of keeping with the snowy moustaches and hair of some three-score winters. He looks completely puzzled, and is bestowing an uneasy sort of attention, for which he feels he must ere long be taken to task, upon a very charming and well-dressed visitor of the other sex, no less a person, indeed, than that *"odious intrigante,"* as Madame la Baronne calls her, the Princess Vocqsal.

She is as much at home here in the War-Minister's apartments as in her own drawing-room. She never loses her *aplomb*, or her presence of mind. If his wife were to walk in this minute she would greet her with amiable cordiality; and, to do Madame la Baronne justice, though she abuses the Princess in all societies, her greeting would be returned with the warmth and kindness universally displayed to each other by women who hate to the death. Till she has got her antagonist *down*, the female fencer never takes the button off her foil.

"You are always so amiable and good-humoured, my dear Baron," says the Princess, throwing back her veil with a turn of her snowy wrist, not lost upon the old soldier, "that you will, I am sure, not keep us in suspense. The Prince wishes his nephew to serve the Emperor; he is but a boy yet. Will he be tall enough for the cavalry? A fine man looks so well on horseback!"

The Baron was justly proud of his person. This little compliment and the glance that accompanied it were not thrown away. He looked pleased, then remembered his wife, and looked sheepish, then smoothed his moustache, and inquired the age of the candidate.

"Seventeen next birthday," replied the Princess. "If it were not for this horrid war we would send him to travel a little. Do you think the war will last, Monsieur le Baronne?" added she, naïvely.

"You must ask the Foreign Minister about that," replied he, completely thrown off his guard by her innocence. "We are only soldiers here, we do not pull the strings, Madame. We do what we are told, and serve the Emperor and the ladies," he added, with a low bow and a leer.

"Then will you put him into the Cuirassiers immediately, Monsieur?" said the Princess, with her sweetest smile; "we wish no time to be lost--now *do*, to please *me*."

The Baron was rather in a dilemma; like all men in office, he hated to bind himself by a promise, but how to refuse that charming woman anything?--at last he stammered out--"Wait a little, Madame, wait, and I will do what I can for you; it is impossible just now, for we are going to reduce the army by sixty thousand men."

While he spoke, Monsieur Stein was announced, and the Princess rose to take her leave; she had got all she wanted now, and did not care to face a thousand Baronesses. As she went downstairs, she passed Monsieur Stein without the slightest mark of recognition, and he, too, looked admiringly after her, as if he had never seen her before. The Baron, by this time pining for more *schwartz-bier*, and another cigar, devoutly hoped his new visitor, with whose person and profession he was quite familiar, would not stay long; and the Princess, as she tripped past the *Huissier* at the entrance, muttered, "Sixty thousand men--then it *will* be peace: I thought so all along. My poor Baron! what a soft old creature you are! Well, I have tried everything now, and this speculating is the strongest excitement of all, even better than making Victor jealous!" but she sighed as she said it, and ordered her coachman to drive on at once to her stock-broker.

The presence of Monsieur Stein did not serve to re-establish either the clear-headedness or the good-humour of the War-Minister. The ostensible errand on which he came was merely to obtain some trifling military information concerning the garrison at Pesth, without which the co-operation of the police would not have been so effectual, in annoying still further the already exasperated Hungarians; but in the course of conversation, Monsieur Stein subjected the Baron to a process familiarly called "sucking the brains," with such skill that, ere the door was closed on his unwelcome visitor, the soldier felt he had placed himself--as indeed was intended--completely in the power of the police-agent. All his sins of omission and commission, his neglect of certain contracts, and his issuing of certain orders; his unpardonable lenity at his last tour of inspection, his unlucky expression of opinions at direct variance with those of his young Imperial master:--all these failures and offences he felt were now registered in letters never to be effaced,--on the records of Monsieur Stein's secret report; and what was more provoking still, was to think that he had, somehow or another, been insensibly led on to plead guilty to half-a-dozen derelictions, which he felt he might as consistently have denied.

As he sat bolt upright in his huge leathern chair, and turned once more to "sublime tobacco" for consolation and refreshment, his thoughts floated back to the merry days when he was young and slim, and had no cares beyond his squadron of Uhlans, no thought for the morrow but the parade and the ball. "Ah!" sighed the Baron to himself as he knocked the ash off his cigar with a ringed fore-finger, "I would I were a youngling again; the troop-accounts were easily kept, the society of my comrades was pleasanter than the Court. One never meets with such beer now as we had at Debreczin; and oh! those Hungarian ladies, how delightful it was to waltz before one grew fat, and flirt before one grew sage. I might have visited the charming Princess then, and no one would have found fault with me; no one would have objected--Heigh-ho! there was no Madame la Baronne in those days-- *now* it is so different. *Sapperment!* Here she comes!"

Though the Baron was upwards of six feet, and broad in proportion-- though he had distinguished himself more than once before the enemy, and was covered with orders of merit and decorations for bravery--nay, though he was the actual head of the six hundred thousand heroes who constituted the Austrian army, he quailed before that little shrivelled old woman, with her mouth full of black teeth, and her hair dressed *à l'Impératrice*.

We profane not the mysteries of Hymen--"Caudle" is a name of no exclusive nationality. We leave the Baron, not without a shudder, to the salutary discipline of his excellent monitress.

CHAPTER XLI
WHEELS WITHIN WHEELS

We must follow Monsieur Stein, for that worthy has got something to do; nay, he generally has his hands full, and cannot, indeed, be accused of eating the bread of idleness. It is a strange system of government, that of the Austrian empire; and is, we believe, found to answer as badly as might be expected from its organisation. The State takes so paternal an interest in the sayings and doings of its children, as to judge it expedient to support a whole staff of officials, whose sole duty it is to keep the Government informed respecting the habits, actions, everyday life, and secret thoughts and opinions of the general public. Nor do these myrmidons, whose number exceeds belief, and who add seriously to the national expenditure, fail to earn their pay with praiseworthy diligence. In all societies, in all places of pleasure or business, where half-a-dozen people may chance to congregate, *there* will be an agent of police, always in plain clothes, and generally the least conspicuous person in the throng. The members of this corps are, as may be supposed, chosen for their general intelligence and aptitude, are usually well-informed, agreeable men, likely to lead strangers into conversation, and excellent linguists. As an instance of their ubiquity, I may mention an incident that occurred within my own knowledge to an officer in the British service, when at Vienna, during the war. That officer was dining in the *salon* of an hotel, and there were present, besides his own party, consisting of Englishmen, and one Hungarian much disaffected to the Government, only two other strangers, sitting quite at the farther extremity of the room, and apparently out of ear-shot. The conversation at my friend's table was, moreover, carried on in English, and turned upon the arrest of a certain Colonel Türr by the Austrian authorities at Bucharest, a few days previously.

This Colonel Türr, be it known, was a Hungarian who had deserted from the Austrian service, and entering that of her Majesty Queen Victoria, had been employed in some commissariat capacity in Wallachia, and taken prisoner at Bucharest by the very regiment to which he had previously belonged. The question was much vexed and agitated at the time, as to the Austrian right over a deserter on a neutral soil, and Colonel Türr became for the nonce an unconscious hero. The officer to whom I have alluded, having listened attentively to the *pros* and *cons* of the case, as set forth by his friends, dismissed the subject with military brevity, in these words:-- "If you say he deserted his regiment before an enemy, I don't care what countryman he is, or in whose service, *the sooner they hang him the better!*" This ill-advised remark, be it observed, was made *sotto voce*, and in his own language. His surprise may be imagined when, on perusing the Government papers the following morning, he read the whole conversation, translated into magniloquent German, and detailed at length as being the expressed opinion of the British army and the British public on the case of Colonel Türr.

I am happy to be able to observe, *en passant*, that the latter gentleman was not hanged at all, but escaped, after a deal of diplomatic correspondence, with a six weeks' imprisonment in the fortress of Comorn, and has since been seen taking his pleasure in London and elsewhere.

To return to Monsieur Stein. It is evening, and those who have permission from the police to give a party, have lighted their lamps and prepared their saloons for those receptions in which the well-bred of all nations, and particularly the ladies, take so incomprehensible a delight. At Vienna, every house must be closed at ten o'clock; and those who wish to give balls or evening parties must obtain a direct permission to do so, emanating from the Emperor himself. So when they *do* go out, they make the most of it, and seem to enjoy the pleasure with an additional zest for the prohibition to which it is subject.

Let us follow Monsieur Stein into that brilliantly-lighted room, through which he edges his way so unobtrusively, and where, amongst rustling toilettes, crisp and fresh from the dressmaker, and various uniforms on the fine persons of the Austrian aristocracy, his own modest attire passes unobserved. This is no *bourgeois* gathering, no assemblage of the middle rank, tainted by mercantile enterprise, or disgraced by talent, which presumes to rise superior to *blood*. No such thing; they are all the "*haute volée*" here, the "*crème de la crème*," as they themselves call it in their bad French and their conventional jargon. Probably Monsieur Stein is the only man in the room that cannot count at least sixteen quarterings--no such easy matter to many a member of our own House of Peers; and truth to tell, the Austrian aristocracy are a personable, fine-looking race as you shall wish to see. Even the eye of our imperturbable police-agent lights up with a ray of what in any other eye would be admiration, at the scene which presents itself as he enters. The rooms are spacious, lofty, and magnificently furnished in the massive, costly style that accords so well with visitors in full dress. The floors are beautifully inlaid and polished; as bright, and nearly as slippery, as ice. The walls are covered with the *chef d'oeuvres* of the old masters, and even the dome-like ceilings are decorated with mythological frescoes, such as would convert an enthusiast to paganism at once. Long mirrors fill up the interstices between the panellings, and reflect many a stalwart gallant, and many a "lady bright and fair." There is no dancing, it is merely a "reception"; and amongst the throng of beauties congregated in that assembly, impassible Monsieur Stein cannot but admit that the most captivating of them all is Princess Vocqsal.

So thinks the War-Minister, who, forgetful of accounts and responsibilities, regardless even of the threatening glances darted at him from the other end of the room by his excellent wife, is leaning over the back of the Princess's seat, and whispering, in broad Viennese German, a variety of those soft platitudes which gentlemen of three-score are apt to fancy will do them as good service at that age as they did thirty years ago. The Baron is painfully agreeable, and she is listening, with a sweet smile and a pleasant expression of countenance, assumed for very sufficient reasons. In the first place, she owes him a good turn for the information acquired this morning, and the Princess always pays her debts when it costs her nothing; in the second, she wishes, for motives of her own, to strengthen her influence with the Court party as much as possible; and lastly, she enjoys by this means the innocent pleasure of making two people unhappy--viz. Madame la Baronne, who is fool enough to be jealous of her fat old husband; and one other watching her from the doorway, with a pale, eager face, and an expression of restless, gnawing anxiety, which it is painful to behold.

Victor de Rohan, what are you doing here, like a moth fluttering round a candle? wasting your time, and breaking your heart for a woman that is not worth one throb of its generous life-blood; that cannot appreciate your devotion, or even spare your feelings? Why are you not at Edeldorf, where you have left *her* sad and lonely, one tear on whose eyelash is worth a thousand of the false smiles so freely dealt by that heartless, artificial, worn woman of the world? For shame, Victor! for shame! And yet, as our friend the Turk says, "*Kismet*! It is destiny!"

He is dressed in a gorgeous Hussar uniform, his own national costume, and right well does its close fit and appropriate splendour become the stately beauty of the young Count de Rohan. At his side hangs the very sword that flashed so keenly by the waters of the Danube, forward in the headlong charge of old Iskender Bey. On its blade is engraved the Princess's name; she knows it as well as he does, yet ten to one she will pretend to forget all about it, should he allude to the subject to-night. Ah! the blade is as bright as it was in those merry campaigning days, but Victor's face has lost for ever the lightsome expression of youth; the lines of passion and self-reproach are stamped upon his brow, and hollowed round his lip, and he has passed at one stride from boyhood to middle age.

He makes a forced movement, as though to speak to her, but his button is held by a jocose old gentleman, whose raptures must find vent on the engrossing topic of Marie Taglioni's graceful activity; and he has to weather the whole person and draperies of a voluminous German dowager ere he can escape from his tormentor. In the meantime Monsieur Stein has been presented to the Princess, and she allows him to lead her into the tea-room, for a cup of that convenient beverage which continental nations persist in considering as possessed of medicinal virtue.

"I have the unhappiness to have escaped Madame's recollection," observed the police-agent, as he placed a chair for the Princess in a corner secure from interruption, and handed her cup; "it is now my good fortune to be able to restore something that she has lost," and he looked at her with those keen grey eyes, as though to read her very soul, while he gave her the letter which had been placed in his pocket-book by faithless Jeannette. "If she cares for him," thought Monsieur Stein, "she will surely show it now, and I need take no further trouble with *her*. If not, she is the very woman I want, for the fool is madly in love with her, and upon my word it is not surprising!"

Monsieur Stein looked at women with hypercritical fastidiousness, but, as he himself boasted, at the same time, quite "*en philosophe.*"

The Princess, however, was a match for the police-agent; she never winced, or moved a muscle of her beautiful countenance. With a polite "Excuse me," she read the letter through from beginning to end, and turning quietly round inquired, "How came you by this, Monsieur?"

Unless it leads to a *revoke*, a lie counts for nothing with a police-agent, so he answered at once, "Sent to my *bureau* from the office, in consequence of an informality in the post-mark."

"You have read it?" pursued the Princess, still calm and unmoved.

"On my honour, no!" answered he, with his hand on his heart, and a low bow.

She would have made the better spy of the two, for she could read even his impassible face, and she knew as well as he did himself that he had, so she quietly returned him the letter, of which she judged, and rightly, that he had kept a copy; and laying her gloved hand on his sleeve, observed, with an air of bewitching candour--"After that affair at Comorn, you and I can have no secrets from each other, Monsieur. Tell me frankly what it is that your employers require, and the price they are willing to pay for my co-operation."

She could not resist the temptation of trying her powers, even on Monsieur Stein; and he, although a police-agent, was obliged to succumb to that low, sweet voice, and the pleading glance by which it was accompanied. A little less calmly than was his wont, and with almost a flush upon his brow, he began--

"You are still desirous of that appointment we spoke of yesterday for the Prince?"

"*Ma foi*, I am," she answered, with a merry smile; "without it we shall be ruined, for we are indeed overwhelmed with debt."

"You also wish for the earliest intelligence possessed by the Government as to the issues of peace and war?"

"Of course I do, my dear Monsieur Stein; how else can I speculate to advantage?"

"And you would have the attainder taken off your cousin's estates in the Banat in your favour?"

The Princess's eyes glistened, and a deep flush overspread her face. This was more than she had ever dared to hope for. This would raise her to affluence, nay, to splendour, once again. No price would be too great to pay for this end, and she told Monsieur Stein so, although she kept down her raptures and stilled her beating heart the while.

"All this, Princess, I can obtain for you," said he; "all this has been promised me, and I have got it in writing. In less than a month the Government will have redeemed its pledge, and in return you shall do us one little favour."

"*C'est un trahison, n'est ce pas?*" she asked quickly, but without any appearance of shame or anger; "I know it by the price you offer. Well, I am not scrupulous--say on."

"Scarcely that," he replied, evidently emboldened by her coolness; "only a slight exertion of feminine influence, of which no woman on earth has so much at command as yourself. Listen, Princess; in three words I will tell you all. Count de Rohan loves you passionately--madly. You know it yourself;-- forgive my freedom; between you and me there must be no secrets. You can do what you will with him."--(He did not see her blush, for she had turned away to put down her cup.)--"He will refuse you nothing. This is your task:- -there is another conspiracy hatching against the Government; its plot is not yet ripe, but it numbers in its ranks some of the first men in Hungary. Your compatriots are very stanch; even I can get no certain information. Several of the disaffected are yet unknown to me. Young Count de Rohan has a list of their names; that list I trust to you to obtain. Say, Princess, is it a bargain?"

She was fitting her glove accurately to her taper fingers.

"And the man that you were good enough to say adores me so devotedly, Monsieur," she observed, without lifting her eyes to his face, "what will you do with him? shoot him as you did his cousin in 1848?"

"He shall have a free pardon," replied the police-agent, "and permission to reside on his lands. He is not anxious to leave the vicinity of the Waldenberg, I believe," he added mischievously.

"*Soit,*" responded the Princess, as she rose to put an end to the interview. "Now, if you will hand me my bouquet we will go into the other room."

As he bowed and left her, Monsieur Stein felt a certain uncomfortable misgiving that he had been guilty of some oversight in his game. In vain he played it all again in his own head, move for move, and check for check; he could not detect where the fault lay, and yet his fine instinct told him that somewhere or another he had made a mistake. "It is all that woman's impassible face," he concluded at last, in his mental soliloquy, "that forbids me to retrieve a blunder or detect an advantage. And what a beautiful face it is!" he added almost aloud, as for an instant the official was absorbed in the man.

In the meantime Victor was getting very restless, very uncomfortable, and, not to mince matters, very cross.

No sooner had the Princess returned to the large *salon* than he stalked across the room, twirling his moustaches with an air of unconcealed annoyance, and asked her abruptly, "How she came to know that ill-looking Monsieur Stein, and why he had been flirting with her for the last half-hour in the tea-room?"

"That gentleman in plain clothes?" answered she, with an air of utter unconsciousness and perfect good-humour; "that is one of my ancient friends, Monsieur le Comte; shall I present him to you?"

This was another refined method of tormenting her lovers. The Princess had one answer to all jealous inquiries as to those whom she favoured with her notice--"*Un de mes anciens amis,*" was a vague and general description, calculated to give no very definite or satisfactory information to a rival.

"Have a care, Madame," whispered Victor angrily; "you will make some of your ancient friends into your deadliest enemies if you try them so far."

She looked lovingly up at him, and he softened at once.

"Now it is *you* that are unkind, Victor," she said in a low soft voice, every tone of which thrilled to the young Count's heart. "Why will you persist in quarrelling with me? I, who came here this very evening to see you and to do you a kindness?"

"Did you know I should be in Vienna so soon?" he exclaimed eagerly. "Did you receive my letter?"

"I did, indeed," she replied, with a covert smile, as she thought of the mode in which that missive had reached her, and she almost laughed outright (for the Princess had a keen sense of the ludicrous) at the strange impersonation made by Monsieur Stein of Cupid's postman; "but, Victor," she added, with another beaming look, "I go away to-morrow. Very early in the morning I must leave Vienna."

He turned paler than before, and bit his lip. "So I might as well have stayed at home," he exclaimed in a voice of bitter annoyance and pique, none the less bitter that it had to be toned down to the concert pitch of good society. "Was it to see you for five minutes here in a crowd that I travelled up so eagerly and in such haste? To make my bow, I suppose, like the merest acquaintance, and receive my *congé*. Pardon, Madame la Princesse, I need not receive it twice. I wish you good-evening; I am going now!"

She, too, became a shade paler, but preserved the immovable good-humour on which she piqued herself, as she made him a polite bow, and turned round to speak to the Russian Minister, who, covered with orders, at that moment came up to offer his obeisance to the well-known Princess Vocqsal. Had he not constant advices from his intriguing Court to devote much of his spare time to this fascinating lady? And had she not once in her life baffled all the wiles of St. Petersburg, and stood untempted by its bribes? Ill-natured people affirmed that another Power paid a higher price, which accounted satisfactorily for the lady's patriotism, but the Autocrat's Minister had his secret orders notwithstanding.

And now she is deep in a lively argument, in which polished sarcasm and brilliant repartee are bandied from lip to lip, each pointed phrase eliciting a something better still from the Princess's soft mouth, till her audience--diplomatists of many years' standing, warriors shrewd in council and dauntless in the field, grey ambassadors and beardless *attachés*--hang enraptured on her accents, and watch her looks with an unaccountable fascination; whilst Victor de Rohan, hurt, moody, and discontented, stalks fiercely to the doorway and mutters to himself, "Is it for this I have given up home, friends, honour, and self-respect? To be a mere puppet in the hands of a coquette, a woman's plaything, and not even a favourite plaything, after all!"

Ladies have a peculiar gift which is enjoyed by no other members of the creation whatsoever. We allude to that extraordinary property by which, without any exertion of the visual organs, they can discern clearly all that is going on above, below, around, and behind them. If a man wants to *see* a thing he requires to *look at it*. Not so with the other sex. Their subtler instinct enables them to detect that which must be made palpable to *our* grosser senses. How else could Princess Vocqsal, whose back was turned to him, and who was occupied in conversation with the *élite* of Austrian diplomatic society, arrive at the certainty that Victor was not gone, as he had threatened--that he still lingered unwillingly about the doorway, and now hailed as deliverers those prosy acquaintances from whom, in the early part of the evening, he had been so impatient to escape?

And yet he despised himself for his want of manhood and resolution the while; and yet he reproached himself with his slavish submission and unworthy cowardice; and yet he lingered on in hopes of one more glance from her eye, one more pressure from her soft gloved hand. He had parted with her in anger before, and too well he knew the bitter wretchedness of the subsequent hours; he had not fortitude enough, he *dared* not face such an ordeal again.

So she knew he was not going yet; and, confident in her own powers, pleased with her position, and proud of her conquests, she sparkled on.

"That's a clever woman," said an English *attaché* to his friend, as they listened in the circle of her admirers.

And the friend, who was a little of a satirist, a little of a philosopher, a little of a poet, and yet, strange to say, a thorough man of the world, replied--

"Too clever by half, my boy, or I'm very much mistaken. Ninety-nine women out of a hundred are natural-born angels, but the hundredth is a devil incarnate, and *that's* her number, Charlie, you may take my word for it!"

And now a strange movement rises in that crowded assembly. A buzz of voices is heard--lower, but more marked than the ordinary hum of conversation. Something seems to have happened. A lady has fainted, or an apoplectic general been taken suddenly ill, or a candelabrum has fallen, and the magnificent hotel is even now on fire? None of these casualties, however, have occurred. Voices rise higher in question and reply. "Is it true?"--"I can't believe it!"--"They knew nothing of it to-day on the Bourse."--"Another stock-jobbing report."--"Immense loss on both sides." These are the disjointed sentences that reach the ear, mingled with such terms as the Malakhoff--the Redan--the north side--General Pelissier, etc. etc. English and French diplomatists exchange curious glances, and at length rumour takes a definite form, and it is boldly asserted that intelligence has that day arrived of the fall of Sebastopol.

Tongues are loosened now. Surmise and speculation are rife upon future events. Men speak as they wish, and notwithstanding the presence of Monsieur Stein and several other secret agents of police, many a bold opinion is hazarded as to the intentions of the Government and the issues of the great contest. Princess Vocqsal scarcely breathes while she listens. If, indeed, this should lead to peace, her large investments will realise golden profits. She feels all the palpitating excitement of the gambler, yet does the hue not deepen on her cheek, nor the lustre kindle brighter in her eye. Monsieur Stein, who alone knows her secrets, as it is his business to know the secrets of every one, feels his very soul stirred within him at such noble self-command.

For a moment he thinks that were he capable of human weaknesses he could *love* that woman; and in pure admiration, as one who would fain prove still further a beautiful piece of mechanism, he steps up to the Princess, and informs her that "Now, indeed, doubt is at an end, for reliable intelligence has arrived that Sebastopol has fallen!"

"Sebastopol has fallen," she repeats with her silver laugh; "then the war has at last really begun!"

Her audience applaud once more. "*Ma foi, ce n'est pas mal,*" says the French Minister, and Monsieur Stein is on the verge of adoration; but there is by this time a general move towards the door: carriages are being called, and it is time to go away, the departure of the guests being somewhat accelerated by the important news which has just been made public. Victor is still lingering on the staircase. Many a bright eye looks wistfully on his handsome form, many a soft heart would willingly waken an interest in the charming young Count de Rohan, but the Hungarian has caught the malady in its deadliest form--the "love fever," as his own poets term it, is wasting his heart to the core, and for him, alas! there is but one woman on earth, and she is coming downstairs at this moment, attended by the best-dressed and best-looking *attaché* of the French Legation.

Somewhat to this young gentleman's disgust, she sends him to look for her carriage, and taking Victor's arm, which he is too proud to offer, she bids him lead her to the cloak-room, and shawl her as he used to do with such tender care.

He relents at once. What *is* there in this woman that she can thus turn and twist him at her will? She likes him best thus--when he is haughty and rebellious, and she fears that at last she may have driven him too far and have lost him altogether; the uncertainty creates an interest and excitement, which is pleasure akin to pain, but it is so delightful to win him back again,--*such* a triumph to own him and tyrannise over him once more! It is at moments of reconciliation such as these that the Princess vindicates her woman-nature, and becomes a very woman to the heart.

"You are angry with me, Victor," she whispers, leaning heavily on his arm, and looking downwards as she speaks; "angry with me, and without a cause. You would not listen to me an hour ago, you were so cross and impatient. Will you listen to me now?"

The tears were standing in the strong man's eyes. "Speak on," he said; "you do with me what you like, I could listen to you for ever."

"You were irritated because I told you I was about to leave Vienna. You have avoided me the whole evening, and left me to be bored and annoyed by that wearisome tribe of diplomatists, with their flat witticisms and their eternal politics. Why did you not stay to hear me out? Victor, it is true I go to-morrow, but I go to the Waldenberg."

How changed his face was now; his eye sparkled and his whole countenance lightened up. He looked like a different man. He could only press the arm that clung to his own; he could not speak.

"Will you continue to *bouder* me?" proceeded the Princess in a playful, half-malicious tone; "or will you forgive me and be friends for that which is, after all, your own fault? Oh, you men! how hasty and violent you are; it is lucky we are so patient and so good-tempered. The Waldenberg is not so very far from Edeldorf. You might ask me there for your *jour de fête*. I have not forgotten it, you see. Not a word more, Count de Rohan; I must leave you now. Here is my carriage. Adieu,--no, not adieu, *mon ami, au revoir!*"

Why was it such a different world to Victor from what it had been ten short minutes ago, from what it would assuredly be the next time they met, and her caprice and *coquetterie* were again exhibited to drive him wild? Was it worth all these days of uncertainty and anxious longing; all these fits of jealousy and agonies of self-reproach; to be deliriously happy every now and then for a short ten minutes? Was any woman on earth worthy of all that Victor de Rohan sacrificed for the indulgence of his guilty love? Probably not, but it would have been hard to convince him. He was not as wise as Solomon; yet Solomon, with all his wisdom, seems to have delivered himself up a willing captive to disgrace and bondage--fettered by a pair of white arms--held by a thread of silken hair. Oh, vanity of vanities! "*this is* also vanity and vexation of spirit."

CHAPTER XLII
"TOO LATE"

For a wounded campaigner on crutches, or a wasted convalescent slowly recovering from an attack of Crimean fever, there are few better places for the re-establishment of health than the hotel at Therapia. It is refreshing to hear the ripple of the Bosphorus not ten feet distant from one's bedroom window; it is life itself to inhale the invigorating breeze that sweeps down, unchecked and uncontaminated, from the Black Sea; it is inspiriting to gaze upon the gorgeous beauty of the Asiatic coast, another continent not a mile away. And then the smaller accessories of comfortable apartments, good dinners, civilised luxuries, and European society, form no unwelcome contrast to the Crimean tent, the soldier's rations, and the wearisome routine of daily and hourly duty.

But a few days after the taking of Sebastopol, I was once more in Turkey. Ropsley, the man of iron nerves and strong will--the man whom danger had spared, and sickness had hitherto passed by, was struck down by fever--that wasting, paralysing disease so common to our countrymen in an Eastern climate--and was so reduced and helpless as to be utterly incapable of moving without assistance. He had many friends, for Ropsley was popular in his regiment and respected throughout the army; but none were so thoroughly disengaged as I; it seemed as if I could now be of little use in any capacity, and to my lot it fell to place my old school-fellow on board ship, and accompany him to Therapia, *en route* for England on sick leave.

My own affairs, too, required that I should revisit Somersetshire before long. The wreck of my father's property, well nursed and taken care of by a prudent man of business, had increased to no contemptible provision for a nameless child. If I chose to return to England, I should find myself a landed proprietor of no inconsiderable means, should be enabled to assume a position such as many a man now fighting his way in the world would esteem the acme of human felicity, and for me it would be but dust and ashes! What cared I for broad acres, local influence, good investments, and county respectability--all the outward show and empty shadows for which people are so apt to sacrifice the real blessings of life? What was it to me that I might look round from my own dining-room on my own domain, with my own tenants waiting to see me in the hall? An empty heart can have no possessions; a broken spirit is but a beggar in the midst of wealth, whilst the whole universe, with all its glories, belongs alone to him who is at peace with himself. I often think how many a man there is who lives out his three-score years and ten, and never knows what *real* life is, after all. A boyhood passed in vain aspirations--a manhood spent in struggling for the impossible--an old age wasted in futile repinings, such is the use made by how many of our fellow-creatures of that glorious streak of light which we call existence, that intervenes between the eternity which hath been, and the eternity which shall be? Oh! to lie down and rest, and look back upon the day's hard labour, and feel that something has been wrought--that something has been *won!* and so to sleep--happy here--happy for evermore. Well, on some natures happiness smiles even here on earth--God forbid it should be otherwise!--and some must content themselves with duty instead. Who knows which shall have the best of it when all is over? For me, it was plain at this period that I must do my *devoir*, and leave all to Time, the great restorer in the moral, as he is the great destroyer in the physical, world. The years of excitement (none know how strong) that I had lately passed, followed by a listless, hopeless inactivity, had produced a reaction on my spirits which it was necessary to conquer and shake off. I resolved to return to England, to set my house in order--to do all the good in my power, and first of all, strenuously to commence with that which lay nearest my hand, although it was but the humble task of nursing my old school-fellow through an attack of low fever.

My patient possessed one of those strong and yet elastic natures which even sickness seems unable thoroughly to subdue. The Ropsley on a couch of suffering and lassitude, was the same Ropsley that confronted the enemy's fire so coolly in the Crimea, and sneered at the follies of his friends so sarcastically in St. James's street. Ill as he was, and utterly prostrated in body, he was clear-headed and ready-witted as ever. With the help of a wretchedly bad grammar, he was rapidly picking up Turkish, by no means an easy language for a beginner; and, taking advantage of my society, was actually entering upon the rudiments of Hungarian, a tongue which it is next to impossible for any one to acquire who has not spoken it, as I had done, in earliest childhood. He was good-humoured and patient, too, far more than I should have expected, and was never anxious or irritable, save about his letters. I have seen him, however, turn away from a negative to the eager inquiry "Any letters for me?" with an expression of heart-sick longing that it pained me to witness on that usually haughty and somewhat sneering countenance.

But it came at last. Not many mornings after our arrival at Therapia there was a letter for Ropsley, which seemed to afford him unconcealed satisfaction, and from that day the Guardsman mended rapidly, and began to talk of getting up and packing his things, and starting westward once more.

So it came to pass that, with the help of his servant, I got him out of bed and dressed him, and laid him on the sofa at the open window, where he could see the light caïques dancing gaily on the waters, and the restless sea-fowl flitting eternally to and fro, and could hear the shouts of the Turkish boatmen, adjuring each other, very unnecessarily, not to be too hasty; and the discordant cries of the Greek population scolding, and cheating, and vociferating on the quay.

We talked of Hungary. I loved to talk of it now, for was it not *her* country of whom I must think no more? And Ropsley's manner was kinder, and his voice softer, than I had ever thought it before. Poor fellow! he was weak with his illness, perhaps, yet hitherto I had remarked no alteration in his cold, impassible demeanour.

At last he took my hand, and in a hollow voice he said--"Vere, you have returned me good for evil. You have behaved to me like a brother. Vere, I believe you really are a Christian!"

"I hope so," I replied quietly, for what had I but that?

"Yes," he resumed, "but I don't mean conventionally, because your godfathers and godmothers at your baptism said you were--I mean *really*. I don't believe there is a particle of *humbug* about you. Can you forgive your enemies?"

"I have already told you so," I answered; "don't you remember that night in the trenches? besides, Ropsley, I shall never consider you my enemy."

"That is exactly what cuts me to the heart," he replied, flushing up over his wan, wasted face. "I have injured you more deeply than any one on earth, and I have received nothing but kindness in return. Often and often I have longed to tell you all--how I had wronged you, and how I had repented, but my pride forbade me till to-day. It is dreadful to think that I might have died, and never confessed to you how hard and how unfeeling I have been. Listen to me, and then forgive me if you can. Oh, Vere, Vere! had it not been for me and my selfishness, you might have married Constance Beverley!"

I felt I was trembling all over; I covered my face with my hands and turned away, but I bade him go on.

"Her father was never averse to you from the first. He liked you, Vere, personally, and still more for the sake of your father, his old friend. There was but one objection. I need not dwell upon it; and even that he could have got over, for he was most anxious to see his daughter married, and to one with whom he could have made his own terms. He was an unscrupulous man, Sir Harry, and dreadfully pressed for money. When in that predicament people will do things that at other times they would be ashamed of, as I know too well. And the girl too, Vere, she loved you--I am sure of it--she loved you, poor girl, with all her heart and soul."

I looked him straight in the face--"Not a word of *her*, Ropsley, as you are a gentleman!" I said. Oh, the agony of that moment! and yet it was not all pain.

"Well," he proceeded, "Sir Harry consulted me about the match. You know how intimate we were, you know what confidence he had in my judgment. If I had been generous and honourable, if I had been such a man as *you*, Vere, how much happier we should all be now; but no, I had my own ends in view, and I determined to work out my own purpose, without looking to the right or left, without turning aside for friend or foe. Besides, I hardly knew you then, Vere. I did not appreciate your good qualities. I did not know your courage, and constancy, and patience, and kindliness. I did not know yours was just the clinging, womanly nature, that would never get over the crushing of its best affections--and I know it now too well. Oh, Vere, you never can forgive me! And yet," he added, musingly, more to himself than to me,--"and yet, even had I known all this, had you been my own brother, I fear my nature was then so hard, so pitiless, so uncompromising, that I should have gone straight on towards my aim, and blasted your happiness without scruple or remorse. *Remorse*," and the old look came over him, the old sneering look, that wreathed those handsome features in the wicked smile of a fallen angel--"if a man means to *repent* of what he has done, he had better not *do it*. My maxim has always been, 'never look back,'--'*vestigia, nulla retrorsum*'--and yet to-day I cannot help retracing, ay, and bitterly *regretting*, the past.

"I have told you I had my own ends in view. I wished to marry the heiress myself. Not that I loved her, Vere--do not be angry with me for the confession--I never loved her the least in the world. She was far too placid, too conventional, too like other girls, to make the slightest impression on me. My ideal of a woman is, a bold, strong nature, a keen intellect, a daring mind, and a dazzling beauty that others must fall down and worship. I never was one of your sentimentalists. A violet may be a very pretty flower, and smell very sweet, but I like a camellia best, and all the better because you require a hothouse to raise it in. But, if I did not care for Miss Beverley,

I cared a good deal for Beverley Manor, and I resolved that, come what might, Beverley Manor should one day be mine. The young lady I looked upon as an encumbrance that must necessarily accompany the estate. You know how intimate I became with her father, you know the trust he reposed in me, and the habit into which he fell, of doing nothing without my advice. That trust, I now acknowledge to you, I abused shamefully; of that habit I took advantage, solely to further my own ends, totally irrespective of my friend. He confided to me in very early days his intention of marrying his daughter to the son of his old friend. He talked it over with me as a scheme on which he had set his heart, and, above all, insisted on the advantage to himself of making, as he called it, his own terms with you about settlements, etc. I have already told you he was involved in difficulties, from which his daughter's marriage could alone free him, with the consent of her husband. I need not enter into particulars. I have the deeds and law papers at my fingers' ends, for I like to understand a business thoroughly if I embark on it at all, but it is no question of such matters now. Well, Vere, at first I was too prudent to object overtly to the plan. Sir Harry, as you know, was an obstinate, wilful man, and such a course would have been the one of all others most calculated to wed him more firmly than ever to his original intention; but I weighed the matter carefully with him day by day, now bringing forward arguments in favour of it, now starting objections, till I had insensibly accustomed him to consider it by no means as a settled affair. Then I tried all my powers upon the young lady, and there, I confess to you freely, Vere, I was completely foiled. She never liked me even as an acquaintance, and she took no pains to conceal her aversion. How angry she used to make me sometimes!--I *hated* her so, that I longed to make her mine, if it were only to humble her, as much as if I had loved her with all my heart and soul. Many a time I used to grind my teeth and mutter to myself, 'Ah! my fair enemy, I shall live to make you rue this treatment;' and I swore a great oath that, come what might, she should never belong to Vere Egerton. I even tried to create an interest in her mind for Victor de Rohan, but the girl was as true as steel. I have been accustomed to read characters all my life, women's as well as men's, it is part of my profession;" and Ropsley laughed once more his bitter laugh; "and many a trifling incident showed me that Constance Beverley cared for nobody on earth but you. This only made me more determined not to be beat; and little by little, with hints here and whispers there, assisted by your own strange, solitary habits, and the history of your poor father's life and death, I persuaded Sir Harry that there was madness in your family, and that you had inherited the curse. From the day on which he became convinced of this, I felt I had won my race. No power on earth would then have induced him to let you marry his daughter, and the excuse that he made you on that memorable afternoon, when you had so gallantly rescued her from death, was but a gentlemanlike way of getting out of his difficulty about telling you the real truth. Vere, that girl's courage is wonderful. She came down to dinner that night with the air of an empress, but with a face like marble, and a dull, stony look in her eyes that made even me almost rue what I had done. She kept her room for a fortnight afterwards, and I cannot help feeling she has never looked as bright since.

"When you went away I acknowledge I thought the field was my own. In consideration of my almost ruining myself to preserve him from shame, Sir Harry promised me his daughter if I could win her consent, and you may depend upon it I tried hard to do so. It was all in vain; the girl hated me more and more, and when we all met so unexpectedly in Vienna, I saw that my chance of Beverley Manor was indeed a hopeless one. Sir Harry, too, was getting very infirm. Had he died before his daughter's marriage, his bills for the money I had lent him were not worth the stamps on which they were drawn. My only chance was her speedy union with some one rich enough to make the necessary sacrifices, and again I picked out Victor de Rohan as the man. We all thought then you were engaged to his sister Valèrie."

Ropsley blushed scarlet as he mentioned that name.

"And it was not my part to conceal the surmise from Miss Beverley. 'She was *so* glad, she was *so* thankful,' she said, 'she was *so* happy, for Vere's sake'; and a month afterwards she was Countess de Rohan, with the handsomest husband and the finest place in Hungary. It was a *mariage de convenance*, I fear, on both sides. I know now, what I allow I did not dream of then, that Victor himself was the victim of an unfortunate attachment at the time, and that he married the beautiful Miss Beverley out of pique. Sir Harry died, as you know, within three months. I have saved myself from ruin, and I have destroyed the happiness on earth of three people that never did me the slightest harm. Vere, I do not deserve to be forgiven, I do not deserve ever to rise again from this couch; and yet there is *one* for whose sake I would fain get well--*one* whom I *must* see yet again before I die."

He burst into tears as he spoke. Good heaven! this man was mortal after all--an erring, sinful mortal, like the rest of us, with broken pride, heartfelt repentance, thrilling hopes and fears. Another bruised reed, though he had stood so defiant and erect, confronting the whirlwind and the thunderbolt, but shivered up, and cowering at the whisper of the "still small voice." Poor fellow! poor Ropsley! I pitied him from my heart, while he hid his face in his hands, and the big tears forced themselves through his wasted fingers; freely I forgave him, and freely I told him so.

After a time he became more composed, and then, as if ashamed of his weakness, assumed once more the cold satirical manner, half sarcasm, half pleasantry, which has become the conventional disguise of the world in which such men as Ropsley delight to live. Little by little he confided to me the rise and progress of his attachment to Valèrie--at which I had already partly guessed--acknowledged how, for a long time, he had imagined that I was again a favoured rival, destined ever to stand in his way; how my sudden departure from Vienna and her incomprehensible indifference to that hasty retreat had led him to believe that she had entertained nothing but a girl's passing inclination for her brother's comrade; and how, before he reached his regiment in the Crimea, she had promised to be his on the conclusion of the war. "I never cared for any other woman on earth," said Ropsley, once more relapsing into the broken accents of real, deep feeling. "I never reflected till I knew her, what a life mine has been. God forgive me, Vere; if we had met earlier, I should have been a different man. I have received a letter from her to-day. I shall be well enough to move by the end of the week. Vere, I *must* go through Hungary, and stop at Edeldorf on my way to England!"

As I walked out to inhale the evening breeze and indulge my own thoughts in solitude by the margin of the peaceful Bosphorus, I felt almost stunned, like a man who has sustained a severe fall, or one who wakes suddenly from an astounding dream. And yet I might have guessed long ago at the purport of Ropsley's late revelations. Diffident as I was of my own merits, there had been times when my heart told me, with a voice there was no disputing, that I was beloved by Constance Beverley; and now it was with something like a feeling of relief and exhilaration that I recalled the assurance of that fact from one himself so interested and so difficult to deceive as Ropsley. "And she loved me all along," I thought, with a thrill of pleasure, sadly dashed with pain. "She was true and pure, as I always thought her; and even now, though she is wedded to another, though she never can be mine on earth, perhaps--" And here I stopped, for the cold, sickening impossibility chilled me to the marrow, and an insurmountable barrier seemed to rise up around me and hem me in on every side. It was sin to love her, it was sin to think of her now. Oh! misery! misery! and yet I would give my life to see her once more! So my good angel whispered in my ear, "You must never look on her again; for the rest of your time you must tread the weary path alone, and learn to be kindly, and pure, and holy for *her* sake." And self muttered, "Where would be the harm of seeing her just once again?--of satisfying yourself with your own eyes that she is happy?--of learning at once to be indifferent to her presence? You *must* go home. Edeldorf lies in your direct road to England; you cannot abandon Ropsley in his present state, with no one to nurse and take care of him. Victor is your oldest friend, he would be hurt if you did not pay him a visit. It would be more courageous to face the Countess at once, and get it over." And I listened now to one and now to the other, and the struggle raged and tore within me the while I paced sadly up and down "by the side of the sounding sea."

"Egerton! how goes it? Let me present to you my friends," exclaimed a voice I recognised on the instant, as, with lowered head and dreamy vision, I walked right into the centre of a particularly smart party, and was "brought up," as the sailors say, "all standing," by a white silk parasol and a mass of flounces that almost took my breath away. When you most require solitude, it generally happens that you find yourself forced into society, and with all my regard for our *ci-devant* usher, I never met Manners, now a jolly Colonel of Bashi-Bazouks, with so little gratification as at this moment. I am bound to admit, however, that on his side all was cordiality and delight. Dressed out to the utmost magnificence of his gorgeous uniform, spurs clanking, and sabretasche jingling, his person stouter, his beard more exuberant, his face more florid and prosperous than ever, surrounded, too, by a bevy of ladies of French extraction and Pera manners, the "soldier of fortune," for such he might fairly be called, was indeed in his glory. With many flourishes and compliments in bad French, I was presented successively to Mesdemoiselles Philippine, and Josephine, and Seraphine, all dark-eyed, black-haired, sallow-faced, but by no means bad-looking, young ladies, all apparently bent upon the capture and destruction of anything and everything that came within range of their artillery, and all apparently belonging equally to my warlike and fortunate friend. He then took me by the arm, and dropping behind the three graces aforesaid, informed me, in tones of repressed exultation, how his fortune was made at last, how he now commanded (the dearest object of his ambition) a regiment of actual cavalry, and how he was on the eve of marriage with one of the young ladies in front of us, with a dowry of a hundred thousand francs, who loved him to distraction, and was willing to accompany him to Shumla, there to take the lead in society, and help him to civilise his regiment of Bashi-Bazouks.

"I always told you I was fit for something, Egerton," said Lieutenant-Colonel Manners, with a glow of exultation on his simple face; "and I have made my own way at last, in despite of all obstacles. It's pluck, sir, that makes the man! pluck and *muscle*," doubling his arm as he spoke, in the old Everdon manner. "I have done it at last, and you'll see, my dear Egerton, I shall live to be a general."

"I hope from my heart you may," was my reply, as I bade him "farewell," and congratulated him on his position, his good fortune, and his bride; though I never made out exactly whether it was Mademoiselle Josephine, or Philippine, or Seraphine who was to enjoy the unspeakable felicity of becoming Mrs. Colonel Manners.

CHAPTER XLIII
"THE SKELETON"

It is one of the conventional grievances of the world to mourn ever the mutability of human affairs, the ever-recurring changes incidental to that short span of existence here which we are pleased to term Life, as if the scenes and characters with which we are familiar were always being mingled and shifted with the rapidity and confusion of a pantomime. It has often struck me that the circumstances which encircle us do *not* by any means change with such extraordinary rapidity and facility--that, like a French road, with its mile after mile of level fertility and unvarying poplars, our path is sometimes for years together undiversified by any great variety of incident, any glimpse of romance; and that the same people, the same habits, the same pleasures, and the same annoyances seem destined to surround and hem us in from the cradle to the grave. Which is the most numerous class, those who fear their lot *may* change, or those who hope it *will*? Can we make this change for ourselves? Are we the slaves of circumstances, or is not that the opportunity of the strong which is the destiny of the weak? Surely it must be so--surely the stout heart that struggles on must win at last--surely man is a free agent; and he who fails, fails not because his task is impossible, but that he himself is faint and weak and infatuated enough to hope that he alone will be an exception to the common lot, and achieve the prize without the labour, *Sine pulvere palma.*

The old castle at Edeldorf, at least, is but little changed from what I recollect it in my quiet boyhood, when with my dear father I first entered its lofty halls and made acquaintance with the beautiful blue-eyed child that now sits at the end of that table, a grown-up, handsome man. Yes, once more I am at Edeldorf. Despite all my scruples, despite all the struggles between my worse and better self, I could not resist the temptation of seeing her in her stately home; of satisfying myself with my own eyes that she was happy, and of bidding her a long and last farewell. Oh! I thirsted to see her just once again, only to see her, and then to go away and meet her never, never more. Therefore Ropsley and I journeyed through Bulgaria and up the Danube, and arrived late at Edeldorf, and were cordially welcomed by Victor, and dressed, and came down to dinner, and so I saw her.

She was altered, too; so much altered, and yet it was the well-known face, *her* face still; but there were lines on the white forehead I remembered once so smooth and fair, and the eyes were sunk and the cheek pale and fallen; when she smiled, too, the beautiful lips parted as sweetly as their wont, but the nether one quivered as though it were more used to weeping than laughing, and the smile vanished quickly, and left a deeper shadow as it faded. She was not happy. I was *sure* she was not happy, and shall I confess it? the certainty was not to me a feeling of unmixed pain. I would have given every drop of blood in my body to make her so, and yet I could not grieve as I felt I ought to grieve, that it was otherwise.

Perhaps one of the greatest trials imposed on us by the artificial state of society in which we live, is the mask of iron that it forces us to wear for the concealment of all the deeper and stronger feelings of our nature. There we sit in that magnificent hall, hung around with horn of stag and tusk of boar, and all the trophies of the chase, waited on by Hungarian retainers in their gorgeous hussar uniforms, before a table heaped to profusion with the good things that minister to the gratification of the palate, and conversing upon those light and frivolous topics beyond which it is treason to venture, while the hearts probably of every one of us are far, far distant in some region of pain unknown and unguessed by all save the secret sufferers, who hide away their hoarded sorrows under an exterior of flippant levity, and affect to ignore their neighbour's wounds as completely as they veil their own. What care Ropsley or Valèrie whether *perdrix aux champignons* is or is not a better thing than *dindon aux truffes*? They are dying to be alone with each other once more--she, all anxiety to hear of his campaign and his illness; he, restless and preoccupied till he can tell her of his plans and prospects, and the arrangements that must be concluded before he can make her his own. Both, for want of a better grievance, somewhat disgusted that the order of precedence in going to dinner has placed them opposite each other, instead of side by side. And yet Valèrie, who sits by me, seems well pleased to meet her old friend once more; if I had ever thought she really cared for me, I should be undeceived now, when I mark the joyous frankness of her manner, the happy blush that comes and goes upon her cheek, and the restless glances that ever and anon she casts at her lover's handsome face through the epergne of flowers and fruit that divides them. No, they think as little of the ball of conversation which we jugglers toss about to each other, and jingle and play with and despise, as does the pale stately Countess herself, with her dark eyes and her dreamy look apparently gazing far into another world. She is not watching Victor, she seems scarcely aware of his presence: and yet many a young wife as beautiful, as high-spirited, and as lately married, would sit uneasily at the top of her own table, would frown, and fret, and chafe to see her handsome husband so preoccupied by another as is the Count by the fair guest on his right hand--who but wicked Princess Vocqsal?

That lady has, according to custom, surrounded herself by a system of fortification wherewith, as it were, she seems metaphorically to set the world at defiance: a challenge which, to do her justice, the Princess is ever ready to offer, the antagonist not always willing to accept. She delights in being the object of small attentions, so she invariably requires a footstool, an extra cushion or two, and a flask of eau de Cologne, in addition to her bouquet, her fan, her gloves, her pocket-handkerchief, and such necessary articles of female superfluity. With these outworks and fences within which to retire on the failure of an attack, it is easy to carry out a system of aggressive warfare; and whether it is the presence of his wife that makes the amusement particularly exciting, or whether Count de Rohan has made himself to-day peculiarly agreeable, or whether it is possible, though this contingency is extremely unlikely, that the Prince has *told her not*, certainly Madame la Princesse is taking unusual pains, and that most unnecessarily, to bring Victor into more than common subjection to her fascinations.

She is without contradiction the best-dressed woman in the room; her light gossamer robe, fold upon fold, and flounce upon flounce, floats around her like a drapery of clouds; her gloves fit her to a miracle; her exquisitely-shaped hands and round white arms bear few ornaments, but these are of the rarest and costliest description; her blooming, fresh complexion accords well with those luxuriant masses of soft brown hair escaping here and there from its smooth shining folds in large glossy curls. Her rich red lips are parted with a malicious smile, half playful, half coquettish, that is inexpressibly provoking and attractive; while, although the question as to whether she does really rouge or not is still undecided, her blue eyes seem positively to dance and sparkle in the candle-light. Her voice is low, and soft, and silvery; all she says racy, humorous, full of meaning, and to the point. Poor Victor de Rohan!

He, too, is at first in unusually high spirits; his courteous, well-bred manner is livelier than his wont, but the deferential air with which he responds to his neighbour's gay remarks is dashed by a shade of sarcasm, and I, who know him so well, can detect a tone of bitter irony in his voice, can trace some acute inward pang that ever and anon convulses for a moment his frank, handsome features. I am sure he is ill at ease, and dissatisfied with himself. I observe, too, that, though he scarcely touches the contents of his plate, his glass is filled again and again to the brim, and he quaffs off his wine with the eager feverish thirst of one who seeks to drown reflection and remorse in the Lethean draught. Worst sign of all, and one which never fails to denote mental suffering, his spirits fall in proportion to his potations, and that which in a well-balanced nature "makes glad the heart of man," seems but to clog the wings of Victor's fancy, and to sink him deeper and deeper in despondency. Ere long he becomes pale, silent, almost morose, and the charming Princess has all the conversation to herself.

But one individual in the party attends thoroughly to the business in hand. Without doubt, for the time being he has the best of it. Prince Vocqsal possesses an excellent appetite, a digestion, as he says himself, that, like his conscience, can carry a great weight and be all the better for it; a faultless judgment in wine, and a tendency to enjoy the pleasures of the table, enhanced, if possible, by the occasional fit of gout with which this indulgence must unfortunately be purchased. Fancy-free is the Prince, and troubled neither by memories of the past, misgivings for the present, nor anxieties for the future. Many such passive natures there are--we see them every day. Men who are content to take the world as it is, and, like the ox in his pasture, browse, and bask, and ruminate, and never wish to overleap the boundary that forbids them to wander in the flowery meadow beyond. And yet it may be that these too have once bathed in the forbidden stream, the lava-stream that scorches and sears where it touches; it may be that the heart we deem so hard, so callous, has been welded in the fire, and beaten on the anvil, till it has assumed the consistency of steel. It winced and quivered once, perhaps nearly broke, and now it can bid defiance even to the memory of pain. Who knows? who can tell his neighbour's history, or guess his neighbour's thoughts? who can read the truth, even in the depth of those eyes that look the fondest into his own? Well! there is One that knows all secrets, and He will judge, but not as man judges.

So Prince Vocqsal thinks not of the days that are past, the hearts he has broken, the friends he has lost, the duels he has fought, the money he has squandered, the chances he has thrown away; or, if he does allow his mind to dwell for an instant on such trifles, it is with a sort of dreamy satisfaction at the quantity of enjoyment he has squeezed out of life, tinged with a vague regret that so much of it is over. Why, it was but to-day that, as he dressed for dinner, he apostrophised the grimacing image in his looking-glass,-- "Courage, *mon gaillard*," muttered the Prince, certainly not to his valet, who was tightening his waistbelt, "courage! you are worth a good many of the young ones, still, and your appetite is as good as it was at sixteen."

He is splendid now, though somewhat apoplectic. His wig curls over his magnificent head in hyacinthine luxuriance, his dyed whiskers and moustache blush purple in the candlelight; his neckcloth is tied somewhat too tight, and seems to have forced more than a wholesome quantity of blood into his face and eyes, but its whiteness is dazzling, and the diamond studs beneath it are of extraordinary brilliance; nor does his waistbelt, though it defies repletion, modify in any great degree the goodly outline of the corpulent person it enfolds. Altogether he is a very jolly-looking old gentleman, and the only one of the party that seems for the nonce to be "the right man in the right place."

Constance listens to him with a weary, abstracted air; perhaps she has heard that story about the bear and the waterfall once or twice before, perhaps she does not hear it now, but she bends her head courteously towards him, and looks kindly at him from out of her deep, sad eyes.

"Champagne, if you please," says the Prince, interrupting the thread of his narrative, by holding up his glass to be replenished; "and so, Madame, the bear and I were *vis-à-vis* at about ten paces apart, and my rifle was empty. The last shot had taken effect through his lungs, and he coughed and held his paw to the pit of his stomach, so like a Christian with a cold, that, even in my very precarious position, I could not help laughing outright. Ten paces is a short distance, Madame, a very short distance, when your antagonist feels himself thoroughly aggrieved, and advances upon you with a red, lurid eye, and a short angry growl. I turned and looked behind me for a run-
-I was always a good runner," remarks the Prince, with a downward glance of satisfaction, the absurdity of which, I am pained to see, does not even call a smile to his listener's pale face--"but it was no question of running here, for the waterfall was leaping and foaming forty feet deep below, and the trees were so thick on either side, that escape by a flank movement was impossible. It was the very spot, Victor, where I killed the woodcocks right and left the morning you disappointed me so shamefully, and left me to have all the sport to myself."--Victor bows courteously, drinks her husband's health, and glances at the Princess with a bitter smile.--"The very spot where I hope you will place me to-morrow at your grand *chasse*. Peste! 'tis strange how passionately fond I still am of the chase. Well, Madame, indecision is not usually my weakness, but before I could make up my mind what to do, the bear was upon me. In an instant he embraced me with his huge hairy arms, and I felt his hot breath against my very face. My rifle was broken short off by the stock, and I heard my watch crack in my waistcoat pocket. I thought it was my ribs. I have seen your wrestlers in England, Madame, and I have once assisted in your country at an exhibition of '*The Box*' but such an encounter as I now had to sustain was more terrible than anything I ever witnessed fought out fairly between man and man. Fortunately a ball through the back part of the head, and another through the lungs, had somewhat diminished the natural force of my adversary, or I must have succumbed; and by a great exertion of strength on my part, I managed to liberate one hand and make a grasp for my hunting-knife.

Horror! it had fallen from the sheath, but by the mercy of Heaven and the blessing of St. Hubert, it had caught in my boot, and I never felt before how dear life was as when I touched the buckhorn handle of my last friend; three, four times in succession I buried the long keen blade in the bear's side; at each thrust he gave a quick, convulsive sob, but he strained me tighter and tighter to his body, till I thought my very blood-vessels would burst with the fearful pressure. At last we fell, and rolled over and over towards the waterfall. In the hasty glance I had previously cast behind me, I had remarked a dead fir-tree that stood within a yard or so of the precipice; I remember the thought had darted through my mind, that if I could reach it I might be safe, and the reflection as instantaneously followed, that a bear was a better climber than a Hungarian. Never shall I forget my sensations when, in our last revolution, I caught a glimpse of that naked tree. I shut my eyes then, for I knew it was all over, but I gave him one more stab, and a hearty one, with my hunting-knife. Splash! we reached the water together, and went down like a couple of stones, down, down to the very bottom, but fortunately it was the deepest part of the pool, and we unclosed our embrace the instant we touched the surface--the bear, I believe, was dead before he got there, and I thought myself fortunate in being able to swim ashore, whilst the brown body of my late antagonist went tumbling and whirling down the foaming torrent below. I recovered his skin, Madame, to make a cover for my arm-chair, but I have never been fond of water since. Give me a glass of Tokay, if you please."

"And did you sustain no further harm from your encounter?" asked Constance, rousing herself from her abstraction with an effort, and bending politely towards the Prince, who was drinking his Tokay with immense satisfaction.

"Only the marks of his claws on my shoulder," replied he, smacking his lips after his draught. "I have got them there to this day. Is it not so, Rose?" he added, appealing to his wife with a hearty laugh.

She turned her head away without condescending to notice him. Victor bit his lip with a gesture of impatience, and the Countess, rising slowly and gracefully, gave her hand to the Prince to lead her back to the drawing-room, whither we all followed in the same order as that in which we had proceeded to dinner.

"Do you not feel like a wounded man once more?" observed Valèrie, gaily, to me, as I stood, coffee-cup in hand, with my back to the fireplace, like a true Englishman. "Is it not all exactly as you left it? the easiest arm-chair and my eternal embroidery-frame, and your own sofa where you used to lie so wonderfully patient, and look out of window at the sunset.

Constance has established herself there now, and considers it her peculiar property. Oh, Vere (I shall always call you Vere), is she not charming? I am so fond of her!"

Slow torture! but never mind, it is but for to-night--this experiment must never be repeated. Go on, Countess Valèrie, happy, unconscious executioner.

"You English people are delightful, when one knows you well, although at first you are so cold and undemonstrative. Now, Constance, though she is so quiet and melancholy-looking, though she never laughs, and rarely smiles, has the energy and the activity of a dozen women when it is a question of doing good. You have no idea of what she is here amongst our own people. They worship the very ground she walks on--they call her 'the good angel of Edeldorf.' But she over-exerts herself; she is not strong: she looks ill, very ill. Vere, do you not think so?"

For the first time since we entered the drawing-room I glanced in the direction of the Countess de Rohan, but her face was turned from me; she was still occupied with Prince Vocqsal, who, old enough to appreciate the value of a good listener, was devoting himself entirely to her amusement. No, I could not see the pale, well-known face, but the light streamed off her jet-black hair, and memory probed me to the quick as its shining masses recalled the wet, heavy locks of one whose life I saved in Beverley Mere.

"Come and play the march in 'The Honijàdy,'" said Ropsley, leading his *fiancée* gaily off to the pianoforte. "*On revient toujours à ses premiers amours*, but I really cannot allow you to flirt with Egerton any more," he added, with a smile of such thorough confidence and affection in his promised bride as altered the whole expression of his countenance, and lit it up with a beauty I had never before imagined it to possess.

"Not *that*," she answered, looking anxiously round, "but 'Cheer, boys! cheer!' as often as you like, now we have got you back again." And they walked away together, a happy, handsome pair as one should wish to see.

I could not have borne it much longer. I gasped for solitude as a man half-stifled gasps for air. With an affectation of leisurely indifference, I strolled into the adjoining billiard-room. I passed close to the Countess, but she never turned her head, so engrossed was she with the conversation of Prince Vocqsal. I walked on through the spacious conservatory. I even stopped to examine an exotic as I passed. At length I reached a balcony in which that structure terminated, and sinking into a chair that stood in one corner, out of sight and interruption, I leaned my forehead against the cold iron railing, and prayed for fortitude and resignation to my lot.

The fresh night air cooled and composed me. A bright moonlight flickered and glistened over the park. The tones of Valèrie's pianoforte, softened by distance, stole sadly, yet soothingly, on my ear. The autumn breeze, hushed to a whisper, seemed to breathe of peace and consolation. I felt that the strength I had asked would be given; that though the fight was not yet over, it would be won at last; that although, alas! the sacrifice was still to be offered, I should have power to make it, and the higher the cost, the holier, the more acceptable it would be. More than once the Devil's sophistry prompted me to repine; more than once I groaned aloud to think that *she*, too, was sacrificed unworthily, that her happiness, like my own, was lost beyond recall. "Oh," I thought, in the bitterness of my agony, "I could have given her up to one that *loved* her, I could have rejoiced in her welfare, and forgotten *myself* in the certainty of her happiness. I could have blessed him thankfully for his care and tenderness towards that transplanted flower, and lived on contented, if not happy, to think that I had not offered up my own broken heart in vain; but to see her neglected and pining--her dignity insulted--her rights trampled on--another, immeasurably her inferior, filling the place in her husband's affections to which she had an undoubted right! Victor! Victor! you were my earliest friend, and yet I can almost *curse* you from my soul!"

But soon my better nature triumphed; I saw the path of duty plain before me, I determined to follow it, and struggle on, at whatever cost. I had lived for her all my life. I would live for her still. Perhaps when I became an old grey man she would know it; perhaps--never in this life--perhaps she might bless me for it in another; but it should be done! Could I but make a certainty of Victor's *liaison* with the Princess, could I but obtain *a right* to speak to him on the subject! I would make him one last appeal that should *force* him back to his duty. I would, if necessary, tell him the whole truth, and shame him by my own sacrifice into the right path. I felt a giant's strength and a martyr's constancy; once more I leaned my head upon the cold iron rail, and the opportunity that I asked for seemed to come when I least expected it.

In such a mood as I then was, a man takes no note of time; I could not tell how long I had been sitting there in the solemn peaceful night, it might have been minutes, it might have been hours, but at length the click of billiard-balls, which had been hitherto audible in the adjoining apartment, ceased altogether, a man's step and the rustle of a lady's dress were heard in the conservatory, and when they reached within six paces of me, Victor placed a chair for Princess Vocqsal under the spreading branches of a brilliant azalea, and seated himself at her side. She dropped her bracelet on the smooth tesselated floor as she sat down; he picked it up and clasped it on her arm: as he did so I caught a glimpse of his face: he was deadly pale, and as he raised his eyes to hers, their wild mournful appealing glance reminded me of poor Bold's last look when he died licking my hand. The Princess, on the contrary, shone if possible more brilliant than ever; there was a settled flush, as of triumph, on her cheek, and her whole countenance bore an impress of determined, uncompromising resolution, which I had already remarked as no uncommon expression on those lovely features.

My first impulse was to confront them at once, and take my departure; but I have already said I suffered from constitutional shyness to a great degree, and I was unwilling to face even my old friend with such traces of strong emotion as I knew must be visible on my exterior. I was most unwilling to play the eavesdropper. I felt that, as a man of honour, I was inexcusable in not instantly apprising them of my presence; yet some strange, inexplicable fascination that I could not resist, seemed to force me to remain where I was, unnoticed and unsuspected. Ere they had spoken three words I was in possession of the whole truth, that truth which a few minutes earlier I had been so anxious to ascertain. I do not attempt to excuse my conduct, I am aware that it admits of no palliation, that no one can be guilty of an act of espial and still remain *a gentleman*; but I state the fact as it occurred, and can only offer in extenuation the fever of morbid excitement into which I had worked myself, and my unwavering resolution to save Victor, in spite of his own infatuation, for her sake in whose behalf I did not hesitate thus to sacrifice even my honour.

"Anything but *that*, Rose, my adored Rose; anything but that," pleaded the Count; and his voice came thick and hoarse, whilst his features worked convulsively with the violence of his feelings. "Think of what I have been to you, think of all my devotion, all my self-denial. You cannot doubt me: it is impossible; you cannot mistrust me *now*; but, as you have a woman's heart, ask me for anything but *that*."

She was clasping and unclasping the bracelet he had placed upon her arm, her head drooped over the jewel, but she raised her soft lustrous eyes to his, and with a witching, maddening glance, of which he knew too well the power, murmured--

"Give it me, Victor, *dear* Victor! you have never refused me anything since I have known you."

"Nor would I now, were it anything that is in my power to give," he burst out hurriedly, and in accents of almost childish impatience; "I tell you, that for your sake I would cast everything to the winds--fortune, friends, home, country, life itself. Drop by drop, you should have the best blood in my body, and I would thank you and bless you for accepting it; but this is more than all, Rose--this is my honour. Could you bear to see me a disgraced and branded man? could you bear to feel that I *deserved* to have my arms reversed and my name scouted? Could you care for me if it were so? Oh, Rose, you have never loved me if you ask for this!"

"Perhaps you are right," she answered coldly, "perhaps I never did. You have often told me I am very hard-hearted--Victor," she added, after a pause, with a sudden change of manner, and another of those soft fond looks that made such wild work with her victim--"do you think I would ask a man I did not care for to make such a sacrifice? Oh, Victor! you little know a woman's heart--you have cruelly mistaken mine."

The fond eyes filled with tears as she spoke. Victor was doomed. I knew it from that moment. He scarcely made an effort to save himself now.

"And you ask for this as a last proof of my devotion. You are not satisfied yet. It is not enough that I have given you the whole happiness of my life, you must have that life itself as well--nay, even that is too little," he added with bitter emphasis, "I must offer up the unstained honour of the De Rohans in addition to all!"

Another of those speaking, thrilling glances. Oh, the old, old story! Samson and Delilah--Hercules and Omphale--Antony and Cleopatra, on the ruins of an empire--or plain Jack and Gill at the fair. Man's weakness is woman's opportunity, and so the world goes on.

"Victor," she said, "it is for *my* sake."

The colour mounted in his cheek, and he rose to his feet like a man. The old look I had missed all the evening on his face came back once more, the old look that reminded me of shouting squadrons by the Danube, and a dash to the front with AH Mesrour and brave Iskender Bey. His blood was up, and his lance in rest now, stop him who can!

"So be it," he said, calmly and distinctly, but with his teeth clenched and his nostril dilated, like that of a thorough-bred horse after a gallop. "So be it! and never forget, Rose, in the long dark future, never forget that it was for your sake: and now listen to me. I betray my own and my father's friends, I complete an act of treachery such as is yet unknown in the annals of my country, such as her history shall curse for its baseness till the end of time. I devote to ruin and death a score of the noblest families, a score of the proudest heads in Hungary. I stain my father's shield, I break my own oaths. Life, and honour, and all, I cast away at one throw, and, Rose, it is for your sake!"

She was weeping now--weeping convulsively, with her face buried in her hands; but he heeded it not, and went on--

"All this I am willing to do, Rose, because I love you; but mark the consequence. As surely as I deliver you this list"--he drew a paper from his breast as he spoke--"so surely I proclaim my treachery to the world, so surely I give myself over to the authorities, so surely I march up to the scaffold at the head of that devoted band who were once my friends, and though they think it shame that their blood should soak the same planks as mine, though they turn from me in disgust, even on the verge of another world, so surely will I die amongst them as boldly, as unflinchingly, as the most stainless patriot of them all!"

"No, no," she sobbed out; "never, never; do you think I have no feeling? do you think I have no heart? I have provided for your safety long ago. I have got your free pardon in a written promise, your life and fortune are secure, your share in the discovery will never be made known. Victor, do you think I have not taken care of *you*?"

Even then his whole countenance softened. This man, whose proud spirit she had so often trampled on, whose kind heart she had so often wounded, from whom she asked so much--ay, so much as his bitterest enemy would have shrunk from taking--was ready and willing to give her all, and to bless the very hand that smote him to the death. He spoke gently and caressingly now. He bent over her chair, and looked down at her with kind, sad eyes.

"Not so," he said, "Rose, not so. I am glad you did not sacrifice me. I like to think you would have saved me if you could; but I cannot accept the terms. To-morrow is my birthday, Rose. It is St. Hubert's day, and I have a grand *chasse* here, as you know. Many of these devoted gentlemen will be at Edeldorf to-morrow. Give us at least that one day. In twenty-four hours from this time you can forward your information to Vienna; after that, you and I will meet no more on earth. Rose, dear Rose," he murmured, as he placed the paper in her hand, "it is the *last* present I shall give you--make the most of it."

Why did she meddle with politics, woman as she was in her heart of hearts? What had she to do with Monsieur Stein, and Government intrigues, and a secret police, and all that complicated machinery which is worked by gold alone, and in which the feelings count for nothing? State information might go to other quarters; fortunes be made on the Bourse by other speculators; her husband wait for his appointment till doomsday, and the attainder remain unreversed on the estates in the Banat as long as the Danube flowed downward from its source;--what cared Princess Vocqsal? She looked up, smiling through her tears, like a wet rose in the sunshine. She took the list from his hand; once, twice, she pressed the paper to her lips, then tore it in a thousand fragments, and scattered them abroad over the shining floor of the conservatory, to mingle with the shed blossoms of the azalea, to be swept away with the decayed petals of the camellias, to be whirled hither and thither by the breeze of morning to oblivion, but to rise up between her and him who now stood somewhat aghast by her side, never, never more!

She put her hand almost timidly in his. "Victor," she said, in a soft, low voice, "you have conquered. I am yours now in defiance of all. Oh, Victor, Victor, you do indeed love me!"

He looked startled, scared, almost as if he could not understand her; he shook in every limb, whilst she was composed and even dignified.

"Yes," she said, rising from her chair, "I will trifle with you no longer now. I know what I do; I see the gulf into which I plunge. Misery, ruin, and crime are before me; but I fear *nothing*. Victor de Rohan! when I leave Edeldorf, I leave it with you, and with you I remain for ever."

They walked out of the conservatory side by side. I do not think they exchanged another word; and I remained stunned, motionless, stupefied, like a man who wakes from some ghastly and bewildering dream.

The striking of the Castle clock roused me to consciousness--to a conviction of the importance of time, and the necessity for immediate action. It was now midnight. Early to-morrow we should all be on the alert for the grand battue on the Waldenberg, for which preparations had been making for several days. I should scarcely have an opportunity of speaking in private to my friend, and the day after it might be too late. No, to-night I must see Victor before he slept: to-night I must warn him from the abyss into which he was about to fall, confess to him the dishonourable act of which I had been guilty, sustain his anger and contempt as I best might, and plead her cause whom I must never see again. More than once--I will not deny it--a rebellious feeling rose in my heart. Why are these things so? Why is she not mine whom I have loved so many dark and lonely years? Why must Victor, after the proof he has given to-night of more than human devotion, never be happy with her for whose sake he did not hesitate to offer up all that was far dearer to him than life? But I had long learnt the true lesson, that "Whatever is, is right"--that Providence sees not with our eyes, nor judges with our judgment; and that we must not presume to question, much less dare to repine. I hurried through the billiard-room towards Victor's apartments; I had then to traverse the drawing-room, and a little snug retreat in which it used to be our custom to finish the evening with a social cigar, and to which, in former days Valèrie was sometimes to be prevailed upon to bring her work. Here I found Ropsley and Prince Vocqsal comfortably established, apparently with no idea of going to bed yet for hours. They had never met till to-day, but seemed to suit each other admirably, all that was ludicrous in the Prince's character and conversation affording a ceaseless fund of amusement to the Guardsman; while the latter's high prowess as a sportsman, and intimate acquaintance with the turf, rendered him an object of great interest and admiration to the enthusiastic Hungarian. Ropsley, with restored health and his ladye-love under the same roof with him, was in the highest spirits, and no wonder.

"Don't run away, Vere," said he, catching me by the arm as I passed behind his chair; "it's quite early yet. Have a quiet weed before turning in." Adding, in an amused whisper, "He's an immense trump, this! That's his third cigar and his fourth tumbler of brandy-and-soda since we came here; and he's telling me now how he once pinked a fellow in the Bois de Boulogne for wearing revolutionary shirt buttons. In English, too, my dear fellow; it's as good as a play."

Even as he spoke I heard a door shut in the passage, and I hurried away, leaving the new acquaintances delighted with each other's society.

In the gallery I met Victor's French valet with a bundle of clothes over his arm, humming an air from a French opera. "Could I see the Count?" "Alas! I was a few seconds too late!" The valet "was in despair--he was desolate--it was impossible. Monsieur had even now retired to the apartments of Madame!" "I must do it to-morrow," thought I; "perhaps I may find an opportunity when the *chasse* is over." And I went to bed with a heavy, aching heart.

CHAPTER XLIV
THE GIPSY'S DREAM

It is a calm, clear night; a narrow crescent moon, low down on the horizon, scarcely dims the radiance of those myriads of stars which gem the entire sky. It is such a night as would have been chosen by the Chaldean to read his destiny on the glittering page above his head--such a night as compels us perforce to think of other matters than what we shall eat and what we shall drink--as brings startlingly to our minds the unsolved question, Which is Reality--the Material of to-day or the Ideal of to-morrow? Not a cloud obscures the diamond-sprinkled vault above; not a tree, not an undulation, varies the level plain extending far and wide below. Dim and indistinct, its monotonous surface presents a vague idea of boundless space, the vastness of which is enhanced by the silence that reigns around. Not a breath of air is stirring, not a sound is heard save the lazy plash and ripple of the Danube, as it steals away under its low swampy banks, sluggish and unseen. Yet there is life breathing in the midst of this apparent solitude: human hearts beating, with all their hopes and fears, and joys and sorrows, in this isolated spot. Even here beauty pillows her head on the broad chest of strength; infancy nestles to the refuge of a mother's bosom; weary labour lies prone and helpless, with relaxed muscles and limp, powerless limbs; youth dreams of love, and age of youth; and sleep spreads her welcome mantle over the hardy tribe who have chosen this wild waste of Hungary for their lair.

It is long past midnight; their fires have been out for hours; their tents are low and dusky, in colour almost like the plain on which they are pitched; you might ride within twenty yards of it, and never know you were near a gipsy's encampment, for the Zingynie loves to be unobserved and secret in his movements; to wander here and there, with no man's leave and no man's knowledge; to come and go unmarked and untrammelled as the wind that lifts the elf-locks from his brow. So he sleeps equally well under the coarse canvas of a tent or the roof of a clear cold sky; he pays no rent, he owns no master, and he believes that, of all the inhabitants of earth, he alone is free.

And now a figure rises from amongst the low dusky tents, and comes out into the light of the clear starry sky, and looks steadfastly towards the east as if watching for the dawn, and turns a fevered cheek to the soft night air, as yet not fresh and cold enough to promise the approach of day. It is the figure of a woman past the prime of life, nay, verging upon age, but who retains all the majesty and some remains of the beauty which distinguished her in bygone days; who even now owns none of the decay of strength or infirmity of gait which usually accompanies the advance of years, but who looks, as she always did, born to command, and not yet incapable of enforcing obedience to her behests. It is none other than the Zingynie queen who prophesied the future of Victor de Rohan when he was a laughing golden-haired child; whose mind is anxious and ill at ease for the sake of her darling now, and who draws her hood further over her head, binds her crimson handkerchief tighter on her brows, and looks once more with anxious glance towards the sky, as she mutters--

"Three hours to dawn, and then six more till noon; and once, girl, thou wast light-footed and untiring as the deer. Girl!" and she laughs a short, bitter laugh. "Well, no matter--girl, or woman, or aged crone, the heart is always the same; and I will save him--save him, for the sake of the strong arm and the fair, frank face that have been mouldering for years in the grave!"

She is wandering back into the past now. Vivid and real as though it had happened but yesterday, she recalls a scene that took place many a long year ago in the streets of Pesth. She was a young, light-hearted maiden then: the acknowledged beauty of her tribe, the swiftest runner, the most invincible pedestrian to be found of either sex in the bounds of Hungary. Not a little proud was she of both advantages, and it was hard to say on which she plumed herself the most. In those days, as in many others of its unhappy history, that country was seething with internal faction and discontent; and the Zingynies, from their wandering habits, powers of endurance, and immunity from suspicion, were constantly chosen as the bearers of important despatches and the means of communication between distant conspirators, whilst they were themselves kept in utter ignorance of the valuable secrets with which they were entrusted.

The gipsy maiden had come up to Pesth on an errand of this nature all the way from the Banat. Many a flat and weary mile it is; yet though she had rested but seldom and partaken sparingly of food, the girl's eye was as bright, her step as elastic, and her beauty as dazzling as when she first started on her journey. In such a town as the capital of Hungary she could not fail to attract attention and remark. Ere long, while she herself was feasting her curiosity with innocent delight on the splendours of the shop windows and the many wonders of a city so interesting to this denizen of the wilderness, she found herself the centre of a gazing and somewhat turbulent crowd, whose murmurs of approbation at her beauty were not unmixed with jeers and even threats of a more formidable description. Swabes were they mostly, and Croatians, who formed this disorderly mob; for your true Hungarian, of whatever rank, is far too much of a gentleman to mix himself up with a street riot or vulgar brawl, save upon the greatest provocation. There had been discontent brewing for days amongst the lowest classes; the price of bread had gone up, and there was a strong feeling abroad against the landholders, and what we should term in England the agricultural interest generally.

The mob soon recognised in the Zingynie maiden one of the messengers of their enemies. From taunts and foul abuse they proceeded to overt acts of insolence; and the handsome high-spirited girl found herself at bay, surrounded by savage faces, and rude, insulting tongues. Soon they began to hustle and maltreat her, with cries of "Down with the gipsy!"--"Down with the go-between of our tyrants!"--"To the stake with the fortune-teller!"--"To the Danube with the witch!" Imprudently she drew her long knife and flashed it in the faces of the foremost; for an instant the curs gave back, but it was soon struck from her hand, and any immunity that her youth and beauty might have won from her oppressors was, by this ill-judged action, turned to more determined violence and aggression. Already they had pinioned her arms, and were dragging her towards the river--already she had given herself up for lost, when a lane was seen opening in the crowd, and a tall powerful man came striding to her rescue, and, as he elbowed and jostled his way through her tormentors, asked authoritatively, "What was the matter, and how they could dare thus to maltreat a young and beautiful girl?"

"She is a witch!" replied one ruffian who had hold of her by the wrist, "and we are going to put her in the Danube. *You* are an aristocrat, and you shall keep her company!"

"Shall I?" replied the stranger, and in another instant the insolent Swabe, spitting out a mouthful of blood and a couple of front teeth, measured his length upon the pavement. The crowd began to retire, but they were fierce and excited, and their numbers gave them confidence. A comrade of the fallen ruffian advanced upon the champion with bared knife and scowling brow. Another of those straight left-handers, delivered flush from the shoulder, and he lay prostrate by his friend. The stranger had evidently received his fighting education in England, and the instructions of science had not been thrown away on that magnificent frame and those heavy muscular limbs. It was indeed no other than the last Count de Rohan, Victor's father, the associate of the Prince of Wales, the friend of Philip Egerton and Sir Harry Beverley: lastly, what was more to the purpose at the present juncture, the pupil of the famous Jackson. Ere long the intimidated mob ceased to interfere, and the nobleman, conducting the frightened gipsy girl with as much deference as though she had been his equal in rank and station, never left her till he had placed her in his own carriage, and forwarded her, with three or four stout hussars as her escort, half-way back on her homeward journey. There is a little bit of romance safe locked up and hidden away somewhere in a corner of every woman's heart. What was the great Count de Rohan to the vagabond Zingynie maiden but a "bright particular star," from which she must always remain at a hopeless and immeasurable distance? Yet even now, though her hair is grey and her brow is wrinkled--though she has loved and suffered, and borne children and buried them, and wept and laughed, and hoped and feared, and gone the round of earthly joys and earthly sorrows--the colour mounts to her withered cheek, and the blood gathers warmer round her heart, when she thinks of that frank, handsome face, with its noble features and its fearless eyes, and the kindly smile with which it bade her farewell. Therefore has she always felt a thrilling interest in all that appertains to the Count de Rohan; therefore has she mourned him with many a secret tear and many a hidden pang; therefore has she loved and cherished and watched over his child as though he had been her own, exhausting all her skill and all her superstition to prognosticate for him a happy future--to ward off from him the evil that she reads too surely in the stars will be his lot.

Once she has warned him--twice she has warned him--will the third time be too late? She shudders to think how she has neglected him. To-morrow--nay, to-day (for it is long past midnight), is the anniversary of his birth, the festival of St. Hubert, and she would have passed it over unnoticed, would have forgotten it, but for last night's dream. The coming morning strikes chill to her very marrow as she thinks what a strange, wild, eerie dream it was.

She dreamed that she was sitting by the Danube; far, far away down yonder, where its broad yellow flood, washing the flat, fertile shores of Moldavia, sweeps onward to the Black Sea, calm, strong, and not to be stemmed by mortal hand, like the stream of Time--like the course of destiny.

Strange voices whispered in her ears, mingled with the plash and ripple of the mighty river; voices that she could not recognise, yet of which she felt an uncomfortable consciousness that she had heard them before. It was early morning, the raw mist curled over the waters, and her hair--how was this?--once more black and glossy as the raven's wing, was dank and dripping with dew. There was a babe, too, in her lap, and she folded the child tighter to her bosom for warmth and comfort. It nestled and smiled up in her face, though it was none of hers; no gipsy blood could be traced in those blue eyes and golden locks; it was De Rohan's heir: how came it here? She asked the question aloud, and the voices answered all at once and confusedly, with an indistinct and rushing sound. Then they were silent, and the river plashed on.

She felt very lonely, and sang to the child for company a merry gipsy song. And the babe laughed and crowed, and leapt in her arms with delight, and glided from her hands; and the waters closed over its golden head, and it was gone. Then the voices moaned and shrieked, still far away, dim and indistinct; and the river plashed sullenly on.

But the child rose from the waves, and looked back and smiled, and shook the drops from its golden hair, and struck out fearlessly down the stream. It had changed, too, and the blue eyes and the clustering curls belonged to a strong, well-grown young man. Still she watched the form eagerly as it swam, for something reminded her of one she used to think the type of manhood years and years ago. The voices warned her now to rise and hasten, but the river plashed on sullenly as before.

She must run to yonder point, marked as it is by a white wooden cross. Far beyond it the stream whirls and seethes in a deep eddying pool, and she must guide the swimmer to the cross, and help him to land there, or he will be lost--De Rohan's child will be drowned in her sight. How does she know it is called St. Hubert's Cross? Did the voices tell her? They are whispering still, but fainter and farther off. And the river plashes on sullenly, but with a murmur of fierce impatience now.

She waves frantically to the swimmer, and would fain shout to him aloud, but she cannot speak; her shawl is wound so tight round her bosom that it stops her voice, and her fingers struggle in vain amongst the knots. Why will he not turn his head towards her?--why does he dash so eagerly on? proud of his strength, proud of his mastery over the flood--his father's own son. Ah! he hears it too. Far away, past the cross and the whirlpool, down yonder on that sunny patch of sand, sits a mermaid, combing her long bright locks with a golden comb. She sings a sweet, wild, unearthly melody--it would woo a saint to perdition! Hark! how it mingles with the rushing voices and the plash of the angry river!

The sand is deep and quick along the water's edge; she sinks in it up to the ankles, weights seem to clog her limbs, and hands she cannot see to hold her back; breathless she struggles on to reach the cross, for there is a bend in the river there, and he will surely see her, and turn from the song of the mermaid, and she will drag him ashore and rescue him from his fate. The voices are close in her ears now, and the river plashing at her very feet.

So she reaches the cross at last, and with frantic gestures--for she is still speechless--waves him to the shore. But the mermaid beckons him wildly on, and the stream, seizing him like a prey, whirls him downwards eddying past the cross, and it is too late now. See! he turns his head at last, but to show the pale, rigid features of a corpse.

The voices come rushing like a hurricane in her ears; the plash of the river rises to a mighty roar. Wildly the mermaid tosses her white arms above her head, and laughs, and shrieks, and laughs again, in ghastly triumph. The dreamer has found her voice now, and in a frenzy of despair and horror she screams aloud.

With that scream she awoke, and left her tent for the cool night air, and counted the hours till noon; and so, with no more preparation, she betook herself to her journey, goaded with the thought that there might be time even yet.

It is sunrise now; a thousand gladsome tokens of life and happiness wake with the morning light. The dew sparkles on herb and autumn flower; the lark rises into the bright, pure heaven; herds of oxen file slowly across the plain. Hope is ever strong in the morning; and the gipsy's step is more elastic, her brow grows clearer and her eye brighter, as she calculates the distance she has already traversed, and the miles that yet lie between her and the woods and towers of Edeldorf. A third of the journey is already accomplished; in another hour the summit of the Waldenberg ought to be visible, peering above the plain. She has often trod the same path before, but never in such haste as now.

A tall Hungarian peasant meets her, and recognising her at once for a gipsy, doffs his hat, and bids her "Good-morrow, mother!" and craves a blessing from the Zingynie, for though he has no silver, he has a paper florin or two in his pocket, and he would fain have his fortune told, and so while away an hour of his long, solitary day only just begun. With flashing eyes and impatient gestures she bans him as she passes, for she cannot brook even an instant's delay, and the curse springs with angry haste to her lips. He crosses himself in terror as he walks on, and all day he will be less comfortable that he encountered a gipsy's malison at sunrise.

A village lies in her road; many a long mile before she reaches it, the white houses and tall acacias seem to mock her with their distinct outlines and their apparent proximity--will it *never* be any nearer? but she arrives there at last, and although she is weary and footsore, she dreams not of an instant's delay for refreshment or repose. Flocks of geese hiss and cackle at her as she passes: from the last cottage in the street a little child runs merrily out with a plaything in its hand, it totters and falls just across her path; as she replaces it on its legs she kisses it, that dark old woman, on its bright young brow. It is a good omen, and she feels easier about her heart now; she walks on with renewed strength and elasticity--she will win yet.

Another hour, the sun is high in the heavens, and autumn though it be, the heat scorches her head through her crimson handkerchief and her thick grey hair. Ah! she is old now; though the spirit may last for ever, the limbs fail in despite of it; what if she has miscalculated her strength? what if she cannot reach the goal after all? Courage! the crest of the Waldenberg shows high above the plain. Edeldorf, as she knows well, lies between her and that rugged range of hills, but she quails to think from what a distance the waving woods of De Rohan's home should be visible, and that they are not yet in sight. Her limbs are very weary, and the cold drops stand on her brow, for she is faint and sick at heart. Gallantly she struggles on.

It is a tameless race, that ancient nation of which we know not the origin, and speculate on the destiny in vain. It transmits to its descendants a strain of blood which seems as invincible by physical fatigue as it is averse to moral restraint. Lake some wild animal, like some courser of pure Eastern breed, the gipsy gained second strength as she toiled. Three hours after sunrise she was literally fresher and stronger than when she met and cursed the astonished herdsman in the early morning; and as the distance decreased between the traveller and her destination, as the white towers of Edeldorf stood out clearer and clearer in the daylight, glad hope and kindly affection gushed up in her heart, and, lame, wearied, exhausted as she was, a thrill of triumph shot through her as she thought she might see her darling in time to warn him even now.

At the lodge gate she sinks exhausted on a stone. A dashing hussar mounting guard, as befits his office, scans her with an astonished look, and crosses himself more than once with a hurried, inward prayer. He is a bold fellow enough, and would face an Austrian cuirassier or a Russian bayonet as readily and fearlessly as a flask of strong Hungarian wine, but he quails and trembles at the very thought of the Evil Eye.

"The Count! the Count!" gasps out the breathless Zingynie, "is he at the Castle? can I see Count Victor?"

"All in good time, mother!" replies he good-naturedly; "the Count is gone shooting to the Waldenberg. The carriages have but just driven by; did you not see them as you came here?"

"And the Count, is he not riding, as is his custom? will he not pass by here as he gallops on to overtake them? Has my boy learned to forget the saddle, and to neglect the good horse that his father's son should love?"

"Not to-day, mother," answered the hussar. "All the carriages are gone to-day, and the Count sits in the first with a bright, beautiful lady, ah, brighter even than our Countess, and more beautiful, with her red lips and her sunny hair."

All hussars are connoisseurs in beauty.

"My boy, my boy," mutters the old woman; and the hussar, seeing how ill she looks, produces a flask of his favourite remedy, and insists on her partaking of its contents. It brings the colour back to her cheek, and the blood to her heart.

"And they are gone to the Waldenberg! and I ought to reach it by the mountain-path before them even now. Oh, for one hour of my girlhood! one hour of the speed I once thought so little of! I would give all the rest of my days for that hour now. To the Waldenberg!"

"To the Waldenberg!" answered the hussar, taking the flask (empty) from his lips; but even while he spoke she was gone.

As she followed the path towards the mountain, a large raven flew out of the copse-wood on her left, and hopped along the track in front of her. Then the gipsy's lips turned ashy-white once more, for she knew she was too late.

CHAPTER XLV
RETRIBUTION

Carriage after carriage drove from Edeldorf to the foot of the Waldenberg, and deposited its living freight in a picturesque gorge or cleft of the mountain, where the only road practicable for wheels and axles terminated, and whence the sportsman, however luxurious, must be content to perform the remainder of his journey on foot. A hearty welcome and a sumptuous breakfast at the Castle had commenced the day's proceedings; but Madame de Rohan had kept her room on the plea of indisposition, and the only ladies of the party were the Princess and Countess Valèrie. Victor was in unusual spirits, a strange, wild happiness lighted up his eye, and spread a halo over his features; but he was absent and preoccupied at intervals, and his inconsequent answers and air of distraction more than once elicited marks of undisguised astonishment from his guests. The Princess was more subdued in manner than her wont. I watched the two with a painful interest, all the keener that my opportunity had not yet arrived, and that the confidence in my own powers, which had supported me the previous evening, was now rapidly deserting me, as I reflected on the violence of my friend's fatal attachment, and the character of her who was his destiny. If I should fail in persuading him, as was more than probable, what would be the result? What ought I to do next? I had assumed a fearful responsibility, yet I determined not to shrink from it. Valèrie was gay and good-humoured as usual. It had been arranged that the two ladies should accompany the sportsmen to the trysting-place at the foot of the mountain, and then return to the Castle. The plan originated with Valèrie, who thus, enjoyed more of her lover's society. Nor did it meet with the slightest opposition from Victor, who, contrary to his usual custom of riding on horseback to the mountain, starting after all his guests were gone, and then galloping at speed to overtake them, had shown no disinclination to make a fourth in his own barouche, the other three places being occupied by an Austrian grandee and Prince and Princess Vocqsal. Had he adhered to his usual custom, the Zingynie would have met him before he reached the lodge. English thorough-bred horses, harnessed to carriages of Vienna build, none of them being drawn by less than four, make light of distance, and it seemed but a short drive to more than one couple of our party, when we reached the spot at which our day's sport was likely to commence.

A merry, chattering, laughing group we were. On a level piece of greensward, overshadowed by a few gigantic fir-trees, and backed by the bluff rise of the copse-clothed mountain, lounged the little band of gentlemen for whose amusement all the preparations had been made, whose accuracy of eye and readiness of finger were that day to be tested by the downfall of bear and wolf, deer and wild-boar, not to mention such ignoble game as partridges, woodcocks, quail, and water-fowl, or such inferior vermin as hawk and buzzard, marten and wild-cat, all of which denizens of the wilderness were to be found in plenty on the Waldenberg. A picturesque assemblage it was, consisting as it did of nearly a score of the first noblemen in Hungary--men who bore the impress of their stainless birth not only in chivalry of bearing and frank courtesy of manner, but in the handsome faces and stately frames that had come down to them direct from those mailed ancestors whose boast it used to be that they were the advanced guard of Germany and the very bulwarks of Christendom. As I looked around on their happy, smiling faces, and graceful, energetic forms, my blood ran cold to think how the lightest whisper of one frail woman might bring every one of those noble heads to the block; how, had she indeed been more or less than woman, a cross would even now be attached to every one of those time-honoured names on that fatal list which knows neither pity nor remorse. And when I looked from those unconscious men to the fair arbitress of their fate, with her little French bonnet and coquettish dress, with her heightened colour and glossy hair, I thought, if the history of the world were ever *really* laid bare, what a strange history it would be, and how unworthy we should find had been the motives of some of the noblest actions, how paltry the agency by which some of the greatest convulsions on record had been effected.

She was fastening Victor's powder-horn more securely to its string, and I remarked that her fingers trembled in the performance of that simple office. She looked wistfully after him, too, as he waved his hat to bid her adieu, and stood up in the carriage to watch our ascending party long after she had started on her homeward journey. She who was generally so proud, so undemonstrative, so careful not to commit herself by word or deed! could it have been a presentiment? I felt angry with her then; alas! alas! my anger had passed away long before the sun went down.

"Help me to place the guns, Vere," said Victor in his cheerful, affectionate voice, as we toiled together up the mountain-side, and reached the first pass at which it would be necessary to station a sportsman, well armed with rifle and smooth-bore, to be ready for whatever might come. "I can depend upon *you,* for I know your shooting; so I shall put you above the waterfall. Vocqsal and I will take the two corners just below; and if there is an old boar in the Waldenberg, he *must* come to one of us. I expect a famous day's sport, if we manage it well. I used to say *'Vive la guerre,'* Vere--don't you remember?--but it's *'Vive la chasse'* now, and has been for a long time with me."

He looked so happy; he was so full of life and spirits, I could not help agreeing with his head forester, a tall, stalwart Hungarian, who followed him about like his shadow, when he muttered, "It does one good to see the Count when he gets on the mountain. He is like *himself* now."

Meanwhile the beaters, collected from the neighbouring peasantry, and who had been all the previous day gradually contracting the large circle they had made, so as to bring every head of game, and indeed every living thing, from many a mile round, within the range of our fire-arms, might be heard drawing nearer and nearer, their shrill voices and discordant shouts breaking wildly on the silence of the forest, hitherto uninterrupted, save by the soft whisper of the breeze, or the soothing murmur of the distant waterfall. Like the hunter when he hears the note of a hound, and erects his ears, and snorts and trembles with excitement, I could see many of my fellow-sportsmen change colour and fidget upon their posts; for well they knew that long before the beater's cry smites upon the ear it is time to expect the light-bounding gambol of the deer, the stealthy gallop of the wolf, the awkward advance of the bear, or the blundering rush of the fierce wild-boar himself; and as they were keen and experienced sportsmen, heart and soul in the business of the day, their quick glances and eager attitudes showed that each was determined no inattention on his own part should baulk him of his prey.

One by one Victor placed them in their respective situations, with a jest and a kind word and a cordial smile for each. Many a hearty friend remarked that day how Count de Rohan's voice was gayer, his manner even more fascinating than usual, his whole bearing more full of energy and happiness and a thorough enjoyment of life.

At last he had placed them, all but Ropsley and myself, and there was no time to be lost, for the cry of the beaters came louder and louder on the breeze; and already a scared buzzard or two, shooting rapidly over our heads, showed that our neighbourhood was disturbed, and the game of every description must ere long be on foot.

"Take the Guardsman above the waterfall, Vere, and put him by the old oak-tree," said Victor, fanning his brow with his hat after his exertions. "He can command both the passes from there, and get shooting enough to remind him of Sebastopol. You take the glade at the foot of the bare rock. Keep well under cover. I have seen two boars there already this season. I shall stay here opposite the Prince. Halloa! Vocqsal, where are you?"

"Here," replied that worthy, from the opposite side of the torrent, where he had ensconced himself in a secure and secret nook, commanding right and left an uninterrupted view of two long narrow vistas in the forest, and promising to afford an excellent position for the use of that heavy double-barrelled rifle which he handled with a skill and precision the result of many a year's practice and many a triumphant *coup*.

Unlike the younger sportsmen, Prince Vocqsal's movements were marked by a coolness and confidence which was of itself sufficient to predicate success. He had taken off the resplendent wig which adorned his "imperial front" immediately on the departure of the ladies, and transferred it to the capacious pockets of a magnificent green velvet shooting-coat, rich in gold embroidery and filagree buttons of the same precious metal. Its place was supplied by a black skull-cap, surmounted by a wide-brimmed, low hat. On the branches of the huge old tree under which he was stationed he had hung his powder-horn, loading-rod, and shooting apparatus generally, in such positions as to ensure replenishing his trusty rifle with the utmost rapidity; and taking a hunting-knife from his belt, he had stuck it, like a Scottish Highlander, in his right boot. Since his famous encounter with the bear at this very spot, the Prince always liked to wear his "best friend," as he called it, in that place. These arrangements being concluded to his own satisfaction, he took a goodly-sized hunting-flask from his pocket, and, after a hearty pull at its contents, wiped his moustache, and looked about him with the air of a man who had made himself thoroughly comfortable, and was prepared for any emergency.

"Here I am, Victor," he shouted once more, "established *en factionnaire*. Don't shoot point-blank this way, and keep perfectly quiet after you hear the action has commenced."

Victor laughingly promised compliance, and Ropsley and I betook ourselves, with all the haste we could make, to our respective posts.

It was a steep, though not a long climb, and we had little breath to spare for conversation. Yet it seemed that something more than the exhausting nature of our exercise sealed our lips and checked our free interchange of thought. There was evidently something on Ropsley's mind; and he, too, appeared aware that there was a burden on mine. It was not till I reached the old oak-tree at which he was to be stationed, and was about to leave him for my own place, that he made the slightest remark. Then he only said--

"Vere, what's the matter with De Rohan? There's something very queer about him to-day; have you not observed it."

I made some excuse about his keen zest for field-sports, and his hospitable anxiety that his guests should enjoy their share of the day's amusement, but the weight at my heart belied my commonplace words, and when I reached the station assigned me I sank down on the turf oppressed and crushed by a foreboding of some sudden and dreadful evil.

Soon a shot afar off at the extreme edge of the wood warned me that the sport had commenced; another and yet another followed in rapid succession. Branches began to rustle and dry twigs to crack as the larger game moved onwards to the centre of the fatal circle. A fine brown bear came shambling clumsily along within twenty yards of my post; I hit him in the shoulder, and, watching him as he went on to mark if my ball had taken effect, saw him roll over and over down the steep mountain-side, at the same moment that the crack of Ropsley's unerring rifle reached my ear, and a light puff of smoke from the same weapon curled and clung around the fir-trees above his hiding-place. A "Bravo" of encouragement sprang to my lips, but I checked it as it rose, for at that instant an enormous wild-boar emerged from the covert in front of me; he was trotting along leisurely enough, and with an undignified and ungraceful movement sufficiently ludicrous, but his quick eye must have caught the gleam of my rifle ere I could level it, for he stopped dead short, turned aside with an angry grunt, and dashed furiously down the hill towards the waterfall. "Boar forward!" shouted I, preparing to follow the animal, but in a few moments a shot rang sharply through the woodlands, succeeded instantaneously by another, and then a scream--a long, full, wild, ear-piercing scream! and then the ghastly, awful silence that seems to tell so much. I knew it all long before I reached him, and yet of those few minutes I have no distinct recollection. There was a group of tall figures looking down; a confused mass of rifles, powder-horns, and shooting-gear; a hunting-flask lying white and glittering on the green turf; and an old woman with a bright crimson handkerchief kneeling over *something* on the ground. Every one made way for me to pass, they seemed to treat me with a strange, awe-stricken respect--perhaps they knew I was his friend--his oldest friend--and there he lay, the brave, the bright, the beautiful, stretched at his length, stone dead on the cold earth, shot through the heart--by whom? by Prince Vocqsal.

I might have known there was no hope. I had heard such screams before cleaving the roar of battle--death shrieks that are only forced from man when the leaden messenger has reached the very well-spring of his life. I need not have taken the cold clammy hand in mine, and opened his dress, and looked with my own eyes upon the blue livid mark. It was all over; there was no more hope for him than for the dead who have lain a hundred years in the grave. This morning he was Count de Rohan; Victor de Rohan, my dear old friend. I thought of him a merry, blue-eyed child, and then I wept; and my head got better, and so I learned by degrees what had happened.

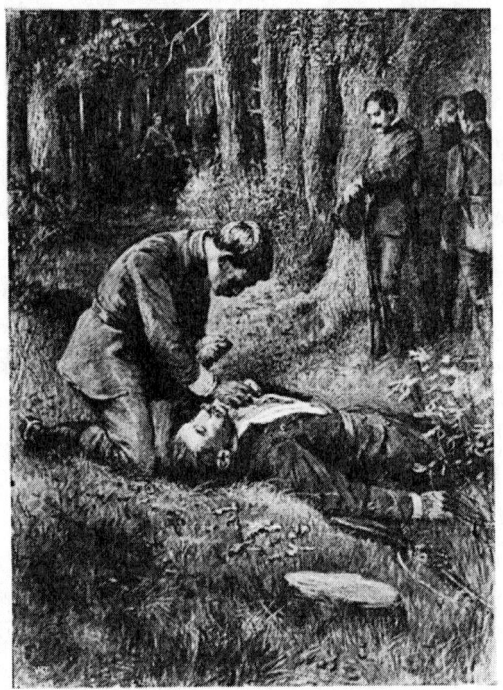

"I might have known there was no hope."
The Interpreter

"I might have known there was no hope." The Interpreter

The boar had dashed down at speed towards the waterfall He had crossed the range of Count de Rohan's rifle, but the Count--and on this fact the forester laid great stress--the Count had missed his aim, and the animal almost instantaneously turned towards Prince Vocqsal. The Prince's rifle rang clear and true; with his usual cool precision he had waited until the quarry was far past the line of his friend's ambush, and had pulled the trigger in perfect confidence as to the result. He, too, had failed for once in the very act of skill on which he so prided himself. His ball missing the game had struck against the hard knot of an old tree beyond it, and glancing thence almost at right angles, had lodged in poor Victor's heart at the very moment when the exhausted Zingynie, staggering with fatigue, had reached his post, murmuring a few hoarse words of warning, and an entreaty to abandon the sport only for that day. As he turned to greet her, the fatal messenger arrived, and with a convulsive bound into the air, and one loud scream, he fell dead at her feet.

Old Prince Vocqsal seemed utterly stupefied. He could neither be prevailed upon to quit the body, nor did it seem possible to make him comprehend exactly what had happened, and the share which he had himself borne so unwittingly in the dreadful catastrophe. The Zingynie, on the contrary, although pale as death, was composed and almost majestic in her grief. To her it was the fulfilment of a prophecy--the course of that destiny which is not to be checked nor stayed. As she followed the body, with head erect and measured tread, she looked neither to right nor left, but her black eyes flashed with awful brilliance as she fastened the dilated orbs on what had once been Victor de Rohan, and murmured in a low chant words which I now remembered, for the first time, to have heard many years before, words of which I now knew too well the gloomy significance. "Birth and Burial--Birth and Burial--Beware of St. Hubert's Day!"

So we bore him down to Edeldorf, slowly, solemnly, as we bear one to his last resting-place. Down the beautiful mountain-side, with its russet copsewood, and its fine old oaks, and its brilliant clothing of autumnal beauty; down the white sandy road between the vine-gardens, with their lightsome foliage and their clusters of blushing grapes, and the buxom peasant-women, and ruddy, happy children, even now so gay and noisy, but hushed and horror-bound as they stopped to look and learn; down across the long level plain, where the flocks were feeding securely, and the cattle stood dreamily, and clouds of insects danced and hovered in the beams of an afternoon sun. Slowly, solemnly, we wound across the plain; slowly, solemnly, we reached the wide park-gates. A crowd of mourners, gathering as we went, followed eager and silent in the rear. Slowly, solemnly, we filed up the long avenue between the acacias, bearing the lord of that proud domain, the last of the De Rohans, to his ancestral home.

Two ladies were walking in the garden as we approached the house; I caught sight of their white dresses before they had themselves perceived our ghastly train. They were Constance de Rohan, and Rose, Princess Vocqsal.

There was deep and holy mourning, there were bitter scalding tears that night in the Castle of Edeldorf. On the morrow, when the sun rose, there was one broken heart within its walls.

CHAPTER XLVI
VÆ VICTIS!

Valèrie de Rohan is Mrs. Ropsley now; she has dropped the rank of Countess, and prides herself upon the facility with which she has adopted the character of an English matron. She speaks our language, if anything, a little less correctly than when I knew her first; never shakes hands with any of her male acquaintances, and cannot be brought to take a vehement interest in Low Church bishops, parliamentary majorities, or the costly shawls and general delinquencies of her pretty next-door neighbour, whose private history is no concern of yours or mine. In all other respects she is British enough to be own grand-daughter to Boadicea herself. She makes her husband's breakfast punctually at ten; comes down in full morning toilet, dressed for the day, bringing with her an enormous bunch of keys, such as we bachelors scrutinise with mysterious awe, and of the utility of which, inasmuch as they are invariably forgotten and left on the breakfast-table, we nourish vague and secret doubts; further, she studies Shakspeare and Burke (not the statesman, but the compiler of that national work which sets forth the pedigrees of peers and baronets, and honourable messieurs and mesdames) with divided ardour, and although she thinks London a little *triste*, believes her own house in Belgravia to be a perfect paradise, and loves its lord and hers with a pure, simple, and entire devotion. Mrs. Ropsley is very happy, and so is he.

"The boy is father to the man." I can trace in the late Guardsman--who relinquished his profession at the Peace--the same energy, the same calculating wisdom, the same practical good sense, that distinguished his youth; but he has lost the selfishness which made his earlier character so unamiable, and has acquired in its stead an enlarged view of the duties and purposes of life, a mellower tone of thought, a deeper sense of feeling as to its pleasures and its pains. He has discovered that the way to be happy is not to surround oneself with a rampart of worldly wisdom, not to cover the human breast with a shield of cynical defiance, which always fails it at its need, but to take one's share manfully and contentedly of the roses as of the thorns--no more ashamed to luxuriate in the fragrance of the one, than to wince from the sharp points of the other. He entered on life with one predominant idea, and that one perhaps the least worthy of all those which sanguine boyhood proposes so ardently to itself; but he had purpose and energy, and though self was his idol, he worshipped with a perseverance and consistency worthy of a better cause. Circumstances, which have warped so many to evil, rescued him at the turning point of his destiny. When he met Valèrie at Vienna, he was rapidly hardening into a bold, bad man, but the affection with which she inspired him saved him, as such affection has saved many a one before, from that most dangerous state of all in which he lies who has nothing to care for, nothing to hope, and consequently nothing to fear. Oh! you who have it in your power to save the fallen, think of this. How slight is the cable that tows many a goodly vessel into port; what a mere thread will buoy up a drowning man; do not stand on the bank and wag your heads, and say, "I told you so;" stretch but a little finger, throw him the rope that lies to your hand; nay, think it no shame to wet your feet and bring him gently and tenderly ashore, for is he not your brother?

The good work that Valèrie's influence had begun, was perfected by the hardships and horrors of the Crimean campaign. No man could witness the sufferings so cheerfully borne, or take his share in the kindly offices so heartily interchanged on that dreary plateau above Sebastopol, without experiencing an improvement in his moral being, and imbibing far more correct notions than he had entertained before as to the *realities* of life and death. No man could take his turn of duty day by day in the trenches, see friends and comrades one by one struck down by grape-shot, or withering from disease, and not feel that he too held life on a startlingly uncertain tenure; that if the material were indeed all-in-all, he had no business there; that the ideal has a large share even in this life, and will probably constitute the very essence of that which is to come. It is a mistake to suppose that danger hardens the heart; on the contrary, it renders it peculiarly alive to the softer and kindlier emotions. The brave are nearly always gentler, more susceptible, than apparently weaker natures; and many a man who does not quail at the roar of a battery, who confronts an advancing column with a careless smile and a pleasant jest upon his lips, will wince like a child at an injury or an unkindness dealt him from the hand he loves.

Ropsley, too, had many a pang of remorse to contend with, many an hour of unavailing regret, as he looked back to the mischief he had wrought by his unscrupulous schemes for his own benefit--the misery, to which in his now softened nature he was keenly alive, that a thoughtless selfishness had brought on his oldest and dearest friends. Poor Victor married in haste, when piqued and angry with one who, whatever might be her faults, was the only woman on earth to *him*. Constance Beverley, driven into this alliance by his own false representations, and her father's ill-judged vehemence. Another old school-fellow, whom he was at last beginning to value and esteem, attributing the wreck of all he hoped and cherished in the world to this fatal marriage; and he himself ere long wishing to be connected by the nearest and dearest ties with those whose future he had been so instrumental in blasting, and who could not but look upon him as the prime source and origin of all their unhappiness.

No wonder Ropsley was an altered man; no wonder Victor's sudden and awful death made a still further impression on his awakened feelings; no wonder he prized the blessing he had won, and determined to make himself worthy of a lot the golden joys of which his youth would have sneered at and despised, but which he was grateful to find his manhood was capable of appreciating as they deserved.

Happiness stimulates some tempers to action, as grief goads others to exertion; and Ropsley is not one to remain idle. Though Edeldorf has passed away from the name of De Rohan for evermore, he has attained a large fortune with his wife; but affluence and comfort alone will not fill up the measure of such a man's existence, and his energetic character will be sure to find some outlet for the talents and acquirements it possesses. Politics will probably be his sphere; and those who know of what efforts a bold far-seeing nature is capable, when backed by study, reflection, above all, common sense; and when blessed with a happy home of love on which to rest, and from which to gather daily new hope and strength, will not think me over sanguine in predicting that something more than a "*Hic Jacet*" will, in the fulness of time, be carved on Ropsley's tombstone; that he will do something more in his generation than eat and drink, and pay his son's debts, and make a will, and so lie down and die, and be forgotten.

It is good to be firm, strong-minded, and practical; it is good to swim with the stream, and, without ever losing sight of the landing-place, to lose no advantage of the current, no lull of the back-water, no rippling eddy in one's favour. It is not good to struggle blindly on against wind and tide, to trust all to a gallant heart, to neglect the beacon and the landmark, to go down at last, unconquered it may be in spirit, but beaten and submerged for all that, in fact. There is an old tale of chivalry which bears with it a deep and somewhat bitter moral: of a certain knight who, in the madness of his love, vowed to cast aside his armour and ride three courses through the mêlée with no covering save his lady's night-weeds. Helm, shield, and corslet, mail and plate, and stout buff jerkin, all are cast aside. With bared brow and naked breast the knight is up and away!--amongst those gathering warriors clad from head to foot in steel. Some noble hearts--God bless them!--turn aside to let him pass; but many a fierce blow and many a cruel thrust are delivered at the devoted champion in the throng. Twice, thrice he rides that fearful gauntlet; and ere his good horse stops, the white night-dress is fluttering in rags--torn and hacked, and saturated with blood. It is a tale of Romance, mark that! and the knight recovers, to be happy. Had it been Reality, his ladye might have wrung her hands over a clay-cold corpse in vain. Woe to him who sets lance in rest to ride a tournament with the world! Woe to the warm imagination, the kindly feelings, the generosity that scorns advantage, the soft and vulnerable heart! How it bleeds in the conflict, how it suffers in the defeat! Yet are there some battles in which it is perhaps nobler to lose than to win. Who shall say in what victory consists? "Discretion is the better part of valour," quoth Prudence; but Courage, with herald-voice, still shouts, "Fight on! brave knights, fight on!"

In the tomb of his fathers, in a gloomy vault, where a light is constantly kept burning, sleeps Victor de Rohan, my boyhood's friend, my more than brother. Many a stout and warlike ancestor lies about him; many a bold Crusader, whose marble effigy, with folded hands and crossed legs, makes silent boast that he had struck for the good cause in the Holy Land, rests there, to shout and strike no more. Not one amongst them all that had a nobler heart than he who joined them in the flower of manhood--the last of his long and stainless line. As the old white-haired sexton opens the door of the vault to trim and replenish the glimmering death-lamp, a balmy breeze steals in and stirs the heavy silver fringe on the pall of Victor's coffin--a balmy breeze that plays round the statue of the Virgin on the chapel roof, and sweeps across many a level mile of plain, and many a fair expanse of wood and water, till it reaches the fragrant terraces and the frowning towers of distant Sieben-bürgen--a balmy breeze that cools the brow of yon pale drooping lady, who turns an eager, wistful face towards its breath. For why? It blows direct from where he sleeps at Edeldorf.

She is not even clad in mourning, yet who has mourned him as she has done? She might not even see him borne to his last home, yet who so willingly would lay her down by his side, to rest for ever with him in the grave?

Alas for you, Rose, Princess Vocqsal!--you who must needs play with edged tools till they cut you to the quick!--you who must needs rouse passions that have blighted you to the core!--you who never knew you had a heart till the eve of St. Hubert's Day, and found it empty and broken on the morrow of that festival!

She tends that old man now with the patience and devotion of a saint--that old childish invalid in his garden chair, prattling of his early exploits, playing contentedly with his little dog, fretful and impatient about his dinner. This is all that a paralytic stroke, acting on a constitution weakened by excess, has left of Prince Vocqsal.

Nor is the wife less altered than her husband. Who would recognise in those pale sunken features, in that hair once so sunny, now streaked with whole masses of grey, in that languid step and listless, fragile form, the fresh, sparkling roseate beauty of the famous Princess Vocqsal? She has done with beauty now; she has done with love and light, and all that constitute the charm and the sunshine of life; but she has still a duty to perform; she has still an expiation to make; and with a force and determination which many a less erring nature might fail to imitate, she has set herself resolutely to the task.

Save to attend to her religious duties, comprising many an act of severe and grievous penance, she never leaves her patient. All that woman's care and woman's tenderness can provide, she lavishes on that querulous invalid; with woman's instinct of loving that which she protects, he is dearer to her now than anything on earth; but oh! it is a sad, sad face that she turns to the breeze from Edeldorf.

Her director comes to see her twice a day; he is a grave, stern priest--an old man who has shriven criminals on the scaffold--who has accustomed himself to read the most harrowing secrets of the human soul. He should be dead to sensibility, and blunted to all softer emotions, yet he often leaves the Princess with tears in his grave cold eyes.

She is a Roman Catholic; do not therefore argue that her repentance may not avail. She has been a sinner--scarlet, if you will, of the deepest dye; do not therefore say that the door of mercy will be shut in her face. There are sins besides those of the feelings--crimes which spring from more polluted sources than the affections. The narrow gate is wide enough for all. If you are striving to reach it, walking hopefully along the strait path, it is better not to turn aside and take upon yourself the punishment of every prostrate bleeding sinner; if you must needs stop, why not bind the gaping wounds, and help the sufferer to resume the uphill journey? There are plenty of flints lying about, we know--heavy, sharp, and three-cornered--such as shall strike the poor cowering wretch to the earth, never to rise again. Which of us shall stoop to lift one of them in defiance of Divine mercy? Which of us shall dare to say, "I am qualified to cast the first stone at her"?

CHAPTER XLVII
THE RETURN OF SPRING

The smoke curls up once more from the chimneys of Alton Grange; the woman in possession, she with the soapy arms and unkempt hair, who was always cleaning with no result, has been paid for her occupancy and sent back to her own untidy home in the adjoining village. The windows are fresh painted, the lawn fresh mown, the garden trimmed, and the walks rolled; nay, the unwonted sound of wheels is sometimes heard upon the gravel sweep in front of the house, for the country neighbours, a race who wage unceasing war against anything mysterious, and whose thirst for "news," and energy in the acquisition of gossip, are as meritorious as they are uncalled for, have lavished their attentions on the solitary, and welcomed him back to his lonely home far more warmly than he deserves. The estate, too, has been at nurse ever since he went away. An experienced man of business has taken it into his own especial charge, but somehow the infant has not attained any great increase of vigour under his fostering care, and the proprietor is ungrateful enough to think he could have managed it better for himself. Inside, the house is dark and gloomy still. I miss poor Bold dreadfully. After a day of attention to those trivial details which the landowner dignifies with the title of "business," or worse still, of vacant, dreary hours passed in listless apathy, it is very lonely to return to a solitary dinner and a long silent evening, to feel that the wag of a dog's tail against the floor would be company, and to own there is solace in the sympathy even of a brute's unreasoning eye. It is not good for man to be alone, and that is essentially a morbid state in which solitude is felt to be a comfort and a relief; more especially does the want of occupation and companionship press upon one who has been leading a life of busy every-day excitement such as falls to the lot of the politician or the soldier; and it has always appeared to me that the worst of all possible preparations for the quiet, homely duties of a country gentleman, are the very two professions so generally chosen as the portals by which the heir of a landed estate is to enter life. It takes years to tame the soldier, and the politician seldom *really* settles down at all; but of course you will do what your fathers did--if the boy is dull, you will gird a sword upon his thigh; if he is conceited, you will get him into Parliament, and fret at the obtuse deafness of the House. Perhaps you may as well be disappointed one way as the other; whatever you do with him, by the time he is thirty you will wish you had done differently, and so will he. Action, however, is the only panacea for despondency; work, work, is the remedy for lowness of spirits. What am I that I should sit here with folded hands, and repine at the common lot? There are none so humble but they can do some little good, and in this the poor are far more active than the rich. Let me take example by the day labourers at my gate. There is a poor family not a mile from here who sadly lack assistance, and whom for the last fortnight I have neglected to visit. A gleam of sunshine breaks in through the mullioned window, and gilds even the black oak wainscoting: the clouds are passing rapidly away, I will take my hat and walk off at once towards the common. Oh, the hypocrisy of human motives! The poor family are tenants of Constance de Rohan; their cottage lies in the direct road to Beverley Manor.

It has been raining heavily, and the earth is completely saturated with moisture. The late spring, late even for England, is bursting forth almost with tropical luxuriance. Dank and dripping, the fragrant hedges glisten in the noonday beams. Brimful is every blossom in the orchard, fit chalice for the wild bird or the bee. Thick and tufted, the wet grass sprouts luxuriantly in the meadow-lands where the cowslip hangs her scented head, and the buttercup, already dry, reflects the sunshine from its golden hollow. The yellow brook laughs merrily on beneath the foot-bridge, and the swallows shoot hither and thither high up against the clear blue sky. How fresh and tender is the early green of the noble elms in the foreground, and the distant larches on the hill. How sweet the breath of spring; how fair and lovable the smile upon her face. How full of hope and promise and life and light and joy. Oh, the giant capacity for happiness of the human heart! Oh, what a world it might be! What a world it is!

The children are playing about before the door of the cottage on the common. Dirty, and noisy, and rosy, the little urchins stare, wonder-struck, at the stranger, and disappear tumultuously into certain back settlements, where there are a garden, and a beehive, and a pig. An air of increased comfort pervades the dwelling, and its mistress has lost the wan, anxious look it pained me so to see some ten days ago. With a corner of her apron she dusts a chair for me to sit down, and prepares herself for a gossip, in which experience tells me the talking will be all one way. "Her 'old man' is gone out to-day for the first time to his work. He is quite stout again at last, but them low fevers keeps a body down terrible, and the doctor's stuff was no good, and she thinks after all it's the fine weather as has brought him round; leastways, that and the broth Lady Beverley sent him from the Manor House; and she to come up herself only yesterday was a week, through a pour of rain, poor dear! for foreign parts has not agreed with her, and she's not so rosy as she were when I knew her first, but a born angel all the same, and ever will be."

Tears were in the good woman's eyes, and her voice was choked. I stayed to hear no more. Lady Beverley, as she called her, was, then, once more at home. She had been here--here on this very spot, but one short week ago. I could have knelt down and kissed the very ground she had trodden. I longed if it was only to see her footprints. I, who had schooled myself to such a pitch of stoicism and apathy, who had stifled and rooted out and cut down the germs of passion till I had persuaded myself that they had ceased to exist, and that my heart had become hard and barren as the rock,--I, who had thought that when the time came I should meet her in London with a kindly greeting, as became an old friend, and never turn to look the way she went; and now, because she had been here a week ago, because there was a possibility of her being at the moment within three miles of where I stood, to feel the blood mounting to my brow, the tears starting to my eyes,--oh! it was scarlet shame, and yet it was burning happiness too.

The sun shone brighter, the birds sang more merrily now. There was no longer a mockery in the spring. The dry branch seemed to blossom once more--the worn and weary nature to imbibe fresh energies and renewed life. There was hope on this side the grave, hope that might be cherished without bitterness or remorse. Very dark had been the night, but day was breaking at last. Very bitter and tedious had been the winter, but spring, real spring, was bursting forth. I could hardly believe in the prospect of happiness thus opened to me. I trembled to think of what would be my destiny if I should lose it all again.

In the ecstasy of joy, as in the tumult of uncertainty and the agony of grief, there is but one resource for failing human strength, how feeble and failing none know so well as those whom their fellows deem the noblest and the strongest. That resource has never yet played man false at his need. The haughty brow may be compelled to stoop, the boasted force of will be turned aside, the proud spirit be broken and humbled to the dust, the race be lost to the swift and the battle go against the strong, but the victory shall be wrested, the goal shall be attained by the clasped hands and the bended knees, and the loving heart that through good and evil has trusted steadfastly to the end.

I may lock the old desk now. I have told my tale; 'tis but the every-day story of the ups and downs of life--the winnings and losings of the game we all sit down to play. One word more, and I have done.

In the solitude of my chamber I took from its hiding-place a withered flower; once it had been a beautiful white rose, how beautiful, how cherished, none knew so well as I. Long and steadfastly I gazed at it, conjuring up the while a vision of that wild night, with its flying clouds and its waving fir-trees, and the mocking moonlight shining coldly on the gravel path, and the bitterness of that hour, the bitterness of all that had yet fallen to my lot, and so I fell asleep. And behold it seemed to be noon, midsummer-noon in a garden of flowers, hot and bright and beautiful. The butterfly flitted in the sunshine, and the wood-pigeon mourned sweetly and sadly in the shade. Little children with laughing eyes played and rolled about upon the sward, and ran up, warm and eager, to offer me posies of the choicest flowers. One by one I refused them all, for amongst the pride of the garden there was none to me like my own withered rose that I had cherished so long, and I turned away from each as it was brought me, and pressed her closer to my heart where she always lay.

Then, even as I clasped her she bloomed in her beauty once more, fresh and pure and radiant as of old, steeping my very soul in fragrance, a child of earth indeed, but wafting her sweetness up to heaven.

And I awoke, and prayed that it might not be all a dream.